GALAXIAS

GALAXIAS

STEPHEN BAXTER

First published in Great Britain in 2021 by Gollancz
an imprint of The Orion Publishing Group Ltd
Carmelite House, 50 Victoria Embankment
London EC4Y 0DZ

An Hachette UK Company

1 3 5 7 9 10 8 6 4 2

A CIP catalogue record for this book is
available from the British Library.

ISBN (Hardback) 978 1 473 22885 6
ISBN (Export Trade Paperback) 978 1 473 22886 3
ISBN (eBook) 978 1 473 22888 7
ISBN (Audio Download) 978 1 473 22889 4

Typeset by Input Data Services Ltd, Somerset

Printed and bound in Great Britain by Clays Ltd, Elcograf S.p.A.

www.gollancz.co.uk

For Elvy May Moylan
b. 11 April 2021
and
Molly Alice Baxter
b. 17 July 2021

EVENT

1973–2057

On 3 December 1973, a small spacecraft passed Jupiter.

The craft, American-built, was called Pioneer 10.

As its makers had intended, the close approach to Jupiter caused the giant planet's gravity field to hurl the craft further and faster than on arrival. And by the time it left Jupiter, Pioneer was moving too fast to fall back into the Sun's gravity well.

Pioneer 10 thus became the first human-made artefact destined to reach interstellar space.

A breakout had been made.

The Sinus Medii, the 'Central Bay', a sea of dry dust, had a striking location: right at the centre of the Moon's permanently Earth-turned face.

Before the events of 2057, however, no human had come here, even though a permanent human outpost orbited the Moon, and descents to places of interest had become commonplace. No human footprints marked the dust of the Central Bay.

By then, however, the Bay had been carefully watched by human eyes for nearly a century.

Two automated probes had come here.

In November 1967 a spidery craft called Surveyor 6 had

landed here, clumsily – and then fired its rocket engine and hopped a few metres over the surface. The purpose had been to test the restarting of engines on the Moon's surface, an essential engineering requirement if astronauts were to be landed on the Moon and sent safely home. The little craft, having achieved its makers' goals, quickly died – but not before it had made an accidental discovery.

This was a chance encounter. The next was intentional, and covert.

In December 1972 the Moon suffered a large impact. This was caused by the guided fall onto the Moon of a discarded, spent rocket, the third stage of the Saturn V booster that had propelled Apollo 17 and its crew to the Moon. During the Apollo programme there had been many such impacts of abandoned vehicle components, the purpose to make the Moon ring with seismic waves, and so afford glimpses of its interior structure.

This was not the purpose of this impact.

No impact before had come so close to the Sinus Medii, to within a few hundred kilometres. This landfall was by design.

And even as the jolt of impact reverberated through the body of the Moon, another small craft, not unlike Surveyor 6 but never publicly named, landed close to its defunct predecessor.

This particular Saturn impact had been an act of concealment. A concealment of the second probe's landing, by one group of humans from others.

This time there was no engine test, no short-lived experiments and observations.

Only watchfulness.

Peace returned to the Moon.

That, and watchfulness. Mutual watchfulness.

Until December 1973, as Pioneer 10 passed Jupiter.

On the Moon, in the Sinus Medii, an eye opened.

An observation was made.

A message was sent.

No reply could be expected for years. There was patience. The patience of aeons.

An eye closed.

After that, again, mutual watchfulness returned.

In 1985 an acknowledgement of the 1973 message was received from the third-level node.

In 2008 an acknowledgement was received from the second-level node.

In 2056 an acknowledgment was received from the first-level node. And a notification of what was to come.

In 2057, on 5 January, it began. In the Sinus Medii, an eye opened once more.

And, in England, a hard rain fell across the face of Tash Brand.

DAY

5–6 January 2057

1

0940 GMT

On Friday, 5 January 2057, in the morning of that day as experienced near the Greenwich meridian, many eyes happened to be turned to the Moon and the Sun: human and artificial eyes, on Earth and beyond. For that morning the Moon, following its own orbit, was sliding into a position precisely between Earth and Sun, so that the Moon's shadow would pass over a swathe of Earth's surface – in the southern hemisphere, across the ocean south of Africa – neatly and precisely hiding the Sun's disc from human eyes across that swathe.

It was a solar eclipse, with the moment of greatest eclipse, the midpoint of totality, due at 0948 Greenwich Mean Time.

A chain of events began at 0940 GMT.

The timing was deliberate, of course. Anticipating the eclipse.

But the primary event occurred at the location of the Sun itself.

The very first human instruments to detect the event were a fleet of solar science probes, launched by many nations, which followed fast, swooping orbits around the Sun, even over its poles, or diving perilously deep into its corona, its outer atmosphere.

This day they recorded baffling, anomalous data, before losing their orbital moorings in space, and scattering like startled birds.

It took eight minutes at lightspeed for the first observable effects – primarily gravitational and electromagnetic, light – to reach the orbit of Moon and Earth. So, as had been intended, the effects arrived precisely at the moment of greatest eclipse.

And, given the line-up of Earth, Moon, Sun, at this moment of eclipse, these effects were first detectable on the Moon's far side – the side closest to the Sun, closer than anywhere on Earth.

The first technology in the Earth-Moon system to record the event, it was later established, was at the Maccone Observatory, an automated deep-space telescope complex near the centre of that averted face, in a crater called Daedalus. For some years the lunar far side, shielded from the Earth's visual brightness and radio noise, had been maintained as a park for astronomy. The Maccone instrument suite watched the sky constantly, in many wavelengths – visible light, radio, infra-red, even gravity waves. And it was equipped to raise automatic alarms if unexpected events were observed.

Such an event was now observed.

The signal set, rich in anomalous data, was immediately flagged as extraordinary. Records were made, summary reports hastily compiled, alerts tagged. This took nanoseconds.

Then it took a fiftieth of a second to transmit the information around the Moon, through the fibre-optic communications network that, in the year 2057, lay draped across the dusty lunar hills like a sparse nervous system.

At much the same moment, visible evidence of the event reached human eyes: in lunar space, the eyes of a dozen multinational crew observing the events of the solar eclipse from the unique perspective of their orbital habitat, Lunar Gateway III.

It was less than two seconds more before visible evidence of the event reached the Earth itself.

And consequences unfolded.

As, in the Sinus Medii, an eye opened to watch the reaction.

2

0948 GMT

At twelve minutes to ten this Friday morning, under an overcast winter sky, Tash Brand was crossing the River Tyne, heading north, on her way home from work at Government House.

The Gateshead Millennium Bridge, built to commemorate a calendar transition that had happened twenty-seven years before thirty-year-old Tash was even born, was showing its age, she often thought. It was pedestrians only, a tilting bridge long since rusted into immobility, and the walkway surface, heavily remodelled, could sometimes be roughed up so you had to watch your step, even in the daylight, at least on a gloomy, overcast, winter morning like this one.

But Tash liked to walk. She took her time.

In fact – this was a few minutes before 0948, as she would remember later – she had already slowed up, feeling calmer the further she got from House with its endless adrenaline-pumping culture of urgency. It was like that even on relatively quiet days, and there were few quiet days. This morning she was emerging from yet another unscheduled all-nighter, this one caused by another attempted landing of French boat people, disgruntled citizens of federal Europe, in the Wash.

She came to a halt halfway across the river, took a breath, leaned against a handrail, and just looked. The light was poor, which wasn't unusual for the time of year – she had grown up in Surrey and had yet to get used to the shorter midwinter days up here, with sunrise only an hour and a half ago. Her father often reminded her of how her mother, Nigerian-born, had never got used to English winter days, even in the south.

But still the view was rich. Behind her the big box of Government House on the Gateshead bank: a monument of smartwood, a righteous carbon sink from its wood pile foundations all the way to its grass-covered roof. You couldn't get more modern than that – or much newer. It was only a year since the English federal government, long decamped from a flooded London and eager to establish its credentials as a uniter of a new England of quasi-independent regions, had moved here after a five-year stay in Birmingham. There had been some controversy about the functions of government being carried out so far north; the comms links made it irrelevant where Parliament sat, of course, but this was felt to be undiplomatically close to the surly English-Scottish international border.

What the hell, Tash thought, looking back. House itself was a spectacular sight, and the views it offered from within could be even more spectacular, when the Sun rose over the North Sea – on a good day, some swore, you could see the turning blades of the huge Dogger Island wind farm, far out to sea. In fact it looked as if it might eventually turn out to be one such good day today; looking back at that eastern horizon now she saw the clouds growing ragged, revealing the deep blue of a winter morning sky.

Meanwhile, to her left, old Newcastle sprawled across its own hilly bank, connected to the Gateshead side by multiple bridges thrown across the Tyne, some centuries old, all of them echoes of originals constructed back when this place had been one terminus of Hadrian's Wall. And the city itself offered a very modern view with its grassed-over roofs, tree-crowded avenues, white-painted buildings – nowadays it had the look of a theme park, so her father often said sourly, when the Sun caught it right.

Not many of her colleagues made this walk, though it was a reasonably short trek to the Manors district, to the east of the city centre, where accommodation for junior workers like Tash had been commandeered when the government had come to town. Most used the traffic tunnel that had been cut beneath the river, for speed and security. Tash, though, actually preferred being forced to take a little more time than the minimum, when she got the chance.

And, she was slowly learning, she liked being close to the river too. Like all British rivers, the Tyne was well controlled, from drainage schemes across the flood plain further west, to the barrier at its mouth on the east coast protecting it from North Sea storm surges. Looking down at the waters, grey in the cloud-choked light, she always had the sense of something bigger than herself, processes shaping the world on a scale far larger than she was ever likely to affect. Even if she was now a worm in the core of the apple of government, as Mel had once called her.

She smiled at that thought. That was Mel Kapur for you – always ready for a smartass put-down in case she ever got pretentious – not to mention Zhi, similarly acidic. Though Tash gave as good as she got. These were her closest friends, since college days, a decade back: herself, Wu Zhi, Mel Kapur. Always in her thoughts, it seemed.

Maybe, standing here, dawdling before going home, her subconscious was prompting her to give them a call. It was an unusual day after all.

She knew that Mel was eclipse-watching over the southern

ocean – aboard Skythrust Two, lucky fiend – and Zhi, luckier yet, was actually up in space, aboard the Lodestone station, ready to make his own observations. Waiting for an eclipse that was due about now, she vaguely remembered. What an experience for them.

The In-Jokes, as they had called themselves ever since a gloomy virus-lockdown term they had shared at Yale. They were all studious, thoughtful. Kind of serious, she supposed now, looking back. They had drifted together as other groups had formed around them – groups often self-identifying around in-jokes of some kind, relics of parties, or through the frat houses which were nothing but extended in-jokes themselves. It was Zhi who, as the three of them had sat gloomily in the corner of some bar one night, had come up with the name. 'We are the In-Jokes. And for us the in-joke is: there is no In-Joke.'

Well, it seemed funny at the time.

Although it had been the Pacific Incident that had caused them to bond for life, she supposed. When the three of them had nearly died in a botched survival exercise, one of Zhi's astronaut-cadet tests: a chopper drop into the water. They worked together, and had got out of there, and had never been out of touch since. Even though their careers had diverged, with Zhi heading for research in space, Mel for astronomy, and Tash, always less academic – her degree subject had been the sociology of science – went into government work. Still they stayed together.

Later, she would remember that was what she was thinking of. Her friends.

What she was thinking of when the Blink came.

And the light went away.

Suddenly, standing there on the bridge, she was plunged into pitch darkness.

And a hard rain fell across the face of Tash Brand.

It was a short, sharp burst out of nowhere, from a sky thick with cloud. Tash, shocked, bewildered, in sudden darkness, turned her head away, fumbled for her hood.

But she staggered, losing her orientation, and stumbled off a kerb, into the central walkway, nearly turning an ankle.

Pitch dark. What the hell? The light had just gone, with maybe a few seconds of fade-out – and she couldn't be sure about that.

It was as if she were deep in the bowels of House, and the power supply had failed. Not that it ever would. *But she was outdoors.*

Somebody screamed, along the bridge. She heard distant car horns.

Pitch dark.

Out in the open, under the sky, for God's sake. You didn't get power-failure blackouts *outdoors*. Standing there, unwilling to move, to take a step, she realised she was thinking like a child, slowly, utterly bewildered, not logically. But she felt helpless as a child, all the control she thought she had had over her world stripped away.

She took a step, stumbled again, nearly tripping on that kerb again.

A rail – she had been leaning on a handrail, that must be just ahead. She reached out, flailing. Found the rail. Clung to it with her gloved hands. Then, with more confidence, she stepped back up to the raised kerb.

She tried to take stock. She was standing on the bridge still, she could feel the rough surface under her feet, she had been looking out over the water. Right here. She thought she heard the lap, now. So that was still here.

She felt a deep, visceral, almost superstitious fear. You didn't get power failures out of doors. So, what else could have happened?

Her sight was gone.

No.

She heard herself sob.

But she had heard that scream, from somebody else on the bridge. Now more voices were calling. Think, Tash. Why would other people be calling out if *you* had gone blind? Why sound their horns?

She clung to her rail and cast about – *there*. A spark of light, like a phone. A way off down the bridge – back the way she had come, towards the south. Was there a vague patch of light in the sky beyond that? Maybe her eyes were dark-adapting—

A phone. The spark of light was a phone. Stupid, stupid. She scrambled in her pocket for her own phone – *don't drop it, for God's sake* – and flipped it open.

A little rectangle of light, dazzling, the usual mundane menu.

'Shit, shit. Thank you, thank you.'

She waved the phone about, like a torch. It shed a glow around her, a few metres in any direction. She was still on the bridge. There was the river, even, returning the faintest of reflections from the glow of her phone.

She felt as if her bubble of perception, her awareness of the world around her, was opening out slowly, slowly. She took a step back from the rail – *her* rail – though she held on to it for comfort, and looked around properly.

Dark everywhere. A sudden night. Below her, the river, now looking a deep, oily black. But above her head one stray light, hanging from the bridge structure somewhere like a forgotten Christmas decoration.

To her left, the city on the north bank was visible, just, with a few lights showing, lit windows, a few ad hoardings. Maybe her eyes were adapting to the dark. To her right the big pile of House on the south bank became more clearly visible too, patches of it shining with the glow of artificial lights, the big clearwood window panels vivid rectangles – but much dimmer than daylight, she realised now.

And there were those people on the bridge with her. She hadn't really even registered their existence before the dark came. More and more glowing pinpoints in the dark, people digging out their phones and watches and headbands. The speckles of light glittered and bobbed, like a swarm of fireflies along the bridge. Everybody seemed to have stopped still, their faces pale masks in the scraps of light.

She no longer felt so existentially scared. *I'm not blind, at least.* But utterly bewildered. She realised that *nobody* on this bridge, across the city, could know what the hell was happening in these first seconds, minutes. Nobody. They all had to work it out, one way or another. Millions of sudden nightmares. And maybe it went much further, too.

And she felt colder, suddenly, and gripped her lapels to close her overcoat tighter – but that was surely just a reflex, imagination. Or maybe not. Had some weather system rushed over? That was possible. Her father had always told her she was of a generation that had grown up blasé, used to freak climate events, of a frequency and severity that his own parents had never known.

But the sky above looked deep black. Not the grey of a regular, thickly overcast morning. Like an overcast *night*.

A streetlight came on, not far away from her on the bridge. Only one – some kind of emergency response? Somebody cheered raggedly. It dazzled her; she turned away.

And more lights were coming on now, she saw, across either bank, across the twin conurbations: more streetlights, more lit-up doorways, and she imagined people fumbling in the sudden dark for switches. On the bridge itself, people were moving now, released from the stasis of shock, going one way or another. Some came running past her, some staring into phones, speaking into them. As if led by the phones' light.

But Tash stayed still, casting around, still trying to figure this out. *The sky* was what counted, not the ground, the people. Something wrong with the sky. The cloud cover had been breaking up to the south and east, she remembered; there had been clear blue sky before. Again she looked that way, beyond House, and to the horizon, the direction of the ocean. She saw no blue sky now. Her eyes, increasingly adapting, saw only a swathe of darker sky where the clouds had broken up.

And she saw *stars*, scattered above that oceanic horizon.

Stars? At this time in the morning?

She still wasn't scared. Not since that first shock had worn off. Just bewildered. Or – awed. Somehow it was all too big to be scary. Bigger than the river, she thought, as the river is bigger than me. You can't hope to control it.

But then, thinking about the sky and the stars, she had a really stupid idea about what was causing this, or at least a connection. *Really* stupid. But it was the only lead she had. And she knew who to call.

She lifted her phone. Her father was calling, she saw. 'Phone. Hold Dad,' she said. 'Get me Melissa . . .'

A smiling face, a shock of strawberry-blond hair. *This is Mel Kapur. If you need—*

'Hey, Mel. When you get this. I'm in Newcastle . . . Just out of the office. Look, it's *dark* here. And – well, where the cloud is broken up I see stars. Stars! And it's not yet ten in the morning,

I think. Look – could it be something to do with the eclipse?'

She had never seen a total solar eclipse herself. But she knew that one was in progress now. When the Sun's light was blocked out by the Moon, if you were standing in the shadow cast by Moon on Earth, yes, there could be stars to be seen in a day-time sky, the planets. But she also knew that during any eclipse the shadow was confined to a narrow track across the Earth, depending on the relative positions of Sun, Moon, Earth. And today that narrow track was where Mel was, in the ocean some-where south of Africa. Half a world away. Not over Newcastle.

But she persisted. 'I know this is really dumb. But this seems to have cut in just when the eclipse was due. Could something – shit, I don't know how to frame the question – we shouldn't even have a partial eclipse up here. Has something, well – gone wrong with the eclipse?'

Mel Kapur's face showed up on her phone now, just a two-dimensional image, but live. Red hair, blue eyes, against a dark background. *That* is *really dumb. Hey, Tash. But, listen, I'm with the Astronomer Royal. If anybody can figure it out, she will.*

Tash tried to take this in. 'So it's – umm, it's happening down there too.'

Right. Well, if somebody turns the Sun off, it's going to be a kind of widespread phenomenon.

'Turned the Sun off? Do you think—'

I don't think anything just now, Tash. Not enough data. We're only minutes into this – well, whatever this is. And, Tash. We ought to try to call Zhi.

Just like Tash's first impulse, to think of friends. 'Yeah. In-Jokes together. He's on the Lodestone. In space . . .' She paged through her phone, hit a link that went through the interna-tional space agency, the NHSA, waited without much hope for a connection on a line meant for emergencies only.

Which this was. She supposed.

Now Tash heard, from the Newcastle bank, what sounded like a crumpling crash, a wailing car alarm, a scream. And, elsewhere, laughter. A police siren howling.

Still the darkness lingered.

'I think I should go back to House,' she said. 'Whatever this is, I think the governments are going to be headless chickens for a while.'

Mel smiled. *So go find your flock. I have to call Jane.* Mel's daughter.

'Tell her Auntie Tash says hi.'

I'll try Zhi as well. And if I find out more here, I'll get back to you. Keep your phone on.

Tash pushed a bud into her right ear. 'Will do. And I should call my dad. Phone, do that now.'

She hurried back over the bridge, watching her step, towards the still brightly illuminated Government House. Every step she took, she hoped the clouds would clear. That the Sun would turn back on. That this would just go away. It didn't.

'Mel. You still there?'

Yeah. Mel sounded breathless, as if she was hurrying too.

'This is going to change all our lives, isn't it?'

More than that, honey. More than that.

Somewhere an ambulance wailed.

And another burst of rain splashed over her face and hair. It felt as if it were getting colder, by the minute. The rain felt like sleet, in fact.

She hurried on, through the disconcerting dark.

3

0948 GMT

Melissa Kapur had had her own grandstand view of the event, in the minutes before she took Tash's call.

Although – even a professional astronomer, and though she was surrounded by other professional and celebrity eclipse-watchers – she had been distracted by the earthly view.

What a view, though.

Skythrust Two was a human-made island in the sky. And high in the sky too, twenty kilometres above the Southern Ocean: above the troposphere, with its clouds and murk. In fact the lower air itself looked like an ocean from this vantage, a deep blue ocean of the sky. Not a shred of cloud above to spoil her view of the Sun, as seen from inside this airtight bubble – a clear-walled observation lounge which sat on a sprawling, open deck – even as the shadow of the Moon had eaten its way across the disc, heading for that magic moment of totality, even as the overall light level subtly dropped, moment by moment.

Nothing to distract her save the astounding bulk of Skythrust itself, an observing platform steady as a rock.

This island in the sky was suspended between two hulls: equally immense cylinders each containing a power plant, the jet engines that controlled the craft's positioning, and other infrastructure. And from everywhere fine carbon-fibre cables snaked further up into the sky to the craft's upper level, the buoyancy farm. This wasn't a sphere like a hot-air balloon, or a torpedo-shape like the old airships; it was a kind of translucent quilt that shone in the strange, dimming light cast by the partially eclipsed Sun – but its upper surface was a solar energy plant that captured some of that light.

And the immense tanks of the farm were entirely empty.

Skythrust was an airship held aloft, not by hot air, helium, or hydrogen – like the old *Hindenburg*, with which she had much in common in terms of fittings and expense – but by vacuum, the ultimate lighter-than-air buoyancy agent. A couple of days back, as the ship had travelled from Johannesburg to this eclipse-watching station, Mel had been taken for a theme-park tour around and *inside* the buoyancy farm, a cathedral built of ultra-light, ultra-strong materials strapped over struts set in octagonal arrays. Two of the ship's designers had bragged their way through the tour, gleefully pointing out that the buoyancy farm was all of an English mile long, and you could have fit hundreds of *Hindenburg*s, whole, inside that mighty volume . . .

Skythrust was an Anglo-Australian design, in fact, developed from immense aerial tankers designed to export hydrogen fuel: a principal product for Australia now, manufactured from water electrolysed by huge, sprawling solar energy farms. She knew that the Aussies liked to say they were exporting sunshine; what better way to carry that sunshine than in a craft built around nothing at all?

But today the spectacular Skythrust was merely a platform from which to observe a greater vision yet. Mel's observation blister was one of several set around the deck, each hosting more passengers, observers protected from an external atmosphere too thin to breathe. And, dominating the centre of the deck space, an array of instruments had been set up to study the unfolding event in the sky, all of them mutely tilted up at the same angle, facing the Sun – just like the faces of the people, Mel thought whimsically.

All the passengers shared a sound system with an optional if enthusiastic commentary. Mel had tuned that out, but she had heard the passengers' gasps as the Moon's leading limb had first slid across the Sun's face – and more as the magic moment of totality approached. And even before totality, the dimming had got to the point where she thought she saw a first star low in the deep blue sky – no, that must be a planet, Venus. A magical sight.

Now she tried to focus on her job. She had to make the most of the observing opportunities of the next few minutes, she knew.

For her to be up here at all, to see the event with her naked eyes, was a kind of treat. Her nominal boss, Charlie Marlowe, England's Astronomer Royal, was buried down in the bulk of the ship, in a big dining area called the Games Room. She would be watching the data feeds as they clattered in, measurements from a bank of instruments ranging from infra-red to X-ray – and, in parallel, providing a commentary for a number of global feeds. Another privileged position, but shut up in a basement, effectively, and hidden from the glorious sky itself. Unlike Mel.

Concentrate, Mel, she told herself. *Be here now,* as her yoga teachers taught her. Such a moment might never come again.

The light dimmed further. Now she was distracted by the unveiling of the corona, the bright, extended outer atmosphere of the Sun – a shining cloud with smooth gradations of brilliance spreading around that central, shocking darkness – a sculpture in the sky normally rendered invisible by sunlight. And then—

Then, the final, perfect alignment of the discs of Sun and Moon. The moment of totality.

And the intensity of the daylight itself dropped, suddenly, dramatically, an effect that extended to the horizon, where an eerie greenish twilight gathered. It was a huge, integrated phenomenon that seemed to shock her, viscerally, a global-scale change, leaving her feeling utterly dwarfed – and, she saw now, a phenomenon beyond the ability of any single instrument to capture.

People gasped, whooped, even applauded. This was beyond her, beyond humanity, for all they tried to capture its fleeting scientific symptoms with eyes, brains, instruments. *This* was why people chased eclipses. And this, she thought, was why people were still sent into space, despite the sophistication of the robots. To *see* stuff like this. You had to be here.

But that moment, as she would later remember it, was when everything changed. For now there was a sudden, shocking *deepening* of the darkness, all across the cloudless, eclipse-morning sky.

It was as if somebody had turned down a dial on some mixing desk, the brilliant blue fading towards black, all the way to that greenish light on the horizon.

For Mel – unlike Tash, it turned out – there was no sudden moment of pitch dark. Skythrust itself still glowed subtly, even in the daylight, even in the midst of a solar eclipse, a glare leaking from the windows of the cabins and halls. Venus shone as bright, just where it had been, she noticed, bewildered.

And, around the position of the eclipsed Sun itself, that corona still shone – looking brighter than before, it seemed, against the darkened sky – and yet a kind of darkness was soon spreading there too, washing out from the black circle at the heart of it all, as if the overall structure were dispersing out into space. It took long seconds before the corona faded away entirely, seconds which she found herself counting out the astronomer's way: 'A thousand and fourteen, a thousand and fifteen . . .'

When the corona was gone, the darkness only deepened further. Now Mel could see stars coming out, joining Venus.

Still the 'eclipse' didn't end.

People began to mutter. Inside the observation bubbles, artificial lights sparked in the gathering dark. Through the shared sound system, she heard the voice of a woman asking plaintively, 'Is that supposed to happen?' Mel thought she recognised the voice – probably some astrological influencer, now utterly baffled.

No. This wasn't supposed to happen. This was very wrong.

Her phone vibrated. She grabbed it, saw a call waiting for her from Tash, pressed it to her head. 'Hold Tash. Call Jane.'

No immediate reply from her eleven-year-old daughter.

'Take Tash, then.'

Hey, Mel. When you get this. I'm in Newcastle . . . Just out of the office. Look, it's dark *here . . .*

Mel tried Jane again. No reply. She tried Zhi. Then Jane again.

And this time Jane answered. *Hey, Mum. I was just going to call. We're watching on TV. And it's getting kind of dark outside.*

Mel knew that Jane was in a rented cottage close to the observatory at Bouldershaw Fell, in Yorkshire, England, Charlie Marlowe's current base of operations and therefore Mel's too.

'Stay indoors, honey.'

I will. I—

'Is Sarah with you?' A second cousin, occasional house-sitter.

Yeah. You want to speak to her?

'No. Just close the doors, tell her to lock up.'

Are you OK, Mum? You're right under it.

Whatever *it* was. Still the sky stayed dark. Many stars were visible now, she saw, in the sky around that blank black disc, as her eyes dark-adapted. How long was totality supposed to be? The number had fled from her mind. Also she ought to be timing this. She was behaving as naively as the baffled influencer in the other bubble. Not like a scientist at all.

But then, this was no ordinary totality.

'Honey, I'll keep in touch. We'll figure out what's going on. Just stay indoors, OK?'

I will. Love you.

'Love you.' She flicked off the connection, made to call Marlowe — but the Astronomer Royal was already trying to get hold of her. 'Charlie, it's Mel, you got me. I'm on my way down—'

No. Don't. Stay up there. A bluff Manchester accent.

On the phone's screen, Charlie Marlowe was a gaudy splash of colour. Sixty years old, she was not tall, heavy-set, and habitually wore loudly colourful trouser suits. Her hair, cropped short, was dyed silver grey. Tash's dad always said she reminded him of Judi Dench as M in the vintage James Bond films. She stood out in any gathering, and, peering into her phone, Mel thought she fit in well against the garish, somewhat ridiculous backdrop of Skythrust's Games Room, a fancy lounge with a chessboard floor and huge playing cards on the walls.

Marlowe said now, *We have enough eyes staring at screens down here. I want a naked-eye view too. Well, give or take an airtight dome. Stay up there as long as it's safe.*

'Safe from what?'

How the hell do I know, on this ridiculous blimp? Atmospheric turbulence? Loss of buoyancy as the heat goes? I wish I was up there with you. Damn it, I'm the Astronomer Royal, and here is the most significant astronomical event in human history, probably, and I missed it. But I need to start making calls.

'Who to?'

Well, the federal English who are paying for this jaunt . . . Or maybe I'll cut a few corners and go straight to the FIS. As once I would have called the old UN Security Council. Of course they will soon start calling me. *Who else would they call? Hey. Was I the first person* you *called?*

'No. My daughter. When I couldn't get her, a friend—'

Good choices. Listen, Mel. I want you to stay close to me in the days to come. As all this unravels. You aren't the sharpest blade in the box, but you may have the biggest heart. I have a feeling that's going to be important. Because this is going to affect everybody on the planet.

Tash was bewildered by that. Marlowe was capable of enormous leaps of intuition, Mel knew. Only minutes into this – event – she seemed to be seeing global implications. 'I'm flattered. I think. OK, I'll stand watch.'

Good. All, we can *do now is watch. Measure.*

'Measure what?' And she bit her tongue; Marlowe wasn't too kind about dumb questions.

Whatever you can think of.

Mel thought that over, looked for the non-obvious. 'Gravity waves?'

Marlowe skipped a beat. *Yes. OK. Good thought. So we can't see the Sun. If this isn't just some optical effect – a radiation effect, hell, I don't know – if the Sun itself has somehow been disturbed – we ought to be detecting that particular death rattle. I'll put in a call to Bouldershaw. Somebody will be making the measurements; make sure we get hold of them.*

Let's just do what we can while we can. I'm going to be relying on you, Mel. Oh, and watch Venus.

'Venus?'

I . . . Voices clamouring in the background. *Who's calling? Already? Oh, hell, I'm coming. Keep safe, Mel.*

And she was gone.

Mel turned back to the sky.

Still that eerie midnight darkness. Stars coming out in numbers now. A big black hole where the eclipse was – the Moon, of course, now occluding the distant stars, as it had been blocking the Sun. But the eclipse should have been long over by now. The Sun peeking around the body of the Moon.

Remembering Marlowe's prompt, she looked for Venus.

And Venus went out, right at that moment. As if somebody had thrown a switch. Mel murmured into her phone to make a log of the timing.

Nobody else on the deck seemed to have noticed.

Now what? Think, Mel. What just happened? Well, we see Venus through the light it reflects from the Sun . . .

Light from the Sun that came directly to Earth took around eight minutes. But the light that came via Venus took a little longer, having first bounced off that world's cloud tops and crossed space to Earth. Now that reflected stream of photons, it seemed, was gone.

This wasn't just some shadow over Earth. There was no light coming out of the Sun, anywhere, in any direction. As if it had . . . gone out?

So, what next?

Upload, dummy. And get confirmation. She made a verbal note of the Venus observation on her phone, the timing, her tentative interpretation.

Around her people were reacting. Laughing. Some called for drinks. Most just stared. She had the sense that Skythrust, massive and solid as it was, suddenly didn't feel like much of a

29

safe refuge. How much more scared would they be if they were higher still, or out in space?

She raised her phone once more. 'Try again for Zhi, on the Lodestone.'

4

0959 GMT

Wu Zhi, aboard the Lodestone, was − though actually in space − the last of the In-Jokes to get the bad news about the Sun, courtesy of Mel's call. Although he was the first of the station's three-person crew to be aware of the day's problems. Ironic when he thought about it later.

But he didn't listen closely enough to Mel's hurried, bewildering call to take it all in, not at first. He thought, at first, the problem was with the corona, the Sun's outer atmosphere.

It wasn't by chance that, on this Friday morning (by Mel's and Tash's time), Zhi had *already* been gazing at the Sun's corona through various monitors, and indeed through a naked-eye window in the wall of the Shelter module they all called the observatory. After all, the whole point of the Lodestone, a station nestled behind the Earth in the planet's long shadow cone, was that, in normal operations, you couldn't see the Sun at all, or most of it.

The Lodestone held its station with the help of a magsail booster − a magnetic trap that caught the wind of charged particles that flowed endlessly from the Sun and washed around the Earth, and so harvested a steady, small but useful force. A force that, when balanced with the gravity of Sun and Earth, enabled the Lodestone to track Earth precisely, and stay within the shadow cone. And thanks to that shadow cone, the station was one of the darkest locations in the Solar System – and one of the best for astronomy. Even away from direct sunlight, space telescopes anywhere near the Earth itself could be blinded by the brilliance reflecting from sea and land and ice – what was left of the ice, anyhow.

So, in the umbra, there were telescopes working in the deep infra-red, seeking elusive traces of ancient radiation, evidence of the early days of the universe, impossible to capture anywhere else. *Big* telescopes. The largest of the station's telescopes was called the L^3T – L-Cubed-T – the Lodestone Ludicrously Large Telescope. And, with other sensors, still more elusive phenomena were studied here – some with instruments sponsored by Jones, Inc. itself, the major engineering contractor behind this station, mostly down to the initiative of its mercurial founder and principal shareholder Serena Jones. The Jones instruments sought traces of dark energy, for instance, the elusive counter-gravity field that seemed to be driving the long-term expansion of the universe itself.

And as for the Sun, you didn't have to wait for an eclipse, you *could* see the corona, any time you wanted, by creating artificial eclipses: carefully positioning your instruments so that the Sun itself was *just* hidden by Earth. Yes, Wu Zhi knew about the corona. Had spent many hours studying it.

But today offered a rare opportunity to do just that. For, if only for a few minutes, the corona would be visible from *two* widely separated locations – the Lodestone and the eclipse track on Earth – offering a chance to study the corona's three-dimensional structure. That was the plan, anyhow.

The trouble was, at the moment of eclipse, the universe wasn't behaving itself.

Just as Mel had warned him, he had already followed that

strange darkening sequence, fifteen seconds or so, as the corona
. . . dissipated. Or something. Eerie. Baffling. Zhi ran the record
through a few times, looking for clues as to what in hell he was
seeing. It was as if the eclipse, impossibly, was going on too
long.

He wondered how his fiancé, Jim Boyd, was feeling right
now. Jim, suspended in space between Mars and Earth, aboard
a spacecraft called Al-miriykh, far further away from home
than Zhi himself. And in the middle of what seemed like a Solar
System-scale anomaly.

He also wondered what the hell to do.

Lodestone was a spoked torus, assembled from over five hundred Jones, Inc. standard Shelter modules mated end to end: a
wheel connected to a central hub via four spokes. The whole
assembly rotated once every fifty seconds or so, to provide a
semblance of Earth-normal gravity in the outer torus, essential
for the health of crew and growing plants alike. The Lodestone contained a life support system that was almost a closed
loop, an ecosystem, of human beings and crop plants. And the
Lodestone, like other modern spacecraft, was able to venture
far from the Earth, thanks to the protection of a magshield, a
superconducting loop capable of repelling the charged particles
of lethal cosmic radiation.

The Lodestone had been a comfortable place to live and
work. Also, fun.

But now here was this anomaly with the corona. Zhi had a
feeling of vague dread.

He was relieved when he heard a familiar patter of running
footsteps, a noise barely muffled from having to travel from a
few modules down the chain that made up the main torus of
the station.

He needed somebody to talk to about this. And the only runner on the ship was Ange Costello, his commander.

'Ange. Hey. Come look. Something's off here.'

She stopped at the door, breathing hard, pushed a lank of greying hair back from a sweat-streaked forehead, took a swig from a water bottle. She showed the flash of impatience Zhu might have expected; nobody likes their running routine to be interrupted. But then this was deep space, and ignoring 'something off' wasn't a viable strategy, long term.

She bent down to see over his shoulder. 'So what's off? The corona? We see it every day. The fact that it's an eclipse should make no damn difference.'

That was the irritating side of Ange; she had a habit of second-guessing what you were about to say. 'Of course not. *Duh*. But it's different anyhow. Take a look. I've run this through a few times.' He glanced at a clock; it was still only a few minutes since scheduled totality. 'Watch the timer. Just at the moment of peak eclipse . . .'

It was, he knew by now, just what Mel Kapur had witnessed aboard Skythrust. There was the glorious eclipse corona. But then that peculiar fade-out, starting at the inner edge of the corona, to darkness.

Ange bent closer; he could smell her sweat, her Lycra shirt. 'Huh. That is odd. Let's run it again . . .'

They watched, and chewed the fat, and watched some more.

'Let's just think about what the corona is,' said Ange, solar specialist — and just a tad pompous with it, Zhi thought. She said, 'The corona is the Sun's outer atmosphere. Sparse, but very hot. Hot enough to be visible from Earth, when the disc of the Sun itself is obscured. Energy pumped into it by solar radiation and magnetism. And now, it just faded away. How?'

Zhi made a conceptual leap. 'But suppose you turned off that flow.'

She frowned. 'You mean, shadowed out the sunlight somehow? How? . . . Never mind. Yeah. If you *could*, the corona gases would quickly dump their energy in radiation. Fading down to infra-red pretty fast.'

'But the corona is light-seconds across. Therefore it would take seconds, a perceptible interval, for the last of the sunlight to, uh, wash through.'

'Just as we see in the recording.'

'Yeah.'

She looked at him. 'So what *could* block the sunlight from the corona?'

This time, no conceptual leap. 'I have no idea. Some kind of shield around the Sun?'

She snorted. 'One. A shield around a fusing mass more than a million kilometres across? Put there in an instant? And two. By "shield", do you imply some kind of artefact? We look for natural causes on this boat, Wu. Not agency. Not for somebody meddling with Heaven.'

Once, in the astronautics academy at Yale, Ange Costello had been his thesis supervisor. Now, all these years later, she was still his thesis supervisor. He might have snapped back about that.

But that was when the master alarm sounded.

Ange glanced over the control panel in front of Zhi. Snapped exactly the right switch.

The alarm dipped to a whisper.

Ange called, 'OK, Harry. You're in the hub?'

Harry Regent was the third of the three crew. His voice came through clearly. 'Doing my shift, checking the readouts.'

35

Ange gave him a second to do that.

The rule was that, at all times, in case some catastrophe hit, at least one person had to be in the heavily shielded hub – their fallback storm shelter at the centre of the torus. The hub was equipped with slaves of all the major control systems of the habitat, so was a good location to spot an alarm, and handle any mishap.

Of course people cheated, came out to help with stuff, for a break, just for company. Not Harry. Harry was a USAF officer. Zhi imagined him sitting in the hub, upright, every sense alert, monitoring the systems in this anomalous situation. As if he were in some Cold War nuclear silo. That was Captain Harry Regent for you.

'All fine in here,' Harry snapped now.

'OK. Zhi . . .' Ange scanned panels of her own. 'I don't see any reason—'

'I've got it. The cause of the alarm. Look here. We're drifting out of position. Only maybe ten metres a minute, but—'

'That can't be,' Ange said. 'I'm looking at the magsail tell-tales right now. Reading exactly as per specification. The sail is thrusting, holding us right where we are supposed to be.'

'Or it thinks it is.' Zhi brought up another display, showing the station's position as determined by radar pulses from satellites in Earth orbit, more than a million kilometres away. 'But the position anomaly is mounting up. And accelerating. And, hey – look at the time record! The problems started just about at the moment of peak eclipse. When the corona started playing up.' He felt an echo of that earlier, almost superstitious dread. 'But that can't be connected. Can it?'

Ange stiffened, almost perceptibly taking on her station commander role. 'OK. Harry, stay down in the hole. Make sure everything is copied down to Earth. But stay in the hole. Let's think this through. We're drifting out of position. What holds us in position in the first place? . . .'

Almost from first principles, Zhi and Ange went through the ship's design logic and systems, one by one. Looking for the flaw.

Zhi knew, as Ange did, that Lodestone was a delicate design. A kind of balance of forces. Strictly speaking Lodestone was a *statite*: a satellite held in orbit, not just by the gravity of Sun or Earth or other bodies, but with the aid of artificial propulsion systems.

A natural station-keeping location for an observatory like Lodestone might have been at the so-called second Lagrange point of the Earth-Sun system – L2, a million and a half kilometres from Earth. Once there, a satellite would stay put – or rather it would be swept around the Sun keeping pace with the Earth, thanks to the combined pull of Earth and Sun. And so the venerable James Webb Space Telescope had been stationed there – indeed it was still out there somewhere, in a silent orbital museum of its own.

But L2 was over a hundred thousand kilometres outside the umbra, Earth's cone of shadow. If you wanted to work *here*, inside the umbra, in this useful place for astronomy, the L2 gravitational balancing act no longer worked. The gravity fields of Earth and Sun, that much closer, pulled too hard on the Lodestone, which would soon have drifted out of position.

And so the station was attached to a magsail: a forty-kilometre-wide superconducting hoop whose magnetic field pushed against the solar wind, the steady stream of charged particles that pushed out from the surface of the Sun (and which washed around Earth's own magnetic field as if it wasn't there). The magsail pushed the station *outward* with the precise force required to compensate for the inward-pulling gravity fields of

Earth and Sun — as required to maintain its orbit in the umbra, keeping in step with the Earth.

The magsail, in fact, had given the station its name, Zhi had been charmed to learn when he had first been assigned to it. In *Gulliver's Travels*, the flying island of Laputa was (implausibly) kept aloft by a lodestone, an immense bar magnet . . .

But right now that delicate balancing act, of magnetism and gravity, was failing.

Ange shook her head, irritated, as she could get when some set of facts made no sense. She glanced over more instrumentation. 'This can't be right. We only have one active component, the magsail, and that is working fine. There's nothing *to* go wrong.'

Zhi said, 'Let's think it through again. We have three forces in balance. The Sun's gravity is about six hundred microgee out here.' An acceleration of about six hundred millionths of Earth's surface gravity. 'Earth itself contributes twenty-one microgee. And the magsail should be pushing us outwards — *is* — at fourteen microgee. Leaving us the balance of six hundred and seven microgee we need to keep us orbiting as we should be.'

'OK,' said Ange. 'And the defect is, Harry?'

'Well, it's pretty big,' Harry Regent admitted. 'Almost six hundred microgee.'

Zhi kept his mouth shut, for fear of Ange's reaction if he said the obvious out loud. Let her say it for herself.

Which she did, eventually. 'The defect is the same as the *whole* of the Sun's gravity. That's not possible.'

Zhi, thinking fast — thinking wildly, he felt — said, 'Harry, copy me your timings, would you? The loss of the corona, and when we started to drift . . . Thanks. Shit. *The timings match.* Just like my readings here. We lost the gravity just as the corona started to fade.'

'Got to be some kind of outgassing from the station itself,' Ange muttered. 'Evaporation. Paint, giving up its moisture in the cold. Got to be.'

Zhi grinned. He couldn't help it. *'Paint?'*

'Even so,' Harry said, more cautiously, 'kind of a coincidence that it gave off a thrust that should exactly match our solar supplement.'

Zhi suspected that Harry was coming to the same conclusion he was, if not Ange. He said cautiously, 'So it looks like the Sun's light switched off. And its gravity, yes? It's almost as if— well, almost as if *the Sun itself has gone away.*'

A screen flashed orange. Another alert signal. Ange tapped the panel, read the text.

'Wow,' Harry said, evidently looking at a slaved copy in the hub.

Zhi was the only one who couldn't see it. 'What is it? The ground checking up?'

'It's not from the ground,' Ange said. 'It's from deep space. A general broadcast.' She looked at Zhi. 'It's from the Al-miriykh. They're in some kind of trouble.'

Zhi tried to think that through. *If the Sun has gone out of Jim's universe too* . . . He shook his head, unable to think further, to think beyond Jim.

Ange rested her hand on his shoulder. 'We'll figure this out. Come on. Let's talk to the ground.'

On stations like the Lodestone, all of the crew's conversations were routinely recorded.

And later it would be determined that nobody on record, anywhere in human space, articulated that hypothesis, that the Sun itself had vanished at 0948 GMT of that day, earlier than Wu Zhi.

5

1002 GMT

On board the Al-miriykh, in space, suspended between Mars and Earth, the master alarm had sounded a little before 1248 hours, Moscow time.

And Jim Boyd, during his short watch at the main control console, had thought he saw – a flash? A change in the light? Just before the alarm clamoured.

So Jim had reflexively checked his watch.

Or rather, watches. He always wore two on his wrist, one set to GMT, so he would know what time they marched to at mission control at Houston – and also Wu Zhi, his fiancé, using GMT on the Lodestone – and the other set to Moscow time, as followed by TsUP. Pronounced 'soup', the Russian mission control was a shack in a grubby suburb in the north of the city. Both controls reported into NHSA, of course, the unified Northern Hemisphere Space Agency, but they were stubborn about their national timekeeping traditions.

Anyhow whatever clock you used, when things went south checking the time *always* paid off, if only when it came to constructing a timeline of events later. If only to apportion blame.

If there was a later.

0948 GMT, then. He scanned the habitat, automatically looking for obvious issues.

This was the core of the Al-miriykh, configured as it was now for its return to Earth. Basically a US-England-Russia-Japan collaboration.

Not that there was a lot to see. A Jones, Inc. Shelter was just a big cylinder, a smart, compact design. Just like the one Zhi was sitting in right now, he thought. The main space-occupier within this particular volume was the storm shelter, a thick, sturdy cylinder within a cylinder, a retreat offering protection when 'foolproof' defences against pressurisation loss or radiation hazards failed. Russian designers were very conservative, and so this thick-walled fallback sat in the middle of the habitat, with such features as its own independent air supply and heating system.

Aside from the racket of the alarm, all seemed well; the various control panels and displays all seemed to show the usual constellation of normal settings.

Now, Jim saw, his two crewmates were reacting to the alarm as he would have expected. Both of them, like Jim, were checking the lightweight pressure gauges they wore on their belts. The most dangerous plausible event that might have triggered the alarm would have been a catastrophic hull breach, maybe through some collision or seal failure, and a rapid loss of air. At the same time Ito Katsuo was confirming readings at the main displays.

And Marina Petko already had the storm shelter open. She glanced back regretfully at the dinner she had been preparing, a thick Russian cabbage soup.

Jim looked around further, wondering what they were missing. Nothing visibly wrong with the structure of the habitat itself.

He slammed a green button to shut down the alarm. 'OK. I'll call it in. TsUP, Al-miriykh. Ah, mission clock shows 1302 your time. We just had a master alarm. Cause unknown. Rapid depressurisation ruled out. Seeking the cause.'

The comms set was smart enough to turn itself on when it heard such a structured message, and transmit it.

Of course there would be no immediate reply. The Al-miriykh was in interplanetary space, having left Mars back in August, and was not due to reach Earth until April, months away – all this after a landing on Mars as far back as May 2055, the start of their fifteen-month tour at Curiosity Base.

April. If they got that far. For now, they were light-minutes away.

All spacefarers – especially American astronauts, Russian cosmonauts – studied dramatic space accidents of the heroic past. Apollo 13 was the most famous, of course, but there had been other incidents. Such as during the flight of Gemini 12 in 1966 when, after a rendezvous radar failure, Buzz Aldrin had hand-calculated thruster burns to get the craft aligned with its target for docking. And the time in 1997 when the Russian space station Mir had collided with a rogue resupply vessel.

The difference was, those crews, even Apollo 13, had had the benefit of support and advice from the mission controllers, in Houston or Moscow, at most only a couple of seconds' time lag away. Jim knew he was shouting into the void; it would be long minutes before support of any kind could come from the controllers at TsUP or Houston.

In the meantime the crew were on their own, facing this problem. But what problem?

'Jim? You OK?'

Marina Petko drifted in the air before him, before the open storm shelter. She was thirty-five years old, short, wiry, compact, dark hair shaved neatly close to her skull, her Russian accent light – her English was better than his Russian. Ito,

Japanese, was similarly short, sturdy. No coincidence. Good astronaut-candidate build, he thought.

'Sorry. Thinking too fast – or too slow.' He glanced around the humming habitat. On good days, it reminded him of a kind of modern kitchen, full of smart, helpful state-of-the-art gadgets. But you didn't get master alarms on good days.

And now the alarm sounded again.

Jim punched the off-button again. 'Not another bloody one.'

6

1016 GMT

Once her confidence had come back, somewhat, Tash Brand had run back from the Millennium Bridge to House. So much for sleep.

The streets had been safe enough. The smart-car traffic had all just stopped when the light failed and pedestrians began wandering around over the roads, so accidents in the immediate aftermath must have been rare – not so rare that she didn't hear the wail of ambulances, though, perhaps caused by people less smart than their cars. Meanwhile, people emerging from brightly lit shops and offices into sudden night seemed to be just as bewildered, if not existentially shocked, as everyone out in the open had been at the moment of – well, nightfall.

It had got a little easier after the first few minutes, when canny managers in council offices began to order the streetlights on. Soon the place had the feel of a sudden, strange but friendly event, and Tash had started to hear laughter, of wonder, even excitement. 'Like a bloody late-night Christmas fair for some folk,' one older man had muttered as he pushed past her.

Still, it was gone quarter past ten before she got back to Government House.

The moment she walked through the big revolving door into the entry lobby with its sign-in desks and security processes, her eyes were briefly dazzled by the brilliance of the light.

And she found herself in a crush of people. Most were trying to get in and back to work, as she was, and chafing at the usual scans and bioscreens. But a handful were heading the other way. Some, maybe, were on official errands that couldn't be entrusted to the net. Others were just heading home. Anxious-looking, probably parents. Tash couldn't remember if the attendance schools had gone back yet from the Christmas break. Home schooling, of course, never let up, and *those* parents might be worried about kids being left alone in homes smart enough to be trusted when things went well, maybe not so much when some weirdness like this closed over the world. *Kitchen. Put the sunshine back on . . .*

She felt somewhat disoriented too, she admitted to herself, to be back in what felt like her own normality. As if the whole weird scene outside had been some kind of dream.

The resulting crush, though, was a slow-moving tide. Growing anxious herself, Tash pushed steadily forward, waving her security card, keeping her phone clamped to her ear, listening for updates from Mel and others. She learned that Mel had even got through to Zhi on the Lodestone, thanks to a friend at TsUP in Moscow, and heard about his problems with positional drift, and his fears for his fiancé Jim, even further out in space.

When she finally got in front of a guard, with a security gate and DNA scanner, she tried to pull rank. 'Natasha Brand. Adviser to Fred Bowles. The science minister . . .'

That title wasn't strictly accurate. Bowles had a lot more responsibilities than just science, but whatever was going on today was obviously science-y, and that was the card she played. It worked to an extent, at least getting her some attention.

And it got better yet as a woman – heavily built, dark complexion, dyed-blonde crewcut, in her thirties – emerged from a secondary scrum behind the security line. Grinning sardonically, she grabbed Tash's arm, pulled her forward.

She was dragged through a door at the back of the lobby, and hurried into a warren of corridors, wood and steel. Heading, Tash guessed immediately, for Situation Room 5, right at the multi-layered core of the building, one of the obvious choices in the middle of an event like this. Not that she had ever been through an event quite like this.

They all but jogged to the first turn, with the woman still holding Tash's arm painfully tight, after which she let go and they merely walked quickly.

Her guide glared at Tash. 'Where in the chuff have you been?'

'Morning to you too, Grace.'

Grace Butterworth was a personal private secretary to Fred Bowles, officially, and bodyguard, unofficially. The gossip was she had once served as a marine.

Tash went on, 'Since you ask, I was on my way home. After a twelve-hour shift on the university bursaries thing. When it . . .'

Grace glanced at her with a trace of sympathy. 'I know. We don't even know what to call it yet. But like I say. You took your time.'

Tash glanced at her watch. It was gone 1040 already – it must have taken her all of twenty minutes to get through the crush. But still, less than an hour since that astounding moment of darkness. 'How was I supposed to know? I should book myself a double shift just in case the Chinese block out the Sun?'

Grace gave her an odd glance. 'Watch your language.' She tapped an ear bud. 'There's already a lot of panicky talk like that. So my buddies tell me.'

More special forces types, a network of minders like Grace, Tash imagined. Maybe they had nights out arm-wrestling.

Grace was right, though. In a crisis you didn't want anyone remotely connected with government to *feed* the disinformation memes that always popped up. Such as by naming a potential enemy without any evidence.

'Anyway, I'm here now,' she pointed out to Grace.

'Good job. He asked for you specifically. By name.'

'Why? Because I'm one of the few advisers the science minister has who actually knows some science?'

Grace snorted. 'Flatter yourself. Because he thinks you know the Astronomer Royal. Or you know somebody who knows her. You do, don't you? And this is obviously an astronomy type of thing, isn't it? I know he spoke to her to get some sensible advice when the MOD wanted to spend that fortune on asteroid deflection. Now he can't get through to her. *You* might. If I were you I'd start making that call now.'

Tash thought about that for one second, as they trotted along. She pulled out her phone. 'Right. Thanks, Grace.'

'You owe me one. Another one.'

'I know, I know.' She tried to call Mel, on Skythrust.

When they got there, Situation Room 5 was already crowded, noisy, the walls covered by huge, glowing screens. There was a central table for the principals, with rows of seats behind for their advisers. People sat, or wandered between the rows, shouting into phones or pressing buds into their ears.

Tash had been in this or similar rooms many times before, whenever a swift response had to be formulated to some sudden crisis – mostly terrorism or cyber-crime or a virus or a weather event, or some combination. Once, the attempted assassination of a junior royal. Nothing, she realised now, on a scale to be compared to – outside. To whatever was going on today. Nothing of the *nature* of this weird, huge phenomenon either.

Still, she did at least recognise the symptoms of an early stage of crisis management in the chaos before her, which was basically a scramble for information. On an interconnected planet of ten billion people, ten billion viewpoints, the problem was generally too much data, not too little. And the first default source of information – of *some* kind of interpretation, rather than just raw data – was always the professional news outlets. That was certainly true today, she saw immediately. On the smart walls, screen after screen showed a lit-up talking head set before darkness, or before a star-spattered sky, depending, she supposed, on whether or not the weather happened to be cloudy at said talking head's location. She did make out a few prominent location labels: London, Dublin, New York, Beijing, Moscow, New Paris . . .

Black skies everywhere, then. Whether it was local day or night. She shivered. It was a shock to have the global scale confirmed so graphically.

And here came Fred Bowles, bustling into the room and through the crowd. Forty-eight years old, his hair grey and thinning, he was a little overweight, a little pale, and looked as if he had slept in his suit. But he always looked like that. And he spotted her.

'Tash. About bloody time. Do you have her yet? The AR? I'm trying official channels of course, but that bloody ship she's on seems just as chaotic as everywhere else this morning.'

Tash had kept her phone clamped to one ear and a bud in the other; she explained quickly that she was trying to make contact through her friend on Skythrust. 'My contact's trying, but the Astronomer Royal is the centre of attention up there too, sir. As you might imagine. So – not yet.'

'Then get a bloody move on. Tell her it's bloody urgent.'

Tash murmured into her phone, trying again to reach Mel.

Grace stepped forward. 'Let me bloody help, sir?'

'How?'

'I'll see if there's an off-duty copper on that airship.'

Tash said, 'It's not strictly an airship—'

'Shut up. Or ex-military. You often find them, places like that. Security guards, for the ship itself or celebrity bodyguards. Get one of them to fetch the Astronomer Royal over. That should sort it.'

'Good thinking,' Bowles said. 'Do it.' He turned to Tash. 'Can't think who else to call, to begin with. But you start with the right person and it all cascades, you find. The right contacts. If you have some kind of astronomical event going on, you call the Astronomer Royal. As long as that's Charlie Marlowe anyhow. And I do need to have some kind of brief ready before the Cobra meeting.'

'What Cobra meeting?'

'Hasn't been called yet. Will be. Apparently the Home Secretary is in Newcastle; she'll chair it. Got to have some kind of handle on this by then. Across the country the chief constables are already calling local major incidents, roping in their emergency response partners – the NHS and WHOCare, the councils, fire, rescue, the environment agency. The usual Gold Command set-up. But mostly doing it without a clue about what they are dealing with, in *this* . . . we don't even have a name for it yet. Just local efforts, we've yet to formulate a national response. Which is what the Cobra is for.'

'Yes. Well, I suppose it is still . . . unravelling.'

'Quite so. Were you outside when it happened? I was in a meeting. We were shown it on TV. It looked to me like, I don't know, a bally awful special effect from some forty-year-old superhero movie. My mother doted on those when I was a kid; could never stand the things . . .'

He seemed to run down, appearing briefly helpless. He sat at the head of the big table, thumbing his phone. Tash just stood there, trying to support him, if silently.

Fred Bowles, Oxford graduate in Displaced Persons Studies, wasn't a *bad* science minister for the English federal government to have appointed, Tash had long thought. Especially since she had heard that as a postgraduate in the 2030s he had gone out to see for himself the post-volcanic Greenland Melt, with its catastrophic flooding and displaced-person consequences from the eastern seaboard of the United States to the north European plain. Out there he had certainly witnessed the role science played in predicting and mitigating disasters. Even so, there was nothing in his educational background that had prepared him for the job — but that wasn't unusual in any modern government system Tash had yet encountered, in her own slowly widening experience.

The real problem was that he wasn't *just* the science minister. Officially speaking he was Minister of State for Universities, Science, Research and Innovation. And in the government bureaucracy, 'science' itself was buried even deeper, in the Department of Business, Energy and Industrial Strategy. So on the rare day when he had to deal with what was clearly, at first manifestation at least, a scientific issue, it was hard for Bowles to focus on the matter.

But if Bowles had a talent at all, Tash thought, it was to surround himself with roughly the right people, from all the disciplines under him, and then ask roughly the right questions — as if on a hunch, and at least giving himself an edge before the shit hit the fan, as Grace Butterworth had once put it.

So asking Tash to find the Astronomer Royal for him was far from the worst start he could have made. Even if, as Tash knew, Bowles had the support of whole committees of government-assembled advisers of various sorts – such as, in this instance, SAGE, the venerable Scientific Advisory Group for Emergencies – all of which Charlie Marlowe adamantly refused to join. Which was probably why Bowles picked her out now.

He seemed to pull himself together, and eyed Tash. 'In the interim, you're the tame scientist, Ms Brand.'

Just as Grace Butterworth had remarked.

'Any ideas?'

'Well, strictly speaking my study area was the sociology and communication of science in the post-2030s era—'

'You're the scientist, Ms Brand. Any ideas?'

'Not really, sir.'

'There's wild speculation flying around. Maybe you can shoot some of it down, at least. The solar eclipse gone wrong?'

She smiled. 'I thought of that. I asked Mel – the Astronomer Royal's assistant on the Skythrust. Sounds impossible, sir – well, but I suppose the whole thing is impossible. An eclipse is just the sunlight shadow of the Moon crossing the Earth. In this case, the totality was over the Southern Ocean – south of South Africa.'

'Well, then, could – I don't know, could the Moon have drifted out of position somehow?'

She said ruefully, 'Not a bad guess, sir. Well, we can still see the Moon from its shadow against the stars; it hasn't moved away from its expected orbital path.' As Mel had told her. 'And even if it had moved, the eclipse shadow would just have shifted across the face of the planet. You wouldn't get the total, global blackout we have experienced.' She thought further. 'Of course, longer term there would be much more dramatic effects. The tides—'

With a wave of his hand he cut off that thread of speculation, which was fruitless for now, she realised. He said, 'Some kind of weather effect, then? I've been on to the Met Office.'

She shrugged. 'I doubt it.' She looked around at the screens. 'Again, it seems to be globally observed, doesn't it? It's hard to believe some weather system could wrap itself around the whole planet simultaneously. And besides, it's a phenomenon that's been observed *under clear skies*, hasn't it?' She thought of that eastern horizon, glimpsed over the North Sea. 'Even here. Where the sky's clear you can see the stars.'

'Umm.' She saw that even as he spoke to her he was accessing information from the screens around him, the phone on the table. 'There do seem to be global weather *consequences*, at least, if not causes. The Met Office are saying it's already starting to get colder than it should for the time of year. The loss of sunlight – I suppose you'd expect that. And if this goes on . . .' He shook his head. 'Come on, Fred. Focus on the here and now. Might all be over in an hour. If not . . .

'What can be *causing* this, then? Something beyond the atmosphere? What, though? What can block out the sunlight? Some bloody great shield, like the geoengineering experiments the Chinese used to tout? Screening out the sunlight to reduce global heating?'

She was impressed by that imaginative line of thought. 'Perhaps, sir. Well, that's about the most realistic guess I've heard so far. But you'd need a pretty big shield to cut out *all* the sunlight, across the planet. We'd have seen the thing being built, or approaching its position . . . And then there's the precision of the thing.' And, she thought, the weird, unprecedented effects like the corona fade-out that Mel had mentioned in her calls. 'Sir, I just don't know.'

Bowles bit his lip, and went back to thumbing his phone.

Tash, standing behind his chair, tried to focus, to follow his lead in abstracting data from a range of sources, all at once. She glanced around at the myriad screens, seeking grounding, a distraction – a headline. But now she saw she was seeing reports covering a wider variety of incidents. Pictures of bonfires, even explosions. Windows smashed. Not just reporters gawking at an empty night sky, though those still predominated.

Grace, still watching her own phone, pointed at one set of screens. 'While we're waiting for the Astronomer Royal and Cobra, sir, maybe we should do something about *that*.'

Tash, squinting, made out what looked like an effort to climb a slim stone pillar. Laughing people, wearing head torches, hammers knocking in chisels as crude pitons. And a bonfire being built at the base.

'Christ,' Bowles said. 'That's the Grey Monument. Newcastle. That's bloody *here*. People are going crazy. It's not been an hour yet!'

'Crazy, or afraid,' Tash said.

Grace shrugged. 'Some people don't need much of an excuse to kick off. There are immediate practical steps to be taken. If you're the ranking minister locally, sir, until the Home Secretary shows up—'

'Christ, yes.' Again a rake of the hair. 'Not thinking clearly. Well done, Butterworth. Never was at my best in the middle of the night.'

'Well, it's the middle of the morning, sir,' Grace said. 'It just feels like the middle of the night.'

'Right. Right.' An aide passed, randomly; he beckoned her over. 'You. What's your name? Listen. Get in touch with the local chief constable. If she tells you she has already called a major incident, tell her it's not enough. Tell her she has emergency powers, authorised by me, to take whatever steps she needs to handle the local situation. We need to calm it down, here of all places. Maybe pandemic lockdown rules would do for a start.' One of a number of civil emergency responses that people were trained in from school days.

'And get *all* the damn streetlights on, even if it is—' He checked his watch. 'Still not much past ten in the morning. What else? Call in off-shift coppers. Make sure the hospitals are staffed to emergency-incident levels. That kind of thing. She will know. Met her once – very capable.' He thought further. 'And get me a line to the Home Office. Suggest the same steps be implemented nationally. Although I wouldn't be surprised if half the Cabinet aren't already making similar calls. Well, we'll get coordinated after the Cobra, but we shouldn't wait for that to deal with what's in front of us now.'

'Yes, sir.'

'And . . .'

Hey, Tash. Mel, in Skythrust, whispering in Tash's ear. *Still trying to get to Charlie for you.*

'Good work, Mel.' Tash waved at Fred Bowles to get his attention, and mouthed 'Astronomer Royal'.

Mel went on, *And I'm still trying to get hold of Jane. She's at the school she goes to in Yorkshire, when I'm stationed at Boulder-shaw. So I'm hoping they will just keep them safe in there until they can be collected. It's all happening so fast I suppose the schools are having to make their own decisions, like the rest of us . . . Tash, if you get a chance, maybe you could – oh. Here's Charlie Marlowe.*

'Put her on speaker. Professor Marlowe? Is that you?'

Well, I know it's me, but who the bloody hell are you?

Tash gritted her teeth.

'I'm putting you on conference. This is Government House. I have Fred Bowles, Minister of State for science and other aspects of—'

Oh, him.

To his credit, Bowles smiled. 'Yes, we've met more than once, Professor Marlowe. Look, it's obvious why I've called . . .' Another aide rushed up, pushed a second phone into his hand. He glanced at it. 'Stay on the line, Professor. I've just been informed we have a Cobra coming up at 1130. What's that, an hour or more off? Home Secretary will be here. I want you on the line, Professor. All right?'

That was an order, Tash could tell.

And Grace, grim-faced, gave him a thumbs-up, and murmured into her own phone. Tash knew that whatever heavy she had found to get hold of the Astronomer Royal wasn't going to let her get away.

But Marlowe wasn't coming quietly. *Oh, wonderful. What a good use of my time, as opposed to actually studying this damn thing, whatever it is. My advice is for everybody to go home and wait it out, one way or another.*

Bowles grimaced. 'I would say we pay you for more than *that*, Astronomer Royal, if I were sure that we pay you anything at all.' He glanced again at his phone. 'They've put us in Conference Room D for the Cobra. I'd better get down there for the set-up. *Stay on the line*, Professor.'

Grace grinned. 'Oh, she will, sir.'

'And where the hell *is* Conference Room D? This place is a damn warren.'

'The aide who brought you the phone will take you. Will you want Natasha here with you?'

'Yes.' He eyed Tash, then paused. 'No. Not just yet. There's a little time. Do me a favour. Go back out and get a flavour of what's really happening out there. Grace, go with her. I think we will need to inject a little realism into the conversation, when it finally happens. Get back before the Cobra.' He looked around, clearly thinking aloud. To the aide he added, 'Keep the

Astronomer Royal on the line. Set up backup links. Oh, and set up a quick security pass for these two when they come back. Right, Room C, Room C—'

'D, sir,' Grace said gently.

As he receded with the aide, Tash murmured to Grace, 'He was almost impressive then. Decisive.'

'Don't let him hear you say that. Doesn't pay to let them get big-headed. Come on, we need to get out of here. I suspect that hour won't seem very long at all, out in the wild.'

They hurried out of the room.

'Any idea where you want to go?'

Tash considered. 'How about a church?'

7

1020 GMT

Aboard the Al-miriykh, the crew worked through the after-math of their alarms.

Jim tried to think it through. 'The first alarm. I thought I saw – I don't know, a flicker in the light – just before the alarm went off.'

Ito Katsuo spun in the air, quickly scanning the displays. 'One thing at a time. The cause of the first alarm is obvious. We lost primary power: the solar power, the panels. All of it. As the alarm sounded, we were already switched over to battery power.' She checked more displays with competent taps. 'Which we are running down right now. Nominal use for outages, they should last eight hours. After twelve hours, we have to make a mandatory internal evacuation to the storm shelter, with all the battery power dedicated to sustaining that. After *that*, a little less than another twelve hours to battery exhaustion, if we are lucky. As you know.'

That was a standard timing, Jim knew. Their two dozen lithium-ion batteries were good engineering, but were designed as backup for short periods when the primary power source, the big external solar panel array, was out of action. Only short outages had been anticipated; the batteries wouldn't last long.

Privately he suspected they might not even make the eight-hour minimum target.

His thinking felt as slow as glue.

'So,' he said, 'the solar panels are offline?'

'Obviously,' Ito said heavily, not quite sarcastically.

'But that shouldn't happen. What can go wrong? The panels are always in sunlight. They are damn near foolproof, the technology is so simple and robust. And decades old.'

That was true. The ship's power system, solar panels and backup batteries, dated back in spaceflight history to the ISS, the International Space Station, and earlier. And between Earth and Mars, unlike in Earth orbit like the ISS, the craft was in perpetual sunlight. Even if it had lost attitude and started to pitch and roll, say, the huge external solar panels, great black sails around the hull, were smart enough to have reoriented themselves to keep facing the Sun.

He said lamely, 'The panels can't have failed.'

Ito shrugged. 'Yet they have.'

Marina said, inspecting the displays, 'And now that second alarm. That wasn't the power system again, actually.'

Which Jim had assumed it must have been. 'Then what?'

'The navigation system. It's lost its lock on the Sun. It's still picking up the beacons at Earth, and the star sensors all seem to be registering. But nothing from the Sun sensors.' She checked further. 'In fact we haven't lost positional information, or attitude. The systems are smart enough to take a majority poll, and maintain position. But they're recording a possible fault with the Sun sensor . . . The system's just confused, I think.'

More bewildering news.

'It occurs to me,' Jim said slowly, 'we should take a look out the window.'

*

58

They exchanged glances.

'For instance, in case we have somehow lost the solar arrays. Let's go see.'

Marina said, 'How could that possibly happen?'

Ito laughed softly. 'What if it has happened, even if impossible? Here we are staring at screens. Of course we should look outside. Maybe even now, nearly a hundred years after Gagarin, human eyes and brains can still make a difference. Perhaps we have been over-trained.'

Marina frowned. 'Mission protocol, though. We should be backing up into the storm shelter, already.'

Jim hesitated. 'OK. But Ito is telling us that at least one system is confused, right now. So the warning is ambiguous. I think the protocols allow us to check a little further, get more data. Let's take a look out there. Come on. No shoving . . .'

They hovered in the air, crowded before a port – a small aperture, thick safety glass, and for once Jim wished the designers had made the view ports larger.

The sky was cut in half.

Jim saw a starscape above, a black plane below – sharp-edged as far as he could see. The plane was a solar panel array, deep black so as to absorb the sunlight energy efficiently. But there was always some reflection, and strong solar illumination usually highlighted the non-absorbing frame, the reflective struts that held the flimsy panels in place.

None of that now. Just that black floor.

'That's array beta,' he said. 'Of course we didn't lose the arrays. There's no indication of a failure of connectivity. And if the arrays had been physically ripped off, catastrophically, we'd have *felt* it.'

'The ship probably wouldn't have survived such an event at all,' Ito said.

'Right. But beta should be in sunlight just now.'

'Well,' Marina said. 'There's no sunlight to be seen out there.' She lifted a handheld screen to record the view. Waved it so it caught the distant stars, Jim guessed.

'Which makes no sense,' Ito said. 'Maybe – what? Did we roll? Is the Sun on the far side of the hull, now?'

'Impossible,' Jim said. 'Even with total instrument failure we'd have felt that, felt any roll.'

They looked at each other.

Marina said, 'Impossible or not, let's go see.'

They crossed the inner space, huddled around a port on the far side of the hull.

'Same view,' Ito said unnecessarily. 'The panels – there's the alpha array.' Another black cut-out. 'And the distant stars. No sunlight here either.'

Marina lifted her handheld monitor. 'I've been running quick visual checks. Eyeballed the sky, with this. The stars are where they are supposed to be. I mean, we haven't rolled. And as you say, we'd have felt it. Our orientation is correct.'

'But no sunlight on the arrays.'

'Correct.'

They drifted away.

'Think it through,' Jim said, trying to slow his speech to match the dull plod of his thoughts. 'We get no power from the arrays. We don't see any technical problem with the arrays themselves, the feeds to the batteries. We haven't suffered any kind of catastrophic failure. The arrays are *there*. And their orientation is correct.'

Marina looked from one to the other. 'We already said all that. You are avoiding the obvious. We all looked out there.

The solar panels are still there. They have no faults. They are providing no output because there's no input. But *there's no sunlight striking the panels.*'

A leaden pause.

'Very well.' Ito checked more displays. 'How can that be? Have we fallen into some kind of shadow? Of a mass of some kind? An asteroid? . . . It would have to be pretty large to occlude us completely. And even if the ground hadn't warned us about the close approach, the proximity radar would have picked it up, oh, days ago. A system which *is* working, I see now. Anything larger than a grain of pulverised asteroid dust would have been flagged as we approached it.'

'Not a shadow, then,' Marina said, growing angry now. 'This isn't playing fair. So what is it?' She glared out of the window again, and pointed. 'The Sun should be – right – *there* . . .'

She pointed into black, empty space.

The master alarm sounded again.

This time Marina went to punch it off.

She glared in exasperation at fresh readouts. 'Another problem. Now our trajectory is drifting. Just minutely, but, yep, we're going off course. Like a steady thrust is being applied. Some kind of air leak?'

'I doubt it,' Ito said. 'Surely this is connected to the big picture.'

Marina glared. 'What big picture?'

Ito said, 'Sunlight gone. So we lose solar power. We lose sunlight navigation. All in an instant. And we start to drift off course, our orbit around the Sun. As if—' She ran down, shrugged.

Jim said, 'You were about to say, as if we lost the Sun's gravity, as well as its light.'

'It's insane,' Ito said. 'It doesn't fit.'

'Quite right,' Marina said. 'The question is, what do we do about it?'

Jim tried to focus. 'That's clear enough, at least. We follow our training. We get in that damn storm shelter, and we close the door, and we wait for some kind of proper feedback from TsUP. And then, when we're sure we know what the situation is, we figure out what we need to do.'

There was no argument; they all pushed through the air towards the storm shelter's sturdy, open hatch.

'But the trouble is,' Marina murmured, 'if something really has happened to the Sun itself — some monster flare, I don't know — TsUP will have their own problems today . . . All of Earth will.'

'They won't forget us,' Jim said firmly. 'Whatever's going on down there.' *And nor will Zhi forget me, no matter what's happening over on the Lodestone.*

He slammed the door closed behind them.

8

1030 GMT

The church of St Joseph's was about twenty minutes' walk away from House, perhaps less.

Grace commandeered a smart car. They made it in five.

But as they neared their destination they slowed up, the car having to inch through a thickening mass of people, all evidently heading for the church. An instinctive response, Tash supposed, as seen in times of crisis in the movies – and indeed what she had come to study. Still a surprising sight, though.

Grace murmured a brief request into her phone.

And by the time the car reached the small gate that led into the church grounds a few minutes later, there was a police drone hovering over the porch, issuing calm instructions for the crowds to step back, be patient. On the whole, the drone was being obeyed.

They were able to get out of the car, into the pitch dark, make their way through the gate and towards the church door, and jump a ragged queue, their way cleared by the hovering drone and its robotic instructions. Tash found herself flinching from the jet-black sky, as if it intended to do her harm.

'I'm impressed they reassigned a drone for us,' she said.

'So am I, if I'm honest,' Grace said, opening up the car doors. 'The police must have every able body out on the streets by now, every drone in the air, just to calm things down. Even so they don't want VIPs like us to get caught in a crush.'

Outside the church, Tash forced herelf to take a moment to look around. The church was a pile of cold Victorian stone — put up in 1859, she knew, so nearly two centuries old. On this day of changes she imagined the waves of civil construction that had washed around this sturdy pile: probably back-to-back terracing for shipyard workers, giving way to uglier mid-twentieth-century inner-city suburban developments — rows of shops and blocks of flats — and now that clutter had been cleared away in turn, leaving the old church as an island of heavy stone in a sparse, park-like landscape of smartwood tenements and grassy swards.

All of it hard to make out today, as the streetlights patchily broke up the strange, sunless gloom.

Within, the church was mostly full. The interior was dark, the church's own lights dim, much of the available illumination coming from people's glowing phones. Tash felt unreasonably glad to be out from under the sky.

They found a seat, an empty pew.

'So,' Grace said. 'Why did you want to come here? I don't know you too well, but didn't imagine you were religious.'

'I'm not. I just found this place when I went walking out of House, in the early days after the move. Peaceful place to pass a lunch time. Now I just wanted to see how people are reacting.'

'Turning to God?'

'Or against Him, maybe.'

'Well, here they all are,' Grace said. 'I guess you return to childhood certainties when something like this happens. We would have. My family.'

Tash eyed her. 'Forgive me, Grace, but I guess I don't know you as well as I should either. Your family were religious?'

'Kind of. More my parents' faith than mine. We were climate refugees, from southern Africa. Scottish descent, and ardent Protestants. Hence my name.' She grinned and clenched a fist. '*Grace*. Which doesn't fit my nature too well. Parents gone now.'

Grace's accent was bland. Tash would never have guessed at such an ancestry.

'You have other family?'

'Just a sister. Still lives in Naples. Italy. That was where we were first given refuge, after the boat crossing of the Mediterranean. I was very young, Ella was smaller. But she moved away from the faith. Married a guy from a Catholic background. She's pregnant, actually. Full term due around about now.'

'Ah. Bad timing.'

'Yes, if everything is going to shit because of all this. The father is long gone also. Anyhow I think my parents would have felt at home in a church like this. And, the Sun going out, maybe it's appropriate. It is all a bit Old Testament, isn't it?'

'Well, I imagine some people might think so—' She dug out a phone that was buzzing softly. Calls from both Mel and Zhi. She said, 'Do you mind if—'

'Take your calls. So long as we're back in time for the Cobra—'
Tash? That you?

'Hi, Zhi.'
And this is Mel. Listening in too.

'I hear you. I'm in St Joseph's, Mel. You remember, Gateshead, we walked here a couple of times—'
Sure.

'I don't have a lot of time, you guys.'
We know, we know, Mel said. *Well, neither do I, if I have to hold Charlie Marlowe's hand through a virtual briefing for your Cobra meeting—*

Jim is in trouble, Zhi said bluntly.

That shut them up.

He summarised the plight of the Al-miriykh. In deep space, powerless, drifting off course.

Tash shook her head. 'I . . . don't know what to say, Zhi. I can hardly imagine it. We're all been bound up by problems down here.'

Well, there are ten billion down there. Only a handful up here.

'All precious, Zhi. All precious.'

Mel again. And how about you, Zhi? How's Lodestone?

We don't have Jim's immediate power crisis. We have a bank of batteries in an emergency and a small nuke reactor — we were in a permanent shadow anyhow; we don't rely on solar power save for topping up the batteries. But we are drifting out of position also. One would assume a common cause, but . . . We will have to fix our drift, eventually. We've the resources to do that, and can be readily rescued if not. And Jim's crew will need to get back on course for Earth. If they have the resources, if they survive that long—

'Zhi, I don't understand,' Tash broke in. She glanced at Grace, who looked as confused as she felt. 'I think I'm behind the curve, here. What are you talking about? *Why* are all the spacecrafts drifting off course?'

We'll work it out, Mel snapped, and Tash was surprised by her ferocity. *We'll science this damn thing, no matter how big it is. The drift is just another clue to help us solve it all. Have faith, guys — if that's not a contradiction. Faith in the science. We will come out of this one way or another.*

Zhi was silent.

Tash said, 'We're listening, Zhi. But while there's life there's hope . . .'

Grace said, standing up, 'Hope, maybe, but no time. Come on, kid. Time to go face Cobra.'

They had been in the church only a few minutes.

Tash followed reluctantly, keeping her phone open.

On the way back, in the car – just as they approached House, with Grace fretting about delays – Mel made another call.

Hey, Tash. We lost Jupiter. I mean it just went out, as a brilliant starlike object, in the deep night sky over this Southern Ocean.

'Umm. I'd like to pretend I'm trying to figure distances and times in my head as we speak.'

Well, try harder, honey. Jupiter is around five astronomical units from the Sun. Five times Earth's distance. So sunlight reflected from Jupiter has to travel ten AU, roughly, to reach our eyes, here on Earth. And since it takes light about eight minutes to cross one AU—

'An hour and twenty minutes.' She checked her watch again.

So we lost Jupiter at 1110 GMT. You know – it all makes sense. Given the vast horror of the loss of the sunlight, the rest is following logically. Even obeying physical law, such as the lightspeed limit. You make sure you tell your minister that. And, like I said. Tell him we will figure this out, one clue at a time. That's the hope . . . the promise.

'We're there,' Grace said, and pushed open the door before the car had stopped.

9

1125 GMT

When Tash had hung up, Mel switched her phone to a display mode, with heavy filters to screen out unwelcome calls.

While around her the Skythrust glowed in the unnatural dark. Fluorescents had been lit up inside the bulk of the gondola so that the whole structure shone from within. Lantern drones hovered over the heads of the guests in the clear-roofed observation sections. Even the quilt of vacuum tubes high above the main ship sparkled with star-like lanterns.

And in the transparent observation bubbles around the perimeter of the main deck, waiters, human and drone, circulated with food and snacks, and the hubbub of conversation was growing louder. It seemed that for better or worse the crew had decided to turn the event into a kind of impromptu party, presumably to keep the passengers relatively calm and distracted.

At first Marlowe had snapped and growled about the light pollution – this was supposed to be an astronomy platform – but after a while accepted there was little more to see, with the naked eye anyhow. So she and Mel stalked the deck, trying to avoid personal contact – especially with anybody who looked like a reporter, a correspondent or an influencer – and after a time Marlowe, trying to think, had even waved away most of the phone calls Mel tried to pass through to her.

At length Marlowe stopped walking, grabbed a tall glass of gin and tonic from a hovering drone, and gulped half of it down.

'Oh, enough of this. You know, Mel, I'm not really *thinking* here. I'm trying to *avoid* thinking, to avoid the obvious conclusion. The causal factor that lies behind all this. Because it's hard for a rationalist like me to bear.'

She paused, and Mel sensed she needed a little help. Paradoxical, but there you were. And besides, Mel suspected she was coming to the same conclusion independently.

'Go on,' she said cautiously.

'Let's look at the evidence again,' Marlowe said. 'The – disturbance – seems to have come out of the Sun, at lightspeed. Or rather the *absence* was experienced at lightspeed. The absence of the light. Eight minutes to the Earth, the sunlight fails. We see secondary effects, the dimming of the corona, of the light reflected from the planets. All clearly regulated by lightspeed. Orderly. Predictable.

'But then the spacecraft out there start to drift. Hard to explain *that* away by a mere blocking of the sunlight. Your friend Zhi on the Lodestone, drifting away from its exquisite point of balance of forces, of the gravity of Earth, Sun, the thrust of their magnetic sail. Further out, the Mars ship, itself on a long, slow orbit around the Sun, bringing it from Mars to the Earth. Now off course – in fact, according to the data coming out of the NHSA, now heading out in a straight line, tangent to their old orbit. As if you whirled a conker around your head and cut the string. It goes flying off . . .'

'There's more evidence, actually,' Mel said. 'Close-in spacecraft orbiting the Sun, Mercury. All losing their orbital paths—'

'And I suspect over a longer period we will see the drift of the planets from their orbits too. May be perceptible already.

We should plot it all,' Marlowe said. 'The timings. Gravitational effects spread at lightspeed. I'm prepared to bet we will find the – the *loss* of gravity – the effects spread out at lightspeed also. It took forty minutes before Jupiter felt it, in his giant bones . . . We should keep checking the gravity wave records too; an event as huge as this surely left some secondary signatures of that kind. Especially within the orbit of Mercury—'

'Yes,' Mel said cautiously. 'But *what event*?'

Marlowe eyed her. 'I think you know as well as I do. The Sun's mass generated its gravity field. The only way we know to remove that field is . . .' She hesitated, as if reluctant to say it aloud. 'Is to *remove the Sun*. Its rest mass. And thus taking away, incidentally, the core furnace that provides us with sunlight.'

Mel had come, reluctantly, to the same conclusion. 'It fits the evidence. And it's not even as if it's a gentle push away—'

Marlowe snapped her fingers. '*Poof*. A magic trick. Or a science fiction teleport. Sun there, Sun gone. Impossible.'

'But we have the evidence.'

'We have the evidence,' Marlowe said severely. 'And one should never deny evidence.'

'No. Do you think we are the first to come up with this?'

Marlowe shrugged. 'Doubt it. Lots of clever people in the world. But we may be the first to shout about it.' She sighed. 'Let's do our duty. Are you still in contact with your pet minister in the English government?'

Mel whispered into her phone.

10

1130 GMT

Cobra meetings were the procedural heart of the English federal government's emergency management strategy, the name inherited from the British predecessor. The latest took place in a small, cluttered conference room in Government House.

The Home Secretary chaired, with the Prime Minister listening in from an aircraft en route from London. There were more virtual attendees than those in the flesh. Tash recognised Cabinet ministers, senior police officers, the Chief Scientific Adviser, the Chief Medical Officer with a representative of WHOCare – the global health service – high-ranking military, and others. Among the group was a disconcerting hologram of the Astronomer Royal, sent from the Skythrust. She seemed to be sitting in a bizarre lounge, with a décor apparently modelled on huge bottles – large, small, cut open, distorted, Dali-esque.

If Charlie Marlowe was there, Mel must be just out of shot, Tash realised.

All the main attendees were crowded around a small smart table at the heart of the room – remarkably small, it seemed to Tash, and remarkably cluttered with pads, pens, water bottles and glasses. Phones everywhere. Tash and other advisers sat back behind the main table, by the walls of the room, clustering behind the meeting member they supported – she and Grace for Fred Bowles, with others.

Tash knew this room was dumber than it looked. Any electronic system could be hacked, so the room, and its many siblings in the building, had no fibres or cables going in or out, save for one heavily shielded emergency link. And it had basically been built into a Faraday cage that blocked electromagnetic radiation – radio signals. The participants too had been screened on their way in, unobtrusively, by a smart doorway. Minutes would be kept as the meeting began, with automated systems backed up for legal reasons by a human stenographer taking notes.

The Home Secretary was Mara Caine, a tough and experienced ex-diplomat, very precisely spoken, with striking crewcut black hair. She came from the right-wing half of England's governing coalition of the Democratic Greens and the English Reconstruction Party. Now she opened the meeting without preamble, saying they should summarise what was known.

'Which isn't much, as I've gathered from earlier meetings. *The Sun is missing.* Correct?'

That was a prompt for the Astronomer Royal's first contribution. Her voice filling the room, Charlie Marlowe confirmed that the Sun had indeed, it seemed, *gone*, all of its mass, all of its fusing heart and roiling layers of hydrogen-helium, and the heat and light it had been shedding across the Solar System for over four billion years.

'We have multiple lines of evidence now to support that extraordinary claim. We have measured the deflection of our satellites, and the inner planets to some extent, arising from the loss of gravity. *The Sun is gone.* And gone at the moment of eclipse totality, 0948 GMT,' Marlowe said firmly. 'As I can confirm myself, having witnessed it.'

Caine leaned forward. 'Yes. My head is full of the emergency, the immediate details. But that itself is a very striking observation, isn't it? An eclipse is not a – a Solar System-wide phenomenon. Is it, Professor Marlowe? It is the casting of a shadow of the Moon on the Earth; it happens at a specific moment, at a specific place—'

'Well, totality lasts a few minutes if you're under the shadow—'

'But for this disappearance to happen at the *moment* of eclipse, here on Earth . . . I don't know how to finish this chain of thought.'

Fred Bowles nodded. 'Home Secretary, you are groping for a key insight, and I commend you. I think you mean that it's as if the event was linked to us, somehow. Us, humanity. Because on this planet, so far as we know, only humans understand eclipses.'

Caine raised her eyebrows. 'Astronomer Royal?'

'I couldn't put it better myself,' said Marlowe. 'Why have the event coincide with an eclipse if you didn't want to draw attention to the – artificiality – of it? Although I haven't got much further in my own speculation than that. Not yet.'

Caine seemed to be trying to think that through. 'I wish you science bods would speak plainly.'

'It's difficult to be plain if you aren't *sure*—'

'Very well. But it seems to me that you are at least hinting that this phenomenon may not be entirely *natural*. That the Sun hasn't just vanished of its own accord—'

'We know of no natural mechanism that can make a star just vanish of its own accord,' Marlowe said. 'Or indeed, any mechanism that could achieve such a feat. But we are a young species, and have been observing the heavens scientifically for a very short time.'

'But it *could* be natural,' Caine said, plodding on. 'If the Sun has fallen into a – another dimension, say.'

'I've heard more ludicrous grant proposals,' Marlowe said, not unkindly. 'Yes, it could be some kind of cosmic flaw. A natural phenomenon. Beyond our current comprehension.'

Tash saw that Bowles was watching Marlowe closely.

Bowles said now, 'But you don't think so, do you? Because of this coincidence with the eclipse, as you mentioned yourself, Home Secretary. Which is a regular, well-understood occurrence – but such an eclipse would mean nothing without intelligent observers to see it. And – only observers on *this* world. A Venusian might see our eclipse unfold, the geometry, but not the experience of the eclipse. Somebody – something – *planned* this. Timed it to perfection. For our benefit. Humans on Earth.'

'You're very sharp, Mr Bowles,' Marlowe murmured. 'And you're quite right.'

'Why, though?'

Marlowe shrugged. 'We are still in the middle of it. I have literally no idea. No sensible one, anyhow.'

Caine frowned. 'But look – if we are looking at some kind of intelligent extraterrestrial intervention here – haven't we thought about this? All those SETI chaps with their radio telescopes, looking for signals from the stars for, for—'

'Nearly a century,' Marlowe said.

She sounded almost wistful, Tash thought. For the good old days when threats from intelligences in the sky were mere theoretical toys to play with.

'Right,' Caine said. 'I know I'm new to this job, and an outsider too . . .'

Tash knew this was a line she played often. The Home Secretary was from the ERP, the English Reconstruction Party, a fairly radical group that advocated the reversal of British devolution among other measures. A group which had now found itself in coalition with Fred Bowles's limping Democratic Greens.

'So don't we have some kind of scenario pack prepared? As we do for a nuke attack or a pandemic or—'

'No,' Marlowe said. 'Those "SETI chaps" tried, Home Secretary, but always got laughed out of the room. But I don't think it makes much difference. I don't think anybody envisaged a situation like *this*.'

Caine sighed. 'Very well. The metaphysics can wait. What we need to do is review the practical actions we have taken, and must take from now on, here in England. Although this is clearly a global phenomenon.' She glanced at a watch. 'I believe it is nearly dawn in New York City,' she said dryly. 'I have observed that those on the night side of the planet when the – cutting out – occurred, seem to have found it hard to credit the reality. Despite the images of the darkness, the urgent calls. Notably the Americans. Let us hope that when President-Elect Cox wipes the sleep from her eyes we will start putting together some kind of international response. I will be taking action points out of this meeting into an international forum which is being set up by the UN – damn it, FIS – for later in the day . . .'

Tash recognised the slip. The old UN, enfeebled by the multiple crises of the 2030s, and facing a swirl of changes among its membership, including secessions from such powerful nations as the US, Britain and Russia – indeed the US and Great Britain no longer existed as the entities they had once been – had more or less gracefully given way to a new body, the Federation of Independent States. This had been an era of global emergencies in which, paradoxically, states and regions had proved to be the principal managers of those emergencies. So the FIS – pronounced 'Fizz' – had inherited many of the old UN's functions, such as UNESCO and the Security Council, but it struck Tash as a somewhat less unwieldy body — 'a second draft of the UN without the deliberate mistakes', as Fred Bowles once said. That had been borne out, maybe, when it had efficiently supported the establishment of WHOCare, 'an NHS for the world', as Tash's dad had put it, 'and about bloody time'.

However, yes, Tash called it the 'UN' sometimes too.

Caine said, 'I know that the Foreign Secretary is holding relevant meetings in parallel with this one. But let's hear how we're getting on in England for now . . .'

So NHS representatives were invited to discuss the psychological impact of the loss of the Sun. Tash leaned forward, interested herself. They threw up a two-by-two chart . . .

Fred Bowles leaned back to murmur to Tash, 'The old presenter's stand-by. Classic.'

. . . A chart that divided the population into four categories: by location on the planet's day or night side at the moment of the Sun's disappearance, and by the weather, sky covered, sky clear. As the Home Secretary had noted, Americans and others who, deep in the night, had had no direct evidence of the Sun's loss barely seemed to have accepted the event at all. Not yet, anyhow. Under the day side, under a *cloudy* sky, the sudden darkness — as in Newcastle itself — had inflicted a deep shock, but one which seemed relatively manageable. But if you happened to be standing under a *clear* sky, and you *saw* the Sun's light vanish in a moment, the impact was much greater.

There followed some discussion of the population's wider reaction so far. According to the reports, accidents, even fatalities, had been few. That was thanks partly to the smartness of the modern built environment, Tash saw. Just as smart cars had stopped when the light went, so had smart planes organised themselves to make safe landings at the nearest airports in orderly swarms. And so on.

But still there was the psychological shock that no smart technology could cushion. There had been the curiosity, maybe, that had drawn many people out of doors to see for themselves – or, alternatively, the fear that had already prompted many to go home and hunker down, even to take their kids out of school. And the edginess that had caused many to go giddy, to dance and sing, drink and shoot up, even to party – or start small riots, the police representatives reported now. In many places, even though so far the power had stayed on almost everywhere, people had lit bonfires as if to defy the dark. Fires that had, predictably, in more than one place, got out of control.

The doctors believed that even if the Sun returned immediately, they would be dealing for many years with cases of mental trauma caused in that first instant.

All this after only a couple of hours, Tash thought.

After a few minutes of this, the Home Secretary wrapped it up. 'OK. Thank you. So the question is, how to go forward.'

'We need more data,' Astronomer Royal Marlowe put in immediately. 'Data has to be the basis of all scientific understanding, which must in turn guide public policy. And that's got to be an international effort. We must collect as much data as we can, from Earth, from space. Especially in these first hours. Share it all, of course. Including records of the vanishing itself.'

'Yes, yes.' The Home Secretary nodded, a little impatiently. 'Agreed. But in practical terms, we must consider recommendations for the near future before leaving this room. The next twenty-four or forty-eight hours . . .'

The pace of the discussion quickened.

Tash was, at first, reluctantly impressed by the detailed discussion that followed. But, watching Fred Bowles, she saw he was growing increasingly restless – as was Charlie Marlowe.

This was an unprecedented crisis — but the English government, like governments around the world, had over the years, or decades, learned how to cope with a stream of disasters unfolding on a world that was still hugely interconnected, hugely interdependent, and hugely vulnerable to such calamities as extreme weather events, pandemics, terrorist incidents. So this situation was new, yet old.

And maybe the human world was a bit more resilient now, with deeper reserves of food and other essentials, shorter supply chains, less material connectivity — but with extreme connectivity of information. Extra redundancy too.

So what quickly emerged from this preliminary discussion was a series of steps that Tash thought were clear, sensible, probably acceptable to a public used to dire governmental warnings — and yet moderate, given that nobody knew how this was going to unfold in the next days or hours.

For instance, schools. The education secretary advised a calm approach. Schools should expect to stay open today through the normal day, as at least some pupils were already on the premises — there could be chaos if all the schools peremptorily shut and parents had to scramble through the dark to pick them up. Today was Friday; maybe they should plan now for schools to stay shut on Monday . . .

Tash thought of Mel and her daughter Jane. She promised herself that she would send a quick heads-up to Mel about this, after the meeting, even if it bent the security protocol a little.

Hospitals. A spate of admissions had to be expected, through accidents in the sudden dark, and the party-time stuff going on in some cities. Longer term, mental health issues to do with the coming of the dark and its continuance. Police and health officials had agreed to move to public holiday protocols for now — as if New Year's Eve, just a few days back, had come again.

The supply chain. Transport would be prioritised for essential goods and services, and kept running as long as possible – roads, rail, by air, by sea . . . For food and other essentials, there ought to be no immediate problem with supplies – save that people always panic-bought at the first sign of any crisis, Tash knew, even in an age of app food. The Home Secretary hesitated about imposing immediate rationing.

People would be encouraged to stay at home, save for essential workers.

The power would be kept on for heating, lighting, as long as possible, with phased shutdowns if necessary. The energy minister warned of spikes in demand at a time when the supply was already stretched by the midwinter. Caine agreed to buy additional megawatts from abroad, including the huge Scottish wind-power farm, New Aberdeen, on Dogger Island.

There was some discussion of the royal family. Tash learned now that there was a pre-existing multi-agency group called RAVEC, the Royal and VIP Executive Control, tasked with the welfare of King George VII and the rest of the family in the face of contingencies like this. Anyhow most of them were still holed up in Balmoral after the Christmas break – although Princess Charlotte, formally Captain General of the Royal Marines and actually a serving officer, was with her unit in Wiltshire.

And so on, and so on.

This was by far the most senior meeting Tash had yet attended as part of Bowles's staff. And she was impressed at how quickly a rough, if short term, strategy was mapped out – quickly, given the novelty of the situation, anyhow. These people were genuinely, conscientiously, and intelligently trying to protect the population who had voted them, or their bosses, into power – and those who hadn't.

Slowly, gradually, Tash felt herself reassured by the evident competence on show.

Until Charlie Marlowe spoke up.

The meeting had already started winding down. The committee agreed to issue public advisories for now, and review the situation if the Sun wasn't back by Monday.

'Thank you all,' Caine said. She looked around the table. 'Of course this is only the beginning. But God knows we have learned to cope with catastrophe. I am sure everybody here understands the importance of on-message speaking—'

But Marlowe cut across the politician. 'Oh, for — is that it? you aren't considering breaking up this meeting with *that*? This isn't enough. Debating whether to close the schools? The bloody *royals*? Is that really as far ahead as you can think? Then the Lord help us all. Because unless all this somehow resolves itself quickly, you will soon *have* to consider the longer term.'

Caine seemed weary, as if longing for the meeting to be over. 'Professor, I think we have all—'

But Fred Bowles, who Tash had noticed had been getting restless himself during the detailed discussions, leaned forward. 'Very well, Charlie. Professor. What's the worst case? If — well, if this goes on?'

'*If the Sun doesn't come back*, you mean? If you can't bear to say it out loud, I will. And I'll try to answer the question.

'Look — I am no climatologist, and there should be some in this room. But it's going to get bloody cold,' the Astronomer Royal said bluntly. 'Well, you know that. The relevant questions are, how cold, and how long it will take to get that cold.' She hefted her phone. 'I've made some order of magnitude calculations while we've been sitting here, which would have been better with some online connectivity. Shoot me down if you know better, any of you.'

Silence around the table.

'Our environment, the environment of Earth that sustains every living thing, relies on sunlight,' Marlowe said now. 'Around a third of the sunlight that hits the Earth is reflected away; the rest is taken into the great planetary systems, the flows of matter and energy that sustain the atmosphere, the oceans, the biosphere, before finally radiating back out as waste heat.

'And now that input has been turned off.

'The good news is we won't freeze immediately. The air will retain its heat, for a while. There is still water vapour in the air – well, water itself is a greenhouse gas. But – today is Friday – by Sunday, Monday, the air will have cooled enough for the water to condense out. Rain first.'

'Then snow?' Bowles asked.

'Snow and frost. By the end of next week, the water vapour will all have gone from the air when it's gone it will get colder, even faster.'

That evoked a few uneasy frowns, Tash thought.

'Then the sea will start to freeze – just the surface at first. Before *that* happens, you see, the relatively warm winds off the sea water will have been moderating conditions on land. But once the ocean is frozen over . . . Two weeks from now, there will be hundred-degree frosts in Britain, for example.

'A month from now and the seas will have frozen down to the equator.

'At that point, many of us should still be alive, actually. In industrial communities at least, as long as the fuel lasts, as long as the machines don't seize up. Think small groups, isolated, huddling. But with the sea frozen, land temperatures will plummet.

'Two months from now the air will snow out. Oxygen first.

'The whole Earth will head ultimately for the temperature of interstellar space. You ask about the worst case, Minister? In sixty days' time, it will be colder than Pluto. After a year, outside of maybe a handful of shelters covered with layers of frozen air, and maybe the denizens of the deepest seas, nothing will survive.'

A bewildered silence.

'Sixty days,' said Fred Bowles.

Caine seemed horrified – as well she might, Tash thought.

'That's – why, that's the beginning of March.' Caine shook her head. 'It isn't some distant abstraction. *March*. We can't possibly take this to the full Cabinet. Let alone the FIS.'

Bowles said, relatively gently, 'I think we must, Home Secretary. And as soon as possible. Charlie – thank you. I'll need you during the international conference calls later—'

Marlowe glared at Caine. 'Home Secretary, what you do is up to you. The sooner you accept the reality, the sooner you will start making realistic preparations, the better. Oh – and even beyond that, we have to consider the implications that we now know we share a universe with an – entity – capable of such a huge and malicious act. In the meantime I will try to get some useful work done.'

And her link from Skythrust fizzed out.

11

1515 GMT

'Is this thing on, Marina? It's kind of hard to see under these dumb emergency lights . . . Also I can't see you too well through the little window of the storm shelter.

'I'm live? OK.

'Let's do this.

'So, calling mission control at Houston, and the TsUP at Moscow, and the world, I guess. This is Al-miriykh. Jim Boyd here, and I hope you can see me. Yeah, the big lunk shivering and waving.

'Our handler at TsUP – and we're very grateful to Josef and the rest for staying at their own posts – encouraged us to make this broadcast. He said that a lot of you, around the world, were listening in to us, even while you are undergoing your own trials. We do appreciate this, very much, being so far away from home. How far? Far enough for it to take minutes, even at lightspeed, for my message to cross space and reach you.

'Let me show you the layout here. So this is our hab module, a standard Jones, Inc. Shelter module, which is keeping us alive as we coast through our eight-month trajectory back home from Mars to Earth. And a darn good job it's doing, I may say, even with the Sun going out on us. Or whatever the hell.

'But, as you can imagine, we aren't keeping too warm in here.

So that's why we have had to retreat, mostly, to this chicken coop in the middle of the floor, that we call the storm shelter. See it over my shoulder? Its main design function is so we can ride out a radiation storm – ha, ironically, the source of which would be the Sun – even if our magshield went down.

'So our ship is still functioning, in the sense of keeping us alive. We are already working on a checklist to bring her back to life, *if* . . . In the meantime our backup systems should keep us safe. We have on-board batteries; they will last for a nominal eight hours of normal functioning, and maybe twelve. After that we will have to retreat into the storm shelter, which will keep us alive for a further twelve hours. In fact we decided to retreat into the shelter now, as much as possible, to save as much juice as we can.

'Recovery, when it comes, will take some time. The first priority will be to bring the solar panels themselves back on line. Then we will begin to reboot our life support systems. Then we'll think about other priorities.

'All of which, I know you understand, is dependent on – well, the Sun coming back. Hard to think of a Plan B if it doesn't, isn't it? For you, too. Well, we will cross that bridge when we come to it.

'You might ask why I'm out here shivering my skinny butt off at all, instead of being tucked up cosy in the storm shelter. Well, like everybody else, we're still trying to figure stuff out about this situation. And on top of all the problems of dark and cold that we share with all of you, this incident has given us an extra glitch.

'When the Sun went away, we quickly found that we were drifting off course. Just a little, but enough for our very sensitive navigation suite to pick it up almost immediately. Well, that baffled us for a while, and even our mission controllers.

'But it's obvious if you think about it. Out here in the dark, coasting, we in the Al-miriykh are totally dependent on the Sun, for our heating – *and also for our trajectory*. So we kicked off from Mars, but we don't blast our rockets all the way home. Instead, very soon after we are away from Mars orbit, we shut down the engines and just coast on our own orbit around the Sun, not following a near-circle like Mars or Earth, but an ellipse: a curve that just touches Mars's orbit at the start, and will just touch Earth's when we get there. And then we will brake into Earth orbit.

'*But now the Sun has gone*. We lost not just its light, but its gravity field too. So we aren't in orbit any more. We are drifting off course, you see – just a little so far.

'And so, by the way, is Earth. All the planets. Which are also in orbit around the Sun, or were. And which is going to cause problems for us all, long term. All humanity.

'But anyhow if this keeps up even for just a day, we will miss our target, the Earth. The longer it lasts, the wider the miss. Now, I'm sure our buddies in the space business will already be working out plans to bring us home whatever happens, but, of course, we would much rather not put that to the test.

'We're working on it too. And the one thing we do need to do is to keep tracking our position. We have inertial guidance systems, all internal, and star-sighting trackers – we use the stars to fix our position just as the first ocean sailors on Earth once did.

'But we also sight on the Sun, and that's one extra fix we need – and one we've lost, of course. Which has thrown the automatics somewhat. So we're coming out here to make manual sightings of the stars and planets, and the Sun when it returns, and *that's* why I'm out here just for now.

'I should sign off, do my chores, and get back in that tin can with my buddies. But I want to emphasise again that we really have been touched by the interest you down there are showing in us up here, in the middle of your own problems. Why, I'm told our little adventure has attracted the highest number of visitors to a space broadcast since Jeff Kraus and Kaui Paku crashed at Imbrium, on the Moon, back in '29, as some of you will remember.

'You know, some good came out of that disaster. All the space agencies worked together to try to help Kraus and Paku, and out of *that* came long-lasting cooperation in space like never before, for instance in the form of the NHSA, the combined Northern Hemisphere Space Agency, which coordinates the space projects of America, Russia, and a slew of other countries. Though not China, as my fiancé Zhi would remind me.

'Anyhow, unlike poor Jeff and Kaui, we can still get through this. All of us. Like all of *you*. TsUP – Houston – planet Earth – this is Jim Boyd on the Al-miriykh, signing out. Godspeed to us all.'

12

1520 GMT

After the Cobra meeting, the formal contacts went international.

As far as Tash could see, a whole hierarchy of meetings was to be set up, beginning with minister to minister contacts at Fred Bowles's specialist level, first with closest allies. These would escalate to heads of government, both one to one and regionally, and finally a FIS Security Council conference call mediated by the Secretary General from Geneva. All of it virtual, of course.

It was happening fast; Fred's first conference, with the Americans, was called for three thirty Newcastle time. That was only a few minutes' notice, for Tash anyhow. But they needed to make fast progress today. Progress that could be demonstrated to the public.

And in all of this, as stressed by Fred Bowles himself, Tash was to keep open her links to Mel and the Astronomer Royal. Charlie Marlowe was the still one scientific authority Bowles felt he could rely on, and he wasn't about to face the President's science adviser without his comfort blanket live on his phone beside him, it seemed.

Fair enough, Mel commented, from Skythrust Two. *I'm already shielding Charlie from other calls, mostly media and pols. Meanwhile we are proceeding under lights to the north, hoping to get to Johannesburg, our home port.*

'No idea what the answer to all this is yet, I take it.'

Tash, we don't even know what the question is yet. Mel's tiny virtual image, hovering above Tash's phone, shook her head with a rueful smile – her smile her best feature, Tash sometimes thought, aside from her strawberry-blond hair. *These bureaucrats sure hit the ground running, don't they? Shame they ain't so quick when it comes to grant renewal time.*

'Oh, that's not fair. Fred Bowles is trying to get his head around a phenomenon that is even more bewildering to him than to you and me. And, bureaucracy, OK, but how else do you get stuff *done*? Some politicians probably are crooks; more are fools. But I suspect most are like Fred. Doing their best. Even if he fears he's not up to the job, deep down. And he has to expect his career to end with the sack, some day. That's if he doesn't get voted out first.'

Well, maybe. I think Jane's generation is growing up to be even more cynical than ours. But also more resilient, given the battered old world we have bequeathed them. But they seem to accept it.

'Is she OK?'

They're keeping her in the school, in Yorkshire. Anybody who would have trouble getting home. They say they'll keep her overnight if necessary.

'My dad asked after her. Said he could have looked in on her if she was anywhere near Newcastle.' She knew Mel had a share in a flat in Newcastle for when she needed to be here with Charlie on government business – before this crisis, mostly grant applications and other funding issues.

That's kind. She'll be fine.

'I think the company would have done Dad some good too . . . So have you spoken to Zhi recently?'

I keep an open channel, Mel said. *Of course all the spacecraft we have up there are vulnerable. Zhi says they are preparing evacuation protocols — meaning, evacuation to some place where they don't rely on solar power. The Moon Gateway astronauts may evacuate to the lunar surface. And there's no change on the Al-miriykh. Maybe we're lucky we only had one human-carrying craft operating in deep space today — but one is bad enough, if your fiancé is aboard. There's no obvious solution there. You know how those missions are pared down to the bone. There is very little margin in fuel for unexpected course corrections.*

Which reminds me — a heads-up for you. There is a longer-term aspect to all this which Charlie Marlowe is already flagging up. You may have heard Jim Boyd himself blurt it out in a broadcast to the world from the Al-miriykh.

Look, the loss of the Sun's gravity is universal. And it's solar gravity that keeps Earth and the other planets in their orbits, just as it constrains the trajectory of the Al-miriykh. So, when the gravity switches off, it's not just a handful of spacecraft that will drift off course. And even if the gravity comes back, there will be long-term effects . . .

Tash thought that through. 'I did hear that but paid no attention. I suppose I was focusing on the fact that we're all going to freeze to death by Easter. So if the Earth's orbit around the Sun becomes . . . distorted? What difference will that make? Nothing good, I'm guessing.'

Nothing good. But it all depends on how long this crisis lasts. If the Sun comes back, as mysteriously as it went away, I guess, and when. Different seasons, basically.

Tash muttered, 'And if the Sun doesn't come back at all?'

Mel hesitated. *Well, all the planets will just drift away. Off into the dark, at their old orbital speeds, heading in whatever direction they happened to be going when the Sun went away. But we will freeze long before that makes any difference.*

A silence.

Tash said, 'One thing I've learned being attached to government is to take one thing at a time. To deal with only what you can control, today.'

Right. So we have to work on the assumption that this isn't an extinction event, until it is.

'I don't think Fred Bowles will put it like that—'

I'd better go. The Captain is monopolising Charlie again, and she looks like she's going to blow.

'I'll keep my phone open.'

Oh, by the way. Uranus went out. Fifteen hundred. Right on cue.

After that, Tash, accompanied by Grace Butterworth, had to dash through House once more to another situation room – F, this time. Well, everybody was rushing today.

They found the room split virtually in two, with the English contingent facing a smart wall which displayed a projection of their American opposite numbers. This had been hastily set up; the conference tables pushed up against one smart wall didn't quite match up with their virtual counterparts.

Still, the two principals were here: Fred Bowles, UK science minister on one side of the virtual partition, and a severe-looking person on the American side.

Tash recognised her from news coverage, as well as the vividly colourful shirt she wore – evidently something of a signature. She was Lee Yamanaka, the President's science adviser, formally Assistant to the President for Science and Technology, and Director of the Office of Science and Technology Policy.

Tash knew little about Yamanaka save that she was from Hawaii.

She made a quick look-up on her secure phone. According to the English government data, Lee Yamanaka had begun her career in the high-altitude observatories at Hawaii itself, and later went back home to run them. Another astronomer, then. Useful, lucky to have her in place. But it all depended on how she got on with Marlowe. Tash had seen enough horn-locking among senior scientists before.

Among the juniors and officials cluttering up the space behind the principals – including Tash herself – other main players stood out, some projecting in from other locations. Sitting behind Fred Bowles's chair, she picked out a virtual representation of Charlie Marlowe, projected from Skythrust, with, no doubt, a slight signal delay as a result.

Then, on the American side, Tash recognised a small, slim woman staring into an old-fashioned-looking phone.

'Wow,' Tash blurted. 'That's Serena Jones.'

Jones looked around vaguely. The use of her name had distracted her; she was able to pick out Tash in the noisy virtual environment around her. 'Was that you, my dear?'

Tash felt herself blush. 'Sorry – didn't mean to be fannish.' She did know Zhi hero-worshipped this woman – indeed, he had formally studied her career for a semester in college.

Jones made virtual eye contact now, and smiled. 'Oh, not at all. Here I am, if not in the flesh. In fact, I guess you're all wondering why I invited you here today.'

A ripple of polite laughter, including the pols.

Tash felt herself helplessly charmed.

Lee Yamanaka smiled. 'Thank you for that, Ms Jones. I suspect this will be a grim enough meeting; breaking the ice is never a bad thing. For the benefit of the record, Ms Jones is here as an unofficial representative of the New Californian Republic and the AFS – the American Free States – and for her technological expertise.'

Jones was around seventy, Tash thought. Her colour was deep, her short-cut black hair flecked with grey. She looked like somebody's grandmother. Well, maybe she was. Not what you'd expect from the founder of Jones, Inc. And Jones had also been a leading figure in the New Secession movement in the United States in the early 2040s, after the chaos of the Greenland Melt and other disasters, and following her own leading contributions to the mitigation of such disasters. No wonder her charisma was so evident, her political contacts so senior. And no wonder she was here, now, in this crisis.

Fred Bowles leaned forward. 'I think you know why we asked you to contribute, Ms Jones. You're the entrepreneur who bought space – that's what they call you, isn't it?'

Amid the stately manoeuvring of egos, Tash knew, he had to remind everybody he was here too, hosting the meeting – if not chairing it, an honour he deferred to Yamanaka.

Jones shook her head. 'Much too immodest. I just waited until the other guys had made all the mistakes, and started from there. But – as for "buying space", talk about *schadenfreude*. When the New York stock exchange opened a while ago it fell twenty per cent before they locked it down. I'm getting poorer, just sitting here.'

Yamanaka nodded, grinning. 'We'll bear that in mind. Thank you, Ms Jones.'

Grace Butterworth murmured in Tash's ear, 'Well, that's the chimp pack hierarchy established. Now we can get on with talking about the end of the world . . .'

Yamanaka opened the meeting formally.

'Thank you all for attending. Usual recording protocols in place.' Yamanaka glanced at the human stenographers, a pair of them on either side of the virtual wall.

'Now, let's just get a sense of our significance here. Or insignificance. We, in this meeting, are part of a worldwide, multi-level communications network, hastily being assembled. For me, a meeting following on from several others already today, mostly domestic, as for most of you, I guess.' Self-deprecating grin. 'If only we could blow the Sun back on with all the hot air, like a birthday candle in reverse, right?'

Polite laughter, led by Fred Bowles. Even, dutifully, from the stenographers, Tash noticed.

Yamanaka went on, 'This particular level is minister to minister, adviser to adviser, between closely allied governments. OK? I should emphasise that I myself am only an adviser to my government, with no political allegiance, power or responsibility. Well, aside from my own quadrennial walk to the ballot box. To remind you, the US and the American Free States have retained for now a common defence infrastructure and command hierarchy. In this emergency I report to the President of the United States – who right now is in the bunker at Raven Rock, by the way. Quite a trial for President-Elect Cox; you'd think this damn thing could have waited for her inauguration at least.

'Later our heads of government will talk formally, and possibly press statements will come out of that. Then there will be contacts across the regions, and with other allies. Ourselves with Canada and the rest of the Americas. You guys in Europe. Similar convocations in Asia, China, Russia and the rest, the Pacific nations . . . All of which is designed to feed into a meeting of the FIS Security Council at . . . I believe at around 2200 GMT, around twelve hours after the, umm, the eclipse, the event.'

She glanced around again, commandingly. 'I don't need to say that the more open we are the better these sessions will work. And I should say that there is much alarm in government circles back home. Alarm and confusion. I mean, as far as we can see, we are facing a threat to all humanity. Do I have that right, at least?'

Nods on either side of the virtual wall.

'Meanwhile our space agencies – including Space Command and Spaceguard, which checks for asteroid threats, for instance – saw nothing of this situation coming, and are at a loss as to how to respond. I know that the Secretary of Defence has spoken of raising the defcon level, or terrorist threat alert levels – but what is there to shoot at?'

Marlowe said languidly, 'I suppose such questions do need asking.'

Yamanaka glanced at her rival suspiciously. Wary, Tash thought, of being mocked. Marlowe had that way with people; Tash wondered if it had helped her further her life goals, or not.

Yamanaka moved on, glancing down at her own smart table. 'So let me suggest a rough agenda. We have little time, of course . . . First item. Background. *What is the Sun?* I mean, how does it work? A thirty-second briefing, please. Second. What can have happened to it? Has it gone out? Forgive the apparent naivety of such questions. We will be asked these questions, and we need straightforward, non-technical, unambiguous answers. Third. *How* did this happen? Fourth. If this goes on – the lack of a Sun in the sky – well, what then? Fifth. What should we do *now*? Have I missed anything?'

'Only the point,' muttered the Astronomer Royal. She got a glare from Bowles, and shrugged. 'Oh, don't mind me. Very well. How does the Sun work? Well, that's simple enough once you know the answer, although it took us until only about a century ago to work it out.

'The Sun is a mass of, mostly, hydrogen and helium. The primordial stuff of the universe. About a hundred times the diameter of Earth, about three hundred thousand times the mass.

'These days we have a whole slew of ways to monitor the Sun, and we have good reason to. For one thing we have learned to be wary of solar storms – Earth can be battered by charged-particle gusts that knock out satellites, even ground-based networks. So you have the Lodestone station watching the corona. Sun-watchers at locations like Mauna Kea in Hawaii—'

Yamanaka grinned, graciously enough. 'My home observatory.'

'There are other observatories in space and on the ground, watching the Sun at visible, ultra-violet, X-ray, infra-red, radio wavelengths – even gravity waves. The Chinese have a very large solar telescope, recently placed in orbit . . . And it's only a few years back that the Benson Sun Probe skirted the photosphere, the surface, closely enough to take a direct sample. Today a lot of these satellites have drifted out of position, by the way, like the Mars spacecraft, the Al-miriykh.'

Fred Bowles raised a finger. 'I presume the Chinese will be taking part in the FIS sessions later.'

Yamanaka nodded. 'We hope so.'

Marlowe went on, 'So we understand the Sun's dimensions pretty well. Or we thought we did.

'And we know how the Sun shines.

'It is fuelled by nuclear fusion. You take four protons, hydrogen nuclei, under enormous pressure, and in a complicated chain of events they ultimately fuse to make one helium nucleus. But that nucleus has a little *less* mass than those four protons. And we know that mass is equivalent to energy, thanks to Einstein, and *that* lost energy is what makes the Sun shine.

'As for your other questions – I can't remember the bloody order – has the Sun gone out? Doubt it.

'Because, you see, the Sun is a pretty big, dense mass and traps a lot of the energy it creates, deep down in its core. That energy is mostly carried off by neutrinos, to which almost everything is transparent and which just zip away. But the sunlight energy that sustains us is carried from the core by gamma ray photons, which get *absorbed* by the dense stuff of the Sun, and then get re-emitted and reabsorbed, over and over. For a single packet of fusion energy, that means it can take a random walk of a million *years* – or more – before most of it reaches the Sun's outer layers, where you have convection, huge fountains of hot gas, helping the heat loss on its way—'

'A million years,' Fred Bowles said, picking out that number. 'And so even if the fusion process in the Sun's core were somehow shut down, it would still – umm, *shine*, for a million years or more.'

'To an order of magnitude, yes. So we know you can't just put the Sun out. Then what *has* happened? Now, you *could* block its heat and light. Put some kind of mega-engineering shell in the way, all around it. Made from the stuff of Jupiter, no doubt.'

Mel whispered in Tash's ear, through her bud. *Remember Yale? Zhi always talks about this stuff when he gets going.*

'Yes. Dyson spheres . . .'

Marlowe was glaring at her through an unreal wall. 'Dyson spheres, did you mutter, Ms Brand? Quite right.'

'So,' Bowles asked cautiously, 'could *that* be what we're dealing with here? Some kind of – container?'

'No,' Serena Jones said. 'Nothing so simple, I'm afraid. I say simple – we're talking about erecting a container around a *star*. I mean, even if we didn't see it being put in place, we would see it *now*, wouldn't we? A big black mass. What we actually see is a star field where the Sun should be. And even if there was a container, the Sun's gravity field would not be affected. Correct, Astronomer Royal?'

'Correct, Ms Jones. Consider our deflected spaceships and

habitats – the Al-miriykh, the Lodestone. The Sun's gravity is no longer pulling on *them*; they are drifting out of their orbits. And,' she said grimly, 'similarly the planets must be drifting off course. Including Earth. As the astronauts have already re-minded the world. And that's something we will have to deal with in the future.'

'So I get the immediate point,' Bowles said. 'I think. A simple shell around the Sun is not enough to explain it all. Even cloaked, we would feel its gravity. Therefore, are you saying that the whole Sun could have been – destroyed? All its huge mass. In an instant?'

'Not at all,' Marlowe said, visibly irritated. 'How could that possibly be so, man? Sorry – Minister. If the whole damn Sun had blown up in our faces it would have taken the Earth with it – after eight minutes of lightspeed delay. And we wouldn't be having this conversation, would we?'

Bowles kept his cool, and Tash knew he was used to getting what he wanted from temperamental scientists like Marlowe. 'Very well, Professor. I apologise for my naivety. Then if you're saying the Sun was not destroyed, but it has evidently *gone*, then as you have said to me before—'

'It must have been moved.'

Tash, even as she absorbed this still-incredible suggestion her-self, carefully watched the other participants. She saw shock, awe, and sheer disbelief – even if many of them must already have heard this.

Serena Jones, though, seemed to be calculating, tapping away at the smart-table surface before her. It was all just an engineering problem for her, perhaps.

After a few breaths Bowles took the bait. 'Moved, then.'

Moved,' Marlowe said. 'We can be sure. We *observed* it, and not just with seven billion pairs of human eyes. We have other evidence.'

She tapped her phone, and images of ungainly, unlikely spaceborne machinery scrolled in the air of this composite room: a skeletal thing, it seemed to Tash, with long girder-like trusses from which blocky components were hanging.

'I mentioned gravity waves. These are emitted when large masses move, or collide, or explode, or collapse. And this is the Southampton University inertial gravity-wave detector – the SIG – out in the asteroid belt. Huge thing, as you can see.

'And *this* baby, it turns out, along with other such probes, picked up a tremendous ripple of gravity waves just as the Sun was – umm, deleted – or rather, after the few minutes it took the resulting lightspeed-limited gravity waves to travel out to the detectors. It was a sharp peak, a plucking – with spherical symmetry. As if a mass had been ripped out of spacetime. De-leted. Neat ripples washed out from the Sun's location. Clearly the Sun has been *moved*. We have *measured* the gravitational consequences of that removal—'

Serena Jones the technologist said abruptly, 'There must be more evidence. For instance, the solar wind should be dis-persing slowly.' She glanced around the room. 'That's a wind of charged particles thrown out of the Sun, a steady blast . . . Magsails, like the one Lodestone uses, rely on that wind.'

'A wind that moves a lot more slowly than light.' Taps on Marlowe's phone. 'Didn't think of that. But I bet somebody did . . . The wind will have been shut off at source, when the Sun was taken away, but there should be a remnant shell still spreading out from the Sun's location . . . Here it is. The termin-ation of that should reach us in . . . a few days.' She glanced up. 'There you are, Minister. A verifiable prediction. Sitting here we've done some actual science. Thank you, Ms Jones,' she said gracefully enough. She looked around the room. 'So it was moved. We have absolutely no idea *how* it was moved. And of course one simpler question we can't answer yet is where it was moved *to*—'

'Professor Marlowe,' said Fred Bowles grimly. 'Let's get back to the point. You just said, *the Sun was taken away*. Isn't there an implication here you haven't addressed, with all this talk of evidence?'

Yamanaka leaned forward and said, 'You're asking, sir, not so much how this happened, but – *who did this?*'

There was a silence. Faint shock, Tash thought.

Serena smiled. 'I think we just crashed through a conceptual barrier here.'

Marlowe sighed. 'And I was hoping to get away without addressing that. If it isn't, even yet, some remarkable natural phenomenon . . .'

'Such as what?' Bowles asked, a little helplessly. 'A monstrous wormhole through which the Sun might have fallen?'

Marlowe nodded. 'That's conceivable, actually. But such an object would have much more mass-energy than the Sun itself. We would *see* it . . .' Her eyes became a little glassy. 'No, it makes no sense at all. The wormhole would have to have the dimensions of a black hole the size of the Sun – the linear size, not the Sun's mass. Which would have to have a mass equivalent to . . . about two hundred thousand suns. The size of a respectable star cluster. *That's* what you would need.' She smiled, ironically. 'Sitting in the middle of the Solar System. We would probably have noticed it,' she said dryly.

Serena Jones shook her head. 'If I may speak. I guess I'm biased, given my own background. But, even if we can never understand the precise mechanism, I believe this event was technological. As you believe, I suspect, Professor. And intentional.

'I mean, we *know* it must be, right? The removal itself was not – not *messy*, like a natural phenomenon. Any kind of wormhole would be messy as hell – a rip in space, radiation everywhere? Like the big black hole in the centre of the Galaxy, huge flows of gas and dust, throwing stars around like firecrackers . . . This was clinical. Precise. A surgical excision.

'Do any of you remember *Star Trek*? Seems to me something just beamed the Sun the hell out of here. Teleported it.

'And, a point I see was raised in previous briefs, the removal was clearly *timed* to coincide with the solar eclipse. The event *must* have been meant as a signal to intelligent creatures on Earth. A signal presumably from some other intelligence. It's actually the only plausible explanation.'

A brief silence.

Bowles said, 'That sounds impossible. But it also sounds like what happened. And the energy you would need to do all that . . . to teleport the Sun?' He looked hesitantly at Marlowe.

Marlowe said, 'We can guess at the power levels required. And that implies a Kardashev Type III culture. By which I mean a Galaxy-scale culture, Minister. Or at least, a culture able to wield energies on the scale of the Galaxy—'

Kay-Three. Tash observed the jargon, noted it in her phone, checked the spelling.

Bowles looked irritated now. 'Kardashev? Didn't he play in goal for Dynamo Moscow?'

Grace Butterworth suppressed a laugh with a snort.

Marlowe ignored that. 'I'm speaking of an enormous amount of energy, very precisely applied.'

'How?' Bowles snapped.

'For now I haven't the slightest idea. Perhaps through some

exotic physics – a reaching down from a higher dimension of space, which I know some of the physicists argue for, to make sense of their equations. Something beyond our ken – for now. Which doesn't mean we can't analyse its effects.'

Yamanaka asked, 'More importantly, *why* would a K-III . . . do this?'

Marlowe looked up. 'We're way out on thin ice here. I really and truly don't want to speculate further. Not without more data.'

Bowles thought that over. 'No. I understand. Well, at least you've given us some kind of frame in which to think about this, Ms Jones, Astronomer Royal.'

'Agreed,' said Yamanaka. 'And I'm getting competing calls. This brief session has been remarkably useful. But I'm afraid we're done here for now. Thank you all.' And abruptly she picked up her phone, stood, walked out of her virtual room.

Marlowe just winked out of existence, like the Sun.

So did Serena Jones, with a regretful smile.

Tash got her stuff together and stood. She saw that the staff, the stenographers, were packing up too – and found Bowles had already gone.

Tash asked Grace, 'That's it? Just like that?'

Grace raised her eyebrows. 'Our lords and masters can be efficient when their asses are on fire. Come on. That was the easy part. Now Fred has to brief the PM . . .' She picked up her phone. 'Oh, by the way . . .'

'What?'

Holding up the phone she smiled, her face transformed. 'I just got a call from my sister. Ella, in Naples. I'm an aunt. This is turning out to be one hell of a day, isn't it?'

13

1800 GMT

Tash got her next call from Mel, on Skythrust Two, around six in the evening.

By then Tash was sitting with Grace in one of the many canteens in Government House, a building that was accustomed to hosting multiple all-nighters, as tonight was likely to be. Sitting, sipping coffee, keeping up to date and preparing, while they waited to be called for some specific task. Phones, personal and work, on the table top before them. The smart walls carrying various news feeds.

Also on the table, snacks. Neither of them was hungry, though Tash guiltily thought she ought to force something down, as her body kept its own time on this timeless day. Even before the Sun went away, she had already just been through an all-nighter. So, caffeine and cakes.

Meanwhile, it seemed, Mel and Marlowe were still observing stuff down there over the Southern Ocean, as Skythrust drifted under a still empty, star-spattered sky.

And what a sky, Mel said softly. *The crew have dimmed the ship's lights, at last. We're sitting under a clearwood dome so transparent we might as well be out in the open. And that stratospheric sky, in this cooling day-night, is getting even clearer as the last moisture condenses out of the air. Wow, what a spectacle.*

The southern hemisphere stars beat out our sparse litter even on a normal night.

Of course most of us, including the Astronomer Royal, keep looking west for any glimmer of the long-set Sun.

But just now we lost Neptune, Tash. Right on the edge of the Solar System. Took all this time for the last of the sunlight to slog out there and back again. Now the whole planetary system is dark. Wow, think of that. Lit up only by starlight.

Grace Butterworth raised her eyes at overhearing Mel's words, whispering from the phone. 'Dark planets, huh. Can't say that's top of my agenda just now.'

Tash grinned back. There was worse company than Grace, even if she was deliberately provocative at times. Just as well since, as the day had worn on, Fred Bowles had made it clear that he expected the two of them to stay close, to stay ready – Tash presumably for her diligence, academic intelligence and smattering of science, and Grace for her reliable muscle, will-power, and ability to get things done.

'OK,' Tash said. 'But *somebody* has to be thinking about that kind of thing, Grace, along with the stress on the National Grid and a bit of petty looting on Northumberland Road . . .'

Mel was still talking, evidently distracted by her huge sky.

. . . I'm worried about Jim, of course. And Zhi too. Oh, the Lodestone seems safe enough; they are a stationary habitat and won't drift far, and the whole thing is encrusted with battery packs. They will be able to survive a long time, and retrieval will be easy. Whereas—

'Whereas Jim's Al-miriykh is a lightweight Mars ferry. Mel, can we set up an open link with Zhi? Just you, me and him. Whatever comes next.'

A frown in the phone's tiny screen. *An In-Joke group hug. But you know what he's like. Withdraws into himself. I can try. I need to check Jane is OK. Later.*

More coffee. More screen-watching.

Word came through confirming that this was indeed going to be an all-nighter, at least. They weren't surprised. There were bunk rooms; Tash and Grace's names had been added to a rota.

'I knew it,' said Grace.

The government as a whole couldn't sleep, locally or nationally, because the population wasn't sleeping.

But after the first few hours, the first frantic round of meetings at ministerial, intergovernmental and ultimately FIS level, it had become clear that there was nothing much to be done about the situation, for now, nothing save for sticking-plaster solutions to the obvious immediate problems. Schools closed tomorrow at least, as the Cobra meeting had recommended, and Tash smiled as she imagined Marlowe's rage at such trivialities. Well, it was something sensible that could be done.

More widely, people were reacting in their diverse ways. There had been a run on the stores, online and otherwise, and a strategic decision had already been made to impose a quick rationing of essential items, notably items like torches and storm lamps, long-life foodstuffs like rice. Almost a reflex move by government agencies, their procedures hardened by decades of disruption of various kinds. There was always panic buying, Tash thought, from floods to pandemics – and now to the vanishing of the Sun.

Meanwhile, as the evening closed in, a lot of people had gone home from work early, if they had gone in at all, to hunker down with their families.

In Newcastle, by now it would have been dark anyhow. The world had started to feel a little more normal– the pubs and bars were becoming crowded, the police were reporting. Cinemas too, especially the big immersive three-dimensional multi-sensory venues. A place to huddle with other people, Tash guessed, and to escape from the world for a while. Similarly the police were reporting that the churches were packed too.

On a national scale the darkened cities were flooded with police resources, amid talk of sending in the army if there was trouble. Generally, however, there was not much sign of the drink- and drug-fuelled riots of which the online tabloids had gleefully warned. Tash had observed this before, in emergencies of various sorts during her own life. When the real crisis came, most people stayed calm.

Grace, though, had different contacts.

She claimed to know survivalist types who were heading for their end-of-the-world bunkers, caches of food and medicine and weapons and such, deep in the countryside. Then again, she said, some of those bunkers were a century old, having been first dug out during Cold War nuke scares. Elsewhere environmental campaigners fretted that the governments would use the crisis as a ploy to open up fossil fuel sources – but such campaigners always fretted about that. Others went to the churches to pray to mitigate the savagery of a vengeful god. And still others were talking about the sunlight shut-down itself as an act of war, waged by some power yet to be identified.

Tash, politely, tried to avoid getting drawn into any arguments with Grace over all these freshly minted conspiracy theories. She vaguely fretted about Grace's apparent relative credulity, though; she seemed to take some of this stuff seriously.

Time wore on.

The weather closed in, as Tash followed through her phone feeds, cocooned as she was in House. Over Newcastle, there had been fog in the afternoon, then rain, and, it was said, some snow inland. Water vapour condensing out of the cooling air. Tash remembered Marlowe telling the Cobra it would take a little longer than that, a couple of days, before the snow came in earnest, but she forgave the Astronomer Royal the hasty, flaky predictions that had been forced out of her. Nobody *knew*.

At about eight, Grace showed Tash a report from Moscow, where it was already midnight. Deep, heavy snow, and a weird hail, covering the streets half a metre deep.

'Granted, Moscow in winter isn't particularly balmy anyhow. Quite a difference from your Astronomer Royal swanning it on her sky boat, isn't it? But of course she's floating around over a nice warm ocean. As is Britain, I suppose. As the ocean cools down slower than the air, so it keeps coastal regions warmer than the deep hearts of continents. For now, Newcastle shivers, but Moscow freezes.'

Tash raised her eyebrows. 'You know some meteorology?'

'I know a lot of stuff that might surprise you. Science was my bag as a kid. That and rugby. Got to Cambridge to study natural sciences . . .'

'Cambridge. I never knew that either.'

'But, halfway through my second year, I was recruited. MI5. I had already been a L.C. Marine reserve cadet, before Cambridge. Recruiter implied that my combination of brains and brawn could be diverted to more useful purposes in the government's employ. Almost a cliché, isn't it? Still, fair enough. Especially when they had me go through a second degree at Edinburgh on politics, ethics, philosophy . . . I'm not just some bodyguard, you see. I'm a scientifically literate adviser to the Minister, *and* a bodyguard.'

Tash thought that over. This was just about the most personal information Grace had ever shared with her. And coming out of nowhere. Memo to self, she thought: get locked down with anyone long enough and you'll get their life story. Second memo: never underestimate.

She extended a hand. 'Well, I'm glad to have met you properly, Grace Butterworth. There are worse people I could be spending this particular evening with.'

Grace took the hand and shook it, with remarkable delicacy, Tash thought. 'Likewise. Does this mean I'm one of the In-Jokes now?'

'In your dreams. More coffee?'

So they sat, and talked, and watched their screens, and responded to a couple of queries from Bowles.

Tash phoned her father a couple of times.

At about nine, King George, secure in his own bolthole at Balmoral with his family, addressed the nation.

In 1940, just as France had fallen, Churchill warned us that if we failed at that moment we might have sunk into a new dark age. Well, Winston, when it comes to dark ages we could show you a thing or two tonight. But I can echo what Churchill went on to say when I promise you that we will get through this trial, whatever it is, however it has come about, however it is resolved. And when people look back in a thousand years' time, they will still say, this was their finest hour . . .

It wasn't a surprise to hear from George at Balmoral. He remained monarch of independent Scotland, as well as of the federation of the English provinces, if not of a proudly independent Wales. And Tash wasn't particularly surprised to hear him quoting Churchill, the go-to source for speeches designed to inspire Britons – even if the country Churchill had preserved in war now existed only as a historical curiosity, a precursor of the modern loose alliance of nations. But she was impressed by that smart allusion to a dark age. Dark it certainly was.

When the King was done, Grace surprised Tash again by producing a small hip flask, with two tiny pop-out cups. She poured out small nips, and passed one to Tash. 'Here. Skye whisky, nectar of the gods. God save the King.' She knocked back her glass. 'I was introduced to it when MI5 sent me for more basic training under his sister.'

'Marine training? Who, Charlotte? You're pulling my leg.'

'Would I? Serving officer, still. Tough taskmaster she was too . . .'

But the whisky failed to warm Tash, and the moment passed, and still they sat in silence.

Waiting.

At about nine thirty, Grace got a message from her sister, in Naples. A 'nutter' had tried to break into the maternity ward where Grace's new little niece was being cared for. 'Yelling about demon babies born on the Devil's day.' Grace glowered. 'I wish I'd been there. I'd have introduced him to the Devil, all right.'

'But your niece is safe.'

'For now.' But after that Grace didn't put down her phone.

Waiting.

A little after ten p.m. Tash's personal phone lit up with a panicky message from Zhi. A relayed broadcast from the Al-miriykh.

Jim Boyd was in deeper trouble.

14

2220 GMT

'TsUP, Houston, Al-miriykh. Jim Boyd here. Speaking to the world, I guess. Thank you to everybody who cares enough to listen in. And love to you, Wu Zhi.

'I am Jim Boyd.

'This is my own damn fault.

'I want to say that from the get-go. Not the fault of the ground controllers, and we are out of synch by long minutes as you know, but I should have waited for advice. And certainly not the fault of my crew, Ito and Marina, who, one way or another, are going to suffer even more because of what I did.

'*What I did*. My choice. My error. I've already downloaded a technical report, and the crew will download more as the events unfold. But I want to say this in my own words, if I can.

'As long as I can.

'OK. Look. Here it is. You know already that when the Sun was – eclipsed, or whatever has happened – we lost our primary source of power: sunlight on our big solar-cell arrays. And we also, incidentally, lost the grip of the Sun's gravity on us, and we started drifting off course straight away.

'Those, you could say, remain our principal issues.

'And you'll know by now too that, among our survival options, we do have battery backup power, and we do have a storm shelter, a small cabin within a cabin where we can retreat.

'The batteries, though, are a finite resource. They are Russian-built and a damn fine product, but they have limited capacities. They are designed for an outage of eight hours. They are said to be comfortably capable of lasting twelve hours, without re-charge. Longer than that it's tricky, but the mission designers have tried out catastrophe-scenario rig-ups where they can be made to last more than twenty-four hours – *last*, meaning keep-ing a crew alive while holding back enough juice for a restart when the power supply is restored.

'But to do that, long before the first twelve hours are gone, you have to retreat to the storm shelter, which has got a lot of thermal insulation, and it's recommended you put on pressure suit layers to keep in the warmth – and, well, you just hunker down in your little hi-tech igloo, while the batteries dribble in the power, and you save all your body heat, and play poker until the cavalry arrives. OK?

'While the main cabin just freezes.

'So, after the first half-hour or so, as we started to realise this situation wasn't going to be resolved any time soon, we started working through those survival protocols. We stowed our key consumables in the storm shelter, along with the pres-sure suits and other bits of clothing – a lot of that stuff was in there already, it's a kind of handy cupboard when not in use. That didn't take long; we were ready.

'And, under TsUP orders, we all started spending most of our time in the shelter from the start.

'But at the same time we were handling the second of our issues, which is that drift off course.

'I spoke about this before. We were concerned about meas-uring that drift. With the loss of data from the Sun sensor we were worried about the stability of the basic position-finding algorithms. And though the other automated position trackers kept working, for now – our star sensors, the inertial tracker and such – we couldn't be sure how long *that* would last, because as the power levels drop the systems automatically shut themselves down, one by one.

'So TsUP asked us to start making manual observations of the stars, with the little sextants we always carry, as long as we could, even before the automated sensors packed up. Because the more checks we made the better handle they would have on our position.

'Fine. Good. We kept at our jobs. I think we found making the star sightings . . . comforting. Something we could actually *do*.

'Ten hours passed. By then we had everything inside the storm shelter, but were still moving around.

'Eleven hours. By then we were going out one at a time, just to stay economical. Making our position reports, calling them in. Eleven hours thirty.

'OK, and here is where it went wrong, and I ain't blaming anybody. Mostly myself, but even me, not so much. I think a combination of factors worked against us.

'We knew the twelve-hour lockdown deadline was coming. But we thought we had half an hour, plenty of time. So, solely on my own initiative, I decided to dash out of the storm shelter one last time, for one final position reading.

'So there I was, alone in the habitat's main area, in my long johns – inside the shelter, we were putting on our pressure suits at the time – when the power started to cut down, seriously. I heard the hum of the air-conditioning fans stop. The water pumps slowing. The main lights flickered, and the low-power LED emergency lamps came on. Long, deep shadows everywhere. And then I heard a deeper hum, fading. I think that was the gyrodynes, the big flywheels we use to help maintain attitude.

'It's amazing how noisy a space habitat is, normally, and now I was hearing it grow quiet, for the first time since we left Mars orbit, I guess, all those months ago.

'I was slow, I admit it. I was listening to it all, trying to figure out what was happening, where we were in the sequence. I don't think I've experienced that kind of power-down before — we never simulated it. I was slow, unforgivably so, to figure out what was going on.

'Then I heard the door slam.

'The door of the storm shelter. And I heard it click locked.

'I saw their faces at the window. Ito, Marina, their palms as they slammed at the door.

'As I said, it's nobody's fault. Certainly not the manufacturers'. But I *think* maybe there is an interfacing issue, with the habitat, a Jones, Inc. product, mostly Californian-built, and the storm shelter, which is itself a smart gadget, but built in Russia. And I think maybe the batteries, draining, gave out a dip in the output, in the overall decline. The shelter detected that fairly abrupt drop in power levels, and interpreted it as some catastrophic failure, and did what *it* was supposed to do. Which was to slam its door shut, to protect the crew within.

'Memo to TsUP and Jones, Inc.: do some more integration testing before you send up another long-duration Shelter-habitat mission.

'Anyhow you can bet that storm shelter door won't open again. Only if the main power comes back, miraculously.

'There's no manual override, if you're thinking of that option. The Russians don't do manual overrides. Yuri Gagarin could have told you that.

'So here you have this ridiculous situation, of my crew safe and snug in a shelter that won't open, and me drifting around in a virtually powerless hab module, with not a sunbeam to warm my face. In my underwear, literally. Having got myself shut out.

'I have to tell you that Marina already figured that without power the temperature in here is going to drop fast. Several degrees an hour? So it's going to get pretty cold in – well, you can do the math. I'm hoping this whole dumb situation will be resolved before then. TsUP are talking to the manufacturers, I know that.

'In the meantime, since you ask, I'm going to keep busy. I'll make notes of the batteries' power output, and on the behaviour of other systems as their power share falls below nominal. All of this will be of use to future contingency planning.

'This is what we do. We record, and we learn, so we can help the next guy.

'Oh, and I will keep on sighting the stars, since it was our one last attempt to do so that has stranded me out here. And with the information that gives, I hope we will eventually be able to bring the Al-miriykh home safe. With all its crew, because I ain't dead yet.

'TsUP, this is Jim Boyd, signing off . . .'

'No.

'Not yet. I have more to say.

'Look, however this turns out, I can't regret it.

'Nobody said getting to Mars and back would be easy, or safe. They did tell me how wonderful it would be, and so it was.

'You'll have seen our science reports, or the summaries. We landed on the Medusae Fossae Formation, a million square kilometres of pumice – hugely ancient, a raft of debris from a long-dead volcano, which had itself formed beneath an equally vanished sea. We *proved* that was what that formation had to be. As if we had discovered that antique ocean.

'But Mars is more than the science. Mars is Mars.

'Just to see these landscapes we had all peered at for so long, through camera images returned by those clumsy, brave little rovers. It had been like looking at a wonderful land through a pinhole. When you're there, when you're down on the surface, Mars is . . . huge.

'It doesn't feel like some small world at all. That tremendous sky, the shrunken Sun. The light is low, and you have this twilight feel, the soft brown of sky and land. And the huge features, the cliffs, the canyons, the craters. All so still, so silent. The track marks from some of those antique rovers have lasted decades. The rovers themselves are still there, you can find them, as if waiting for a call from their distant makers.

'I don't regret any of it. How could I? I just wish you could have been with me, Zhi.

'Oh, and please don't dock my pay over this. I know that's the Russian way.

'Or the crew's pay.

'Zhi, I love you.'

15

6 January 2057, midnight GMT

Midnight, Mel recorded – a new day, after this longest of days – and still no sign of the deleted Sun in a star-littered southern sky.

And Skythrust Two, in this unending night, had reverted to type – or rather to its designers' primary purpose. It had become a party boat, a kind of vast sybaritic resort floating above the troposphere, with lights blazing in the night, and the overlapping sounds of music and laughter and the chink of glasses, even the clatter of cutlery on midnight-feast plates. It was a kind of defiance, Mel thought. After all, the great vacuum-lift ship relied on solar energy just as much as did the Al-miriykh, out in space. But Skythrust had a hell of a lot more battery capacity aboard than the fragile Mars ferry, and even a small nuclear plant as backup.

But it felt cold enough here, Mel thought, on this deck, even under a clearwood, air-conditioned viewing blister.

She and the Astronomer Royal, with a few other dogged types, sat side by side in low-slung deck chairs, wrapped in coats, leggings, blankets, even big fur-trapper lined hats. Keeping up this vigil of the empty sky, as pointless as it seemed right now. They were accompanied by a handful of other watchers, human reporters and a couple of drones humming in the air.

Observing the observers. There was some interest in their professional perspectives, evidently.

But there was nothing to say. Because there was nothing to see.

Nothing, Mel supposed, other than a glorious night-time panorama. The atmosphere could never have been more transparent, with whatever moisture there had been in the stratospheric air above having long condensed out. And, tonight, there wasn't even the impediment of the zodiacal light – the background interplanetary glow reflected by the debris in the plane of the Solar System, lit up by the Sun on any other night. No Sun, no glow. Even the equatorial belt of human-launched satellites and debris, usually a thin, sparkling band, was invisible tonight, without the sunlight to catch it.

This, she realised, must have been the best night to observe the stars themselves from the location of Earth since the Sun had lit up more than four billion years before. Some thought.

Then, just after midnight, one of her phones buzzed.

Just as Marlowe's did likewise. With a rueful glance at each other, they consulted their screens.

Mel's message was from Zhi. 'Shit,' she said.

'I see your shit and raise you. You first.'

'News of Jim Boyd. The fiancé of my friend on—'

'I know who he is by now. As does the whole world, I fear.'

'Well, he still seems to be OK. But the internal temperature in that thin-walled habitat is still dropping steadily. Down to freezing soon.' She checked the time. 'Two hours since the shut-down? Sounds about right.'

Marlowe grunted. 'I suggest you look up the symptoms of hypothermia.'

That was the kind of seemingly unfeeling remark from Marlowe that, Mel had learned, was best left unanswered. She touched a tab to listen to a little more of Zhi's message. *His crew, locked in that storm shelter, with all his own warm clothing . . . What can they be feeling? What a screw-up . . .* 'So, you've got worse shit than that?'

'I'm following feeds from around the world. The virtual meeting of the FIS Security Council has reconvened. Finally. Thank the Lord that's gone above my level for now. I suppose our pal Fred Bowles will be supporting that, briefing his own superiors, the other ambassadors . . .

'And, look at this. At the moment of nominal sunrise, in any given place, people have been congregating. Maybe that's the right word. Just coming out of their homes as dawn approaches, or when it should be happening in their location. New Zealand, Australia. As if it's one massive New Year's Day celebration. . . There's no logic to it, of course. And a profoundly depressing response.'

Mel felt faintly irritated. 'Well, what are we supposed to do? Charlie, you can't condemn people for reacting this way. With . . . *awe*. Surely that's a natural, even appropriate human reaction.'

'I suppose so, actually. We, Melissa, are scientists, and we can't let *awe* hobble our capacity to think. But what religious fables do remind us, though, is that once people believed they lived in a universe shaped by *intention*. By the intention of a god or gods, or other primordial beings, whatever. The Renaissance was our painful awakening from that fundamental belief. Well, I'm afraid this whole contemporary episode of ours is a cosmic phenomenon that does indeed reek of intention. Even that hard-as-nails politician Mara Caine seemed to see that much.'

'You mean the timing of the, umm, disappearance, to coincide with the eclipse.'

'The action itself, the deletion, is almost beyond our imaginations. Perhaps it's meant to be. But the link to the eclipse is clearly deliberate. A message. And as we've seen from the beginning a message that could only have meaning for minds on Earth, minds capable of interpreting that strange shadow. In some sense this is all for *us*. Our task now will be to figure out what that message is, what we must do next.'

'If we survive long enough to figure out anything.'

'There is that.'

Mel tapped her screens again, longing for a fresh call, yet at the same time dreading any coming in – certainly any from Jane, her daughter, who she hoped was sleeping quietly in her school in England.

16

6 January 2057, 0100 GMT

Jim Boyd's cabin temperature had indeed fallen below freezing about midnight.

So Tash learned, following the feeds on her phone.

In Government House the long night stayed quiet, relatively. Quiet for Tash and Grace anyhow. They had both supported Fred Bowles, as he in turn helped prepare the English Federation's representative to the FIS Security Council for that level of meeting. And with that done, right now Fred was locked in with his own subordinates, advisers and peers, including the Chief Scientific Adviser, the Chief Medical Officer, police and military chiefs, considering next steps. Tash and Grace could only wait for a call.

She wondered if everybody else was holding their breath. Waiting to see if this strange nightmare of cold and dark would end. Everybody in the world, waiting.

A little after one, she and Grace made a decision to attempt to get some sleep.

Together they made their way through the cool warren of corridors that was House – a crowded warren tonight with so many people working over – and found the small overnight accommodation suite they had been allocated: two bunk beds, a minuscule bathroom and a coffee pot, empty.

They agreed one would try to sleep while the other covered the phones, taking turn and turn about. In the end Grace, who among her other superpowers seemed to possess an ability to thrive on a lack of sleep, volunteered to take the first shift awake. Some animal part of Tash was glad of it.

So Tash changed, washed, and cleaned her teeth with ministry-supplied brush and toothpaste, while Grace went out hunting down coffee refills.

When she lay down, Tash felt too wired to sleep, too exhausted to stay awake. But she was determined to lie here, asleep or not.

While, gradually, her thoughts crumbled.

She did sleep, but only lightly, and in fragments.

Kept waking up fretting. Furtively checked her phones, out of sight of Grace.

Mostly checking for news about Jim Boyd.

At around two a.m., Jim, still cheerful – or putting on that face – still compos mentis, was monitoring his own heartbeat, finding it high, and reporting the results.

I'm doing what I can, he said through a throat tight with the cold. *I came out here in my damn underwear. So I'm improvising. Pulling on every stray bit of clothing I can dig out. I'm looking at the insulation we have cladding the walls, behind the hygiene panels. I'll get at that.*

I know the theory. My body is doing what it should be doing. I'm shivering, heart pumping, my body burning up stores of energy in a last-ditch attempt to keep my inner core warm. My vital organs. I'm still wearing my med sensors – we're supposed to wear that stuff inside the storm shelter – so anybody who chooses can follow my vital signs. Maybe I can provide some data on the advance of hypothermia in a healthy young male – youngish –

even if I don't recommend you make the same mistake I did . . .

Amid the grand spectacle of a whole world shivering in the dark, Tash, along with much of the human race, found the small human story of Jim Boyd, stuck out in space, utterly compelling. Hardly surprising for her since he was the fiancé of a friend, though Tash had never met him personally. But it was also a neat, self-contained story in its own right, on a night of overwhelming events.

Maybe it was always this way, a means for mere humans to comprehend such immense disasters. *Saving Private Ryan*, about a survivor of the Second World War. *Refugee Tears*, about a survivor of the 2030s border clashes between China and Russia – a phase of a long-lasting, slow-burning conflict in which Zhi's own father, conscripted, had been killed.

Saving Jim Boyd. Except there seemed no way to do that.

Tash fell asleep to the calm murmur of his voice.

When she woke Boyd seemed more confused.

I'm trying to take my damn heartbeat but now it says it's slower than normal and that can't be so . . .

It was four a.m., Tash saw. The Russian mission controllers of Al-miriykh weren't releasing the predicted cabin temperature any longer. It had to be far below zero. She sent another sympathy message to Zhi on the Lodestone, but – even if it ever got through the habitat's mission controllers – as with its predecessors she got no reply.

Tash made to get out of bed, but when she opened the door to the tiny lounge area Grace, sitting there, shook her head. 'Nothing's happening. Get some rest while you can, because you never know when you'll get another chance. Listen to an old soldier.'

'I thought you were an old marine.'

'Classified.'

She was right, of course. The morning would see chaos, and mountains of work, come daylight or darkness, sunshine or frost. Besides, some deep, frightened part of her, she suspected, just longed to escape back into the oblivion of sleep.

She went back to bed.

Her next wakening was seven a.m.

Surprised she had slept so late, and apparently deeply, she bundled out to the lounge, quickly paging through the relevant feeds on her phone.

The Sun was still absent. That was the first thing she checked.

The second was the latest report from the Al-miriykh, not from Jim but his crewmates. A recorded summary, on repeat.

. . . It got worse around six a.m. UTC . . .

Which was a common astronaut's standard timing, the same as GMT, Tash knew.

. . . We couldn't reach him. We were locked in. He was in a rage. He ranted at us, the TsUP, God, you name it. Then he started ripping off his clothes – what little he was wearing, just layers of stuff he had found lying around in the cabin, and bundles of insulation from the walls. Even his med sensors, ripped right off. He said he was too hot. *Stuck in here, we couldn't stop him. Then he moved out of sight, and we don't know where he is now, what he's doing . . .*

Grace walked over. She glanced at the feed. 'Look at those body temperatures. It's over for him.'

Tash longed to return to sleep.

She dumped her phone and headed for the tiny bathroom.

17

0947 GMT

'Melissa.'

Mel, huddled on a couch, had dozed off, to her surprise.

She only discovered this when she was shaken awake, rudely, even roughly. She was still in the Skythrust observation blister.

The Astronomer Royal was standing over her.

'Charlie? What the hell? . . .'

Marlowe pointed to the black, star-specked sky, through a crystal-clear observation roof. '*Look* at that.'

A flicker of hope that she must mean a returned Sun quickly died. Of course not; the whole sky would be blue once more if so. Still, she looked in the direction Marlowe was pointing.

And was dazzled.

A very bright star. A brilliant pinprick, high in the sky, bright enough to light up the sea below, like a shard of a full Moon. No, much brighter than that. Bright enough for her to pick out the smooth lines of Skythrust itself.

Marlowe grinned. 'Well? *That* just appeared. What do you think?'

'Umm. A star? It's in Centaurus, right? But not one of the regular constellation stars. No, obviously not, far brighter than any star I see up there. Magnitudes more. Venus, Jupiter . . .

No, of course not that either, far too bright . . . And of course, no sunlight to be reflected. Wake up, Mel. A nova? Supernova?'

Marlowe grinned. 'That's the least stupid thing you've said so far. But I don't think so. I mean, what are the odds of such an event, a naked-eye supernova, a once in a millennium occurrence, in the middle of all this? And—'

And the 'star' winked out.

The world was perceptibly darker.

'Damn it,' Marlowe said. 'You *saw* it, didn't you?'

'Yes, of course.'

'How long did that last? Two minutes maybe? No matter. I have some data at least, and the automatics will have harvested a lot more . . . Give me a moment.'

It was more like six or seven as she worked the numbers.

'There,' Marlowe said at last, triumphantly. She held up a small multi-purpose sensor. 'Can't you see? I got its spectrum. *It was the Sun*, Melissa. Not a nova – the Sun. Our Sun. The spectrum proves it. That's sunlight.'

'But the light *came from far off*. Out in the Kuiper Belt, I'm guessing. Beyond Neptune. Hell, never mind guessing, I can work it out from the intensity.' She tapped at a screen. 'Here we go. About as bright as, umm, eighty full Moons. If it's as dim as that, it must be around ninety AU away, ninety times as far out as Earth is from the Sun – or as Earth is usually. And I – shit!'

Mel had to smile. 'Something surprising, Astronomer Royal?'

'I'll say. Because ninety AU is *precisely* where you get to if you travel at the speed of light for twelve hours, from the position of the Sun, outward.' She tapped at screens. 'I wonder if we can get an observation from that Mars ship, the Al-miriykh. If we can get some kind of triangulation we can confirm that.'

'I suspect they might have their hands full.'

'Ah. Yes, probably. There will be other eyes in the sky, though. How long ago did the Sun vanish? Must be seven, eight minutes already. And – yow!'

Light flooded the world.

Mel threw an arm over her eyes.

18

0948 GMT

When it happened, Tash was still stuck with Grace in their hospitality suite in the bowels of Government House. She was absorbed in breaking down summary police reports from around the country, in preparation for further briefings later in the day. And so not looking at her phone for once.

Grace, sitting across from her, reached over and shook Tash, not unkindly. And, grinning, held a brilliantly lit phone screen in front of her face.

'What the hell? . . .'

'Not hell but heaven, kid. It's back!'

'What is? . . . Oh, shit. The Sun?'

Grace paged through her phone to a screen with rolling news.

Meanwhile, Tash saw, the news feeds to the wall screens were catching up. Sunlight everywhere. Dawn skies, sunset skies, bright noon skies, from across the day hemisphere of the planet.

Frost melting in the Sahara. Remarkable sights.

Grace said, 'It reappeared at just the same time as it disappeared yesterday. To the second. Well, probably more precisely than that, but that's the best that the media can do.'

'To the second? . . .'

Grace just laughed. 'Our lord and master is calling already. Fred Bowles. Now that everything Cobra and the Security

Council discussed is probably redundant, the government needs to reset. See you later.' She stood, made for the door, then hesitated. 'Out of interest. When you're free of all this, when you get out of this wooden box, where's the first place you'll go?'

Tash thought she was jumping the gun a little, minutes after the return. *What if the Sun went away again?* She wondered if she would always be anxious now, like a once-abandoned child, that the Sun would some day go away again.

But maybe most people would react this way, with utter relief that it seemed to be *over*, without questioning any more. Like plugging in a kettle immediately after a power outage.

'Where would I go?' She thought of the chapel around the corner. St Joseph's. 'Back to the church,' she said.

'Why?'

'Seems appropriate. I dunno. Then, back home to Dad.'

Thinking of that, she sent her father a hasty text message.

He pinged her back almost immediately. *All well. Do your job.*

'Grace, what about you?'

'The pub. But not before I call my sister in Naples. See you at Fred's office.' She left, slamming shut the door.

Tash sat on the couch, paged through her own messages. From Zhi, From Mel.

She found a straight news channel. She scanned through images of a sunlit Britain. Images taken from the air and space, and from the ground – very bright images, landscapes and cities, covered in snow and frost, all under a brilliant blue sky, what with all the clouds having condensed or rained or snowed out in the global twenty-four-hour night. People rushing outdoors, thronging. One eager commentator wondered if a single astronomical event had been so intensively celebrated across Britain since the solstices and equinoxes of prehistoric times.

Now she turned to Zhi's message, and found it in mid-flow, evidently on repeat.

. . . French engineers who had studied the storm shelter engineering aboard Al-miriykh found a protocol to unlock the shelter as soon as power started flowing in the solar panels again. Long before the batteries will be charged, of course. So Ito and Marina just burst out of there, still in their pressure suits, and at first they couldn't find him. In the end — well, there he was . . .

Blurry images. A huddled form, floating weightless in the air, inside a bundle of rags. A naked back. Frost on the flesh. Rocks, oddly, scattered around, some drifting in the air. Images only minutes old, Tash saw from the time-stamp.

He'd stripped completely in the end, Zhi said. *And — this. Apparently not unknown in hypothermia cases. They call it 'terminal burrowing'. You can see he actually broke open sacks of Martian rock samples, and pulled it all together around him in that space.*

A fresh call came in. Mel, on Skythrust.

Tash? Hi. You OK?

'I'm fine. I slept through the end of the world in the belly of the English government. I haven't seen all your calls . . . You?'

Listen, Tash. You need to focus. This isn't over. Charlie Marlowe is full of energy, of ideas. The timing, all of it, has surely proved that this was a deliberate act, by some — intelligence — and it was aimed at us, at humanity. If we didn't know it before. But this thing has limits.

'Limits? But *this thing* can manipulate the Sun—'

It has limits. So Charlie says.

'Oh, yeah? Such as?'

Lightspeed.

Look — we made an observation, just before the Sun, ah, reappeared. We saw the Sun, far off, low in the sky — far away, like a brilliant star, but it was definitely the Sun — the spectrum proved it. Very brilliant. It was in the constellation of Centaurus. Just a couple of minutes. And then the Sun returned to the sky – its normal position.

Tash felt fuzzy; her thinking seemed slow. 'Data overload, Mel. And the interpretation is—'

Charlie got it immediately. Well, she is the Astronomer Royal.

Suppose you take away the Sun, at lightspeed, or near it. You transport it out of the Solar System – out beyond the planets, more than three times as far out as Neptune. Twelve hours out. You leave it there for – well, we don't have the timing of the sighting, yet. Maybe two minutes. The Sun's still shining, light spreading in all directions – including back towards the centre of the Solar System.

Then *you bring the Sun back, at lightspeed. Which takes another twelve hours.*

'Ah. OK. I see. The two-minute image of the distant Sun *just beats the Sun itself* as it races back home. And we saw that star-like Sun shine for . . .'

Two minutes, Mel said triumphantly. *Then, when the Sun itself is set back in its place at the centre of the Solar System, a new pulse of sunlight washes out over the planets, reaching the Earth itself eight minutes later. Precisely the sequence of events we saw. Well, I say precisely, it's all still unfolding, we still need to examine the instrument records more carefully.*

It was deliberate, then . . .

. . . Give me that – oh, hell, yes, it was deliberate.

That was Charlie Marlowe's voice. Her sudden interruption startled Tash. The voice sounded hoarse.

And you, anyone who has the ear of government ministers, must understand that clearly, from the off. We have reams of evidence now that this event was deliberate, and targeted. At us, at humans. Reams. It starts at the moment of eclipse, an event that only occurs here on Earth, at that precise moment. The Sun is held away for twenty-four hours — our terrestrial day! This was no cosmic flaw, a random event. Somebody did this. If ever there was a doubt about that—

'Why?' Tash demanded. 'That's what my boss will want to know. Not how this was done, but why?'

Good question. Of course you must ask it; if an action is deliberate you must seek the motivation. I can't even guess — not yet. But I can tell you that this — this existential monster — evidently has limits. Its very actions betray that. Lightspeed for one. Huge as it is, powerful as it is, it kneels before Einstein!

And, listen. You have to think of the bigger picture. Make your superiors see. This — thing — this intelligence — it comes from beyond the Earth. This is the day of the Blink . . .

And that would turn out to be the first time Tash heard that label for the event.

But, Marlowe went on, *this is also the day we found life beyond the Earth. This is the day we were contacted by extraterrestrial intelligence. This is a dream of the ages — of decades of SETI dreams. This day! And everything we know about the universe, about ourselves, is transformed.*

'Some first contact,' Tash murmured.

So it was more Christopher Columbus than Carl Sagan. You play the hand you're dealt.

Tash shook her head. 'God or not, extraterrestrial intelligence or not, it has killed some of us. Many of us, across the planet. We haven't yet counted the dead. And it killed Jim, our friend's fiancé—'

So it did, Marlowe said savagely. *It may kill me. It may kill us all. But I can understand it. I can. And so I will. So will we all. Remember that, all of you. I — what, now? Very well . . .*

She's taking another call, Mel said. *Sorry about that. I . . .*

'You sound exhausted.'

I am. Haven't slept. And – it's the sixth of January now, right?

'Go sleep,' Tash said. 'No, go talk to your daughter. Then sleep.'

Hell of a way to start the new year. I wonder what the rest of it will be like . . .

And in the Sinus Medii, an eye closed.

YEAR

2057

19

January 2057

In the last week of an extraordinary January, Tash Brand more or less ordered the In-Jokes to put aside their demanding schedules and get together properly – well, over their phones – for the first time since the Blink. As opposed to swapping occasional scrappy messages.

Even if Wu Zhi could only show up virtually, courtesy of a link from a microgravity rehab facility at Houston, where he had been taken on landing from the Lodestone.

Tash herself was stuck here in Manors for now, in her government-funded flat – into which she had moved her father, Noel, since Blink Day. But living within walking distance of Government House helped a lot. And she wasn't about to tell him so, but in the fallout from the Blink, her Dad's help with such irrelevances as meals and laundry had been invaluable.

Mel Kapur, meanwhile, had been brought back to England in the wake of Charlie Marlowe – and on this particular night Mel had asked if she could bring along Charlie too. To Marlowe's chagrin, both were stranded in Newcastle, some way from their home observatory in Yorkshire, and still, frustratingly, unable to get any significant science done of their own. Indeed Tash, Mel and Charlie had another meeting to attend later that evening.

The problem was that Marlowe's very visible role on Blink Day had elevated her to the status of a kind of celebrity adviser to the English government and its allies, on the Blink and all manner of related science phenomena, and Tash had seen a lot of her – and so of Mel. Well, they had plenty to advise about. The whole world was data-gathering, it seemed, trying to figure out what just happened. Government centres like House were sinks of expertise and knowledge, to which experts of all kinds were summoned – inasmuch as there were any experts about such an event as the Blink, Tash supposed – in advance of more hierarchies of international consultations. Ultimately, maybe they would even take some action.

And meanwhile, off in the shadows, Tash knew, other groups were organising too: the conspiracy theorists, the millennial prophets and their followers, the bunker builders. A whole new meme set had been inserted into humanity's paranoid soul.

As the last of the January sunlight bathed the house, they finally sat down together – Tash, Mel, Charlie – in the flat's tiny lounge, while Noel fussed around in the kitchen making tea. As for Mel's daughter Jane, she generally seemed mysteriously to discover overdue homework assignments whenever her mum's old fart friends got together, and she was sleeping over with a school friend.

And here was Wu Zhi, even, a big image projected from Houston thrown on a wall screen, showing him to be locked into a full-gravity-support exoskeleton that didn't whirr *too* loudly.

For a moment there was peace, calm, togetherness. This was what it was about, for Tash. In times of angst her instinct was always to gather, to nurture. Even just to hug, damn it, even if only remotely.

But any traces of serenity on Zhi's face were fleeting. The grief, the anger, were all too raw.

Everybody was still following the travails of the surviving crew of the Al-miriykh. After the Blink, with sunlight restored, and power flowing through the spacecraft's systems again, at least the immediate danger to life had been averted. Now the crew were struggling to get their craft back on a new Earth-rendezvous course, using their emergency-measures solar sail to compensate for the twenty-four hours of drift they had suffered on Blink Day. The various national space agencies were cooperating, putting together contingency rescue plans in case of under- or over-correction with this clumsy improvisation.

And the astronauts themselves had completed what examinations of Jim's body they could manage, before paying their own respects. Five days ago, Tash had come home with her father to watch the final, bleak, unreal-seeming ceremony that followed – the whole world, it seemed, had watched – as the airlock hatch had finally been opened, and the body, wrapped in an improvised shroud, had been consigned to a sunlight that no longer seemed friendly or eternal. It had all looked like some movie special effect to Tash.

She knew that amid the global trauma of Blink Day, there had been a handful of high-profile deaths like this that had particularly grabbed wider attention. It was always this way, at times of national disaster or terrorist outrage or pandemics. You sought symbolic deaths, of the hero medics, the bereft children, the serene elderly who had seen so much before. This time it was Jim Boyd, lost Mars astronaut, symbolising a whole damaged planet.

As for Zhi, Tash had heard hints that Serena Jones herself had commandeered a ship, one of her corporation's wholly owned experimental craft, to bring Zhi, Jim's fiancé, down quickly from the Lodestone's quiet watch in the renewed shadow of the Earth. Tash had felt unworthy as she speculated that maybe

Jones was just seeking some favourable publicity. But maybe there was a nobler motive; since then there had been hints of Zhi's participation in some new project of Jones's. If so, Zhi hadn't said a word. Not even to the In-Jokes.

And, probably, Mel and Tash had glumly concluded, not to his own family. Of whom there only seemed to be his mother, herself – apparently – a formidable space scientist, still based in China, called Wu Yan. The only time the other In-Jokes had ever met her – or rather, glimpsed her – was when she had shown up in the wake of their notorious cadet-training near-death experience. And even then she seemed to be there to check on Zhi's health, to berate him coldly at his stupidity for getting in such a mess, and to rail at the supervisors of the test. As opposed to comforting her son.

Now, as the Al-miriykh inquiries unwound, Zhi had watched helplessly, Tash knew, and grieved silently for his fiancé.

Well, here he was today, with them all, if only for a while, if only in spirit. And if the In-Jokes were all the true family Zhi had, she was glad he was here . . .

But even so he seemed distracted to Tash, as if he had some ulterior reason even for joining this little gathering.

The apartment block creaked and swivelled, as the last January sunlight, low but strong through the windows, shifted.

Charlie Marlowe looked around, amused. 'My parents owned a house like this. An early smartwood build. Always turning like a flower to the Sun.'

'I guess we're used to it,' Tash said. 'We had a place like this before, years ago, when my mother died . . .'

'The '39 pandemic,' Noel called from the kitchen.

'Then, after Dad retired from the security business, and I started working in House – Government House – I moved here.

This estate was part of the redevelopment of much of the region when they moved the government up here, and I didn't have a lot of choice. I think we quite like it though. Nostalgic. 2030s chic.'

'Never got used to it myself,' Marlowe said. 'Being shifted around every couple of hours of daylight.'

'Maybe that's the astronomer in you,' Mel said with a smile. 'You need a sense of your own orientation in space and time.'

Marlowe snorted. 'And *you* need to spend less time with pop-psychology journalists, as on Skythrust. What babble. I'm prone to seasickness, as you may have observed on that flying toy, and that's a lot more likely explanation . . .'

Tash was aware that Zhi was not contributing. Behind his screen, he looked blankly from one face to another, as if they were talking some unknown language.

Noel came bustling in with a tray of tea cups, a pot, a jug of whitener. 'Sorry to take so long,' he said as he set the tray down on a small central table. 'Damn food printer on the blink again. Government-issue tat. Tea for everyone? Good to meet you by the way, Astronomer Royal.'

She smiled back. 'Only the King calls me that, Mr Brand. I'm Charlie.'

'I'm Noel, then. Noel Brand. Very good to meet you anyhow.'

Marlowe eyed him. 'Noel, huh? I'm guessing we're around the same age. Wrong side of sixty? And is there a trace of a Manchester accent? My parents were Britpop fans too.'

He sat. 'Ha! Guilty as charged. Not that it ever meant anything to me. Old folks' music. I grew up on Korean pop. Remember that?'

'No, Dad,' said Tash with mock weariness.

Noel swivelled towards Zhi's image, making a visible effort, Tash saw, to include him in the conversation. 'Maybe you'd know some of that stuff? The K-Pop classics. I once saw Black-pink live—'

'Oh, *Dad*—'

'No, no. It is fine,' Zhi said dryly. 'China and Korea are after all in the same hemisphere. Easily confused. But I was never a fan of such elderly music.'

Impulsively Mel reached out towards his screen, pulled back her hand. 'Always too serious, huh, Zhi?'

The screen relayed the soft sound of a ringtone. Zhi stared down, presumably at a phone out of shot. Then, with a stiff, formal smile, he said, 'I apologise. I have set the alert level to significant only. Of course, that does depend on your definition of "significant".'

Tash sensed the tension among the rest of the group, as Mel, even Noel, almost visibly longed to check their own phones. *What now?*

All save Marlowe, in fact, who sipped her tea serenely. 'That's the skill of it all right, at a time like this. Plenty of facts coming in, of one kind or another. And non-facts. The trick is to iden-tify what's true, let alone significant, and to use that to make sensible guesses. All in order to brief the politicians, which will be the fate of Tash and myself in . . .' She checked her watch.

Tash tried to reassure her. 'We've a couple of hours yet, and it's only a short drive back to House.'

Mel said, 'Tash, have you heard about the big conference the FIS is planning for the summer? To debate "global responses".'

'Sure. England is putting in a strong bid to host it.'

Marlowe snorted. 'Of course we are. Thus the governments start scrambling over each other to secure a piece of whatever new world order emerges from this latest catastrophe.'

'Well, you're being cynical, but that's not a bad thing, is it?' Noel asked. 'That's sort of what happened through the climate crisis in the end. A new world order, as you put it, but a better order at the end than at the beginning. After much foot-dragging and foolishness and disputes.'

'Maybe so. Oh, I suppose there are similarities. This Blink is another global threat, demanding a global response. And for sure the Earth's systems will take another beating. But otherwise this is quite different – an existential event of a different character. And a different order of magnitude.'

Noel frowned. 'That's pretty alarming, if vague. But then I suppose it's your job to alarm us all.'

She smiled. 'I wouldn't say it's my job. Call it a perk.'

'As far as I can see it's not been so bad, so far. Not here. I mean, a day of darkness that scared everybody half to death. Maybe we're tougher up north. Like a cloudy midwinter day for us, no worse than that.' He looked up at Zhi. 'I know there were casualties. But the worst after-effects so far seem to be those big storms in the southern oceans. Even they could be just seasonal, some are saying—'

Marlowe shook her head, decisive. 'I'll excuse your sloppy thinking, sir, since you are not my student, nor a journalist, nor a science influencer. Or a politician. And you are serving me tea. But you are getting your news from idiots. You have to think it through. We all do. And to do that you have to have a grasp of the numbers.

'We are still in the immediate aftermath of the Blink, essentially. Look – we lost sunlight for a whole day. Correct? That one day of our natural energy supply is equivalent to the energy output of our technological civilisation over maybe thirty *years*. Surely you can see that it must have delivered a huge shock to the Earth's natural systems.'

To Tash's relief, Noel responded to that mild put-down with a smile. 'An interruption in the flow. My wife was a plumber.

Tash's mother. She always said you don't want an interruption in the flow.'

Marlowe smiled. 'A plumber?'

'Family business. They came over from Nigeria. Was running quite an enterprise, when she died.'

'I'm sorry.' And Marlowe glanced at Mel. 'You lost her in 2039, you said? The pandemic. I suppose this is off-topic. But, Mel, I seem to remember you once told me you lost your father about that time.'

'He had family in India. Went back there during a famine, got killed in a separatist attack.'

'And,' Zhi put in, 'I lost my father when I was young also. He was a soldier, drafted to fight in a border skirmish with Russia.'

Marlowe looked at them all. 'So is this what drew you lot together?'

'I guess so, yes,' Mel said. 'In part, anyhow. We met at college. We found we were all – well, half-orphans. Zhi and Tash were only children – and I have one brother, Paul, who studied theology, and is now off in some kind of religious community in Oxford. Have hardly been in touch with him since our parents died. Totally different path to mine.'

Tash snorted. 'Brought together by our dodgy family backgrounds *and* a shared catastrophic lack of social skills.'

Marlowe nodded. 'There are worse bases for friendships.'

'We never talk about this,' Noel said gently. 'Family. Your Mum. I'm sorry, honey.'

'Oh, Dad.' Tash leaned over and rubbed her father's back. 'Nothing to be sorry for. Never was, never will be.'

'Anyhow you did get it right,' Marlowe said, smiling at Noel.

He looked puzzled. 'Got what right?'

'About the weather. In a cartoon way. About the storms?

Interruptions in the flow of energy? So, yes, on Blink Day the warm summer air over the southern hemisphere cools down a bit, loses some moisture – rain mostly – and as it grows cooler and denser, accumulates in high-pressure systems. While it's snowing harder in the northern hemisphere winter. Then the Sun rises once more, the energy pours in, the air suddenly warms up, the moisture evaporates – and, in the south, everything's become unstable. Especially over the ocean. So, storms, as we see now.'

'With human misery as a consequence,' Tash said. 'Which is what's at the top of the politicians' agenda for now.'

Marlowe seemed irritated by that, Tash thought. 'Of course it is. Always the immediate, the short term. But these post-Blink consequences should last only days, weeks, while the Earth's systems find their equilibrium again. Or a new equilibrium. It's going to be the longer-term effects that we really need to worry about. And not just the climate adjustments.'

Tash frowned, imagining Fred Bowles and the rest of the English government hearing this in an hour or two. Any heads-up she got on this the better. She asked gently, 'Well, what longer-term effects, Charlie? What exactly?'

And Zhi spoke up. 'Longer-term effects like *this*. Downloading.'

Tash quickly set up another wall to display his new feed. The smart surface picked up the data, magnified it.

An image of the Moon.

Weeks after the full Moon of the eclipse, this was a gibbous Moon, more than half full, and apparently a live image. Tash could just about make out the rest of the disc of the Moon, a deep grey – lit up by the reflected light of the Earth, she knew that much at least. This image was set against a background of stars, the sunlit portion not bright enough to obscure them.

Tash felt embarrassed to ask. 'So, the Moon. What are we meant to be seeing?'

Two astronomers and one astronaut turned to her with evident surprise. Mel asked, 'Can't you see it?'

Noel patted Tash's hand. 'Never mind, sweetie. I can't see it either. Just as well we've got the Astronomer Royal herself to explain it to us saps.'

Charlie grinned. 'OK, we deserved that. There's a couple of things. Obvious at a glance. The darkened limb, against the stars – that's not quite right. You can see more of the starry background than you should be able to, at this point in the Moon's orbit.'

In her head, Tash tried to translate this into terms that Fred Bowles would understand. 'OK. And that's because the Moon has – moved? I mean, I know it orbits the Earth—'

'It's a little too far away,' Mel said, taking pity on her. 'The orbit has changed. So the visible disc is a bit smaller, against the background stars.'

'And not just that,' Zhi said. 'Look at the surface features. I'll enhance the Earthshine so you can see it clearly.'

It was as if a bright beam shone on the shadowed portion of the Moon's surface, in real life only dimly lit by reflected sunlight.

And now the complete, familiar Man-in-the-Moon pattern emerged, Tash saw – a landscape of huge craters and seas of lava dust. Down there somewhere, a handful of human artefacts: the old museum-piece probes, the historic Apollo sites, the modern bases inhabited by multinational crews rotating down from the orbiting Gateway station. All very familiar.

But not quite, she saw as she looked more closely. There was the Mare Imbrium, the Man's right eye. And *he was looking away*, as if his head had turned right, a little.

'Shit,' she murmured. 'Sorry, Dad. The Moon has — turned?'

'Good,' Marlowe said. 'You see it. Well done. Sorry to be patronising again. But you're right. The Moon is a little further from the Earth than it was. *And* it's rotated on its axis, relative to the Earth. It always did wobble a little — libration, we called it — but otherwise, that's the first time the Moon has started to turn away from us for billions of years. Well, we expected this; the models predicted it. But I concede it's another thing to see it with your own eyes.'

'This is to do with orbits,' Tash said slowly. 'Isn't it? When the Sun disappeared, its gravity switched off. And so the Almiriykh, on its way back from Mars to Earth, started to follow the wrong orbit home. But Mars and Earth too—'

'Followed the wrong orbits also,' Marlowe said. 'Correct. And so *they* are back in orbit, but not in the same orbits as before. Same as all the planets. And Earth's orbit is — distorted.

'You understand that the Earth's orbit was never a perfect circle in the first place? It's an ellipse, slightly flattened off the circular. Or was. Its perihelion, the point when Earth comes closest to the Sun, is in January — about now, the northern winter, a couple of weeks after the solstice — and the aphelion, the furthest, in July, in the middle of our northern summer. So our summers were always that bit cooler than the southern hemisphere's. Well, now that ellipse has got more elliptical. We astronomers say the eccentricity of the orbit has increased — it's roughly doubled, in fact. The perihelion is the same — the same distance at northern winter. But the aphelion is increased — that is, Earth will be further away from the Sun during our summer. So those differential warming effects are going to be magnified. Colder summers in the north. Harsher winters in the south.'

'And,' Noel said grimly, 'I bet we are all going to find out about the implications of that in the weeks and months to come. Correct?'

'As the climate systems try to adjust, as wind and rain patterns become scrambled, reaching for a new equilibrium . . . Afraid so.'

Tash pointed. 'And the Moon?'

'That's more complicated,' Mel said. 'The Moon is in orbit around the Earth. So when the Earth went off course, the Moon was dragged after it. But the multiple influences were complex—'

'It's finished up in its own, new, more eccentric orbit around the Earth,' Marlowe said grimly.

Tash tried to think that through.

Her father got there first. 'Tides,' he said. 'That's going to muck up the tides.'

'Correct,' Marlowe said. 'The effects are already visible regarding the ocean tides. Well, those tides are metres high, easily measurable. But there are rock tides too. The Moon's gravity, and the Sun's, raise tides in the crust of the Earth a few centimetres high. The effects of *that* will take longer to work out. But they will come.'

Tash frowned. 'What effects?'

Mel shrugged. 'Land slips. Earthquakes. Even volcanic eruptions, possibly.'

Impulsively, it seemed, Noel grabbed for their hands: Tash, Mel. 'Tough times ahead, then, however all this works out.'

Tash smiled and squeezed back. 'Dad, just have some pity on me as I try to help government ministers and civil servants understand all this.'

'*And more,*' Zhi said abruptly, from behind his screen. 'There is more you need to stress, Astronomer Royal. You must speak of *agency*, to the governments. Convince them of it.'

*

Noel seemed alarmed. 'Zhi – agency? What do you mean?'

Mel squeezed his hand harder. 'He means, this isn't a natural phenomenon, global and severe as it is. Not just a, a Chicxulub comet strike. Something *did* this to us. Or somebody. There is agency behind all this. And that's how we have to think of it, how we react.'

Zhi said, 'Of course this is nothing new. Professor Marlowe has been saying this from the earliest meetings. It's obvious, isn't it? And here in Houston I have been privileged with further data, gathered elsewhere. Data I think you should ask to see before you speak to your ministers again.'

There was a tense silence.

Tash nodded, and murmured a command. 'OK, Zhi. The channel's still secure, the flat's systems. I'm government, remember. They set me up with this in case I ever needed some kind of confidential briefing at home. And—'

'Not me, though.' Noel made to stand. 'If you lot have sensitive things to say to each other—'

'Please stay,' Charlie Marlowe said. 'I trust Mel, so I trust Tash, so I trust *you*. But, actually, Zhi is right. Some of us have been calling this out since Blink Day. The surgical precision of the removal of the Sun. The eclipse timing. These are all hallmarks of intelligence – and signals aimed at intelligences on Earth, us. But somehow it is – ignored. As if we dare not speak of it. I understand the need to avoid paranoia, even panic. But the sooner all this is out and understood and assimilated, not just by the scientists and politicians but by the public, the sooner we will be able to handle it all. Collectively, I mean.'

Noel frowned. 'A being able to transport suns. Some first contact. I thought the theory was that advanced civilisations, advanced in technology and such, would be advanced ethically too. That was always the dream. I remember the remake of *Contact*, what, in the 2030s, with that terrible avatar of Carl Sagan . . . They would come to help us, cherish us.'

Marlowe shrugged. 'They – or it – *may* be ethical. But in their own value system. We think it's ethical to eliminate viruses, don't we? We drive them to extinction if we can. Influenza. The 2030s Covid strains. Maybe to *it*—'

'We're just viruses?' Noel asked. '*That's* a thought. Talk about Carl Sagan, he must be turning in his grave. And I suppose taking away the Sun for a day isn't evidence of a kindly nature. Look, I do need to make some more tea. Fill me in, Tash.'

Tash felt numbed. She had put off thinking about this aspect of things. *Above my pay grade.* She was almost scared of what she might learn next.

As her father bumbled out to the kitchen, she tried to hide her own anxiety.

'Look, we aren't completely in the dark,' the Astronomer Royal said. 'There has been some speculation before – not about this event particularly – but about events of this kind. Agents of this kind. Of this *scale*. Theoretically, I mean. And, if they exist, how intelligences might reshape the universe on huge scales.'

Tash frowned. 'You're talking about the – what was it – the Kardashev types? You brought that up on Blink Day. I had to check the stenographers' spelling . . .'

Marlowe nodded. 'In part, yes. That's a starting point at least.

'Kardashev. Soviet Union, scientist in the last century. A Kardashev Type I culture masters energy on a planetary scale – meaning, all the sunlight that falls on it. So we aren't *there*, even, not yet. A K-II masters energy on a stellar scale. All of a star's output. Dyson spheres, if you know what they are. And a K-III masters the energy output on the scale of *all* the stars in the Galaxy. Hundreds of billions of them.'

Kay-Three.

'Now, to move the Sun, in an instant – let me remind myself of the numbers—' Marlowe tapped at her phone on the table top before her, squinted a little at the screen. 'OK. To move the Sun, to teleport it, you would surely need to master energies equivalent to the mass-energy of the Sun. E equals m cee squared, remember. Ten times the energy of the largest supernova explosions.'

'So,' Tash said cautiously, 'too big even for your—'

'K-III culture? Well, I figure it would take a century or so of its energy budget, but it could be done.'

Noel came bustling back with the tea, and a heap of biscuits, Tash saw, warm from the printer. '*Kay-Three*, huh. Sounds like another Korean pop star. Sorry. I'll pour the tea.'

'So,' Tash said carefully, 'the entity we are dealing with—'

'People are calling it *Galaxias*,' Zhi said. 'Here in Houston anyhow. A name is a name. Nobody seems to know who coined it. Galaxias. We have named it. Even if all we know about it is that it can move the Sun.'

'Galaxias,' said Marlowe softly. She swiped her phone. 'I ought to know about this. Here we are: *Galaxias*, Greek or Roman name for the Milky Way, as visible in the sky. Named for the spilled milk of a goddess. Root of our word "galaxy" of course. Also the name of a type of fish,' she said dryly. 'Fine. Call it Galaxias; it needs a name, as long as we understand there's no implication of gender or motherhood. The label doesn't matter.

'But I do think we are dealing with a single entity here, effectively. So, a singular name – yes. It. Not *they*. Monstrously powerful, but one entity.

'And yet it hides, even though it doesn't need to hide from *us*, surely.

'How do I know it hides? *Because the Galaxy looks unmodified.* It is a Galaxy-scale entity, it *must* be to master such energies as we have witnessed, yet none of its works are visible. And it must have been able to stop anybody else building anything significant too – upstarts like humanity, perhaps. No Dyson spheres, anywhere. If such traces existed we would have found them by now. This is why I believe it is a single entity, though I know some disagree. Because we see not a trace of *it*, or any vanquished rivals. We know it exists. It hides as a unity. It must *be* a unity.'

Mel pursed her lips. 'I should say this is pretty controversial. I suspect if you polled most scholars, even if they accepted the hypothesis of intelligence, they would argue for a strongly unified culture rather than a single entity—'

Marlowe shook her head. 'No. The control is too precise, too universal for that.'

'Good grief,' Noel said. 'A single beast that moves suns. Maybe we should just build a whacking great temple and bow down and worship—'

'No,' Marlowe said sharply. 'I won't have language like that . . . Sorry, Noel.'

Tash smiled ruefully. 'So you should be. I think you sometimes lack perspective, you scientists, you and Mel . . . You should see the polling that crosses Fred Bowles's desk. Right now fifty per cent of people seem to think this is an act of God – and I can testify to that, every time I pop into the local church it's packed out. Another forty per cent think it's all the fault of the governments, or some secret cabal of scientists and oligarchs. Or the Blink was something to do with a big Chinese spaceborne weather control project, which has been a popular meme for years. Only the final ten per cent think it's all — scientific, astronomical. And even to them, a debate as to whether this Galaxias is a single entity or some kind of alien federation would be pretty abstruse.'

Mel said reluctantly, 'My own brother has been putting out posts about religious interpretations. Paul, the radical theologian. And *he* has been saying it's all an act of God, and we should be respectful.'

Marlowe looked aghast. 'Really? Your own brother? Did I ever meet him?'

Mel smiled thinly. 'No. You'd remember. He's a very *clever* radical theologian, and can argue well.'

Marlowe snorted. 'Makes you wonder if humanity is worth saving at all.' Then some of the energy ran out of her. 'I don't mean that, of course. It's just that sometimes one despairs . . . But anyhow this is no god, Noel, yours, or brother Paul's, or otherwise. *We know it's limited to lightspeed.* Remember that. It has some proven limitations, at least.

'And as a material entity it must need — engines — of some kind to have achieved this. Moving the Sun. Not miracles. We are looking for such engines, or their traces. In the vicinity of the Sun — around the orbit of Mercury, for instance. And out in the direction of Centaurus, about where it put the Sun, there *is* some flaky evidence — various TNOs being deflected.' She glanced at Noel, seeking understanding. 'Trans-Neptunian objects, comets and moonlets and dwarf planets. It's as if big — masses — have been assembled out there. Huge unseen engines. We *think*. The data is patchy. Things orbit slowly out there, and they are sparse, but the results we have so far are — puzzling.

'But it's all technology. Big, but not miraculous. Since when did God need scaffolding? And anyhow the biblical miracles were small fry in comparison to *this*. Even Joshua's miracle day, when the Earth's rotation was stopped. A K-II, a star-scale culture, could have pulled *that* one off. A god? Puny Yahweh! Any tea left, Noel?'

But even as Noel went out to refresh the pot, Tash saw that Zhi was distracted. Looking away, to something off screen.

'Zhi? You OK?'

'Fine, fine. Just – bending a few rules. Charlie, Mel, I hadn't realised how far you'd got in your thinking. But there's something else I have here. I wasn't sure it even existed . . . Now I am. I just got confirmation of access. Look – when you meet your ministers. There's something else you need to know about – if the Americans haven't done the decent thing and fessed up already, and they probably won't have.'

Mel shrugged. 'Nothing I've heard.'

'Nor me,' said Tash.

Charlie glared. 'Get to the point.'

Zhi said, 'I got a tip from some friends back home. China.'

Tash tried to puzzle that out. 'Your mother?' Who, Tash knew, was a senior space scientist in her own right, who, it had always seemed, had never had much contact with the son who had gone to the West to build his own career.

He didn't reply.

Mel said, 'Never mind the provenance. *Something else*, Zhi? What?'

'Something else that might be connected to Galaxias. On the Moon.'

There was a startled silence.

Tash said, 'Look, Zhi, don't get yourself into any kind of trouble. I know about government security. I spend my life inside it. You're a hero astronaut, but that won't save you if—'

'I know, I know. And I'm sorry. I know I'm dragging you all into . . . indiscretion. But I saw a chance to get this stuff to you. I thought it was important. We should be sharing. Besides, there's no point being a tragic hero without leveraging it every now and again.'

A half-smile.

Tash and Mel shared a glance. *That* was a flash of the old Zhi.

'Tash, set up your smart wall . . .'

Tash rebooted the wall with a soft command. The Moon image, approaching fullness, was replaced by a shadowed hemisphere, its features only dimly visible.

Zhi said, 'The new Moon around the moment of eclipse. Lit by Earthshine . . .'

But now, Tash saw, a spot near its centre was flashing, on, off.

'So,' Mel said. 'I take it we're back to Blink Day, right?' Frowning, she stood and walked over to the wall. 'You're highlighting this feature?'

Tash asked, 'Do you know what it is?'

'Sure. Every amateur astronomer does. Its location is the most significant thing about it. Or was – now, with the whole lunar hemisphere out of whack, it's lost its title.'

'What title?' Tash asked.

'This is the Sinus Medii.'

'Correct,' Zhi said. 'The Central Bay – right at the centre of the Moon's Earthside face, as was. Jules Verne's lunar travellers saw it . . . Never mind. And it has some history. So I've been finding out – yes, all right, thanks to leaks from my mother, who has her own agenda, needless to say . . .'

Tash and Mel exchanged glances. Charlie Marlowe leaned forward to see better.

'The Americans landed a pre-Apollo spacecraft there, in the

153

Sinus Medii. Surveyor 6. No crew, of course. This was back in the 1960s. They sent it there just by chance, they could have sent the probe anywhere on the surface – it was really just a technology test bed. NASA didn't *report* anything unusual about the mission.

'But it turns out that they, and successor agencies, have been quietly watching the site ever since, from lunar orbit, from telescopes on Earth and in space. And, I learned since I got here, NASA even dropped a *second* probe there, a few years later, under cover of an Apollo mission. Entirely covert.'

Tash glanced at Mel, wondering where the hell this was going.

Zhi went on, 'Well, the Moon got more attention than usual even as Blink Day wore on, as it became obvious it was turning on its axis, relatively. Obvious to the astronomers. And one American instrument, a lunar low orbiter, right at the end of the twenty-four hours, saw *this*.'

He tapped at, presumably, an out-of-shot phone. New images splashed on the smart wall.

Evidently the Moon again. But a landscape, now.

'This was the scene just before the Sun returned. Low-light imagery; basically you are seeing by Earthshine . . .'

Tash saw what looked like an ordinary lunar scene – if you could ever call pictures beamed back from the Moon *ordinary*. A rubble-strewn ground, ellipses that must be foreshortened craters. The colours were odd, the ground greyish – the sky littered with stars, all of which would normally be drowned by sunlight, in a lunar day, leaving only the Earth to be seen.

But this wasn't like the usual human-touched lunar landscapes Tash was used to seeing. No Neil Armstrong footprints here, no habitats covered in radiation-shield dust. Just a low mound in the foreground. A heap of dirt.

Zhi said, 'A deep lunar midnight, at the Sinus Medii. But the visibility was good enough to pick up – three, two, one – *this*.'

In that static scene, the sudden movement startled Tash.

A projectile. A glittering pellet that was fired out of that innocent-looking mound of lunar dirt, and went sailing into the sky. As if a small cannon had been fired, right from the heart of the face of the Moon.

None of them spoke. Mel and Tash just stared, as the sequence was repeated, twice, three times.

A montage of images with explanatory overlays followed. There were multiple views, measurements made with multiple instruments – and multiple types of instruments, Tash saw, including a spectrometer, which gave clues as to the composition of the projectile.

Which had just streaked away, a blur receding from sight.

'Wow,' Tash said.

Zhi watched their faces. 'I'm not going to say a word. Not yet. Let's pool our thinking.'

Marlowe asked quietly, 'How big? That – projectile.'

'About half a metre across,' Zhi said. 'Roughly spherical.'

Tash asked, 'How long has *that* been up there? The mound, the – the artefact, whatever, that fired that shot.'

'Well, we can't know that—'

Mel said, 'OK. So we saw it by accident, in 1967, through that Surveyor.'

'Correct. The Surveyor photos had shown some kind of structure, visibly poking out of the dirt, a cylindrical hole cut in the top. Even the dust pile looked too symmetrical to be natural. Also the Americans thought they saw evidence of *ice* inside that hole in the crest, maybe shadowed. Just a reflection; the Surveyor had no sampling gear.

'That's about all. Don't ask me more; all of this is classified, and I've seen little of it. As I said, the Americans sent up just one more lander, kept it quiet. Just watched, for decades. Not an unwise policy. But the structure, whatever, can't have been doing anything but watch, in return.'

'Watch what? Who?'

'Given the location,' Marlowe said dryly, 'right at the centre of the Earth-facing hemisphere, I'd guess it's been watching Earth. Us.'

Zhi nodded. 'I think that's the best theory they have. They being the American intelligence community, coordinating with some covert bits of the old NASA and its successor agencies. The probe runners. The old SETI theorists had a name for a probe like this. A lurker. It just sits and watches you, without revealing its existence. Anyhow I only have partial information on this thing, all acquired since the Blink. So I do know the US agencies have monitored this mound, this artefact, for decades. But now it's all hotting up.'

Tash frowned. 'What do you mean?'

'*There's a Chinese team up there now.* A human team.

'They were sent down from the Lunar Gateway after Blink Day — after, presumably, the American imagery of this — firing event — was hacked. The Chinese are running a lot of industrial projects on the Moon, so they have plenty of infrastructure up there, a lot of cover. And much of it in Copernicus. A big, bright nearside crater. Now a lot of them have moved into Medii. The Chinese are being very cautious, as you can imagine. And secretive. They have left the US probes alone — I mean the Surveyor and the spy probe. They keep just out of its field of view — but they have also masked off the mound from the US probe's view.'

'What was it made of?' Tash asked. 'The . . . cannonball.'

'Good question. As far as the Americans can tell from the spectrometry – *ice*. Just water ice. About a kilogram by mass, we think. A fat snowball. But it may have some kind of protective covering we can't see, to protect it at the speeds it seems to be going. There is a lot of dust in the plane of the Solar System, although it's heading out of that plane . . .'

Marlowe was intensely interested in that. 'What kind of speeds?'

'As far as we could track it, it was still accelerating, hard. Multiples of G. We don't know how it's propelled, by the way. No sign of fuel usage – no infra-red signature – nothing like a rocket exhaust, or a sail . . . We *don't know*. We don't see any reason for it to slow anywhere short of lightspeed itself. By *we* I mean the American analysts who are studying this thing.'

Tash shook her head. 'A bucket-load of water ice? What's the point of that? I thought we were talking about a galactic intelligence!'

Marlowe said cautiously, 'We can only speculate. But, Tash, you could store a lot of information in water, if you chose. You yourself are pretty much a bag of water containing information coded into complex biomolecules. I'm not suggesting this – system – is using DNA itself, but the principle stands.'

'OK,' said Tash, trying to think this through. 'But even if you could, theoretically, who would *choose* to send a message in water ice?'

Mel said, 'That's a better question. Maybe somebody to whom water is . . . everything. We know that there are water worlds out there. I mean, exoplanets with nothing but deep ocean, no land breaking the surface . . . So maybe this is a clue as to the origin of Galaxias. If so – how exciting!'

Noel said evenly, 'But aren't you missing the point? *Where was this sent to*? Do we know?

157

Zhi smiled. 'Another good question. Well, we don't know where it will end up. But we do know where it is heading, right now: for the constellation of Ophiuchus. North of Sagittarius, the zodiac constellation. If you go that way long enough you would finish up above the centre of the Galaxy.'

Mel said, 'But it's not even travelling at lightspeed, yet. Correct? It would take millennia to get that far—'

Marlowe shook her head. 'Ophiuchus: I think I have an inkling . . .' She dug out her phone. 'Catalogue. Ophiuchus. Barnard's Star . . . Zhi, can you download some better data on that missile's trajectory? . . .'

With that projection, it took Marlowe only minutes to get the answer she apparently sought.

'Barnard's Star. I knew it. The next system out beyond Alpha Centauri, nearly six light years away.'

Tash asked, 'You're saying that's where the pellet is heading?'

'Well, possibly,' Marlowe said. 'When you factor in the relative motions of Sun and star over the next few years. And a logical destination. But what's there waiting for it? Barnard's is a red dwarf with just one planet, as I recall.'

Zhi frowned. 'Take a look.'

Mel said, 'But the system's very well studied—'

'We shouldn't rely on anything we thought we knew before. *Take a look*. Find a recent observation.'

Marlowe nodded to Mel.

Mel paged through data coming into her phone.

'. . . OK. Not sure I see the point of this. There are frequent all-sky surveys that check out nearby star systems, known exoplanets, regularly. Let's see. Particularly, find out if there's anything new since Blink Day.' She murmured into her phone again.

When the results evidently came in, seconds later, Mel looked puzzled, Tash saw. She tapped her phone, waved it at the wall, as if seeking a better signal.

'There is something. A new set of observations, which . . . They've been flagged as anomalous. An instrument glitch.' She shrugged. 'For what it's worth . . .'

On the smart wall, up came a blurry image of a star, and an even more blurred image of three planets of some kind.

'These are the best recent images I can find quickly. Taken a couple of days back, actually with L³T. Umm, that's Zhi's own Lodestone Ludicrously Large Telescope, in deep space.'

Marlowe got up, crossed to the wall image, and stared at it. 'Barnard's has one planet.' She tapped the second planet icon, and the third.

The images magnified. Tash saw fuzzy splashes: worlds with banded clouds, like Jupiter or Saturn.

Mel snapped unhappily, 'I know. If so, what the hell are these? Well, we *thought* Barnard's had only one planet,' she said, paging through her phone. 'Turns out we were wrong. Running some quick analyses . . . These two are about half the mass of Jupiter each. One is at asteroid-belt distance from the star, the other not far in from where Jupiter would be. Oh, this is rubbish. These worlds can't exist. We should have seen them. We've been spotting exoplanets for decades . . . Oh, shit,' she said. 'I found an independent observation. Similarly not believed. They're real, all right, Charlie. Missed by the automatics because – well, I suspect the AIs aren't trained to look for stuff like this, planets appearing out of nowhere. They just read them as data anomalies.'

Tash said, 'My head is spinning. So what you're saying is that an alien cannon, hidden on the Moon, spat a gob of water at alien planets that didn't even exist last month.'

'I know,' Mel said, sounding unhappy. 'On any other day, in any other year, that might seem strange.'

Zhi said earnestly, 'Mel, widen your search. Nearby planetary systems. Find other, recent, anomalous observations. There's no reason why there should be just one.'

She glanced at Marlowe, who nodded.

'On it.' But as she worked she shook her head. '*Why?* Why do it this way? Why conceal whole planets? If we haven't got everything wrong here.'

'Maybe it's all about security,' Tash said.

Mel frowned. 'What about security?'

'Sorry. Government hack speaking. And Dad used to be a specialist consultant on cyber-security for the Met.'

Noel nodded, cautiously listening.

'You get to think in these terms. It was when you were talking about concealment and so on, of the cannon and these planets. Also I was wondering *why* anybody would communicate between the stars with chunks of water. Well, maybe that's the answer. *Security*.' She looked at Mel uncertainly. 'It makes sense, doesn't it? Even on a tight-beam relay, the chance of some bad guy picking up a beamed signal is *much* higher than intercepting a small packet of ice. It's a low-tech way to do it, but it would be secure.'

'That makes a lot of sense, yes,' Marlowe said. 'Thank you. I didn't think of that. I *wouldn't* have thought of that. You are right, Zhi; this is why we must share all we know – all of humanity, actually. It's the only way we are going to figure it out. Yes, it's a somewhat paranoiac pattern that fits the observations. The moving of the Sun was a huge stunt, obviously, and very visible. But aside from that, it's all been . . . creeping around. An ice-pellet message fired from a hidden station on the Moon? Fired at cloaked planets?'

Zhi nodded. 'This is the question. So who is Galaxias hiding from? Who does it *need* to hide from?'

Marlowe said, 'Maybe nobody specific. It's solitary, as I said. It hides by reflex. Maybe waiting for some hypothetical threat. A threat like us, maybe. If we were to – *emerge*.' She pronounced the last word quite savagely.

'I found more,' Mel said.

'What?'

'Planets.'

She waved her hand over her phone, throwing more images on the wall. More planetary systems, Tash saw.

Mel said, 'I ordered up a sweep of recent anomalous, to-be-confirmed-or-discarded observations of nearby systems. I suspect people are embarrassed by these data sets and the academic journals will have trouble accepting them . . .' She smiled grimly. 'Sometimes it's *good* to be able to namedrop the Astronomer Royal.'

'And you found something,' Zhi prompted her.

'I did. Only two more systems so far. The next out, beyond Barnard's, is Altair, in the constellation of the eagle. About seventeen light years away. We thought it had no planets at all. Now it turns out it has *twelve*, at least . . .'

More images. The outer six worlds were Jovians – the outermost, a hundred thousand times as far from Altair as Earth was from the Sun, was so big it was technically a brown dwarf, halfway to a star.

'Of the inner planets, there are five Earthlike, or larger. The fourth planet – Altair e, I guess – is slap in the middle of the habitable zone, and may be Earthlike . . .'

Zhi actually smiled. 'You're confusing Tash. Probably. Tash, think of Altair a as the star itself. So the first planet to be discovered is b, the second c—'

Mel shook her head. 'Anyhow, we saw *none* of these worlds before the Blink.'

Marlowe seemed to be drinking in this information. 'And you said one more system?'

Another slide; more blurry worlds.

'This is 55 Cancri – in the constellation of Cancer. Actually a double star system. It has five planets – well, we knew that already. But what's *changed*, in this case, is the fourth in terms of distance from the star, the fifth to be discovered – 55 Cancri f, formally, it's called Harriot, after a long-dead astronomer. Half the mass of Saturn. *Now* we see it has a big moon – it looks oceanic, a big water world, probably kept warm by tidal influences. We'd have spotted it before . . .'

'So,' Marlowe said. 'I think I see a pattern. There must have been a wave of – unveilings. Camouflage dropped – from as far out as 55 Cancri, at least. And this was all done years ago, so the images came heading in at lightspeed, the camouflaged systems unmasked, from our point of view, one by one. Because, presumably, that concealment doesn't matter any more. Or it wasn't *going* to matter any more by the time these lightspeed images reached our telescopes, after Blink Day. And on Blink Day itself the installation on the Moon fires off at least one message bundle back, to the nearest – station . . .'

Tash felt faintly disturbed. 'What does all this concealment say about the psychology of – whatever it is we're dealing with?'

Mel frowned. 'Nothing good.'

Zhi stared at 55 Cancri. 'How far away is this one?'

Mel didn't seem to hear. 'There may be more, umm, masked stars. We need to report this to the international councils, continue to check—'

'*How far away is 55 Cancri?*' This time Zhi shouted his question.

Shocked, Tash looked up. 'Hey, buddy. Take it easy—'

'*How far?*'

'It's all right,' Marlowe said, calm. 'It's hardly a secret. Forty-one light years, Zhi. Forty-one. OK?'

Zhi seemed to be thinking hard. His eyes scrunched closed. 'Forty-one light years,' he muttered. 'Times two. Lightspeed.' Then he opened his eyes, looked around as if waking. 'I know.'

Tash longed to be able to hold him. Or shake him. 'Know what? What do you know, Zhi?'

'Why it is here. Galaxias. Or at least, why it is here *now*. The timings all fit.'

Tash was bewildered, and Mel looked the same. 'Zhi – the timings of what?'

'Something we did. I *think*.' He looked around again. 'I must talk to the people here. And NHSA.' He stood, grabbed a jacket from a chair behind him.

'Zhi. Wait. Don't go like this.'

'There's probably little time. We can't waste any more of it. I, I—' He seemed to run down. 'I'll be in touch.'

His image winked out.

Tash was the first to break the silence. 'Wow. OK. So what's the plan?'

Mel, looking weary, just shrugged. 'I'll have to put together some kind of formal report on what we have found tonight. In your living room, Tash!'

Marlowe said, 'Yes, we have to report this. Recommend further searches, analyses. Let's make a start.' She reached for her phone.

'If it's going to be a long night,' Noel said, standing. 'I'll go put more tea on.'

Mel said. 'I wish I knew what Zhi is thinking. He's just gone haring off again. If we knew what he was after we could help him.'

'Or stop him,' Tash murmured.

But, as it turned out, before the end of the month Mel learned she would soon find herself travelling again – and, this time, with Zhi.

20

February 2057

The smart plane, a State Department loan, small, fast and nimble, ducked down out of the low clouds that blanketed much of the coastal plain around Anchorage.

Alaska from the air looked . . . odd, Mel thought.

This was the state capital, a city of white blocks of relatively new developments scattered like a giant's toys around an older, dingier core. Clearwood windows returned sparkling reflections, a sign of the climate-migration population boom this most northern of the old union's states had enjoyed, or suffered, in the last few global-warming decades. But in the wider landscape beyond, as the plane came down through turbulent air, Mel saw open ground that itself looked unusual. Dimpled. Pitted, scarred, the low sunlight casting distinctive circular shadows, as if from lunar craters.

Meanwhile, though this was still winter, there wasn't a trace of ice or snow to be seen around the city – indeed, nothing truly wintry until she ducked her head and peered to the north, where at last she caught glimpses of ice. She shouldn't be surprised, really; despite its reputation southern Alaska hadn't been a snowy wilderness for much of her own lifespan, probably. Maybe, post-Blink, that was going to change.

And in the meantime, she knew, much of the US administration was holed up here – including the President's science adviser, who they were here to brief. Even if, she knew, Lee Yamanaka had no real idea what kind of news they were bringing.

She turned from the window to look back at Zhi, stiff in his exoskeletal support, her only companion on this flight. Or rather she was *his* companion, on a trip that had been set up through contacts via Marlowe and Fred Bowles.

On the surface this was Zhi's mission: to share his insight into the Blink's timing, to leverage it to help Serena Jones persuade the US government to respond to the Blink event in some quixotic fashion, it seemed – a project whose details Mel herself was yet to learn. But this was a fairly sensitive diplomatic moment too, Mel had come to realise. They had news the US government needed to learn, and which it might not like learning. So, leak it through a low-level contact like this, and let it filter up before the formal stuff. And to hell with the weight of responsibility poor low-level Mel might be feeling.

Right now Zhi was buried in his reading materials, phone images and sketchy graphs and charts, including what looked to Mel like engineering cutaways. A clue to what he had to present, maybe.

Zhi himself had changed so much since the Blink, as much as anybody she knew, she thought, or more. Once, before *that* day, he would have been bagging a window seat, peering out at this climate-changed landscape, speculating, hypothesising – a still young, curious, supremely bright astronaut-scientist. Everything was different now – everybody was different – but Zhi particularly was transformed, lost in his own reclusive obsessions.

But then he had a right to be. He had lost somebody close, through the Blink. He wasn't alone in that, especially if you included those left bereaved by the ongoing aftermath of the event. Still, it made it personal – and for Zhi, the loss had been horribly public.

At the same time, though, Tash and Mel, gossiping, had speculated that maybe Zhi, who had always seemed the least academic of them, was emerging as some kind of tormented, mixed-up genius. After all it had been a key insight of *his* – the timing of the lurker signals – that had unlocked that bit more of the enigma that was Galaxias, even if he was still reticent about the details, even to his closest friends, to Mel and Tash. He was the one invited to the Winter White House. He was the one Serena Jones had co-opted as a public face of her still-secret space project. Maybe they had been too close to see him clearly, over all these years . . .

And maybe there was still some kind of competition going on with his remote, aloof, space-scientist mother . . . *You're here to support him, Mel. Not psychoanalyse.*

The plane made its final run-in. From above, a new airport was a compact criss-cross mesh of short runways and scattered buildings, blocks of reflective white and silver. The plane ducked down into this complex along a startlingly steep descent curve, touched down with scarcely a jolt, and rolled quickly to a halt.

Zhi folded up his phones with a snap, glanced out of the window, and got up without a word or a glance back at Mel.

A car drew up at the bottom of the debarkation escalator, sleek, smart, its hull white, marked with the roundel logo of some US federal government department.

As they deplaned, the car's gull-wing doors opened. Out climbed a bulky figure, a woman, swathed in a thick black coat. Under an impressive fur hat, her face was broad, dark. She waved at them.

Mel recognised her immediately, and she suspected Zhi did too, given his slight hesitation.

Mel walked up, hand extended. 'Professor Yamanaka. We virtual-met on Blink Day, in the English government briefing. I was supporting Charlie Marlowe.'

Yamanaka grinned as she enclosed Mel's hand in her own gloved paw. 'Melissa Kapur, right? Charlie always speaks highly of you. And, Wu Zhi?' Another handshake. 'Now you I would have recognised anyhow. After the Al-miriykh tragedy – your personal connection to that – I'd say you have the privilege of owning one of the most famous faces on the planet. But I guess you would give it up in a flash—'

'Yes, ma'am,' he said stiffly.

'Come, get in the car. Alaskan air can still cut through . . .'

They clambered in, the doors folded down around them, and the car drove off, evidently knowing its destination. The air temperature inside quickly climbed. Mel tentatively slipped off her gloves.

'Yes, the cold.' Yamanaka sat facing away from the direction of motion, looking back at the two of them. 'And I do admit my ageing bones miss the warmth.'

'You're from Hawaii,' Zhi said.

'That's right. Which has its own problems, even after more than a month since the Blink. Did you know that with the anomalous tides, there have been beachings of dolphins, even whales? . . .'

Leaving the airport compound, the car slid smoothly along a broad avenue lined with stocky, modern buildings, some smartwood, some not. There was little traffic on the road, no pedestrians to be seen on the wide sidewalks.

Then, abruptly, the car dipped a little, swaying to the right before recovering. Mel grabbed a handhold.

Yamanaka smiled at her. 'Don't be alarmed. The ground here is notoriously uneven. You'll get used to it.'

'Permafrost,' Zhi said.

'Correct,' said Yamanaka. 'Or the lack of it. Lenses of ancient ice, underground. When they melt, the water soaks away or evaporates, and the ground just subsides. It's been a global-warming phenomenon since the last century – since long before the big Migrant Relocation programmes kicked in, oh, fifteen years ago or more. Certainly before the US federal government moved up here after the DC floods.' She laughed, genial. 'Maybe not enough attention was given to fixing the holes before the President moved in.'

Mel, not a particularly social animal herself, and with Zhi taciturn beside her, admired the way this very senior figure, the President's science adviser, was effortlessly putting them at their ease.

'But the Winter White House facilities themselves are impressive. I shouldn't promise anything, but if your pitch is good enough you might get a tour.'

Zhi looked faintly concerned, Mel thought. She said, '*If* the pitch is good enough . . .'

Now Yamanaka frowned. 'You can understand we have been in a rolling crisis here since Blink Day – as all governments have been. A situation, I suspect, which will go on for years, decades – and, between us, I'm not sure even President Cox understands this yet. I have to tell you that whatever the merits of your proposal, when you and Serena make it, there simply may not be the resources to follow it through.'

Now Zhi looked angry. Before he could speak Mel took his hand in hers.

'My advice is to just stay calm,' Yamanaka said, observing them. 'Everybody expects you to be nervous . . . And everybody knows you have a burden of grief to carry. You'll likely get some hard questioning, but we're here to listen, believe it or not.'

Mel thought that Yamanaka would not be so complacent if she knew *all* Zhi had to tell her today.

The car pulled smoothly off the road and approached a white-painted wall maybe three metres tall, with a barred gate. National Guard in black uniforms and visors patrolled, and drones buzzed overhead. Beyond the gate, at the end of a short drive, the Winter White House was a blunt box. Ultra-modern, and indeed white. Mel longed to dig out her own phone, to send pictures of all this back to Jane, at school in England. But she knew it would never be allowed.

The gate opened with what seemed like reluctance.

As they got out of the car the building's main door, wood-faced but with a visible metal substructure, swung open for them.

Yamanaka led the way forward. 'Come through. You should be cleared, but there are the usual retinal, face ident checks. Also, put your hand on the pad as you pass – you know the drill. Oh, and the voice check. Repeat after me: "Mary had a little lamb . . .'''

Once through the security barrier, Yamanaka strode down a brightly lit, sparsely decorated corridor. 'Most of the offices are subterranean, actually. Here we are, my own office, pro tem . . .' A side door opened for her as she approached, and she ducked inside.

Mel and Zhi followed.

The room, brightly lit by ceiling panels, was another box in the plain white that seemed to be the only colour scheme in here. A desk with one big padded chair behind it, a couple of office chairs before it. More chairs stacked in one corner.

'Let me get this place set up . . .' Yamanaka tapped the walls in a couple of places, and hatches opened to reveal a coffee maker – already steaming, and Mel wondered if this room had known Yamanaka was coming from the moment her car headed this way.

Yamanaka briskly shrugged off her heavy coat, threw it on the chair stack. Her outfit beneath was a billowing trouser suit, brilliantly coloured. Flamboyant in this pallid place, Mel thought. And Hawaiian, no doubt.

'Please. Be comfortable. Well, as you can be. Hang your coats on the back of the door. Sit down.' She gestured at the chairs before the table. 'I'll fetch coffee, if you both . . .'

Mel and Zhi complied, Mel a little uncomfortably. Yamanaka's vigorous big-scale hospitality now felt a little intimidating. Mel was suddenly aware of how *junior* they were, to be bearing the news they had to impart.

Yamanaka dumped three coffees on the desk top. 'Please, sit. The coffee is not bad, printed or not.' She sat.

Mel sipped the not-bad coffee.

Zhi stacked his phones on the desk and looked around. 'The place seems . . . sterile.'

Yamanaka raised her eyebrows at his frankness, and smiled. 'I guess so. Look, this is a new facility, newer even than most of New Anchorage, and in the build they prioritised utility and security over comfort, let alone aesthetics. But right now, post-Blink, this is one of the few US government facilities where you'll actually find senior government players, like – well, like me, and I'm about the most junior of that pantheon.

'You see the response across the nation, of course. The National Guard at their stations. Martial law in some places. Civic leaders and the hospitals geared up for mass casualties from – well, whatever comes next. We all grew up amid calamities, didn't we? We're used to it.

'As for the federal government, since Blink Day we've been operating a COG protocol. Continuation of government. So senior officials, from the President and Vice-President downwards, are scattered across US territory in the bunkers, such as here, NORAD in Colorado. Some of these facilities are many decades old, but still serviceable if you *really* need to be safe. The President herself is in Raven Rock, under Pennsylvania. I've been there, actually. Baby Boomer chic. I guess you won't know what that means. Most of the congressional leaders are at the Mount Weather emergency operations centre in Virginia – in the Mole Hole, they call that one, the Strategic Command underground bunker from where they once planned to fight nuclear wars.

'In a crisis the President usually has most of her senior advisers close by, such as, well, me, her science adviser, and the Chairman of the Joint Chiefs of Staff, her National Security Adviser, the Secretary of State, the directors of the CIA and FBI, the White House counsel . . . Oh, and her political advisers. I think President Cox is leaning on us all a little, just now, because—'

'Because she's feeling out of her depth,' Zhi said abruptly, surprising Mel.

Yamanaka sipped coffee, raised her eyebrows. 'Well, that's obvious enough. She was only elected in November, of course. One of her first actions post-Blink had to be to postpone her own inauguration. Yes, she's bewildered.' Yamanaka hesitated, studying them. 'You need to understand where the President's head is right now. Look – if you'll forgive me, you're both pretty young. And the young often have a different perspective to us older folk. Before you make your pitch to me, let me give you a little context.

'When I grew up, climate change was hitting the country

hard. The interior was desiccated, especially once the aquifer and glacier water supplies dried up. Colorado, California too. Elsewhere, flooding, massive incursions of the ocean in the south-east, over Florida, Louisiana, Georgia, the Carolinas. No surprise that those states led the Secession. And of course the major flooding events along the east coast.

'But, you know what? We adapted and survived. We, working with the Canadians and Mexicans, I should say, who took a lot of our emigrants. We put in place massive technological fixes where we could. And, of course, we moved people. Whole new cities sprouting like mushrooms in the Appalachians, in the Canadian north. But we got through it all, by God. *You* grew up with this. *We*, my generation, had to deal with it. And I think, in the end, over the course of my life, I can feel proud of my country. Hell, even of most of my presidents. Proud of what we did.

'But now President Cox is going to have to live up to that standard, even exceed it.'

'Because of the Blink,' Zhi said.

'Because of the Blink. You know, we have a whole set of National Response Scenarios, guidance on how to deal with various calamities, natural or human, as dreamed up and war-gamed over decades. Of course along comes the Blink, which is like nothing anybody ever foresaw. The Earth is in a different *orbit* now, damn it. Everyone knows we weren't prepared. How could we be?

'And then this is an unusual crisis, psychologically. The sheer abstract nature of it doesn't help. Lights in the sky. You have a high anxiety level anyhow among a public that has grown up against a background of disasters. Do you know about Freud's analysis of fear? He said you can have a kind of rational fear of something specific, but then there is a free-floating fear which is always there, and just attaches itself to any candidate cause it can find. A neurotic fear. Freud called it "dread". I think that's exactly what many of us are feeling now, in the face of this huge, abstract threat, Galaxias. Dread. And so anyhow now there is the usual panic buying, the survivalists retreat to their bunkers, the Mormons flee to Utah where Jesus will return to Earth.' She looked at Mel, a little uncomfortably. 'The – religious hypothesis – is a strong one in this country. The idea that this is some kind of punishment from God, or *a* god. Despite all the specific scientific evidence, those doubters overlap with other groups who think it has all been some kind of hoax.'

Zhoi nodded. '*Puny Yahweh.*'

Mel Tash remembered Charlie Marlowe's facetious conversation – on Blink Day itself? She'd used those words then. And she'd repeated the phrase in many conversations and broadcasts since.

But Yamanaka said now, 'It would help us all greatly if the Astronomer Royal did not utter those words publicly again. Not on my watch anyhow. Nothing good ever came from provocation . . . I leave that with you.

'And in the meantime,' she went on, 'our government has to keep everybody fed and safe. Anyhow that's what our mint-new President is having to deal with, even as she learns the way to the White House lavatory.'

Zhi nodded. 'I am Chinese. And we have a word: we are a culture that dreads the return of *luan*, of the chaos of a disorderly past.'

Yamanaka smiled. 'Maybe we Americans need that as a loan word.'

Mel thought all this over. 'We need to understand how the President is thinking. Even as she's coming to terms with the job. That's why you're telling us this.'

'Yes. But on the other hand – I'm on your side. I think. My impression is that it's some kind of positive proposal. Yes? You mean to *do* something. If so, if it's of any value at all, *I want your pitch to get through.*' She said this with a vehemence that surprised Mel. 'And that's why I'm speaking to you. Look – I'm basically an exobiologist – I'm no psychologist. Let alone a politician. We have to deal with the disasters to come. *She* has to, President Cox. But I think, right now, she *needs* something that is positive, not just – anti-negative. Something we can do, and build, that will not only do us some good, but maybe make us feel better about ourselves. And thus help us wage the wider war to come.'

'You're right,' Zhi said calmly. 'I understand. America . . . *does* stuff. And I hope you will welcome Serena's proposal, which, yes, is a positive act. But—' He glanced at Mel.

She nodded back. *Now's the time.*

'We have something else to tell you,' Zhi said.

Mel put in. 'Something sensitive, diplomatically speaking. We think—'

Zhi blurted, '*It's because of something America did that Galaxias is here now.* This is my own hypothesis. That's what I believe.'

And Yamanaka just stared, frowning.

Mel glanced from one to the other. *So much for the diplomacy, Mel.*

She said, 'Professor Yamanaka, you've been sent the briefings Charlie Marlowe prepared for the British government. The latest data—'

'On the Blink?'

'And its causes. As much as we have figured out.'

Yamanaka showed a flash of impatience. 'Summarise for me.'

Mel spoke carefully – but she had worked alongside Charlie Marlowe for years, which had toughened her up for this kind of presentation. 'To begin with, we believe that Galaxias, the name given to this phenomenon, is a conscious agent with Kardashev Type III energy resources. The Kardashev types—'

'I know. Go on.'

She summarised Marlowe's argument about the displacement of the Sun, and what it implied of Galaxias's restriction to lightspeed. And she spoke of the revealed planetary systems: Barnard's, Altair, 55 Cancri. And the discoveries in the Moon, the ice packet fired from the lurker –

'I have been briefed about the lurker. At least I have been now. I never heard of that installation on the Moon before the Blink. Plausible deniability, they told me in the end. I had heard rumours of the revealed planetary systems . . . Which does make me wonder what else I don't know. Or haven't been told. We are grateful for the sharing, of course. Go on, please. What has America got to do with it?'

'Well, the lightspeed limit puts boundaries on Galaxias's ability to respond to events. Actually, it was Zhi here who figured that out. And who made predictions, made us *look* for evidence we never expected to find. The changed planetary systems. Never imagined . . .'

She nodded to Zhi.

He said evenly, 'It was Galaxias's evident lightspeed limit that made me think of this. That and the fact that the ice-mass probe was fired off at close to lightspeed itself. I wondered where it was going. And how long it might take to get there. And, if it did carry a message, how soon we might expect some kind of reply.'

Yamanaka nodded. 'Go on.'

'Right. The lurker shot seems to be aimed at Barnard's Star, the nearest of these — camouflaged — systems. And the *furthest* we've spotted in this set of changed systems is forty-one light years away. 55 Cancri.

'But — just suppose this isn't the *first* signal the lurker has sent from the Solar System, to 55C. Possibly via Barnard's, Altair, possibly direct. The question is, why should any such signal have been sent at all? *Because of something we did.* That's what I believe, and others.'

Mel wondered which others. Not herself, Tash, Marlowe. Zhi was evidently engaged in conversations on another level, with some shadowy cabal of truth searchers.

He said now, 'I believe that the monitor on the Moon, whatever it is, may have been watching us — well, possibly since before we were human at all, let alone spacefarers. And now it has observed us doing — *something* Galaxias wouldn't like.'

Yamanaka frowned. 'And what exactly?'

Zhi nodded, comparatively calmly, Mel thought.

'That's where the timing comes in. Let me work through the logic, and you'll see for yourself. The lunar probe sees this *action* of ours, and sends a report to its neighbouring, umm, stations. You would think the more distant the target, the more significant that target must be as a — a *node* in some communications network. And the data gets to 55C—'

'After forty-one years. OK. And if a response was sent back it would have reached the Moon at least forty-one more years after that.'

'Maybe a response was sent immediately; maybe there was some preparation. I think there was as much as a year's delay at one end or another — maybe because Galaxias wanted to time its response to coincide with our solar eclipse . . . Sorry. I'm running ahead. My head is too full of this stuff. I believe a response to that first report was received, from 55C, no later than 2056. And, as we know, the Blink has occurred in 2057.'

'But you're trying to convince me that this chain of responses was set in motion because of something *we* must have done . . . my mental arithmetic is awful, 2056 or '57 minus twice forty-one years . . . The signal to 55C must have been sent maybe around 1973, 1974? Why that date?'

Zhi took a breath. 'Because – I believe – at that time we humans did something that we had never done before. Something extraordinary.

'On 3 December 1973, an American spacecraft called Pioneer 10 passed Jupiter. In fact on that day it reached periapsis—'

'Closest approach to the planet,' Mel put in.

Yamanaka the exobiologist nodded a subtle thanks.

'Yes,' Zhi said. 'Only about a hundred and twenty thousand kilometres above the cloud tops. And there was a gravitational slingshot. As the mission designers had planned, Pioneer reached escape velocity. *Solar* escape velocity—'

Yamanaka got the point all at once, very visibly, Mel thought. Her jaw dropped, she sat back, she thumped her smart table top with her fist.

'My God. At that moment Pioneer 10 became the first human-made object to escape the Solar System – in principle, right? It had the energy, it had the velocity, and all it had to do was to coast on out, beyond the orbits of Saturn, Uranus, Neptune. Energetically speaking, it had *already* escaped from the Sun's gravity well. At that moment in 1973.'

'Exactly. Pioneer is long inert by now,' Zhi said. 'But still sailing out of the system, never to return. A sister ship followed it – Pioneer 11 – and then the Voyagers, and then—'

'I know, I know.' Yamanaka waved that away. 'But your point is, Pioneer 10 was the *first* of our ships to get away, right?

To break out. And – something on the Moon was watching.'

'Yes. And so the lurker at Medii sent a report to 55C – maybe to Barnard's, Altair too. But I bet 55C is the key node. A light-speed interval later—'

'The response comes back. It comes *now*.' Yamanaka scribbled numbers on a pad. 'Or at least, with this gap for the timing, the solar eclipse coincidence . . . And then, the Blink. My God.' She sat up straighter. 'It all fits. I need to check this over, but – I think you sold me.

'We'd been sending out radio signals for decades, and nobody cared about *that*, evidently, but as soon as we start sending physical objects out of the System – wham. The door is slammed in our faces.' She shook her head in bewilderment. 'And, hell, this is so sensitive, diplomatically, politically. So we have a covert US probe babysitting this ET thing on the Moon for decades? And then we have the Pioneer, another US probe, triggering this huge existential response. *As if it's all our fault.'*

Mel nodded. 'You'd like to think no rational person would apportion blame.'

Yamanaka eyed her. 'There are probably no rational persons even in this room. Welcome to the world of politics. The US will be accused of cover-ups, of hubris, of further cover-ups yet . . . Well, we did cover up the discovery of the lurker.'

'That's why we brought this to you first, Professor Yamanaka,' Mel said. 'Maybe we can help.'

She explained Fred Bowles's strategy. Fred had foreseen this kind of response, so by sending Mel and Zhi to this briefing, he was trying to smuggle in as much as he could discreetly – so that Yamanaka could take it to her government in the best way she saw fit.

'OK,' Yamanaka said, evidently thinking fast. 'So we can figure out a defence about this Pioneer thing before the shit storm. Good. Thank you. Smart move by Fred, and thoughtful. Well, OK, with preparation time we'll handle it.

'But beyond that – we know a bit more about Galaxias now, don't we?' She frowned. 'Why, there's even a subtext of – contempt. The casual revelation of those exoplanets – think about it. For us to be allowed to see the reality of those systems *now*, after more lightspeed delays, the masking must have been dropped at 55C as soon as the Moon signal reached there – and, presumably, the other nodes dropped their masks as an instruction through some kind of command chain that was sent back out. Yes – I'd call that contempt.' She looked at Zhi sharply. 'So, Zhi. You really figured this out yourself?'

Zhi actually blushed. 'Well, I was surrounded by the right people, who had access to the right data—'

'Bullshit, with respect,' Mel said.

Yamanaka said, 'Agreed. You deserve a hell of a lot of credit. If you're right. So. What have we learned? That we have been watched for decades by this – lurker. At least decades, possibly for much longer. We dare to send one flimsy probe out of our own system, and the response is a report sent up through some kind of communication chain.

'After which, the Blink.' She nodded. 'What can that be seen as but a warning? We are being – contained.' She smiled, grim. 'Which I fear is unacceptable. Anyhow, Zhi, here you are with some cunning plan, it seems. What do you and Serena Jones have to offer us in response to Galaxias?'

He smiled back. 'A spaceship,' he said softly. 'The ship that will allow a human crew to follow where Pioneer 10 went. Whether Galaxias likes it or not.'

Mel herself hadn't heard of this. It was a surprise. Startling, even.

Yamanaka stared at Zhi.

Then she grinned hugely. 'Hell, yes. Wu Zhi, I'll get you and Serena Jones in front of President Cox. Count on it.'

21

March 2057

Energised by Zhi's pitch, Lee Yamanaka hastily organised a minister-level conference – a preliminary pooling of scientific findings on the Galaxias crisis – to be held a couple of weeks after Zhi's and Mel's visit.

This was to be hosted in her homeland, Hawaii. A boost for that Blink-battered island, Tash knew.

And an early acceptance by the English Federation was a crucial step in giving the event authority and cachet – not to mention securing funding. Tash knew Fred Bowles was more than glad to travel out himself, having pushed his government to take part. Fred had always believed the world had to work together to overcome this crisis, an agenda he did everything he could to advance at his own relatively junior level. Even if all they *could* do for now was talk: gathering in one conference chamber or another, talking, talking.

So they flew out. The core of the British contingent was Bowles himself, Grace Butterworth as security, Tash, along with Marlowe and Mel.

And, to everybody's surprise, Zhi's mother.

Wu Yan had flown to England to visit her son, if briefly; she hadn't seen him since his return from the Lodestone, and this was a last chance before he was due to disappear into a

high-security Jones, Inc. facility in America, to pursue his new
passion, Jones's new proposal for some kind of Galaxias-defying
spacecraft. Tash had no real idea how that meeting, between
mother and son, had gone. Anyhow, given Yan's presence in
England, it had taken only a little In-Joke diplomacy to draw
Yan into this journey, and for her to gain an endorsement from
her own government.

The flight to Hawaii itself was enormously long, and mar-
ginally hazardous thanks to traces of volcanic ash in the air, a
lingering remnant of a so-far minor eruption on the flanks of
Mount Rainier – an event Grace followed closely, always aware
of her family, still stuck in Naples, itself an uneasy volcanic
province. And there were also diversions and cancellations
because of the latest storms in the Pacific. One, hurricane-
strength, had hit Hawaii itself not long ago.

Tash understood, everybody did, that all of this was related
to the great disturbance of the Earth in its orbit on Blink Day.
Air, oceans, the liquid rock under the crust, even the planet's
iron core, all were sloshing, sloshing. And people were dying,
dying.

Still, when Fred and his entourage arrived the night before
the conference itself, and Yamanaka in gratitude for their support offered a tour of her own observatory, Bowles readily
accepted.

Even though they had to climb a mountain.

Their smart bus toiled up a road surface that looked to a
nervous Tash like it needed some significant renovation, with
crumbling edges and even a couple of potholes.

But that was a distraction from the gradual opening up of a
spectacular view from this mountain on Maui – second largest
island of the Hawaii group, and birthplace of Lee Yamanaka.

And at last, towards the end of this steep, inadequate road, Tash glimpsed the stubby form of their destination, the observatory itself: the Daniel K. Inouye Solar Telescope, as Lee Yamanaka had proudly told them. Beyond that, nothing but hazy, smoggy sky above, a sea of cloud below, brilliant white. The sense of altitude was remarkable, Tash thought. Intimidating.

The bus rolled forward, working through the last leg along a rougher track. After one particularly heavy jolt Tash grabbed the hand of Mel, sitting alongside her.

Charlie Marlowe, opposite, raised her eyebrows, to Tash's chagrin.

Wu Yan, sitting behind them, saw this too. Yan leaned forward and patted Tash's shoulder. 'My son always said this of you, Natasha. A nervous traveller.'

Tash exchanged a look with Mel, as they released their hands.

Wu Yan was slim, elegant, startlingly tall. Ever since she had been added to the party Tash and Mel had both been off balance, Tash thought. After witnessing a decade of frosty distance between mother and son, here they were sharing gossip with her. *People are complex*, Tash thought. Sometimes she thought that was all she had learned in her whole life.

'Me too,' Mel said, covering an awkward gap. 'Nervous, I mean. I'm tougher than Tash here, but I do admit I even got airsick a few times aboard Skythrust.'

'A *few* times,' Charlie Marlowe murmured.

Tash broached the taboo subject. 'Zhi has travelled to the Lodestone, a million kilometres from Earth, and I get airsick crossing the Tyne Bridge. Surprising he talks to us at all.'

'He values your friendship very highly,' Yan murmured. 'As do I. Especially since his loss.'

Neither of them quite knew what to say. Wu Yan was a conundrum, Tash thought.

Well, in the post-Blink world, China itself was a conundrum. From the beginning their response had been cautious. The Chinese offered help where it was needed with the various post-event disasters as they unfolded, although it was suspected that they were covering up problems of their own.

But they were clearly also working through their own investigations of the phenomenon, on Earth and in space – especially on the Moon, it seemed, from rumoured surveillance reports. Up there they were pursuing what looked, from afar, like large-scale experimental industrial projects – as well, it seemed, as establishing a heavy presence of their own in the Sinus Medii, close to the water-cannon alien installation.

Still, they had promised to attend this event, and to contribute to a planned end-of-year major FIS session.

And here was Yan, a distinguished astronomer and space scientist, fulfilling that first pledge. Tash had heard cynical suggestions that Fred Bowles was seeing potential in the relationship between Zhi and Yan, fractured as it was, in the global response to Galaxias. The hero astronaut of the West, this prominent thinker of the East, son and mother. A bridge-building element. That was the way, she was learning, that skilful politicians worked. With the people around them.

But Yan *was* Zhi's mother, nonetheless, and she was here. So Tash covered Yan's hand on her shoulder with her own, briefly, before Yan sat back.

And then the bus lurched, throwing Tash back in her seat and making her gasp.

Grace, ex-military, was of tougher stuff, and liked to show it. 'Oh, come off it, Brand. You're only three kilometres up. I'd die of boredom before anything up here managed to kill *me.*'

Lee Yamanaka squinted up at a faintly smoggy, orange-tinted, volcano-ash sky. 'Well, I wouldn't be so sure. We have

185

had casualties up here. Nobody dies of boredom, mind you. We'll reach the observatory soon, but you've had a long day . . . Let's take a break before we face all that. Bus, hold it here. Rest mode.'

The bus rolled a little further, apparently seeking a scrap of level ground. When it settled it reconfigured, with the walls silently ballooning out, and the struts and frames of the windows seeming to melt away.

At last it was as if they were sitting in a bubble of faintly tinted glass. The passengers' seats swivelled to face each other, small tables popping up out of the floor.

When this was all in place Grace came up and patted Tash's hand. 'You just sit tight, you poor dear. I'll go fetch you some coffee.' She squeezed through to the back of the bus.

But Tash saw now that Fred Bowles looked a little sickly too, as well he might. Even if he hadn't been climbing a mountain, nowadays Bowles probably wasn't used even to being outside the bowels of hive-like official buildings like Government House. Since Blink Day there had been an upsurge in general craziness, as might have been predicted, and in Britain one junior minister already had only just survived an assassination attempt.

But Bowles was studying the scenery gamely enough. Especially the observatory itself, at the summit of this peak.

Tash, looking that way, saw what looked like a modern-art interpretation of the classic dome shape of an optical observatory: a faceted pillar on which stood a vaguely hemispherical structure, but with multiple triangular facets. From here, Tash knew, astronomers had been studying the Sun for around forty years, long before the Blink. Now, of course, solar observations were more significant than ever.

As Grace handed out coffees from a tray, Bowles pointed. 'And that, I'm guessing, is our destination?'

Yamanaka smiled, a little apologetically. 'The installation itself isn't all that impressive – no astronomers peering through eyepieces like Percival Lowell – in fact, no permanent human staff at all since about 2040. There is a VIP visitor centre, but the very air isn't very healthy out there any more, not since the volcanism, the ash, the damage done to the ozone layer—'

'Sunburn and cosmic radiation.' Fred smiled. 'Even politicians read the news, Prof Yamanaka.'

'But I did want to bring you up here. It's just . . . I love this place. As you know I was born here myself, on the island. Did the work that was the basis of my own doctorate right here, at this facility. And that's why I'm using this as the conference venue. I need to grab your attention, and you won't forget *this* trip.

'Charlie, your ongoing analysis of the entity we must call Galaxias has struck me profoundly. I know that others globally have converged on similar models: the K-III intelligence, supremely powerful, solitary, hidden. Although there are plenty of naysayers who believe we can *never* understand Galaxias, because we always anthropomorphise. Project our own fears and hopes – no, the fundamentals of our very nature – onto the unknown.'

Marlowe shrugged. 'That's a valid objection. All we can do is be aware of our own limitations.'

'Anyhow to deal with this, we need to talk, talk, the science advisers, the ministers – we senior scientists, the astronomers, the exobiologists, the planetary scientists, the sociologists . . .'

Bowles nodded. 'The FIS plan a big science conference in July, as you'll know, and their major heads-of-state summit planned for November. After nearly a year of data-gathering.

That's when we expect to be able to start making significant post-Blink decisions, as opposed to the disaster-response mode we are all in at the moment.'

'Yes. November seems a long way away, but there's wisdom in it. But we need to get some kind of understanding, a governmental handle on all this, *now*, if only because our stance towards Galaxias may soon be defined by the more proactive project the Jones people are developing.'

'Their rocket ship.'

'Right. That's exactly why I bring people up here, both the senior scientists and the government flunkeys—'

'None taken,' Bowles said with a grin.

Yamanaka shifted in her seat, and looked out through the bus bubble. 'Of course nothing is as it was. There's post-Blink smog, even up here, and it is hampering our work to some extent. For our work is astronomical.

'This telescope was actually built to study the Sun itself, decades before the Blink. And that's what we've continued to do since it happened, with a rather higher profile. There are spaceborne instruments too. The best of them can resolve the Sun's surface down to a detail of around a thousand kilometres – something like a thousandth of the Sun's diameter – and we can see surface oscillations, the result of sound waves bouncing around in the interior, on a timescale of about five minutes. Sometimes I think the Sun is like one – vast – clock. Exquisite. And now some bastard has come along and taken that clock away and shaken it up.'

Charlie Marlowe turned, raised a hand to shield her eyes, and looked towards the setting Sun, just for a few seconds. 'Well, that's logical. Stars aren't meant to be teleported around the place. And the process evidently wasn't particularly smooth.'

'Quite. The whole solar interior seems to be *sloshing*. And so we're seeing resulting disturbances to the magnetic field, which are generating solar storms and suchlike – minor for the moment, but that might not last. Which won't be good news for us . . . But we still don't know, of course, *how* this was done. *How* the Sun was moved in this way.'

'Except,' Marlowe said, 'maybe we do.'

She milked the shocked silence, Tash observed, expertly.

Bowles shook his head, half admiring the intervention, half irritated. 'What a reveal. You didn't get to be Astronomer Royal by accident, did you?'

'I will be covering all this in my presentation.'

'Which even I haven't seen,' Mel groused.

Bowles grinned. 'Just tell us, damn it, you showboater.'

Marlowe smiled. 'OK, guilty as charged. I'm speaking now – informally – on behalf of a network of researchers, mostly archivists actually. None of what I have to say has been peer-reviewed, let alone published. I thought I'd wait until I saw you in person, Lee, before—

'Sorry, Fred. I'll get on with it. In fact we do think we have the faintest of handles on *how* it moved the Sun. Because we think we have found some evidence of the presence of Galaxias, deep in the heart of the Solar System, *before* the Blink. And we have *that* because we've been studying Mercury.' She glanced at Bowles. 'The planet closest to the Sun. This was part of a wider survey of the Blink's effects on all the planets—'

'Just get on with it,' growled Bowles. 'What have you found?'

Marlowe said simply, '*Negative matter.*'

Bowles frowned. 'OK. That's new to me.'

Tash glanced at Mel. 'Me too. Like antimatter?'

'Not that,' Marlowe said. 'Antimatter and matter mutually annihilate, when brought together. Negative matter is different, although the abundance of negative matter might be similar to that of antimatter: less than one part in a million – probably much less than that. Up to now we haven't been sure if negative matter exists at all—'

Mel prompted, 'Charlie, you should be clear that you don't mean dark matter, or dark energy either, the mysterious missing fractions of the universe—'

'None of that. This is different stuff. Matter and negative matter don't destroy each other, like matter-antimatter. But they do repel each other. *Gravitationally*. Or, strictly speaking – matter attracts everything, matter *and* negative matter. But negative matter repels everything, both ordinary matter *and* negative matter. Hypothetically.'

Tash tried to work through that. 'So is every particle of negative matter alone, then? Because it pushes away everything else?'

Wu Yan smiled. 'Good thinking. Not quite. I am not unfamiliar with these ideas. Negative matter does *feel* other forces, in particular electromagnetic. That's where it's unlike dark matter or dark energy, you see, which don't . . . So if you charge up a cloud of negative matter, you can in principle arrange for electromagnetic forces to hold the cloud together, against the negative-matter push – because gravity is pretty weak on short scales, much weaker than electrical forces. As far as I know, that's how we think negative matter might occur, deep in intergalactic space – far from normal matter – in big, diffuse clumps.' She looked at Marlowe. 'So now the Astronomer Royal is going to tell us what this has to do with the Blink.'

'All right. Look – let's get back to Mercury. So we were studying the effects of the Blink. As it's the innermost planet, Mercury got quite a jolt when the Sun disappeared. A jolt that's increased the eccentricity of its already eccentric orbit by around a third. We don't have good eyes out there at the moment. We're expecting savage surface-melting episodes, rock tides, volcanism of some kind . . .'

'Yes, yes,' Yamanaka said. '*And*—'

'And, just as we studied Mercury post-Blink, some bright spark had the idea of trawling through data sets archived just *before* the Blink itself. We wanted to verify the change in Mercury's orbit, old against new.'

'Jolly good,' said Bowles, a trifle more impatiently. 'And what have you got?'

'Well — very little yet. We know Galaxias has capabilities orders of magnitude beyond our own. We can estimate those capabilities in terms of gross energy and power. But how that power is wielded – mostly we can only guess.'

Bowles prompted, 'But—'

'*But*, when the Sun was moved, there was a little leakage.'

Yamanaka said, 'Something you detected at Mercury?'

'At Mercury.'

Marlowe dug out her phone, flipped it open, and flung images onto the bus's smart transparent walls – data, graphs, what looked to Tash like a sketch of a planet's orbit. 'Help yourself to any of this stuff. It will all be uploaded globally soon. Look . . . Here we have the orbit of Mercury, a few hours *before* the Blink, and then from a few seconds before. And—' She plucked out a planet-orbit image, expanded it with a wave of her fingers. 'Its position just *after* the Blink.'

'You found something,' Yamanaka breathed, staring.

Bowles just sat quietly, waiting.

Tash had to smile. Fred Bowles knew his scientists. You had to be patient.

'Yes, we found something,' Marlowe said. 'Mercury's orbit was perturbed, just a little, in the last seconds *before* the Blink.

A slight signal, but a definite one, and – anomalous.' She threw more pages of data, images, notes into the air. 'Cut a long story short, the best model we came up with was—'

'A push,' Grace Butterworth said. 'Negative matter. Even I could see that coming, given all the trailers.'

'It's very tentative, the data ambiguous. But we *think* that possibly there was a sort of – compressive – effect working all around the Sun, just before the Blink.' Marlowe mimed this, cupping her hands, pushed them towards each other. 'As you might get from a shell of negative matter enclosing the Sun. And some kind of side-lobe of that compression, yes, pushed Mercury out of position, just subtly. Over a few minutes—'

'*Pushed*, not pulled,' Yamanaka said. 'Which is why you are talking about negative matter—'

'As the only generator of antigravity we know about, right. We got some data out of this, fragmentary, but we're hoping it's enough to pin down the theoretical modelling of the phenomenon. Maybe negative matter's antigravity field is mediated by a boson, like the graviton for regular gravity, and if so we may determine limits for its mass—'

'Perhaps later for the details,' Fred Bowles said mildly. 'So. What now?'

'Now,' Marlowe said, 'we keep gathering data. We keep hypothesising.'

'And on *that*,' Wu Yan said, 'we do agree. Good work, Professor Marlowe. We know Galaxias sent us a message, with the Blink. Now we have to figure out what that message means. And how we should respond.'

Fred Bowles looked at them thoughtfully, and sipped his coffee. Then, a hum from his jacket pocket. He scrambled for his phone.

A comms panel in the bus flashed.

And a bangle Wu Yan wore lit up.

'Another hurricane blowing up out of nowhere,' Bowles said, studying his phone. 'Brazil, this time. Damn it. My apologies, Lee – we'll have to cut this short and get back.'

Yamanaka nodded. She hurriedly gave the bus its orders.

The walls began to collapse inward, a slow, silent implosion.

The Hawaii event went off much as Mel had expected.

Following Fred Bowles's personal agenda, Tash tried to involve Wu Yan as much as possible, to engage her in discussions, to have her meet people.

Mel observed all this, of course. 'So you're playing geopolitics, *and* helping your buddy reconnect with his mother. You always were a multitasker.'

Tash just grinned.

It had gone as well as it could, without producing any solid ways forward.

But Mel never expected that the next time she saw Wu Yan, just a month after Hawaii, it would be on the Moon.

22

April 2057

The formal invitation came from Wu to Charlie Marlowe, evidently on behalf of the Chinese government – a rare open gesture to western scientists, though not so rare as it had once been.

The Chinese were notoriously secretive about their space activities, and even the Moon was big enough, generally, for them to stay hidden from all but the most carefully positioned spy satellites. Now, though, they were evidently up to something in the Sinus Medii – and drawn there, evidently, as it was the location of the Galaxias artefact. Nobody knew precisely what they were doing, but even the Chinese could hardly blockade such a sensitive area. In fact they were, it seemed, actually working in sight of the lurker – and so necessarily in view of the other national and international teams drawn here since Blink Day.

So maybe now they were going to the other extreme, by actively inviting nations and institutions to come visit.

Whatever, the invitation came. And Mel was sent up as the representative of her boss, who was too busy to go herself. '*This* time,' Charlie had growled. 'Make the most of it.'

Whatever the political logic, Mel, for sure, wasn't about to lose the chance.

*

The journey out was predictable, but predictably astonishing.

A Skylon flight to orbit.

The days-long ride to the Moon aboard a Jones, Inc. Moon-Earth shuttle. The docking at the Lunar Gateway. Mel spent some of the journey wondering what tweaks had needed to be made to the mission profiles of the various craft now that the post-Blink Moon was in a new orbit around the Earth.

The descent in a scarily fragile lander . . .

She blogged every detail for Jane, her daughter, who at least feigned interest in her replies. And she kept the In-Jokes informed. Noel, Tash's dad, said he thought going to the Moon now was like going to Antarctica had been when he'd been young. A few generations after the Scott and Amundsen days, they had been sending for plumbers and builders, rather than heroes.

Maybe. It felt extraordinary to Mel.

Once down on the Moon she spent another day in a reception dome, getting used to the gravity, undergoing medical checks, and being fitted with a surface suit from an extensive store containing all sizes.

Then, finally, Mel completed the very last leg of the journey, by rover, twenty kilometres from her landing area, to the Sinus Medii.

And there, the long shadows stretching before her, Melissa Kapur climbed out of the last of the chain of vehicles that had brought her here, and stood at last on the surface of the Moon.

The rover had delivered her to a small survival and supply station. It was a squat cylinder a couple of metres tall, maybe a dozen across, half-buried in the dirt, surrounded by a jet-black solar-cell blanket. There was a small emergency stash of air canisters, food packs, what looked like medical infusers, as well as power packs and radio transceivers.

Even as she and her ride companions stood there, smart cables snaked down from the rover to plug into the energy blanket.

This was evidently a multinational site. The survival station itself was adorned with the flags of many nations as well as the FIS – the American states, the British nations, the Russian, the Chinese, the green of the African Commonwealth. And the upper surface of the station was inlaid with a helpful compass rose.

Distracting details.

On the Moon!

She looked down at herself. Her pressure suit was brilliant high-vis orange, adorned with a gaudy cross of Saint George, the flag of federal England, on her left shoulder. As it was intended to do, the orange clearly stood out against the colour of the ground, dirt which looked a little like beach sand, pocked, pitted, and scarred with footprints and tracks – her own footprints which, as everybody knew, would last a million years if they weren't overlaid in the next couple of minutes by the passage of more booted human feet or vehicle wheels she took a hasty photography. Everybody did. When she looked away from her footprints, the dirt itself seemed bright under a pitch-black sky, more complex in texture than she had imagined, with hummocks, even individual grains, casting long shadows in the low sunlight.

So much for the detail. Now the big picture.

She turned, trying to orient herself. Thanks to the compass rose she could tell that it was off to the lunar north-west that she saw an object oddly like an artist's easel – a gaunt frame standing on three legs, and, fixed to the frame, instruments and what looked like a decayed solar energy panel. She recognised it immediately. This was Surveyor 6, of course, the old American probe – and the first human artefact to land in this place, once the centre of the visible face of the Moon. She knew that the second craft to land here, the Americans' dedicated spy probe, had long since been removed.

Not far from the Surveyor, though, was another puzzle, a patch of ground that glimmered, oddly, almost like a lake of some blackish fluid, she thought, like crude oil – but no oil could flow here. A solar energy blanket, like the one near the survival station? It seemed to have a different, more organic texture. A single suited figure seemed to be standing guard over it.

Then, turning slowly anticlockwise, a little way away from the blanket, she saw a kind of fenced-off compound, maybe fifty metres across. A single dome-shaped habitat stood within the fence. And there were people, maybe a dozen of them, standing together in pairs or threes, or moving around with casual Buzz Aldrin Moon hops. Human beings, moving, working together, here on the surface of the Moon. From a distance these lunar workers looked similar, all encased in heavy-looking pressure suits, their visors gold as hers was. Upgrades in the suits from the old Apollo days were obvious, though, just as were featured on her own suit: strong-looking hinges at the joints, a glimmer of exoskeletal support, copper-coloured frames around the limbs and back. She was too far away to make out any ID, or even national flags, though the suits were bright with non-lunar colours, red, electric blue, green, for ease of spotting.

Some of her companions from the ride drifted over that way, some lugging gear from the rover. If these workers were speaking to each other she wasn't being copied in.

But she did glimpse what most of the people inside the barrier were working around.

At the centre of the fenced-off area she saw a low mound of dirt, shallow, sprawling, its summit rising maybe two metres from the base landscape, its contours softened by the ubiquitous dust.

She recognised the morphology with a shock. She had come a hell of a long way, she thought, since she had had her first, remote glimpse of this back in January at Tash's flat. Now she was here, *it* was here, no more than fifty paces away from where she stood.

It would have seemed unremarkable to her, had she happened on it: a bit of geology, probably, unusually symmetrical, not particularly out of place in this arid landscape of ancient volcanism and impact-processed dust. But now this mound was ringed by instruments, and patrolled by drones hovering overhead, presumably carefully positioned so their low-gravity rocket-exhaust squirts caused no disturbance. The equipment of people from many nations, gathered here to this part of the Moon, patiently working. Studying.

Unremarkable the mound might look, but that was why they were all here.

'This is all still very new.'

She turned.

A lunar explorer stood beside her, in a chunky, sky-blue pressure suit. She was tall, and Mel recognised the smiling face through the visor before she spotted the name tag on the chest, below a Chinese flag.

Wu Yan said, 'Sorry. I didn't mean to startle you.'

'Oh. No problem, Yan. Thank you for inviting me, us. Is it already a month since Hawaii?'

'Indeed. Walk with me. I will show you what I can of the Chinese installation here. You are not the only non-national guest, but I will give you the private tour . . .'

Yan bounced away, an easy, expert bunny hop.

Mel took a step forward, more clumsily.

They set off, not for the alien mound, but towards that patch of reflective surface, the 'oil slick' Mel had seen to the north-west. They might have been walking across a stretch of desert on Earth.

'Your first time on the surface? Don't worry,' Yan said, not unkindly. 'You'll get used to it.'

Mel grunted. 'If I get the chance. I only have a couple of days. But I would have grabbed this just for a couple of *hours*. The whole world is crowding here now, to the Sinus Medii, or trying to . . . But Charlie thought she needed a close-up view of her own. An impression. So your personal invitation was very welcome. And meanwhile my daughter, Jane, is either prouder than she's ever been of me, or more mortified. Umm. Sorry. I gabble when I feel out of my depth.'

'No apology necessary. We all need distractions these days, I think. Not that home itself isn't a distracting enough sight, even from here.' She pointed upward. 'Take a moment. Look.'

They paused, leaned back a little, Mel breathing hard. And peered up at the Earth.

Once the home world would have been directly overhead, from this point. Now it was off-centre. Mel had never been here before. Still, that lack of symmetry was disturbing. Right now the Earth itself was around three-quarters full, Mel estimated, and she could make out a scatter of city lights in the darkened crescent, looking like gathered-up stars in that black slice of disc. It was early afternoon in England, as Mel knew well, having been in touch with Charlie Marlowe in Gateshead only a couple of hours ago. So the hemisphere she saw now was centred on the Atlantic.

Where a brilliant swirl of cloud obscured much of the familiar shapes of continents and ocean.

She said softly, 'A storm so big you can see it from the Moon.'

'Storm Malacoda,' Yan said. 'Named for one of Dante's demons, I believe. I fear it will be a long time before we give such storms any names but hellish ones.'

'Christ. From here it's like Jupiter's red spot, plastered on the Earth.'

'Well – you're an astronomer; you know that's an exaggeration. But that's how it must feel to be under a hypercane.'

Mel knew that this huge atmospheric disturbance was actually an indirect consequence of rock tides, induced by the Moon's changing orbit around the Earth: tides in the planet's very crust. Those stresses, building for weeks, had finally triggered a massive quake in the Atlantic sea bed, near Iceland, a major land slippage. That was a zone prone to instability anyhow, a place where continental plates were born from currents in the mantle that underlay Earth's crust.

And because of that undersea slippage a tremendous amount of heat, very localised, had been injected into the ocean, and the air above.

The resulting storm structure was thousands of kilometres across, and inflicted thousand-kilometre-per-hour winds at its margins – as much as three times as strong as most major storms. It was so tall it threw water-vapour clouds high into the stratosphere, which blocked out the sunlight, and added to the ongoing disruption of the ozone layer by various volcanic events. The whole of both Atlantic coasts had been battered, locked down.

People called it the first truly extreme event since the Blink.

'You mentioned your daughter,' Yan murmured, sympathetically.

'She's safe. With friends in England. And Zhi is safe too, I believe.'

'Yes, so he tells me. Busily working on the new Jones, Inc. project, somewhere on the west coast of America. Far from the Atlantic, at least.'

'So,' Yan said. 'Come. Walk further with me, and let us talk of other things. Do you understand where you are? On the Moon, I mean. The Sinus Medii, of course. Once the very centre of the visible face of the Moon, as seen from Earth. But the Moon has its own intrinsic geography.' She pointed. 'The nearest Apollo landing was Apollo 14, about three hundred kilometres to the west. Now a Smithsonian site . . .' She turned. 'The bright crater Copernicus is about seven hundred kilometres *that* way, roughly east-south-east.'

'Right. Which is where the Chinese have their main base.'

Yan hesitated. 'I wouldn't put it like that. This is the Moon; under space law it is beyond the sovereignty of any nation. I would admit that there is a concentration of Chinese-owned facilities at Copernicus. But we may own the equipment we brought here without owning the land it stands on. Exploit the minerals we extract with authority permissions, and the payment of suitable dues.'

Mel nodded, knowing this wasn't any kind of sophistry. 'You're working within the Outer Space Treaties.'

'Indeed. We need no permission to work here, within the law. We're under no obligation even to talk about it. But, in these post-Blink days, we believe it may be useful for you, and the rest of the world, to understand what we are doing here. And why. We being the Chinese government, its space agencies and so on. This is why you, and other witnesses, are invited.

'We want you to see, not the detail so much, more the thinking behind it. For our work here is shaped by our global philosophies. And they are not identical to the West's. Perhaps you will have learned something of this from Zhi.

'We are not explorers, you know – not on the Earth anyhow. Not conquerors, or exploiters, in that sense. Not by nature. To us, China is the centre of the world, and always has been. That is a foreigner's clichéd view of us, of course, but it carries some truth. An ancient polity that saw off assaults by invaders from steppe nomads to the predatory British, even as we absorbed their ideologies and technologies, and they stole ours in turn . . .

'And in the last century, as the climate changes have come to dominate, and new ways of working and trading have evolved, so have we. For decades the talk has been of a new Silk Road, a trading network spanning Eurasia and beyond, with China as the hub. We have rail links as far as Germany to the west, and – it is under construction, or was before the Blink – a rail tunnel planned under the Bering Strait, to the Americas in the east. Across Asia and beyond, gold, rare earths, agricultural and industrial products already flow along vast networks of transport links and pipelines. Perhaps you heard the slogans. Peace. Connections. Co-prosperity. Networks.'

'You are hinting this is how China's response to Galaxias as a whole will be shaped. Some kind of – mutual cooperation. With the rest of humanity?' Mel thought it over. What would Tash make of this? Why was she being told all this, here? 'And, *cooperation with Galaxias itself*, somehow? Is that why you are running these experiments in full view of the lurker?'

Yan smiled. 'That's very perceptive. Wait and see. Actually we don't have a formulated strategy yet. I have learned that the western view of China is largely a cliché. The inscrutable foreigner. Try to think of us as a nation, very smart, very rich, very *old*, and pursuing very advanced technological pathways in response to the extraordinary events of this year – and, indeed, before. Much of it in plain view. I will tell you one thing we have learned: the one thing we do know is that we don't know enough, not yet . . .' She walked on, and Mel followed.

They paused at the edge of the 'oil slick'. The guard, in a sky-blue suit similar to Yan's, stood back, watching them calmly.

That glimmering surface, black, gleamed with reflected sunlight, Earth light. Mel saw that it was a roughly circular formation, spread so thinly over the lunar ground that she could make out the contours of hummocks and depressions in the dust beneath – even what looked like miniature craters.

Small mounds of machinery stood around its edge, apparently inert. A framework of ladders and walkways had been set up over the slick itself, evidently for inspection or repair.

'So,' Mel said. 'Another solar energy plant?'

'Indeed. More than that. Well, an experiment.'

Mel leaned to look closer. 'The technology is new to me. It looks like – black foil? The way it's just draped across the ground. And very fine.'

'Yes. It is not foil. Much finer than that, much finer than any energy-capture blanket manufactured before. More – exquisite.'

'OK. Maybe ten, twelve paces across?'

'About that. It's around a hundred square metres in area, at the moment.'

At the moment. An odd thing to say. 'And those walkways above it – for inspection?'

'Indeed. This is an experimental facility; inspection is constant, including by human eyes. Well, everything we do up here on the Moon is experimental. The technology pre-dates the Blink, of course – though not this installation. Once we knew the significance of this location, we moved the experiment here. Tell me what else you see. Lean down. Take a look at the very edge . . .'

Mel found her suit was flexible enough, just, for her to kneel down. There was an authentic sensation of soft, loose, giving lunar dust under her knees. Bending, she thought she saw texture in the surface of the foil-like sheeting. Fine lines, almost like silvery wiring.

And she saw a soft red glow, all around the rim of the foil sheet. It was hard to make out in the bright sunlight.

But that periphery *advanced*. Almost invisibly, imperceptibly unless she looked away, back again. Creeping out over the lunar dirt. It took a couple of minutes of watching before she was sure. That black sheet was *growing*, covering one lunar dust grain at a time . . .

She stood up, startled, and would have lost her balance if Yan hadn't taken her arm.

'Tell me what you see,' Yan said.

'A self-replicating solar panel?'

'This is something of a test bed. But, yes, that's the principle. This is a solar energy sail, growing across the regolith. Or out of it. The sheeting is essentially aluminium – lunar aluminium, very fine. Now, a sail this size can capture—'

'Let me figure it. A hundred square metres. So the solar power input would be around a hundred and forty kilowatts—'

'Most of which we collect. This is a very efficient technology. Now, such a power level is capable of extracting perhaps three grams per second of aluminium from the lunar soil. The extracted metal is fed through a network of fine capillaries, almost like veins, to the rim . . .

'And so it grows. At its current size it might grow in radius by perhaps half a millimetre per minute . . . Like a fast-growing flower, the growth is just fast enough to see with the naked eye. But at such a rate, this experimental rig is capable of doubling in size *in less than three days*. And of course the growth is exponential; the larger it gets, the quicker the aluminium is extracted, and the faster it grows, and the larger it gets . . .'

Mel looked around. 'OK. You say this is just an experimental set-up. Of course you will have fifty per cent downtime when the Sun isn't above the horizon—'

'But the poor battered Moon still enjoys fourteen days of sunshine at a time.'

'And, more seriously, there's a lot more to making a solar energy panel than extruding aluminium from the lunar soil. You'd need heavy metals . . . Ah. But you have Copernicus.'

Yan just smiled.

'I am an astronomer after all,' Mel said. 'An impact crater, and a comparatively recent one. *That* is why the Chinese have gone to Copernicus?'

'You have it. Heavy metals are rare on the Moon – but, we believe, may be mined from the remains of the asteroid impactors that lie buried under such craters as Copernicus. And, yes, the younger the better.

'This is not yet industrial-scale. For now, at least, we test the principles, the control technologies. We do see this as the basis of a long-term strategy, though. Such technologies as this, representing a massive extension of energy-gathering and manufacture capabilities – and cheap, once the principles are established – will generate huge transformations on the Moon and beyond. And enormous profits for the Chinese corporations holding the patents.'

Mel grinned. 'Which is why you are mounting this demon-stration – here, where the action is right now on the Moon. To impress the watching foreigners. And, I dare say, watching dignitaries back in Beijing.' She glanced over at the mound, the unprepossessing centre of this place, all this activity. 'And, I'm guessing, it's no coincidence you are running this trial in full view of *that*.'

Yan said, 'All this pre-dates the Blink. But everything is dif-ferent now. We have new motives. Yes, we moved this rig here deliberately, so that the lurker, hopefully, will observe.'

Mel thought that was a thrilling, disturbing thought. What-ever they were planning with this technology, the Chinese *wanted* this enigmatic visitor to witness it. She wondered what the long-term implications were of that, for the Chinese overall strategy. And, maybe, she thought, for all their futures.

Mel realised she herself was being used as a kind of conduit of contact here, in the face of the alien, between the two polar-opposite rival cultures on Earth. She would have to discuss this with Charlie, she knew. Report it formally, even. As Wu Yan knew she would, of course.

'Come,' Yan said. 'Let's walk over to the lurker. I know that's what you've really come to see.'

Her visit wasn't yet done.

Still Mel made out little she hadn't seen before: the mound of lunar dirt, the people, all contained inside a security fence that she was still on the wrong side of.

At the fence gate stood another blue-suited guard, actually armed, with some kind of handgun at her waist. It was the first gun Tash had seen on the Moon.

Yan submitted to a retinal scan by a handheld scanner pressed against her faceplate. Mel was apparently signed in by Yan, but even she had to show a badge on her arm, lift her own sun visor to allow her eyes to be inspected.

At last they were waved through, into the compound.

It was a place of busy study, as Mel could immediately see from the activity within. Drones like small tractors rolling around, or hovering on squirts of rocket exhaust. People in suits like semi-deflated balloons bouncing over the scuffed ground. There were American workers, three or four in the score or so active here, bearing on their arms the flags of the US or of the secessionist states. But most of those working here were of other nationalities, in this site that had not long ago been an American monopoly.

Mel wondered what furious arguments, what uneasy political compromises, lay behind the evident rough and ready governance of this place. The patrolling guards, all armed, all wore blue suits, and Chinese flags emblazoned on their chests. After the Blink the Chinese had evidently been the first to come here in force, to take charge. Now the Chinese seemed intent on keeping the probe from harming any humans nearby, if it even could, and stopping harm coming to the probe from humans – and all the while keeping a boot on the neck of this extraordinary location. Yet they welcomed her, if perhaps grudgingly.

But as Yan tactfully led her through the small crowd and towards the centre of the compound, Mel's awareness of the people around her, their gadgets and fences and instruments, the glares they targeted at each other and the guards – all of that faded away.

Because here, at the centre of it all, was the alien.

It wasn't much to look at.

It didn't even take long to walk around, if you ignored the obstructive people in the way. Overall, at first glance, it certainly looked more like a bit of lunar geology than anything artificial. Just as she had seen in the first images, a flat-topped heap of regolith, a roughly conical mound maybe ten metres across, maybe two tall.

But Mel knew what to look for from her briefings. A closer inspection had revealed surprises – including the very first anomalous observation, seen all those decades ago in the re- trieved Surveyor images. For, from its landed vantage, with its elevated camera, Surveyor had glimpsed an opening in the top of the mound – an opening which, even in the crude photography of the time, showed a glint of ice. And that was a problem, Tash knew. Ice was suspected to exist on the Moon in shadows and deep-buried lodes, but any exposed to the surface vacuum and sunlight should have long sublimated away. Not only that, after reflections and highlights had been analysed by that second, dedicated probe, it was soon realised that the ice block within that mound was *faceted* – jewel-like. Artificial, or at least modified by artifice . . .

Artifice that had become obvious in the aftermath of Blink Day, when a sphere of ice, apparently data-laden, had been fired into the lunar sky from this very location.

Yan led Mel in a slow walk around the mound. 'There's still plenty of water ice in there. Or at least, a layer of water ice laid over a kind of plinth of rock – a fine, perfectly circular plate – underlying the whole thing, and covered by the dust. We detected all this through non-intrusive scans. We took a sample from the plinth, just a few grains. But we haven't yet had the courage to take a sample from the water.

'Still, scans prove that the ice mass within is – ice. Water, down to the molecular level.'

Mel smiled. 'Once Zhi said the lurker's message missile was probably nothing but a fat snowball.'

'In a sense, he may be right.'

Mel nodded. 'It makes a certain kind of sense. Charlie was quick to figure it out. There seem to be water worlds at the strategic locations we have spotted, at Barnard's, Altair and 55C. If Galaxias originated on a water world, it would naturally use water-based technology when it moved out into space. That much fits.

'And the logic of the lurker strategy makes sense too. I mean, *we* looked for the alien remotely, through telescopes, optical, radio. But we also sent probes to the planets of our solar system, physical objects equipped to look for life directly, on the spot. And if you want to watch Earth you couldn't find a better place to watch it from than the centre of the Moon's Earth-facing hemisphere. As this place used to be anyhow.' That snagged Mel's imagination again. 'Wow.' She stared at the inert, silent mound. 'What if we could communicate with this thing? What kind of records might it have kept of our past? It could be a treasure trove.' She sighed, thinking about that. 'But "lurker" is a pretty pejorative label, isn't it?'

'But perhaps appropriate,' Yan said. 'When those old theories of lurker probes were dreamed up, not everybody was happy with the idea of a silent alien spy, watching us evolve and reporting to its masters on our progress. And the fact that the name is being used now is an indication of how suspicious many of us still are.

'And – ah. Look over there.'

Now, Mel saw, very near the mound itself, a new activity was beginning. A group wearing green vests over their pressure suits – the green of the African Commonwealth – was setting up a kind of screen close to the aperture at the top of the mound, near the hidden icy lens.

The workers were clumsy in their suits, but even before the screen was attached to the summit, Mel saw how it lit up with images.

She glimpsed the whole Earth, and then a melange, of oceans, landscapes, aerial shots. Animals in the sea, forests on the land. People, walking, waving, working, smiling . . .

'They're trying to speak to it,' Mel said, wondering. 'I imagine this must all have some kind of international authorisation.'

'Indeed,' Yan said. 'Well, on the face of it – isn't it a good idea? There are more structured experiments to come. You can imagine – lists of prime numbers, various alphabets . . . An-other old fantasy. How do you communicate with the alien? With mathematics? Well, now we can try – and, I think, the hope is that if Galaxias recognises us as worthy it will – spare us. If not answer back.'

Mel nodded. 'It's not a pious hope. If the Blink *was* intended as a message to us, then maybe we ought to try replying. Any way we can.'

'We've had many applications for messaging of various kinds – beyond the scientific I mean – from national governments, corporations, religious groups, individuals. There is pressure to let people through, but security is tight. We fear rogue states trying to message this thing for their own advantage, or corporations trying to access its technology, even to patent it, and the relevant law is very unclear . . .

'But most attempted communication is harmless enough, futile or not. However, we spoke earlier about China's strategy towards Galaxias. We do believe that one thing we should *not* try, at this point, is to *challenge* Galaxias.'

'You mean, like the Jones, Inc. spacecraft project,' Mel said carefully. 'You oppose that? Even though your own son is involved.'

'I can't stop him. Of course he is driven by grief and anger as much as by curiosity, as by science. He lost somebody on Blink Day – as many others were lost, and have been since. No wonder he wishes to strike back. Which is why the lurker is so heavily protected here.' She smiled through her visor. 'Now. You have spent rather a long time in that suit. Is there anything else you need to see before we take a break? . . .'

23

May 2057

A month after Mel returned from the Moon, she and Tash got an invite from Wu Zhi, to California, where Serena Jones was going public with her 'Project Breakout' scheme. So they hastily flew across the Atlantic, and then on across the continent.

They ran late.

Such a journey couldn't be taken for granted any more. Most transatlantic flights had been cancelled altogether because of the aftermath of the hypercane. And now the biggest new problem was a kind of low-grade solar storm.

The Earth's iron core was sloshing: another after-effect of the great jolt of the Blink, still working its way through Earth's huge mass, its ponderous systems. As a result, the planet's magnetic field, produced by that disturbed core, was weakening – and so failing to shield the world from the energies of a still turbulent Sun, itself another Blink aftermath. So winds of high-energy particles from space battered an orbital infrastructure of habitats and satellites, and in places reached down to the Earth's surface, causing comms disruptions and power outages. Current surges had melted cables, even.

It was possible, some said, that the Earth's magnetic field could collapse altogether. Or the poles could flip, north changing places with south. That had happened forty-two thousand years back, the 'Laschamps Excursion', which appeared to coincide with the extinction of the Neanderthals, a branch of humanity.

And so on.

Tash knew that the experts called these phenomena, the Atlantic hypercane, the solar storm, *global geophysical events*. Like Krakatoa in 1883, the Boxing Day tsunami of 2004: events which transcended the customary human scale, and which had global effects, physically, economically. And, ministers like Fred Bowles had been warned, the aftermath of the Blink was bound to feature many more such events.

And so, after limping across the ocean, the plane had flown low over a North America with whole communities gone dark, roads clogged with stationary vehicles, trains stranded on their tracks.

They went through papers and other material in their different specialities through the whole flight. Their buddy Zhi had invited them over, but they were here to work.

Mel continued to be a trusted set of eyes and ears for Charlie Marlowe, as she had been from Blink Day – and the Astronomer Royal remained a go-to source for public comments on new developments, and a focus for the continuing astronomical and theoretical study of Galaxias and all its works.

And Tash was here to report back on Jones's pitch to Fred Bowles, of course. Since Lee Yamanaka had extracted support for the Jones, Inc. space project from a somewhat distracted President Cox, Jones and her associates had mostly kept quiet about their plans – until this big reveal. Fred Bowles insisted he had to know what this was all about before committing any funding from a cash-strapped post-Blink England. As was suspected of China too.

Tash knew that the endless diplomatic dance, or power

plays, went on. You might have thought that the evident in-trusion of the overwhelmingly powerful Galaxias would – as some SETI contact optimists had always hoped – have made humanity realise at last how small and weak and limited it was. Not yet it hadn't. You hadn't gone to war with anybody, despite the planetary instabilities and pressures on various frontiers and resource lodes, and behind the scenes you kept working, but your ambassadors pointedly ignored each other at cocktail-party receptions. That was politics, Tash was learn-ing. Diplomacy.

On the other hand, she knew, those same relatively stable (for now) good diplomatic relations only fed some of the wilder con-spiracy theories going around, many of them gleefully relayed to her by Grace Butterworth. Theories such as there *was* no Galaxias at all, and the Blink and all its consequences were the machinations of some international cabal intent on total mind-control of the population. And the Blink itself was obviously a mass hallucination due to drugs in the water supply and brain viruses transmitted through phones.

Sometimes Tash wondered, vaguely, uneasily, if Grace herself was drawn to such ideas, so enthusiastically did she relay them.

When Tash had talked this over with Mel, she had said she wished it *was* some kind of James-Bond-villain cartel, because it would be a hell of a lot easier to overthrow than the authentic Galaxias.

At last the plane started its final descent. Tash and Mel both checked their phones, hoping for better signals than the plane's systems had been able to afford them in the air.

Mel glanced over. 'At last.'

'Right. We'll be running.'

'Any more from Noel, by the way?'

'His cataracts, you mean?' Another minor fallout from the

Blink: intense solar ultra-violet getting through a patchy ozone layer and damaging human eyes. Minor unless it was you. 'Nothing new. The usual grumbles. Sometimes I think he's older than his years, you know?'

'Grumbles like what?'

'Well, he says there's hardly any birdsong to be heard.' She glanced down at her phone, thumbed through messages. '"Some bloody spring," he says here, just today. "Worse than the climate-collapse days."'

Mel pulled her lip. 'That's the magnetic field disturbances, maybe. Affecting migrating birds? I'm just guessing.' She tapped her own phone, looking stuff up. 'I don't think anybody *knows*. There's too much going on. You can't follow it all. You can't even filter it, prioritise it effectively. Hmm. I wonder if that's a sign that we are close to some kind of collapse. A collective brainstorm.'

Tash glanced over. 'Or individual brainstorms.'

Which was, of course, a reference to the deeper reason why she and Mel had done their best to wangle their way onto this trip. To get to Zhi, who had been buried for long, silent weeks at the heart of Serena Jones's project. For the In-Jokes to keep secrets from each other for so long, such big ones anyhow, was pretty much unprecedented. Maybe this was too big to leak, even to friends.

Or maybe the evening was drawing in for the In-Jokes. Well, one way or another, here they were.

The plane made its final descent. The landscape beneath opened up.

From the air, Jones's development centre looked like nothing so much as an elderly, disused airport. Mel pointed out landmarks like wind tunnels and scarred runways.

This had once been the NASA Ames Research Center, Tash knew – latterly it had become an NHSA facility, still formally owned by the rump US but now standing in American Free States territory. They were somewhere in northern California, not far from the venerable Stanford University, and close to an old US Navy air base – these proximities presumably being reasons for this facility's location in the first place. Lots of history, of a sort.

Tash remained underwhelmed.

By the time the plane had cautiously taxied to a halt close to the shabby, much-repaired building that was hosting the event – apparently it had once been the site's main cafeteria – Tash and Mel were very late indeed. They got out of their seats as soon as they could, grabbed their phones and carry-on luggage – for now trusting their hold baggage to the gods of automation – and clambered down the stair that had unfolded from the side of the plane.

Then, defying stern automated safety admonishments blaring from loudspeakers, they just ran across the tarmac, over a stretch of lawn, through a tangle of trees – twenty-year-old carbon-munching trees in every public place, Tash had time to reflect, even in an old aeronautical centre in the middle of a desiccated California – and made it to the building itself.

Where Zhi was waiting for them in person. He was propping a door open, alongside a security guard with a Jones, Inc. spaceship-and-swoosh logo on his jacket.

Zhi said, 'Shit, you're late.' But he gave them both buffed kisses on the cheek as they were security-swiped by the guard's wand, and then turned and led them, at a near run, down a corridor towards what looked like the door to a brightly lit auditorium. His exoskeletal support, worn under his clothes, creaked and hummed.

'Good to see you too,' Mel said dryly, as she struggled to keep up. 'Apologies for getting held up by the end of the damn world. Zhi, you're wearing a *suit*.'

'I held a couple of seats at the front . . .'

The auditorium, when they reached it, was a cavernous box with an oddly greasy, smoky smell, Tash thought. This really had once been a cafeteria, then. A crude stage had been set up at the far end of the room, a podium and a row of chairs. Serena Jones was already standing at the podium. Before her, more chairs in neat rows, crowded with suits. A murmur of conversation. Light and camera drones hovered.

Zhi hurriedly guided them to the promised pair of empty seats at the front, waved them to sit. Then he turned, leapt up onto the stage, and took his own seat.

Mel called, 'Good exoskeleton work there, Zhi.'

He flashed them a nervous smile.

Mel's hand slipped around Tash's, just for a second, a squeeze. 'It's still him,' she murmured.

Tash squeezed back, let go.

And Serena made ready. A tap of the microphone on the podium, a push at her old-fashioned spectacles.

She began to speak.

'OK,' she said. 'Now we're all here. At last.'

Zhi raised a hand in apology.

But Serena, slim, elderly, elegant, in a smart suit, waved him back. 'No, no. You're the star of the show, Wu Zhi. And in a way this is all *your* idea. Your inspiration anyhow. If we can't wait a moment for you to greet your friends . . . Nothing is stronger than friendship. Right? Not the woes of the world. And certainly not the, the *whim* of some kind of galactic superpower, if our current interpretation of what's happened to us all over the last five months or so is any guide.'

She faced her audience. '*Whim*. I use the word advisedly. Because when an absolute power reigns absolutely, that's what we are subject to. The whim of the God-Emperor Galaxias. Well, we Americans have been fighting off monarchs and other autocrats for nearly three centuries so far . . .'

A positive-sounding murmur indicated to Tash that Serena was, predictably, hitting the right note.

Tash knew that this event was intended for the global press, as well as the space industry investors who Serena wished to draw into collaboration, and the governmental and scientific types of all sorts including Tash and Mel themselves. It was the launch of a big, ambitious, multinational technological project, before an audience that might have been expected to be sceptical. But Tash, in those first moments, sensed nothing but unstated support.

Maybe Serena was, fundamentally, right to try this, whatever the detail of the project turned out to be — whether it worked out or not. People needed to hear something positive. To know that somebody was going to *do* something. That positivity, she knew from Mel, was what had attracted Lee Yamanaka to the project in the first place, on behalf of her President. Which did mean, Tash reflected, the audience might not be as critical as they ought to be. An easy sell for Serena Jones, then, who had made a career out of selling the expensive and outlandish.

Now Jones waved her hand. 'So, welcome to this magnificent . . . cafeteria.'

Good-natured laughter.

'And welcome to what is now officially the Jones, Inc., Charles F. Hall Research Center. Yes, I did it; I bought up NASA Ames. Like buying a piece of the True Cross to any space buff, right?

'Well, I didn't have to strike a very hard bargain. I think it's fair to say that the glory days of Ames were over long before the unwelcome arrival of Galaxias. But nothing can take away the history of this place, and its association with the name of Pioneer – yes, including Pioneer 10, the first ship to get out of the Solar System, and, apparently, which had caused all this hoo-hah. For the greatest triumphs of that line of spacecraft were designed and built here.

'But did you know that the Pioneer name has a history that dates back to the first American ventures into space? Pioneer 1, in fact, was the *very first* craft controlled by NASA to reach space, just a year after Sputnik – though it was launched by the Air Force – and even though it never reached orbit, it did make it to the Van Allen radiation belts, and so delivered some crucial scientific data as well as engineering experience.

'Well, back in those days NASA was young and fast-growing. And it took over this place, which had already been a long-standing aeronautics laboratory of some renown. Ames was always one of NASA's smaller centres – but far from the least significant. For, inspired by those very early satellite experiments, the Ames directors, ahead of their time, had already made a pitch to design and build a new range of smart but well-engineered and robust craft, basically intended for the first interplanetary missions. So the later Pioneers, after those illustrious 1950s predecessors, would be sent to monitor the Sun, and to Venus . . .

'And, most famously of all, Pioneers 10 and 11, which became the first probes to reach the outer planets. Famously or, now, notoriously.

'Which is why we are here today. Right? *Because NASA Ames built Pioneer 10.* And, as my colleague here has convincingly argued' – she waved a hand at Zhi – 'it was Pioneer 10's achievement in achieving solar escape velocity – in leaving the Solar System, in December 1973, first in terms of kinetic energy and later in terms of literal distance – that has brought *you* here today.'

She opened her arms wide and looked to the sky – or the ceiling anyhow, Tash observed wryly.

'*You*. I'm talking about *you* up there! You, Galaxias! If you can hear me, through that toy you left on the Moon?'

More laughter, if uneasy. Jones spoke on.

'Yes, *you*. You realised that fragile robot craft, stealing a little momentum from Jupiter, barely able to limp out of the System, was a precursor to what was to follow. And more craft – another Pioneer, the Voyagers, others, each one heavier, long-lasting, more sophisticated – did indeed follow. Each of them with some primary target in our Solar System, but each, too, eventually pushing that little bit further into the gulf of interstellar space – *and never to return.*' She smiled at the audience. 'You know, as a kid I myself imagined travelling on some early starship, and going out and collecting those fragile old Pioneers, and bringing them back here to Earth. Hang them from the roof of the Air and Space Museum, right?

'Well, it looks like the future isn't going to work out that way, doesn't it? Because *you* up there, Galaxias, didn't like what you saw. And so you sent us the Blink, a warning. Right? An order, to stop right here. The planets may be for us, but not the stars – not now, not ever. Because *you* have taken it all.

'That's what we think is in your mind, anyhow.

'Well, guess what. *We ain't stopping.* And that's what today is all about.

'Let me make clear what we're planning here.

'We're going to send humans out to where only robots have been before. Yes, humans, a human crew.

'We're going to build a starship.'

She stepped back, sipped some water, waited for a reaction.

Which seemed mixed to Tash.

There was some polite applause − almost mandatory in response to lines like that. Some stronger enthusiasm, even a rebel yell from somewhere. But also caution. Unease.

As well there might be, she thought. Since January the power of Galaxias had been evident, like it or not. And since Jones had pitched to Yamanaka her idea of sending a human-crewed spacecraft out of the Solar System − a basic pitch long since leaked − nothing had been heard of the detail of *how* she was going to achieve this.

She was going to have to be damn convincing, Tash thought.

But here was Serena Jones, stern but frail-looking, defiant. Even as she stood there, the applause swelled again.

Mel whispered to Tash, 'She's the student in front of the tanks in Tiananmen Square. Fragile. Magnificent.' She held up her phone. 'Jane and her pals are loving this.'

'Or she's bluffing . . .'

Serena seemed aware of the same doubts. Now she grasped the podium, glared around. 'A crewed starship. Or at least, interstellar-capable. With people aboard. And we're going to build it, or its components, right here.

'As you can guess, it ain't going to be cheap. Nothing in space ever is. This will be another Project Apollo − though shorter, sharper, perhaps more clearly focused − and it could well consume as high a percentage of the nation's GDP as Apollo in its heyday. Which is a sign of the backing President Cox and the US administration are giving this thing, as well as our hosts, the American Free States.' She gestured to the back of the room. 'And all this is thanks to our key political and corporate allies.'

A rumble of noise, people twisting in their seats. Among a sea of heads, Tash thought she recognised the colourful bulk of Lee Yamanaka, the President's science adviser, grinning broadly.

Mel whispered, 'We've come a long way since Zhi and I took the Pioneer thing to Lee in Alaska.'

Tash patted her hand. 'You changed the world.'

'And the specific reason you are all here,' Jones went on, 'is that we are launching today a request for proposals from potential subcontractors. I have to tell you that there was no competitive bidding when we got the contract, a bid we made through NHSA but backed by the American federal government. We got a sole source contract, not really the done thing, but, well, we *were* the sole source of the idea.

'But we can't build this alone, clearly. Aside from the propulsion and power – I'll talk about that – there's a whole slew of subsystems that need innovative thinking. Comms, data management, radiation-proofing, life support. Because *nobody has done this before*. No human. Nobody has flown so far, so fast, for so long. We're going to have to figure out how to do it all. We will build on proven systems where possible, but that ain't always going to *be* possible, because there *are* no proven precursors. So we invite tenders. We are also, of course, issuing announcements of opportunities to the science community. This is a vessel of exploration, of science, after all. And as to *how* we are going to build this—'

Jones raised her arms, looking almost messianic, Tash thought.

'Well, in management terms, we are going to do it the way they built Pioneer 10. That's how. And that's why you are sitting in what will now be known as the Charles F. Hall Center.

'Charles Hall, who spent his entire career at NASA Ames, was project manager for the interplanetary Pioneers, and it was he who delivered the Ames Center's greatest successes. So what more suitable name could we give the old place now? And when Hall took over, one of the first decisions he made was to commandeer this big old cafeteria as office space. So here we are again.'

Ripple of laughter.

'Hall has always been one of my own personal studies in how to run complex, indeed cutting-edge, technical projects successfully.' She emphasised her points with fist-pumps. 'You bring talented people together, you encourage them to express themselves, you brainstorm solutions to problems. You hold your meetings standing up! So after a couple of hours everybody gets uncomfortable, and that's one sure motivation to wrap things up fast.

'When the project is under way, you *keep things simple*. You break it down into *achievable stages*. You use stuff that's *worked before*. When you have a working design, you *freeze* it. Rigid change control: you modify only if you really have to.

'And you deliver *fast*.

'We *can* deliver fast. I can announce now that we're planning to do our main testing and build out at the Lodestone, in Earth's umbra. Jones, Inc. has always part-funded that facility in order to be able to use it as a zero-gravity skunkworks.

'We can *build* fast. I'm announcing now that we will aim for a conclusion of stage one, a test flight of the propulsion system, by the end of the year. Ideally earlier.' She grinned, wolfish. 'Maybe you can tell I'm looking forward to this.

'That's *how* we will build this. But what I haven't told you yet is *what* we are going to build. Well, when you are going somewhere new, further than anyone has gone before, you need a new technology. Like this.' She raised one hand, snapped her fingers.

And a hologram image appeared in the air over the stage. Everyone turned to look up – including Zhi, Tash noticed. She wondered, not for the first time, how much he knew in detail about what he was getting into.

The 'ship' was mostly a wide, barely concave dish. A dish or a sail, Tash thought, made of some wispy material, so that background stars were visible through it. And it was spinning, slowly. At its centre was a short, boxy, rectangular hull.

The whole thing looked like an immense umbrella, blown inside out.

Somebody yelled out from the audience. 'That some kind of a ramscoop?'

'You could call it that,' Jones said. 'I should say this depiction, meant for clarity, isn't to scale.' She snapped her fingers again; the dish grew wider and flatter, the 'handle' of the umbrella shrank to a speck by comparison. 'Yes, it is a ramscoop. The scoop itself is made of graphene – the lowest-density substance we could find – in fact a netting, so the surface density is even lower than that. The main hull is assembled from standard Jones Shelter modules, each twelve metres long.'

'And how big is that darned dish?'

'Oh, about the diameter of planet Mercury.'

That interrogator seemed to splutter. 'Are you crazy?'

'No. That's how big it needs to be.'

'To do what? What the hell are you going to scoop up? Not interstellar dust, or hydrogen . . .'

'Something more fundamental than that. Madam, this is a *dark energy drive*.'

Jones let them take that in.

Tash had no idea what it meant.

Mel evidently knew enough to be stunned to silence.

So did much of the audience, it sounded like. A scatter of uncomfortable laughter.

'OK,' Jones went on. 'Conceptual shock time. But, look – the engineers among you will know what the benefits of a ramscoop are. Any ramscoop. You don't need to carry any propellant! You just sail through the medium of choice, sucking stuff in and using it for its energy – as a jet engine takes in oxygen from the air. There have been studies over decades, maybe a century, of ramjet starships taking in the interstellar medium, as you suggested, madam. Which is largely hydrogen, the cooled-down wind from the stars. Maybe you could collect it up and use it as fusion fuel, as in the heart of the Sun . . . but the practical details turned out to be intractable.

'Dark energy, though . . . Dark energy is a kind of energy field that pervades the whole universe – from the scale of this room up to the largest superclusters of galaxies. And it is a kind of expansion field, relentlessly pushing the whole *universe* apart . . .

'Do you know what this stuff *is*? Well, I don't either, but since the Blink we have been playing around with it in our Lodestone skunkworks – along with other advanced technologies – and we think we know ways to tap it.

'But all we really care about is that *it is energy*. Almost vanishingly sparse, which is why my damn scoop is so big! But it is everywhere, and if we could tap it we could *go* anywhere. And, indeed, return, as a bonus. As I said, I believe we, Jones, Inc., *can* tap dark energy. And *that* is how we are going to send a crewed ship out of the Solar System.

'Ladies and gentlemen, we live in an ocean of soup. And we of Jones, Inc. may just have invented the spoon.'

That provoked a tension-busting laugh.

'OK,' Jones said. 'So that's the proposed system. Information packs are being downloaded to you now. But let's get back to the purpose of the technology, the mission itself – *which is of course a mission to break out of the Solar System.'*

That was met by a stunned silence, for a few heartbeats.

And then, some scattered applause. Another rebel yell, two. Murmured conversations.

Jones spoke on, steadily. 'Yep. I hear your reaction. Now, I listen to the debates. I know that many of you will think this is just an appalling idea, to do what Pioneer 10 did before, to do the *one thing* we believe Galaxias doesn't want us to do. Why it wants that, we can only speculate. But Galaxias musters overwhelming force; it can impose its will, you may say. So what's the point in defying it?

'I can give you several answers. One is, *what if we are simply wrong*? What if we are somehow misreading the meaning of the Blink, the motivation of Galaxias – even its nature, that it is some kind of Galaxy-spanning organism, or even a single entity . . . let's test our understanding. Let's see what's really out there, a God-like interstellar beast – or just a fleet of beat-up Klingon birds of prey, cloaked so we can't see 'em, crewed by folks not much smarter than we are. Or less! And let's see if it really does intend to stop us breaking out of the Solar System.

'Let's see if it *can*. Nobody *knows*! And we can't base our whole future as a species on guesswork. Let's go out there and *see* if it stops us.

'Or test whether it *can* stop us. I mean, can it? Fooling around with the Sun is one thing. What if it can't stop us as individuals, at the level of a single ship? Just as you can stomp an ant's nest, but can't necessarily kill every damn ant in the process.' A rueful grin. 'I grant that's not a very reassuring metaphor. But we ain't going to know unless we go find out, are we? Isn't that what science is for?

'Look – we are proposing a test of the hypothesis that we now live in a cage. Whether we break out or not, we will know where we are – better than we know it now.' She glanced at her phone. 'OK, that's enough from me – almost. Two more things to tell you.

'The first is the name of the ship.' She grinned, and waved a hand at the gauzy model beside her. 'Given all I've said, maybe you can guess at that. Pioneers 10 and 11 went to Jupiter and beyond, and are now sailing out of the Solar System. Pioneers 12 and 13 went to Venus. And so I give you – *Pioneer 14*.'

That drew applause, slow at first.

'Thank you – thank you. Well, we have a ship, and we have yet to name the crew. But I can announce the mission commander.'

People started standing up. More enthusiastic applause.

'You're ahead of me. It was Wu Zhi here who figured out the Pioneer 10-Galaxias timeline in the first place – and it was Zhi's presence at my side that convinced President Cox to buy this programme in the first place.'

Whooping and cheering.

'Here he is! Here he is! The next Neil Armstrong, if you will . . .'

She called out his name again, but the applause drowned out her voice.

Zhi got out of his chair, solemn-faced, arms raised, facing the camera drones and raised phones all around him.

Mel had to yell in Tash's ear. 'That's not *our* Zhi. He'd have been terrified. Self-conscious. Both. But he looks . . .'

'Determined,' Tash yelled back, feeling as dismayed as Mel sounded. 'Or obsessed?'

'They really are going to do this, aren't they? *He* is going to do it. We came all this way to see him. But we've lost him, Tash. Right here, right now.'

Mel grasped her hand. 'Let's hope you're wrong.'

The discipline of the audience broke down, and people rushed the stage, surrounding Zhi and Jones. Overhead drones bathed them both in an almost heavenly light.

Still holding hands, Mel and Tash retreated to the back of the room, out of the old cafeteria, and found their way outside into the muggy Californian air.

24

June 2057

As soon as she got out of the packed plane at New Diaspora, and made it into town on a crowded open bus, Tash started to suspect that if it hadn't been for the Moon-suit-green jackets the In-Jokes had each promised to wear she wouldn't have a chance of finding Mel or Zhi. And the secessionist capital's big 1957-themed summer party would have had to go ahead without their meeting.

They'd decided on this meet-up in the relatively happy wake of Jones's California briefing, herself, Mel and Zhi: a drunken moment for Tash and Mel, less so for Zhi, who was already in astronaut training. The venue was Zhi's idea, surprisingly, something about it attracting him particularly. Well, it had seemed like a good idea at the time, Tash thought now, a way to keep in touch. But the journey in had been bad enough, the transport links, inadequate for this new city even without the festival, usually packed. But now she was here . . .

A big open sky, blue with a few streaks of high cloud, the Sun high. A beautiful, harmless sky, for once, and without any of the clutter of a big old city like Newcastle to obscure the view. She longed to stay on the bus. Hide under a seat, even. The sky had seemed harmless on 5 January.

She looked down at the security of the ground. Took deep breaths. Focused on the day to come.

Which way to go from here?

They'd decided to meet under the big statue of a kneeling Elvis Presley that had been set up at the centre of the park, the kilometre-wide green sward that dominated the heart of this great bowl of a city. Indeed, right on the very spot that Elvis, resting comfortably on one knee, chin resting on fist – striking a pose – seemed to be staring down at, in the images boosting the festival. The problem was, everybody else seemed to have had the same idea, and, even from the approaching bus, Tash could see it was a mob scene.

She shrank back from that too.

What made it worse yet was that she kept losing her phone signal. *No service.* She knew this was a global problem, arising from the increasingly tattered post-Blink state of the world's infrastructure. *No service.* She suspected that for generations like hers who had grown up in an interconnected world with effectively infinite bandwidth it was like the voice of Galaxias itself, goading humanity one by one: *No service . . . No service . . .*

They had all been too busy to think it through properly, to give 1957 Day the reflection it deserved. Tash had vaguely assumed that Diaspora's biggest public event since the Blink was going to be a big hit – a day of escape from the pressures of the age, as its organisers evidently intended. But she had also assumed that most people would join in remotely via feeds, rather than in person, despite the connection problems. That was how events went nowadays – wasn't it? Maybe not, not since the Blink, despite the subsequent travel problems. Not today anyhow. People still wanted to get together, it seemed; they wanted to *be* here, in a crowd of their fellow humans.

So, doggedly, Tash climbed out of the bus and made her way through the crush, heading vaguely towards Elvis. Collisions were frequent. At least most of the bumps and barges were unintentional – and softened by the layers of clothing everybody was wearing. Summer solstice it might be officially, here in the northern hemisphere, but it felt a lot colder: more like an early English spring day, Tash thought. But, given the drift of the calendar, the term 'summer solstice' had no meaning any more.

It was an ordeal. Tash led most of her life indoors now, in regulated secure environments. She found herself shrinking back from the human chaos.

Then Tash caught a flash of the lurid green she was looking for, off in the distance. Mel or Zhi, it had to be – no, Mel, her strawberry-blonde hair, brilliant in the sunlight, was unmistakable. Tash jumped and waved, dressed in the same green.

Mel spotted her, waved back, and they started to make their way towards each other.

When they finally met they embraced, looked each other up and down, and laughed. Then they linked arms and pushed on through the crowd. Aimless at first, just heading away from the central knot around Elvis.

Their green coats drew stares.

'Shit,' Mel said. 'I know these things were my idea. I kept trying to persuade Jane to come over with me, you know, but the coats were the final straw for an eleven-year-old.' She fingered her own lapel. 'This *is* the nearest thing I could find to that ugly lunar green. Well, the idea was to stand out in a crowd. But, wow, yours is even worse.'

'Have to admit it wasn't my choice,' Tash admitted. 'Didn't have the time. Grace Butterworth found me something in the end – remember her? She travelled with me and Fred Bowles to Hawaii, when—'

'I remember. Tough character. With the niece in Naples?'

'We've all been so damn busy in House.'

'Since the hypercane? I don't get much chance to follow the news.'

'Well, the aftermath of the storm is still unravelling. You know that in the end we had to evacuate whole cities from the western coasts, Greater Liverpool, New Bristol.' Brand-new cities built only decades ago to accommodate populations fleeing from the climate-collapse sea level rise, now overwhelmed in their turn. 'The Irish mainland got it worse—'

'I know,' Mel said. 'It's that way all around the Atlantic periphery, isn't it?'

'It's difficult to get any sleep, let alone to get any clothes shopping done . . .' Tash hesitated. 'Zhi made no promises about wearing Moon green, you know. Or even about showing up. Even though coming here was his idea.'

'Oh, he'll be here. Reminds me, I did get a fresh message last time my phone worked. Forget Elvis. Now we're supposed to meet him near something he called the slave market exhibit.' Mel glanced at a phone map – retrieved from memory, Tash saw – and looked around. 'Over that hill. Although I don't know why the crowds should be more sparse there than anywhere else. All these collisions, this Brownian-motion stuff, are wearing me out . . .' She eyed Tash. 'You more so, I think. Correct?'

Tash tried to tough it out, then gave in. 'It's just the people, Mel. And that big open sky.'

Mel squeezed her hand. 'The sky, I know. Do you ever follow the medical analyses? It's all about the Blink – and where you were on the day, how you experienced it. When it happened, I mean, the loss of the Sun. If it was the middle of the night – well, you woke up to a missing dawn. If you were indoors, something funny about the light outside the window. But if you were caught outside, in the daylight – pow. Lights out, with just a little afterglow from the corona. It was visceral, shocking, totally disorienting, as if a chunk of your reality had come loose. To the extent that people have acquired mild phobias about being outdoors. People like you. It's a recognised syndrome. We're all affected by the Blink, and how we experienced it.'

Tash had heard of this. The syndrome had been recognised even on the day 'Maybe. It seems pretty weak.'

'Not at all—'

'It doesn't seem to have affected you.'

Mel rubbed her nose. 'Well, I was studying the sky. Not outdoors, contained in a bubble on that dumb airship. It was already an unusual morning because of the eclipse. It was shocking, but, well, with Charlie's help I think I was scienceing it pretty quickly.'

A family, a couple of kids, came by, and Tash couldn't help but flinch.

Mel smiled. 'And here are all these people. We all got phobic about crowds long before Blink Day because of all the pandemics, right? You're not alone in that. Come on. Maybe it will be easier away from the centre.'

So they linked arms again and walked, following a path leading to the foot of that hill.

'So how is your dad?' Mel asked.

Tash was feeling vaguely ashamed, and was glad of a change of subject.

'Like everybody else, I guess. Wishing it would all go away. Safe enough, though. I think he's glad to have me close by.'

'I bet he is. Jane's lucky if I fly through the stratosphere overhead once or twice a month . . .'

Now they were climbing the hill, both soon panting, and the conversation faltered.

Tash glanced back as the view opened up, of Elvis, and the smartwood tower of Council Hall that loomed behind him, and the sprawl of greenhouses on the hillsides beyond – in fact the greenhouses were new, an improvisation in the face of the mixed-up climate, an attempt to keep agriculture going in this cold Blink summer.

Tash knew something of the story of this new city of Diaspora. Back in the 2040s the Council Hall, or a predecessor structure, hastily thrown up, had become a seat of government as a new polity had evolved from what had been a vast refugee camp sheltering the climate-displaced from New York State and other eastern regions. That had been the beginning of the Secession, as the states harder hit by the climate collapse had begun to look to their own affairs, independently of the federal government, and then to link together in a new alliance – a different federation. 'From a food riot to nationhood,' Tash had heard it sourly described by one diplomat, an envoy of the rump United States.

Now, even this far inland, the Hall itself had been visibly battered by the hypercane's winds and rain – although restoration work was under way, as Tash could see, great sheets of smart plastic wrapping swathes of the building like bandages.

And, spreading over the hills beyond, tent cities. In this new polity there had been barely time for a single generation to come of age, Tash reflected, before the fresh calamity of the Blink had forced further migrations as, back in the east, stretches of states once safely inland were being abandoned altogether.

'Ironic,' she said.

As she walked on Mel produced small bottles of water from deep pockets in her green coat, passed one to Tash. 'What is?'

'Look at all this. A world that has just coped with one decades-long trauma in the climate adjustments, now hit with another.'

Mel sipped water. 'Actually Charlie Marlowe argues that it's no coincidence. It's probably *because* we just became powerful enough to do stuff like adjust a planet's climate, even if by accident, that Galaxias has shown up right now. Pioneer 10 was a kind of proxy of our capabilities – unacceptable capabilities, from its point of view, it seems.'

She seemed to be tiring quickly.

Tash took her hand as they walked on, more slowly. 'You OK?'

'Yah. Just out of condition. We travel all the time, you know. Or Charlie does, conferences and ministerial briefings all over the world, as everybody runs around trying to get a handle on things. Travelling, immobile in one seat or couch or office chair after another. But you do need to be face to face if you're talking to the FIS Secretary General. And where Charlie Marlowe goes, I have to go.'

'That's good, isn't it? To be valued.'

'Yes,' Mel admitted. 'It feels good to be *doing* something. Even if it is just giving repetitive briefings and fending off dumb questions, over and over. Charlie complains about the lack of time she has to do any actual *thinking*. But ten per cent of *her* time is probably more productive than a hundred per cent of most people's.

'So I travel all the time, but I never walk anywhere.' She smiled. 'I do my yoga moves, like we did at college? In hotel rooms. Every morning, every night. Three sun salutes. If not for that I'd be stiff as a board.'

'For me it's twenty-four-hour stays in House. At least you're seeing the world.'

'Huh. Conference room by conference room . . .'

They stepped back to let a group pass. Densely packed, adults and children alike, they were singing some kind of hymn, and carried crucifixes and palm leaves, they looked like, brandished in the air. And they all wore pale blue T-shorts emblazoned with a slogan:

PUNY YAHWEH?

Tash and Mel exchanged a glance. 'Bloody Charlie,' Mel murmured. Every time Tash was confronted with religious explanations for the Blink, she would hear that damn phrase of Charlie Marlowe's. They pushed on.

The hill got steeper yet. This was the Appalachians, after all.

'Let's keep pushing it,' Tash said. 'At least we'll warm up. Some midsummer day this is.'

Mel smiled ruefully, panting harder. 'Only midsummer by the calendar now, my friend. The old calendar, I mean. And not that we have a new calendar yet. But we're already feeling the effects.'

'Of Earth's new orbit?'

'Right. Our whole year is stretched out! By about twenty days overall. The calendar has already slipped by six days since Blink Day — we think. So the next winter solstice is going to be tenth of January, next year. Drifted from twenty-first December. And so on. Our whole calendar is going to drift and shift, and we will have to figure that out.' She smiled. 'We do bullshit a lot about this, travelling. What about birthdays? Isn't Elvis here because of a birthday? His hundredth, maybe?'

'Not quite,' Tash said. 'I looked it up.'

Mel smiled. 'You always were the nerdy one who'd do that.'

'Apparently it's a hundred years since he became truly famous – appearing on something called the Ed Sullivan Show, online – or maybe on television back then. Still, it makes you think. Will you celebrate your birthday by the old calendar or the new?'

The crowd of people around them was thinning as they climbed. And now Tash saw they were approaching the brow of the hill, probably to Mel's relief.

'Then there's all the religious festivals,' Mel said, puffing. 'The Pope is already consulting with the astronomers about Easter. That's set by the Church's rules to be on the Sunday following the first full moon on or after the spring equinox. As an algorithm, that still works, even if the dates of the equinoxes and full moons are going to be different now. I think they call it the *Computus*. Then there's Ramadan, Rosh Hashanah . . . The religions and traditions will just have to find their own ways to adjust. And as for the Chinese New Year—'

'My ears are burning.'

Here came Zhi, as if out of nowhere, marching down from the crest of the hill. Wearing a luminous lunar-suit green jacket.

They gathered, stood together a little ill at ease. Hesitating.

'In-Joke group hug,' Mel ordered.

They joined in a circle, arms around each other's shoulders.

But it didn't feel the same, Tash reflected sadly. It was kind of stagy. Going through the motions. Too much distance be-tween them, if not literally. Maybe they were growing too old for this.

Or maybe it was just Zhi's exoskeletal support getting in the way, she thought, suppressing a grin, feeling the rods and joints under his jacket.

They broke the hug, rather awkwardly.

Mel said, 'Come on, let's get this darn hill done.'

They climbed on, Zhi walking back the way he had come between Mel and Tash. Tash could hear that mechanical whirr as he stepped.

'I didn't mean to jump out on you.' He held up his phone. 'The signal strength is a little better up here. So I tracked you, and suddenly there you were. What did you think of Elvis?'

Tash shrugged. 'I had heard of him. Recognised the music. Part of the soundtrack of our lives, I suppose.'

'More like our parents',' Mel said. 'Even our grandparents'.'

Zhi said, 'My Jim was a big fan, you know.'

'Of Elvis?'

'Liked to dress up, though he couldn't sing a note. He could be surprisingly camp in some ways, for a deep-space astronaut. Anyhow, there's a kind of competition going on, concerning Elvis. All this is about anniversary days. You know about Elvis's—'

'We heard.'

'The original idea for today, 1957 Day, came from the Russians – did you know that? – who pointed out that this year is the hundredth anniversary of Sputnik 1, the first space probe to reach Earth orbit. An anniversary of us, humanity, doing something magnificent. Even if it was all about the Cold War, back then. There's a display somewhere . . . Let's all big up Russia for a day!'

Mel said, 'I suppose you could see it as another act of defiance against Galaxias. *We* did that.'

'Maybe. But then other people starting digging up other anniversaries to tack on. Births of famous people. Writers and such. I can see why.'

Tash nodded. 'In the middle of a bad time, look back to the good.'

'Well, it felt like the right thing, to me. To celebrate all we have done. How far we have come. Whatever that damn Galaxias does to us, we mustn't forget. Not ever.'

Tash thought that sounded like the authentic Zhi. Not nostalgic. Angry.

'Anyhow,' he said now, 'one of today's hundredth anniversaries is the signing of the treaty that established the European Union. Or its precursor organisation, not the one that was re-established a few years back — whatever. It was a big deal in terms of international cooperation, in its time. And *their* anthem was the Ode to Joy. Beethoven's Ninth. So, right now, people are voting on their phones for preferences for music to be played later. Big scale stuff. First option: either the Ode to Joy, the famous 2036 all-mech performance, or Elvis doing "Always On My Mind".'

Mel hummed a phrase. 'I think I know that one.'

Zhi said, 'Well, cast your vote. It's just over the hill, by the way.'

'What is?' Tash asked.

'The slave market.'

'You've been posting about that,' Tash said. 'How you wanted to see that particularly . . . Your public posts on the Jones sites, I mean. I have been following you, Zhi. So, how is Pioneer?'

'Well enough. Test flight in September, they are saying now. October maybe.'

'That soon?'

'Progress is smooth. I mean, it's mostly standard components, the Jones Shelters, the secondary drive systems. It's just the dark energy propulsion system that's novel. But we're confident the theory will work out.'

'I hope you're right,' Mel murmured. 'Since your ass will be on the line.'

Zhi shrugged. 'If I'm fit and ready. Of course the mission has to be crewed, whether by me or not. *Humans have to go*. It's a – gesture. For our kids. Our generation's, anyhow. What kind of world we want them to grow up in. What kind of *regime*. You'll know more about this than I do, Tash – our generation isn't having a lot of kids. Not even at the replacement level, globally. Even before the Blink. Look at the three of us.

'You can see why. *Our* parents grew up somewhere around peak population, and we were born into a world where we felt like we were in the way, just another burden on a creaking planet. And I have a feeling we passed that on to the next generation.' He looked away. 'Jim and I were planning to do something, sometime in the future. Maybe surrogacy, maybe an adoption. We wanted to be parents, I think.'

Mel and Tash exchanged a glance. Without a word, they grasped Zhi's hands, one on each side.

And they walked on until they crested the hill.

Where they paused, panting.

They were overlooking another broad hollow in the Appalachian landscape. A shallow lake. A tent city on the far shore, festival goers camping out.

And in the foreground, before the lake, was a strange tableau: a kind of wooden stage on which stood rows of human beings, old, young, many ethnicities. All naked, shackles around their ankles.

People were walking past this, staring, smiling uneasily, looking away. The 'actors' kept their eyes downcast, Tash saw. Camera drones hovered overhead, but nobody was taking pictures.

'My God,' Mel said.

Zhi nodded. 'The one thing I really wanted to see, today. This is the two hundredth anniversary of the largest slave auction ever held in US history. They called it "The Weeping Time". These people will stand here all day, without food or drink. Whatever the weather. All day.'

'Quietly magnificent,' Tash said, moved.

Mel grunted. 'I wonder if Galaxias is watching somehow. And if it understands.'

Zhi glanced at her. 'Good thought. Look, you two – I know you think I have got myself lost in the project, the work.'

Tash eyed him. 'Well, haven't you?'

'Not totally.' He seemed to force a smile. 'I'm glad we decided to do this. *Us*. We ought to cherish each other more. If not today, when? From what I understand, it's believed that Galaxias is alone. Right? A cohesive entity, maybe even a single individual.'

Mel nodded. 'That's what Charlie has argued from the beginning. You'd need a tightly integrated culture at least, to maintain your hold across a Galaxy—'

'So Galaxias *has* no friends. Only potential enemies, like humanity. And that's its problem.'

Mel held them both back, and they clasped hands in a ring. 'Quite right. And we mustn't forget who *we* are.'

'Right,' Tash said.

Zhi grunted. '*Damn* right.'

A ripple passed through the crowd. Suddenly everybody was watching their phones. Some started swarming over the crest of the neighbouring hills, heading back towards the centre of New Diaspora.

Zhi glanced at his own phone, scrolled quickly through it. 'The result of the plebiscite is in. *Look* at this.'

They all peered into his phone. Once again Tash was looking over the park at the centre of New Diaspora, the looming Council Hall behind it.

And that tremendous statue suddenly stood up, swaying, smiling, fifty metres tall.

'Ha!' Zhi said. 'People are running and screaming . . . The Elvis monster comes to life.' He put his arms around Mel and Tash. 'Take that, Beethoven!'

And, over a lilting piano phrase, Elvis began to sing. As the words scrolled in the air before them, the In-Jokes sang along.

As did everybody in the landscape, as far as Tash could tell.

But at that strange moment of togetherness she had a stab of doubt. A doubt about whether, when this day was done, the In-Jokes would ever stand together like this again.

25

July 2057

Tash learned early that the much-anticipated FIS-sponsored international science conference on the Galaxias crisis, and the highest-profile such event so far, was to be held at the Royal Society of Edinburgh, opening on 1 July. A cooperative effort by the English and Scottish governments. This was basically a technical-level session meant to provide input to a heads of government session in November, tentatively planned for New Aberdeen — if the British governments could swing that one too.

A couple of days before the event a memo from Fred Bowles's office informed his staff that a single helicopter would be travelling up to Edinburgh from Newcastle — and anybody who didn't get a place on that flight could either make their own way, or watch online.

Tash knew she had to be there. If anything came out of these conferences relating immediately to English government policy, it would have to be absorbed first by Fred, as science minister, and then interpreted and implemented by his team. So the closer to the source she got, the better.

And Tash had to be there for another reason. Because the increasingly controversial Jones, Inc. space mission was to be debated: in an international forum for the first time. And because of that Zhi had promised to come, along with Mel enabling, another In-Joke reunion – and Zhi's mother, Wu Yan, back from the Moon, would be one of the Chinese team joining in the global debate. In the middle of a worldwide trauma, and given Zhi's involvement in the Pioneer project, Tash and Mel feared that this might be the last chance for mother and son to attempt a rapprochement. Or, Tash thought more cynically, if Fred Bowles and others had their way, a last chance to exploit a relationship that might end up being crucial to East–West relations. But she thought even more cynically that probably the Chinese wouldn't have put up Wu Yan once again if she hadn't already proven how good she was at polite deflection.

So Tash made damn sure she was on that chopper flight.

Only to find that the Royal Society of Edinburgh wasn't in Edinburgh any more.

Tash had known Edinburgh a little. Her father had Scottish relatives – an excuse to go north of the border sometimes, although Noel hadn't tried for dual citizenship after the break-up of the Union. Since then there had been drastic changes. In the closing stages of her flight, low over the city, Tash saw gondolas working their way around the castle mound, and along the straight-line canal that marked the route of what had once been Princes Street. As the climate had decayed, the swamp that had been drained to make room for the New Town centuries before had slowly and stubbornly returned.

Then the chopper headed back south, passing over the new suburbs on higher ground that had sprawled out from the old city in the wake of the climate adjustments, and then expanded further, with increasing confidence, since the political independence of Scotland in the 2040s. The venerable Royal Society of Edinburgh, itself a precious relic of the Scottish

Enlightenment, had ended up relocated to a kind of business park called New Fala, in the foothills of the Lammermuirs. From the air, the new main building was a sprawling monument of smartwood and steel, with smaller satellite installations around it – specialist labs and libraries, Tash saw from her phone map.

She felt a twinge of disappointment. This was a fine piece of architecture, but could have been anywhere. Maybe as she got older she might have to get used to similar twinges. A nostalgia for an erased past.

The chopper descended towards a concrete apron close to the main facility, and landed smoothly. The passengers debarked, accompanied by rolling smart suitcases, and lugging carry-on bags. Tash emerged under a Sun that was high, bright, and shed some decent warmth. Even if it was further away from the Earth than it should be on this July day.

And Mel was here, waiting on the tarmac, with Jane, her daughter. A pale redhead like her mother, but with darker eyes – perhaps her father's, who none of the other In-Jokes had met – Jane smiled politely enough at Tash, her mother's old frat friend.

'Come on,' Mel said, briskly splitting Tash off from the rest of the Bowles party and leading the way into the nearest of the buildings. 'I know you're running a little late, I'll get you through. Any luggage?'

'It can find its own way.' She glanced back uneasily, hoping that was true.

At gate security, the formal entrance to independent Scotland, Tash had to pass through DNA and retinal scans – and give that day's English Federation four-digit pass code, a new but old-fashioned procedure that still had a chance of working when the power went down.

Then, inside the building, Mel led Tash and Jane away from the main group and through a broad concourse.

Mel said as they hurried on, 'The conference is already in session. The introductory remarks. Yes, you're *that* late. Charlie Marlowe is handling it actually. I figured you could skip that.'

Tash had to smile. 'You did, did you? So where are we going?'

'To see Yan and Zhi, of course. I waylaid them both when they landed – just like you – Charlie figured it was the only way to get them in the same room, by just descending on them first chance I got. And I figured you would want to be there. If that's a problem—'

Tash grinned. 'It's exactly what Fred Bowles would have wanted. I'll need to send a couple of texts.' She pulled out her phone to do so as she walked, to Grace Butterworth, to others of Fred's aides.

Mel went on, 'Charlie Marlowe has promised to look in on us when she's done – did I say she's giving the conference introduction? Everything's bound to be a scramble, these things always are. Actually, today, if Charlie had her choice, she'd have been watching the eclipse.'

That puzzled Tash. 'What eclipse?'

'Precisely. What eclipse? There should have been an annular solar eclipse today, visible in some parts of the world. Which happens – *happened* – when the Moon crossed in front of the Sun, but a little further from the Earth in its orbit. I mean the old orbit, and even that was slightly elliptical. And because the Moon's disc was too small to cover the Sun's disc completely—'

'Oh. You got a ring of sunlight around the Moon? An annulus, a ring. So, an annular eclipse. I remember.'

'Not as spectacular as a total, but still quite impressive. Now all that is gone. Cancelled, by Galaxias. The Moon *will* clip the face of the Sun this time – but no more total eclipses, ever again, and we haven't even got a finalised timetable yet for when the next eclipse of any kind will happen. Anyhow I think Charlie wanted to be out there as she would have been *before*, with her eclipse glasses and so on. Kind of a symbolic defiance.'

Very visual. 'The press would love it.'

Mel led them through a door into a long, brightly lit corridor.

'I booked a green room down here. Zhi and Yan should be there, if they haven't already found a way to escape . . .'

Jane was staring at her phone as she followed. 'It's trending, actually, Mum.'

'What is?'

'What you were talking about. Eclipse-watching. It's a thing. Especially if you're under the track that the eclipse should have been seen from. Which is . . . Don't know where that is.'

'Geography,' Mel muttered to Tash. 'Just a disaster area at school. And I'm no help, what with the way the borders have all washed to and fro in our lifetimes.'

'I think there's a sort of flash protest,' Jane said. 'I *think*. People are saying, we want our eclipses back.' She giggled. 'I bet half of them never knew what an eclipse was in the first place. Without a mother who hangs around with astronomers, lucky me.'

Tash coughed back a laugh.

Mel pursed her lips. 'A mother who *is* an astronomer, actually. Tell your friends to wait until 26 December.'

'Why?'

'Because that day there should have been another total eclipse.'

Tash said, 'Really? Two in one year? I didn't think that was possible.'

'It's rare, but possible. Or *was*. The Christmas eclipse. That's what we would have called it, probably.'

Jane hastily manipulated message holograms above the surface of her phone. 'Wow. I put that in, and I'm trending already.'

Mel said with a grin, 'Mothers never get any credit.' She paused at a door. 'Here we are.'

Tash and Jane followed her into a small, brightly lit room, which Tash assessed quickly, with an experienced eye.

Airless. Hard upright chairs. A long table with bottles of water, plates of some kind of snack covered in paper. Even a few bottles of wine, the obligatory alcohol. It was a classic green room, thought Tash, being a veteran of many such establishments after having supported Fred Bowles at venue after venue.

And here sat Wu Yan. Alone.

Zhi's mother was grave, dressed all in black, her lined face framed by short-cut hair, black streaked with a little grey. She looked tired, Tash thought, as a first impression. Calm — she always was calm in Tash's experience — calm, tall, elegant. But tired.

She smiled, though, as they came in. Smiled and nodded. 'Hello, Tash, Mel. You must be Jane! Nice to see you again, and to meet you, Jane. Take a seat. Have some water. Some of these . . . biscuits, on this plate. I think that is what they are.'

And before they had a chance to reply, Wu Zhi burst in through a second door.

He stood there in the doorway. He gave a nod of acknowledgement, but didn't speak, didn't sit. Instead he started to walk up and down at the head of the room. Tash recognised the stiffness of his posture, the curt, angular movements. The usual astronaut's exoskeletal support, under his clothes. He seemed distracted, perhaps listening to a private feed in his ear.

Wu Yan, however, smiled sadly. '*Now* he returns. Just in time for biscuits.'

'I'll pass,' Jane said, sitting briskly. Mel sat beside her.

Tash, dumping her carry-on bag, sat near them. 'So why don't you come sit down too, Zhi? Still wearing that darn exo suit? More comfortable standing, is it?'

Zhi raised a hand, flexed his fingers; the arm made a whirring sound.

Jane stared.

Zhi grinned at her. 'I only do that to show off, you know.'

Wu Yan sniffed. 'Exos are bad for you to wear too long. You know that. You'll atrophy.'

'Yes, Mother. And they are bad for you too if you put them on and off too often, the way *you* do. Anyhow I won't be here long before I'm back in microgravity at the Lodestone . . . Tell you what, Mother, I'll leave you this exo. When I'm out in deep space you can make it march up and down and bark commands at it and pretend it's me.'

Mel frowned. 'Zhi, don't speak to her like that.'

Mel was a mother herself, Tash reflected.

'And I heard that too.'

Charlie Marlowe came bustling into the room. She wore a smart trouser suit – well, Tash conceded, as smart as the Astronomer Royal ever got. 'Sorry to be late. Got away as quick as I could, though I'll have to be back soon, I'm supposed to be chairing the second session. It turned into a Q&A. Who the hell asks questions at introductory remarks? I had to skip the fire exit instructions.'

'I should be there too,' Yan said quietly.

'We'll make sure you don't miss your slot,' Marlowe said.

She glanced at Mel. 'I'm not sure if I'd ever have spoken to a friend that way. Not without falling out. You characters really are close.'

'They *are*,' Jane said, staring at her phone again. 'All I got when I was growing up was Auntie Tash and Uncle Zhi.'

Even Zhi had to laugh at that. 'Well, you're still growing up,' he said.

She glanced up at him. 'I made you smile. Who's the grown-up now?'

Yan angled her head. 'Has she got a point, Zhi?'

Zhi pursed his lips. 'And why don't you get to *your* point, Mother? About how you think Pioneer 14 is a bad idea. No – since I'm involved, it must be an *immature* idea.'

'Am I that obvious?'

'Yep.'

'Well, I am afraid the argument is obvious too,' Yan said softly. 'That's the reason I'm here. The Chinese party, in fact. You, my son, your team, and those who have backed you, may be making a terrible mistake.'

And Tash sat back, surprised.

Zhi walked back and forth, the same few steps, a little stiffly. 'There was me thinking you might have come over to support me.'

'I am not alone in my scepticism. Most of my colleagues too. China hasn't yet formalised its position about the Jones mission, but—'

'Well, Mother, my colleagues would say otherwise. And much of American public opinion. President Cox believes in us, though she hasn't told me so to my face.'

Marlowe seemed reluctant to speak. 'I feel as if I'm an umpire here, of a fight I don't want to see happen. But, and I'm in a position to know this, Zhi, nobody much outside America – the two Americas – is too enthusiastic. I suspect a majority think we should do nothing at all right now. Nothing precipitate. Nothing that might, umm, *anger* Galaxias yet. Not until we know we *need* to risk doing that, and know what the consequences might be.' She glanced at Yan. 'Also – and this probably isn't the place to air it – everybody knows the Chinese are also up to something, on the Moon and beyond. I know you've shown us stuff – you brought Mel to the Moon! But you are fending us off with scraps. It would help if *some* of the final goal could be made public—'

'We are not in a position to do say more,' Yan said.

Mel, Tash, Marlowe shared glances. The same Chinese line, still.

'The philosophical principles we can discuss at this conference, but—'

Zhi snorted. 'Philosophy! What use is that?'

Marlowe spread her hands. 'Well, Zhi, since we are dealing with an unprecedented phenomenon – a phenomenon that we barely have a handle on, barely a shred of evidence, but which sprawls across multiple scientific and epistemological categories – I'd say we have nothing much *but* philosophy to guide us. As we try to use the known to make at least some sense of the unknown.'

Zhi said, 'Well, what we *know* for sure is that Galaxias seems to have responded to the Pioneer 10 breakout by making existential threats, if only implicitly. And damaging our world significantly. Do you know how many deaths have already been caused, post-Blink? Galaxias intends to bottle us up, it seems. As Serena Jones says, what we need to do is to break out, to find out if it really is blockading us, and to show it we won't put up with—'

'No,' his mother said patiently. 'Or, rather, that is one interpretation. That is, *bottling us up*. Another interpretation is that
Galaxias is trying to educate us. Clumsily perhaps, but—'

That word seemed to make Zhi explode.

'*Educate?* Where's the proof of that? And educate us into
doing what?'

Marlowe sighed. 'If you let her speak she might tell you.'

Zhi glared around the room. Tash thought she had never seen
him so impatient.

But, at length, with another clunky, whirring movement, he
finally sat down. 'Oh, very well.'

Yan spread her hands on the table.

'Good. Look – as for any Chinese position. We don't have a
solution to announce. Not yet. Not even a plan as cockamamie
as the Pioneer project.'

'Good word,' Jane said with relish, and she noted it down in
her phone. '*Cockamamie*. Is it Chinese? Or is it swearing?'

Mel hushed her.

'But we do think – we *theorise* – that we know something
about the nature of Galaxias. And where it came from, how it
came to be. Why it is here, I mean the background motivation.
Call it philosophy or deduction, a hypothesis built on a slim
foundation of fact—'

For a moment Zhi looked as if he might reach for her hand,
but pulled back. 'Mother, I think you could drop the scientific
caution, just once.'

Yan frowned and thought about that. 'Actually I am not sure I
can. We believe, you see, that the scientific assumptions hidden
behind *your* plan to challenge Galaxias are mistaken. Because
you are mistaken about its nature.'

'How?' Marlowe snapped. 'Get to the point.'

Wu Yan, considering her words, held her hands in a praying position before her lips.

'Reflect on this. There are those, including the Americans, who think – who *behave* as if Galaxias is a conquering force. I have heard the words used often. It has *blockaded* Earth, as if to force us into submission. As besieging armies, like the Mongols in medieval China, once starved cities into surrender.'

'Before butchering the population,' Zhi murmured.

'But Galaxias is *not* a Mongol horde. Save for the Blink, it has not touched us. One action, granted a pretty destructive one, but one action alone, and now it waits for us to draw our conclusions.

'And we believe, you see, that this is a reflection of its nature. Galaxias is not a conqueror. It is not even *expansive*, as we are.'

'Expansive.' Jane looked that up on her phone.

'But it may have cause to fear cultures that *are* expansive. Perhaps from encounters in the past. It may see *us* as potentially threatening.'

Tash felt vaguely baffled by all this. *What would Fred Bowles do, if he were here?* Ask tough questions. Questions he probably couldn't ask in public, or in any session likely to be recorded.

She said, 'OK. You people keep saying Galaxias commands the power of a Galaxy. Well, then – if it thinks us a threat, why not just wipe us out, without any warning at all? Could it do that?'

'Indubitably,' Marlowe murmured. It could destroy the whole Earth. 'With only a fraction of the energy it took to move the Sun.'

'It may have its own code of ethics,' Yan said now. 'Well, it must. Perhaps it is averse to taking life indiscriminately . . .'

And Tash remembered Marlowe's bleak comparison with the 'ethics' of wiping out a harmful virus.

'Ethics?' Zhi shook his head. 'Tell that to my lost fiancé, his family. Mother, tell that to those thousands who have died since Blink Day, in the volcanism, the storms. I grant that it has not simply destroyed us—'

Marlowe said now, 'But even that could be seen as an ethical act. *Depending on the ethical system*.

'No – let me finish.

'My own instinct is that Galaxias seeks gestures that seem – small. To it, anyhow. Comparatively speaking. It doesn't build a huge beacon on the Moon; it builds a – a water pistol. It doesn't destroy us; it evidently warns us. It is conservative. So perhaps its goal is not to preserve life as such but *energy*. Mass. It preserves the *potential* for life, for longevity. On cosmic scales, anyhow. If that's the case, you see, it *would* be rational, even ethical, to contain expansive, destructive species like us. Who grow so fast we just burn up our resources, on a planetary scale for now, maybe on an interstellar scale in the future – at least, until our expansion wave hits the speed of light and we finally crash and burn. That's "the light cage". There are plenty of mathematical models predicting just that. Maybe it seeks to contain us, as opposed to destroying us, before we wreck a few hundred star systems and crash anyhow.'

Tash nodded. 'OK. I could buy that. But why move a star? Why not just the Earth – even the Moon?'

'Or just stop the Earth rotating, like Yahweh?' Marlowe grinned.

Tash and Mel exchanged unhappy glances, and Tash remembered the slogan worn by those cultist types at New Diaspora.

Mel said, 'Charlie, I think everybody would be happier if you stopped kicking Yahweh.'

Marlowe shook her head. 'I recall what we said before. Those are K-II stunts. Stellar-scale energies. Galaxias wanted to *prove* to us, conclusively, that it is K-III. Galactic scale. If not greater. And so it makes a K-III gesture. You can take some crumbs of consolation. It hasn't destroyed us yet. And if we don't alarm it perhaps it will continue to leave us alone. And, within those parameters, we may be safe.'

Zhi snorted. 'Safe? That seems a reach. How can you know that?'

'I don't know it. But we have evidence, of a sort. Negative evidence, evidence of absence. Remember the Fermi Paradox? If life arose on Earth, how come it hasn't arisen everywhere? How come other species haven't built starships – or at least sent radio messages we can hear? There's been time for civilisations to rise and fall across the Galaxy, over and over. Why don't we see them?' She glanced around, looking them each in the eye. 'Because Galaxias stopped them, that's why.

'Because *the Galaxy is big enough for only one K-III*. That's the definition of what K-III is. And if it is suppressing everybody else from becoming K-I or K-II, as it seems to have stopped us – and if it *were* to spare us – maybe we will actually be protected, in a sense, in the future. If we can live with Galaxias, we don't need to think about provoking other threats.'

'Perhaps,' Wu Yan said slowly. 'And isn't it a corollary that, for fear of provoking Galaxias, we must learn to live together peacefully?'

Zhi grunted. 'Maybe. Or maybe it doesn't matter whether or not we fight each other. We'll still be in a prison with only one gaoler. You may have trouble selling that as good news. If we can't expand, economically, physically—'

Yan said, 'But we humans have not always been so expansive as in recent centuries – indeed, once we were not so at all. Look – once our deepest ancestors were animals, among a suite of animals, wandering around the planet, looking for food. Oh, we emerged from Africa several times over, and walked out across Eurasia, all the way to the Americas, Australia . . . The economists say we *diffused*. Like a gas, filling a space. It's thought that just before farming was developed we were doubling our numbers every few thousand years. *But—*'

'But then we did develop farming,' Marlowe said. 'And the consequences included booms and crashes, starvation and gluttony, war and peace – peasants and empires. And, ultimately, the light cage. That's the growth paradox, right there. Any culture that expands into interstellar space at anything like our own historic rates is *bound* to hit the lightspeed limit, to crash and burn in a few centuries or millennia. Taking out a chunk of the universe's usable resources in the process.'

Zhi got up and walked again, exoskeleton creaking. 'I love you all dearly, but, just like my mother, you spend too long *getting to the point.*'

'No,' Mel said, '*I* think I know what you're getting at. You don't *have* to expand at breakneck speed. The slower you go, the further you can go. And if Galaxias has gone really, really slowly, so it didn't crash into lightspeed before it had covered the whole Galaxy—' She peered into her phone, manipulated dancing images in the air above it. 'Say a hundred times a hundred times slower – no, slower than *that* – you'd grow so slowly that . . . You could cross the Galaxy well within lightspeed.' She sat back.

Yan smiled. 'You are paralleling our own thinking. Chinese thinking.'

Tash said, 'So, if I get this right, Galaxias didn't expand. It didn't conquer. It *diffused*. Too slowly to fall into any light cage trap of its own.'

'And moved quietly,' Yan said. 'Touched the stars lightly. So lightly we don't see any evidence of – modification. Building.

Crossed the Galaxy, still a single culture.' She nodded at Marlowe. 'Indeed, some of us believe it is a single being, perhaps, a galactic mind with thoughts carried at the crawl of lightspeed. And, just as Galaxias failed to fall into any light cage, so, we think, *it must stop others falling into the same trap.* Otherwise we would see them: the Dyson spheres, the antimatter rockets, the interstellar wars, visible across light years.'

Jane was wide-eyed. 'What a pity.'

Zhi grinned. 'You said it, kid. And so it decided to teleport our Sun out to the Kuiper Belt? Somewhat drastic response to Pioneer 10. Just one ship! Just one frail little probe!'

Yan said sadly, 'Probably every light cage catastrophe would have started with just one frail little probe.'

Zhi stood again, walked stiffly around the table. 'Mother — even if you're right — this is about more than science. The decisions we make now might shape the whole future of humanity, for ever. And for all your lectures about the dangers of light cages and the like, do you really believe it will be healthy for humans just to — to sit here on Earth — with every independent choice shaped by the fear of Galaxias and its retaliation, for ever? At least now, *right now*, we can *do* something. In a few generations, if our space technology withers, or even our willingness to push back — is stagnation not a danger too?'

'Of course it is.' She hesitated. 'But there is a greater danger of doing something — foolhardy. Precipitate. Obvious, even. We must do more than — than not attack Galaxias. We must show it we have learned the lesson it gave us. It must *believe* we will *never* threaten catastrophic expansion.'

Zhi looked as if he wanted to argue some more.

But Tash held up her hand. 'Hang on, Zhi. I've been around Fred Bowles and his like long enough to be able to recognise what your mother said as a politician's answer.'

Yan smiled. 'I am flattered. I think.'

'That wasn't a denial. More an evasion. I think you have secrets. With respect. You may not endorse the American plan, but . . . *I think the Chinese do have some scheme.*' Somehow convincing Galaxias we are harmless. Though I can't imagine how you would do that.

Zhi stood and glared at his mother. 'And you won't tell *me*? About any of this? Even what you are doing, personally, now?'

Yan stayed calm. 'My son, do you have a sprint setting on that exoskeleton of yours?'

He frowned. 'I don't understand.'

'I am attempting a joke in the English idiom. Forgive me. You always did run before you could walk.'

There was a brief silence.

Then Jane laughed softly.

Charlie Marlowe said, 'She's got you, son. Never cross swords with your mother.'

Zhi forced a smile, but it was an angry expression, and Tash could feel the tension. 'Right,' he said. 'And tell that to the light cage cultures Galaxias has . . . *mothered.*'

He walked noisily out.

Yan seemed bewildered. 'I hope he isn't too upset by any of that. I – oh, dear.'

Jane leaned over the table and took her hand. And she held that hand tightly, as Yan suddenly appeared to be fighting back sudden tears.

Charlie Marlowe rocked back in her chair with a sigh. 'You know, if only we could just get along . . . Imagine the progress we could make. Look at our stumbling response to the climate crisis. Wars broke out over *that*. Now we have an alien incursion. Can we not work together?'

Yan took her time replying, once again. 'Professor Marlowe, I am working with a group of very smart, highly qualified, deep-thinking people, back home. We are the world's largest nation by far, possibly the richest and most powerful, and arguably the most politically stable. We have seen the United States fracture in my lifetime . . . What need have we of your assistance?

'But *we – do – not – trust – you,*' she said, emphasising the words with gentle slaps of the table.

Marlowe said, 'And if you do come up with some concrete plan, must we trust *you* to act for us?'

'It is the only way . . .' She seemed to falter.

Tash said, 'Even if it's costing you your relationship with your son.'

Jane squeezed Yan's hand harder.

'We'll bring him back to you,' Tash said earnestly. 'We promise.'

'We'll find a way,' said Mel.

We better had for the sake of the world, Tash thought, feeling caught between sympathy, cynicism, and an awful sense of global responsibility. If mother and son could not work on this together, what hope the rest of humanity?

Yan bowed her head.

It was a ferociously long day.

But even as the technical sessions ran down, it was made clear to Tash and her colleagues that attendance was expected of them at a series of 'cultural exhibits' set out in the main hall by various groups, displaying a variety of responses to Galaxias and the Blink: artistic, philosophical, and several religious. Mel showed Tash a party in blue PUNY YAHWEH? T-shirts.

The one that fixated Tash especially was a choir, of a couple of dozen adults, who appeared to be dedicated to the worship of Galaxias. They sang by memory. Their tenet was that Galaxias had meant to plunge humans into the dark as a punishment, hidden from a light that sinners did not deserve. And so, they had all had their eyes surgically removed.

26

August 2057

The Edinburgh conference ended without any more significant meetings between mother and son, Yan and Zhi – Yan's handlers seemed to see to that.

But another opportunity of sorts for a rapprochement came up a month later. For by then Wu Yan was participating in another exotic lunar-manufacturing experiment – and this time on Earth, and, to Tash's initial surprise, in the Americas, on a plateau in Oregon called the High Lava Plains. But the American Free States' government had responded positively to a Chinese request for resources, partly for political advantage – particularly over its rival, the rump US – and also for the chance of learning about the Chinese experiments themselves. And the AFS too saw an advantage in getting Wu Yan out there, for political leverage, for publicity through imagery featuring her own now-familiar face against an American background.

So, Tash and Mel started to work out an itinerary to get Zhi out to Oregon.

Officially he was to be a kind of goodwill ambassador from the American hosts of the Chinese project – one the Chinese would find hard to turn away. Unofficially, as far as Tash could see, he was being used yet again as a sort of out-in-the-open spy on his mother's project.

It was becoming a pattern, Tash thought. 'It's a long shot,' she told a sceptical Mel, 'but it's cheap, and it's worth a try.'

In the end an invitation was forthcoming, over Wu Yan's signature – though, in the end, and to Tash's intense disappointment, she would not be present herself on the day.

Mel herself was sent out in advance to find her way around the facility. Then Tash followed with Zhi.

And as it turned out, to complicate everything, the meeting was to take place on the very day the surviving crew of the Al-miriykh, the jeopardised Mars mission, were due, at last, four months late, to return to Earth. But maybe that was a good thing, Mel and Tash decided. If things went bad – or even if they went well – there couldn't be a better day for Zhi to be with the In-Jokes.

If not his mother. Tash had a very hard time trying to read how Zhi felt about that absence.

On the day itself, after a very early start, a Jones, Inc. shuttle plane, carrying Tash and Zhi, descended from an iron-hot sky to land at the Chinese experimental site.

It was a little before midday, local. As they waited on the plane while its engines closed down, Tash could see Mel herself emerging from a small white dome of a shelter. Wearing a broad-brimmed hat against the strength of the Sun, she walked alone to the plane.

There was little else *to* see. This so-called 'High Lava Plain' really was just a plain, a kilometre and a half above sea level, thrust into a blue dome of sky – free of cloud, a rare sight in a world of turbulent post-Blink weather.

The set-up itself was largely automated, Tash knew. She saw a few buildings nearby, scattered bits of machinery, evidently components of the test rig. But further out there seemed to be more complex knots of machinery, more activity. Tash thought she glimpsed movement, slow, deliberate. Enigmatic. Not a human in sight. Space manufacturing technology, brought to this strange corner of the Earth.

Zhi, in the seat beside her, was staring into a screen. Tash glimpsed scrolling readouts, a sketchy cartoon of a stub-winged spacecraft high above the curve of the Earth, a couple of human faces, their talk too soft for Tash to make out the words. The surviving astronauts of the Al-miriykh, talking to their mission controllers, their capcoms. The day's other priority. Zhi seemed aware of nothing else – not even the fact that the plane had landed, maybe.

Tash tentatively reached out to him. 'Hey. We're down. Mel is coming—'

'They just ejected. The lander, I mean, from the rest of the complex, the Shelter.' He tapped to bring up a clock. 'On time, just after nine a.m. local time here. Now they only have the service module for last-minute tweaks to the trajectory.'

The service module was a small propulsion unit, Tash knew. 'So,' she said, 'they're falling—'

'Towards re-entry.'

Falling into the air of Earth in a landing module that looked, in the images Tash had seen, like the mutant offspring of an Apollo command module, a squat cone atop a thick heatshield, but with stubby space-shuttle black and white wings. The lander was an emergency lifeboat that should never have been needed. The original mission plan had been for the whole remaining stack, Shelter and all, to be decelerated smoothly into Earth orbit, and then docked with one of the low orbit stations up there, tucked safely inside Earth's magnetosphere.

Well, the Blink had put paid to that plan. After drifting off course for a whole day without solar gravity, the crew had had to burn up most of their remaining fuel to correct the ship's course, and had used their emergency-only solar sail to get a little more deflection. The remnant ship had at last reached Earth – but with not enough fuel left to slow up sufficiently to make orbit, to achieve a docking. And so now, desperately, the surviving astronauts – like the wounded Apollo 13 crew on the way back from the Moon – were just going to have to hurtle direct into the atmosphere and lose their final kinetic energy to friction from the air of Earth.

Tash had been surprised to learn that this particular lander had made the trip to Mars and back twice before, without needing to be used. A high-tech lifeboat, emergency only. Now its time had come. And already this veteran of space was falling down through the sky of Earth.

Tash knew there would be few such missions in the near future, for in the face of the Galaxias crisis the multinational Curiosity Base on Mars was being mothballed, its crew returned home.

'We won't see anything from here, will we? I know that's naive—'

Zhi shook his head curtly. 'Not from here. And nowhere for an hour, maybe more, before they hit the atmosphere.'

She took his hand. 'That hour's going to seem like a year. Let's get out of here. Come see Mel.'

Zhi scrambled out first.

Tash, emerging from the plane, stood at the top of a mobile stair, cautious in the brilliant light – and immediately aware of the thinness of the dry air. She took her time, breathed deep, looked around.

She faced a stark landscape, a flat plain of brownish pebbles and dust. The human presence was slight.

Nearby, that huddle of buildings, evidently what passed for an air terminal here. Small clusters of enigmatic bits of machinery, perhaps waiting to be deployed, or else flown out. And, in the distance, that more complex site. At its heart Tash glimpsed what looked like a pool of black tarmac on the ground.

And, humans or not, there was motion everywhere, if slow, ponderous. Robots, evidently. Several squat, complex, truck-like machines were rolling and digging and scraping in the dirt. Around that central black circle, she saw now, a kind of spiral groove expanded out into the bare landscape, evidently being dug out by the machines. Save for Mel coming from her domed shelter, no humans were visible, though there were more domes scattered across the landscape, brilliant white, with Red Cross markers on their flanks. Relief stations, presumably.

Drones flitted everywhere, insectile, faintly buzzing. Away from this complex, she could see nothing else for kilometres, out to a horizon only slightly dust-obscured. All very enigmatic, she thought, as she cautiously descended the stair. An enigmatic Chinese space-tech experiment being run in the heart of North America.

But that wasn't so strange any more. In the wake of the Blink, Tash knew, having burrowed herself through the dusty heart of the government system, that the major nations were actually communicating and cooperating pretty effectively – even inward-looking China, even nations in relative turmoil like the US and its secessionist offspring – as were international agencies from the FIS and subordinate agencies on down, including NHSA, the space agency. And even now Chinese vessels, ships and planes and satellites, were very visibly helping with the monitoring of the approach of the stricken Mars ship, basically an outcome of an American project, as it headed for a hopeful splashdown in the South Pacific.

Cautious cooperation, then, when it really counted. Tash hoped it stayed that way in the coming months and years. But then, she knew, she always had been an optimist.

At last she reached the ground, following Zhi.

As she moved out of the shadow of the plane, the sunlight seemed to hit hard – not in terms of heat, but brilliance. She flinched and scrabbled for sunglasses. And when she breathed, she found she gasped a little, even after the mild exertion of the stair. She was reminded of times when she had landed in Denver, and felt a similar high-altitude breathlessness getting off the plane.

At the foot of the stair, Mel stood waiting for them. She was wearing a dust-streaked coverall, a broad hat, and a healthy layer of sunblock cream. 'Here.' She handed over wide-brimmed hats, like her own. 'Welcome to the guided tour, by the world's worst guide. Is this the strangest place we three ever got together? And I've been here a couple of days already. Lucky me . . .'

Tash took her hat gratefully. Zhi took his in a kind of resentful silence, though he put it on.

Mel smiled. 'Just be easy on yourselves for a while. Remember, you're a mile high, as our American hosts insist on measuring it. The air is thin, and the Sun strong – especially given the damage done to the stratosphere and ozone layer. We shouldn't stand around in the light. In fact I'm the only person live on site today. The regulars fly down to safer locations when they can.'

'No Wu Yan,' Tash said.

'No Wu Yan. Not yet, not as far as we know. The machines do everything, after all. Well, that's the idea. So it may seem a little quiet to you. I take it you don't need any comfort breaks before—'

Zhi growled, 'That whole damn flight was a comfort break.

This *day* is a comfort break, isn't it? Let's just get on with it.' And he marched straight for the enigmatic manufacturing complex, his exoskeleton creaking.

Mel and Tash shared a glance, and followed him.

'This is probably as good as it gets,' Tash murmured softly as they walked.

Mel shrugged. 'At least he's here.'

They walked along a broad road of little more than compressed rubble, Tash saw – laid over a landscape that was itself pretty much rubble, with only a few of what looked like desert flowers to break the crimson monotony.

'Pretty rugged place,' Tash said.

'And old,' Zhi called over his shoulder. 'Not much has happened here since the Miocene five million years ago. I looked it up. When the line that would lead to humanity was still splitting off from a whole gaggle of ape types, around the world. And, just about then, a big geological event right here.'

'Correct,' Mel said. 'A huge magmatic eruption. It created immense basaltic domes, which were then eroded to rubble – and the remains were uplifted by even more heroic geological forces to this altitude. So, the result: a lava beach higher than some mountains. Earth really is a remarkable planet.' She kicked a rogue pebble off the road surface. 'And this particular bit of it is very useful for the Chinese. Basalt pebbles, dust, dry as a bone, rich in aluminium – among other things – under that thin air.'

'I think I get it,' Tash said. 'I'm no scientist, remember. I just have to *listen* to scientists. And some of it sticks. That's why the Chinese came here. Because it's like the Moon. It even *feels* like it's halfway to the Moon.'

'Geologically, yes,' Mel said. 'We can't replicate lunar conditions on the Earth – not on any scale, anyhow. The vacuum, the low gravity and so on. But this place is a reasonable facsimile in terms of the rocks underfoot, at least. And the intense sunlight, the aridity. So here, the Chinese are trying out new industrial techniques for eventual transfer to the Moon – and indeed other rocky worlds – proceeding step by step towards the goal—'

'Just like Jones, Inc.,' Tash put in. 'Right, Zhi? You bend my ear about *your* methodology often enough. Step by step, each step another design decision validated . . .'

But he didn't take the bait, or wasn't listening. Marching along, he was staring into his phone.

Mel, following with Tash, glanced at her own phone.

Tash asked, 'No news from space?'

'Not really,' Mel said. 'Still a while before the entry begins. They've gone quiet. The crew. They are committed now. All they can do is wait until they fall into the air, and hope they got it right.'

For, as Tash knew well enough by now – as the whole world did – if the lander came down at too steep an angle it would plunge too fast into the atmosphere, and burn up. But too shallow an angle and it might just skip off, like a stone bouncing from the surface of a pond, and fly off back into deep space. Tash knew that options had been explored for reaching the crew even so, by sending some kind of fast mission after them. But the best estimates were that the crew's consumables would be exhausted long before such a retrieval could be made.

'All they can do is wait,' Mel said again. 'And that's all you can do, Zhi. Come see your mother's latest toys . . .'

They walked on.

'So,' Tash said as brightly as she could. 'The Chinese project, then. Step by step?'

'Indeed. They seem to be developing and testing a suite of

new technologies, new designs. Even new ways of *thinking* about machines. The stuff here on this basaltic plain on Earth, even the rigs on the Moon itself, are test beds, development sites, to allow the work to develop further, to reach the ultimate goal.'

Zhi glared over his shoulder at her. 'What "ultimate goal"? Nobody seems to know. Outside of the Beijing high-ups anyhow. Fear of failure, is it?'

'Well – call it academic caution.'

Zhi just laughed. 'Not politics at all, then. We, under Serena Jones, have done it all out in the open, from the beginning.'

Tash grunted. 'Oh, come on, Zhi. Not all of it. As far as I know you haven't even said where you're going yet.'

'Well, the American nations do continue to operate a capitalist economy, Tash. There is such a thing as commercial confidentiality. So we hold details back. We have said *what* we are trying to do. We are emulating Pioneer 10; we are pushing out of the Solar System, with a crewed craft. The whole world knows that. Whereas the Chinese—'

'Whereas the Chinese, perhaps,' Mel said with a smile, 'are waiting until they have something that works before bragging about it. Anyhow this isn't a commercial competition, Zhi. But if it were, Serena is at a disadvantage. Because fewer people will want to buy an edge-of-the Solar-System space drive, no matter how advanced, than efficient extraterrestrial industrial technology.'

Now Zhi looked around at the installation they were approaching with, it seemed to Tash, an academic kind of curiosity that overrode even his other tensions, if briefly.

Mel just smiled. 'I knew that would hook you. Come. Let me show you.'

*

Mel walked them up to the edge of the spiral ditch that in turn enclosed that sprawling black 'oil slick'. They stood just inside the shade of a big sagging canopy, to Tash's mild relief, one of the structures she had spotted from the plane.

She looked around. Machines toiling around the periphery, digging trenches, moving dirt. The buzz of drones overhead. She felt bewildered at the sprawling scale, the slow, patient movement everywhere.

She tried to observe it component by component, imagining debriefs to come. The black 'slick' turned out to be a kind of pavement, jet-black blocks of some hard rock, larger than household bricks, fitting together with what looked like microscopic precision. And at the far side of the pavement she saw a spidery machine setting down more blocks, one at a time, in a dead-straight trench cut in the dirt. Beyond *that* she thought she saw more movement, a spray of dirt and small fragments thrown in the air. Another machine, digging a trench for the next line of bricks?

Away from the pavement itself, beyond the toiling bricklayer and the digger, she saw other enigmatic structures: robots moving slowly, some on wheels or rollers, others on spindly, spidery legs. All *handling* stuff, picking it up, putting it down.

And at one location she saw what looked like a miniature factory, a few metres on a side. Toy-like trucks, themselves loaded by other digger machines, rolled up to dump dirt into a hopper on one side of the factory unit. Meanwhile, on the other side of the factory, metallic bars were extruded, to be carried away by still more truck-like machines.

There was something intriguing, if somehow disturbing, about all this autonomous, apparently leaderless work. Perhaps it was like an ant colony. And yet she was prepared to bet that the dumbest of these machines, even the humble ditch-digger, was smarter than any ant.

Mel murmured, 'So what do you make of it?'

Zhi was looking at his phone.

Tash tried to reply. 'Well . . . I can see there's a process here. Little trucks, with skips being loaded up with rubble by those – digger types – over there. The trucks go to that complex of buildings over *there*, and they dump the fill into scoops at one end, and out of the other come . . . ingots of some metal. Aluminium, I guess? . . . '

A whirring noise overhead; she ducked when she saw a drone, one of the cloud, hovering closer, under the canopy.

'You're quite safe,' Mel murmured. 'The drones are much too smart to be any danger to the site itself, or a visitor. In fact the drones are the brains of the outfit – and its nervous system, with the transponder links they maintain between the different components. A distributed machine intelligence.

'You are looking at a process, yes. Look – you have machines of different specialities. Miners of various sorts, gathering dirt, water perhaps, which is carried to serve as feedstock for mineral extraction. Aluminium is key, but there are other valuable products to be had in the local geology.

'Then the extracted minerals are taken to fabricators of various kinds. One machine makes bricks for this pavement, others use aluminium to make machine parts. Still more sophisticated machines use those parts to build *other* machines. Such as more miners or extractors or fabricators. All of it controlled and co-ordinated by the drones. And all powered by sunlight, by the way. There are extensive solar energy capture blankets beyond – more of which can be produced by the fabricators.

'And all of this is a process of which the only end goal, for now, is the laying of this pavement. But on that pavement, you see, will eventually be built another set of buildings as you see over *there*, all essentially constructed from local resources.'

Tash remembered what Mel had told her of what she had seen on the Moon: the solar energy blanket growing in the light. This was evidently some kind of extension of that technology. Not just a solar blanket: a whole installation now, *growing* out of the dirt, in the sunlight.

It was baffling. She should have been pre-briefed back in Government House.

She said, 'This is all about self-replication, isn't it? Machines that grow. Reproduce.'

'Correct,' Mel said. 'Machines that can make more machines, copies of themselves, from the local resources. The theory is old, the practice is still being worked out. What I can't guess at yet is what the Chinese are going to have these smart industrial machines *do*. In the context of Galaxias, I mean. I'm guessing something big—'

Zhi's phone pinged. He lifted it. 'Updates from Al-miriykh.'

All of Zhi's consciousness, Tash saw, was focused on his phone's screen.

'They just ejected the service module, after a last course-adjustment burn. That's it. Nothing else they can do until they are in the atmosphere and their aerosurfaces start to work. For now they have no more control than does a bullet fired from a gun.'

'How long?' Mel asked calmly.

'Fifteen minutes,' Zhi said. 'That's all. Well, a lot less if the entry fails and they skip off . . . Fifteen minutes until they are down in the ocean, grinning at the helicopter crews come to pick them up. Or not.' He looked at her, apparently helpless. 'Longest fifteen minutes of my life coming up, since Blink Day itself, and I lost Jim.'

Mel shepherded them both forward. 'Sit in the shade, both of you. I'll fetch more drinks.' She walked off to the nearest dome shelter.

Zhi sat on the machine-created basalt-block floor, stiff in his exoskeletal aids, and he stared at his phone, the cryptic images and figures scrolling in the air above it.

Mel returned from the nearest shelter with iced water, handed out glasses. Then she sat beside Zhi, took a glass herself, and pulled out her own phone, evidently to track the astronauts' entry.

Tash fought the impulse to get out her phone too.

'All on track,' Mel murmured.

'The controllers are saying the guidance is perfect,' Zhi said. 'On track as best they can tell. Just eight minutes until the blackout. They are falling head first into the air. The crew will be seeing brilliant light now, beyond the windows. Ionised gas, curtains of it glowing all around the lander . . .'

A long silence.

Then, 'Eighteen hundred kilometres downrange from the splashdown target. And, and . . . *there*. Blackout. On time. Two minutes, if they come through it. The ionisation blocks the radio signals.'

Mel sighed. 'We know.'

Zhi hunched, eyes closed, rocking. Tash reached out to him, but Mel shook her head.

They felt like the longest two minutes of Tash's own life.

Then a hiss of static, a distorted voice.

Zhi held up his phone.

Mel stared at her own phone. 'An aerial tracker saw them. Gliding, gliding. Eight hundred kilometres downrange, just where they should be.'

She tapped her phone, for audible sound. Tash heard radio voices, mostly incomprehensible. Cheering in the background, and the raucous voice of some capcom. *We got them! We got them!*

Zhi folded over on himself, collapsing into tears. 'Oh, oh shit . . .'

The In-Jokes crowded together, knelt beside him, held him. He stayed hunched over, unresponsive.

And, beyond, Tash saw the patient robots working, working. Pushing out this island of artifice on the ancient plain, brick by basalt brick. She thought it was the strangest thing she had ever seen, leaving aside the Blink itself.

Then a message came in, for her. From Fred Bowles's office.

Having visited this mock-up of the Moon surface, next month Tash was to travel to the Moon itself.

27

September 2057

'I just never imagined I'd be doing this myself,' Tash said to Grace Butterworth.

Or rather yelled to her, over the noise of the RAF helicopter that airlifted them out of Gateshead into a murky, volcano-ash sky, headed north towards Thorness.

Grace, ex-military herself, looked at home strapped into the confines of a bucket seat. Tash thought she would never have guessed that there was a cute photo of Grace's nine-month-old niece Billie tucked under her bullet-proof vest. But even as she spoke, Tash noticed Grace never took her eyes off Fred Bowles, or rather the back of his head a couple of rows of seats ahead of them, as he earnestly went through material on phones and tablets with a couple of his advisers.

Grace said now, 'Doing what? You mean a ride in a chopper? A plane would be quicker, but choppers fly lower, under the volcanic ash—'

'No, not that. Well, yes, me, in an RAF chopper. But mostly, *me*, going to the Moon!'

'Oh, right.' Grace grinned, and ran a hand over her crewcut hair. 'I know. Well, I did this bit once before – the ride into space at least. Training on military hardware in low orbit. Fred has never flown either. He *has* to go. England has to establish a presence at Sinus Medii, in that Monument Park that's grown up there.'

The Park had grown out of the gathering, in the last few months, of streams of international visitors to the lurker on the Moon, many of whom had left behind tokens and messages. Similarly nations, corporations, churches, colleges, and other groups had sent small probes to the area, carrying inscriptions or tokens. It had grown into Earth's more or less spontaneous cultural response to the startling presence of an alien artefact on the Moon – and, apparently, to one you could see, even could have touched without the security barriers. As opposed to the immense invisibility of Galaxias itself.

Soon, inevitably, the Park had been formalised, and under FIS governance was hosted fairly graciously by the Chinese, who had a more significant presence on the Moon than any other nation. But security had got tighter after a number of attempts to challenge the 'spawn of Galaxias', as some called it, with displays of obscenity, defiance, threat.

And now it was the turn of the Federal States of England to make a formal contribution to the Park. As Tash had understood it, the English monument itself was already up on the Moon; now she was flying up there with a party for the formal unveiling.

Grace went on, 'The PM had to send a Cabinet minister with our contribution, and it had to be Fred, didn't it?'

Mel, sitting behind them with Charlie Marlowe, herself buried in work, leaned forward and yelled over the noise of the chopper. 'Logical, yes. He's the science minister. It's his domain—'

'No,' Grace said. 'It's not that. He's senior enough to be a weighty presence. Junior enough to be disposable.'

Tash suppressed a grin. 'Don't let him hear you say that. Oh,

I think he knows. There was some talk of sending a royal, but the King himself vetoed that. Also Fred's going because we're still bidding for November, the big FIS conference, the heads of state. England's *got* to host that. We can't afford to build the big stuff like this Chinese factory effort on the Moon, or even Zhi's firecracker spaceship. But we do know how to put on a diplomatic show.'

Mel nodded. 'I did hear they are thinking of hosting it in New Aberdeen this time. Although I suppose that might mean sharing some credit with the Scottish and the Dutch . . .'

Mel and Grace started to debate that.

Tash turned back to her phone, the latest messages, the talking heads whose voices whispered through the buds in her ears about current government issues.

She couldn't concentrate on any of it.

She looked out of her window, and down on post-Blink Scotland: glassy sheets of water that were the relics of floods from the hypercane storm in April, sprawling structures of pale plastic set up to protect emergency food crops from the unseasonably cold weather. All chaotically assembled amid still-young carbon-capture forests, relics of the last global crisis . . .

She was going to the Moon! Holy shit. And one other, at least, of the In-Jokes would be with her – the second time for Mel in a few months. Maybe Zhi would be watching. Although, she thought sadly, probably not.

It seemed no time at all before the pilot quietly spoke in their ears to announce the beginning of the descent into Thorness, on the west coast of Scotland. And Tash, peering out of her window again, saw an airfield, with kilometres-long runways, stripes on the ground.

No, this was not an airfield – or not any more. A spaceport.

*

The passengers were hustled off the chopper, across a few metres of tarmac, and into a surprisingly primitive terminal building.

Here, detached from their luggage and carry-ons, they were sorted into rough seniority groups and bundled through a boarding process that Tash quickly found intrusive, even by the standards of such procedures. In a small cubicle she had to strip naked, and pass through a shower and body scanner before being allowed to dress in her own clothes once more. Meanwhile the clothes themselves had been irradiated.

They had all been warned about a dress code. The recommended costumes were coveralls and soft, slip-on shoes. Only a couple of the group had bent the rules too far, had their own clothes confiscated, and emerged in compulsorily imposed and ill-fitting RAF blue flight suits. Tash actually felt a faint twinge of envy over the cool-looking suits. Very adolescent of her, she thought.

After this, she was reunited with her colleagues in a small, sparse lounge. Here they collected secure clones of their phones and other gadgets. Fred Bowles was back at work already, going through red-box briefings on a tablet. And Charlie Marlowe too sat alone, speaking quietly into the air while paging through her phone.

Tash sat with Mel and Grace at a small table. Only clear water to drink, she saw. 'So this is space travel,' she said. 'That check-in process was somewhat thorough.'

Grace, her own phone in her hand, just shrugged. 'You're going into space on a military-class machine. What did you expect? And *this* is an RAF base, or was. Built during the Second World War, let out as a science and technology park for a few decades, then taken back as a spaceport.' She grinned. 'The potholes filled in, the runways lengthened a bit. This was a while after the RAF was given responsibility for supervising Britain's access to space.'

Mel asked, 'Why not the RASF?' She emphasised the 'S'. 'I always wondered. If it's now an air and space force . . .'

Grace just gave her a look. 'I was in the Marines. I haven't a lot of time for these fly-boys and their toys. But − change "RAF"? Are you mad, or just a traitor?'

Tash smiled.

An orderly came by, subtly beckoning.

Grace stood up. 'Time to board.'

The interior of the Skylon IV-B was less roomy than Tash had expected, but maybe more like an airliner than she had thought, with rows of conventional-looking seats in pairs set in a passenger compartment that represented, she surmised, only a small percentage of the volume of the long, sleek hull she had glimpsed from the transfer bus.

But then, as Mel had told her as they boarded, most of that volume was taken up by fuel. 'And that's hydrogen,' she murmured. 'The lightest element. Needs a lot of tankage.'

So Tash sat with Grace beside her, Mel and Charlie just behind her, Bowles and his team ahead. Tash's seat was smart, and seemed to mould itself to her body as she sat down, with a rest riding up and gripping her neck and head, not uncomfortably, and a kind of heavy-duty belt swathing her belly.

Grace was already busy on her phone, supervising something or other.

Before her own seat swallowed her up, Mel reached forward and gripped Tash's shoulder. 'Enjoy the ride, kiddo.'

'Hope so,' Tash said. 'And, whether or not I keep my lunch down, I want to tell Dad all about it. You know, I think he's proud of me and where I have got to, but he's not particularly interested in the mechanics of government. A spaceplane ride, though . . .'

'I know. They won't let us record stuff, of course. Last time I tried to remember it all for Jane, the first time. My daughter,' she said for Grace's benefit.

Grace nodded. 'I remember. How old? Twelve?'

'In December.'

'She'd be the perfect age for this, probably.'

And then, with a curt announcement over a PA, the Skylon began to roll forward.

The windows were tiny, and awkwardly placed. There was a virtual display array hanging in the air before Tash's face, but it was hard to follow the details – naturally Tash hadn't followed Grace's advice to look it all up in advance.

But still, the experience soon became extraordinary.

With the plane already rolling, somewhere in back huge engines lit up, working in 'jet mode', as she understood it, for now burning hydrogen from those big tanks in oxygen drawn from the atmosphere. A roar gathered for maybe five seconds – and then the craft leapt forward, thrusting her deep in her chair.

Grace didn't turn her head, but when she spoke, her voice carried. 'Runway's five miles long. And they do still brag about it in miles, God bless the RAF . . .'

The plane tipped up without warning, and flung itself into the sky.

Tash could *feel* it, feel how she was lying on her back. Visualised the dark blue needle climbing through the air, murky and turbulent as it was. And now she felt the thrust build up, pushing her back into her seat. She had been told it would be no worse than three gravities, no more strenuous than a scare-the-punters amusement park ride, but it *felt* a lot more than that, felt as if some huge open hand was pushing down on her ribs, her belly.

Then, only perhaps ten seconds into the flight, a shudder, a rattle – almost as if they had struck some physical barrier – and a sudden smoothing out, a reduction of the ambient noise.

'Through the sound barrier already,' Grace yelled – unnecessarily loudly now.

Tash dared not turn her head to look out of the window, but the seat-back display in front of her showed how the ground just fell away, the runway stripes soon lost in the wider countryside, the sky around her deepening to a rich blue.

'Here's the trick,' Mel called, behind Tash. 'To get to orbit in a single-stage ship you need an engine that works in different modes. So we fly like a jet plane until we get to Mach 5, maybe forty kilometres up, and *then* we switch over to using liquid oxygen from our internal tanks to burn what's left of the hydrogen – rocket mode. That's about a minute into the flight . . . which is . . . now!'

A sharp transition. The thrust in Tash's back felt tougher, sharp-edged. But then, here was a different mode of engine pushing a much lighter vehicle, now mostly devoid of its fuel. Of course it would feel tough, rattly . . .

It seemed to go on and on.

And the cut-off, when it came, was another brutal transition. Not so much a loss of thrust as a feeling of being hurled forward, against her straps, then a fall back into her seat. A crash, not a cut-out.

It was over, then.

Tash sat back, breathing hard. Through her tiny window she saw black sky, a curve of bright blue Earth, like a strip of a photograph of a tropical sky. She felt her stomach churn as she moved her head. Weightlessness!

'And now you're in orbit,' Grace said. But her voice was choked.

Tash turned in surprise. She saw tears rolling down Grace's cheeks.

Impulsively Tash reached for Grace's hand. She felt scar tissue under her own palm. 'Hey. What's wrong?'

'Oh, it's just – sorry. Don't tell the fly-boys I blubbed, they're big-headed enough already. It's just that it's all so *magnificent*, you know? We did this! We dumb humans! We built planes that can fly into space! Even the British! Even if . . . And now this bastard Galaxias comes along and – what? Tells us to stay in the playpen?' She shook her head, dug out a tissue, blew her nose.

Even if there's no Britain any more, Tash completed the line.

When she sat back and looked around at her companions, she saw Charlie Marlowe folding out her gadgets, her phones and a tablet, as if this was just another office to work in.

And soon Grace was taking an efficient-looking nap. Tash tried to let go of her hand, but Grace, in her sleep, hung on.

In the hours that followed, Tash and the rest of Fred Bowles's party transferred to a Jones, Inc. EarthMoon, a clumsy, irregularly shaped habitat that did nothing but cycle endlessly between Earth and Moon.

Then the three-day journey itself, coasting to the Moon, and watching the whole Earth recede. Mel got nauseous, space-sick, which turned the habitat into a hospital ward you couldn't leave. There was always one, said the crew, and being a one-time veteran like Mel was no guarantee of immunity.

Even Charlie was sympathetic. Not Grace, however.

Then a transfer to the Lunar Gateway, another habitat, this one in permanent lunar orbit.

Six hours later, a final descent to the lunar surface in a Moon-Lander, a big, spherical, spindly-legged Jones, Inc. creation.

On the surface, a transfer to another Jones element, a Moon-Hab, for a couple of days of orientation, suit-fitting and training. Clumsy fun.

Then a fifty-kilometre ride in a big lunar rover – a MoonBus, yet another Jones design. Jones really did have this technology sewn up, Tash reflected.

An hour of slow-motion jostling in their suits.

And *then* Tash's own first footsteps on the Moon.

She hadn't been allowed out of any of the various vehicles before this moment.

Climbing off the rover, like everybody else Tash made her own 'Armstrong footprint', a travellers' ritual like crossing the equator, her own one small step in the lunar dust, the boot cleats clearly visible in the crisp ground, the low sunlight. A hasty photograph, then she moved on.

Thrilling, astonishing, all of it. Just as Mel had described to her after her own jaunt earlier in the year.

And she was *here*. She had come to the Sinus Medii, and the lurker. She looked around slowly, carefully, keen to remember it all, here on the airless Moon, under a black sky in which Earth and Sun hung like lanterns – in this place where Earth had once rested at the apex of the sky. Why, she didn't even feel afraid of the big black sky. *This* wasn't the sky that had betrayed her in Newcastle, she supposed.

Look at me, Dad!

But, once away from the rover, the landscape's outstanding feature turned out to be a wall: a big circular barrier of what looked like melted rock, maybe five metres tall. Like some fortress. And outside the wall a line of figures in deep blue

283

pressure suits. Blue, the signature of the Chinese on the Moon.

And *that* was where the lurker was, she knew. Behind that wall.

She soon learned that they could only pass through one of the few gateways in this wall, evidently heavily guarded. And to get there, the English party had to walk a half-kilometre from where the MoonBus had dropped them.

So they all moonwalked: Fred Bowles the science minister, Charlie Marlowe the Astronomer Royal, their entourage. They were trailed by a few English and other British nationals who had shared the MoonBus with them. These were longer-stay residents, mostly scientists or habitat support staff, here for six-month assignments, roped into today's chore – and probably glad of a change of routine, Tash soon realised.

A handful of Chinese guards shadowed them, at a distance. Almost politely.

This security was all routine, Grace told her gruffly. No lander was allowed to approach closer than fifty kilometres to the lurker site, and no human-carrying vehicle at all was allowed any closer than half a kilometre from this outer perimeter, this wall – not even the zippy rovers used by the FIS-controlled security forces. One such vehicle had carried the only significant cargo the English party had brought to the Moon, the box that contained their nation's contribution to the fast-growing Monument Park. Now a team of local volunteers were lugging, by hand, these last metres, a coffin-shaped package that had been brought all the way from Gateshead.

But the hike wasn't a chore. Walking on the Moon was deceptively simple, Tash found, rather to her delight. You really did just bunny-hop your way around; it was easy, almost instinctive, even in the heavy vacuum-proof, radiation-proof suits they all had to wear. And the suits were smart. Every so often one of the novices did make a misstep, and the suit would right itself, thanks to a built-in exoskeleton.

Tash's helmet was so big, her field of vision through the visor so wide – the Sun's glare so expertly filtered – that sometimes it was as if she wasn't wearing a helmet at all. It certainly didn't get in the way of her view of the ground under that high black sky.

A ground that itself seemed more interesting, close to, than she had expected. It was a heavy dust, pitted with craters that could be the scale of a footfall on a dry, sandy beach on Earth, or much smaller, or much larger – many too wide for her to make out properly from a human-eye-level perspective, she was sure. Craters within craters, and overlapping. Here and there the sunlight glistened off some reflective grain, embedded in this dust that itself was the product of billions of years of impacts. A world of debris. And yet when she turned her head, the angle of the sunlight changed, and she perceived different colours, from a washed-out grey to a kind of tan.

Thus, the Moon. Exotic, churned-up dust, and a handful of people stumbling across its surface. And that wall, around an alien artefact.

A wall that did indeed, she judged now as she approached, look like it really had been made by melting rock – lunar basalt, she supposed.

At the wall itself, at the gates, more security. Armed guards, and drones of various kinds patrolling a heavily surveilled sky.

Tash understood the security was necessary – and not that difficult to implement. The tentative colonisation of the Moon had been a political success – well, compared to most human politics. The Artemis Accord, agreed by spacefaring nations, based on old space law principles and drawn up before a new wave of landings in the 2030s, had held together pretty well.

On the whole, it seemed, people up here cooperated; the Moon itself was more alien than any terrestrial differences —and was a lethal place besides.

But the lurker had provoked different reactions. There had been too many threats against it, from various groups on a ravaged Earth, for any chances to be taken. It did the authorities no good to stress the theory that the lurker was just a probe, not a part of Galaxias itself – that striking at it would be useless. This was all there was *to* strike at. Hence the wall.

At last gates were thrown open.

There were final security checks as they passed through the Moon-rock fortress wall itself. Tash had long since lost count of how many times the party and its cargo had been checked over to get here, starting with the transport from Government House itself up to Thorness.

Then, finally, once through the gates, they spread out, apparently unconsciously, Tash thought, and looked around. None too subtle guards, some Chinese, some with FIS peacekeeper emblems, dispersed among them, watching carefully.

And within the wall Tash saw an enclosed patch of lunar terrain, littered with *stuff*: flags, photographs, models, statues, even a few flickering hologram images. Tributes to the alien.

The single most obvious human landmark visible within the wall's curtain was what looked like a squat boiler, a cylinder metres high, panelled with what might be aluminium, surrounded with a kind of ribbing, for structural strength or heat management, maybe.

Fred Bowles, breathing hard with the effort, murmured over their shared radio link, 'What the hell is that?'

'I'm not sure,' Charlie Marlowe replied, 'but I believe it's Chinese. Their tribute to the Park. I'll try to find out.'

Bowles just snorted. 'Well, that's just typical.' He glanced around at his entourage. 'Makes our contribution look like a Christmas cracker toy. But – quality rather than quantity, eh? Let's hope Galaxias has good taste.'

'Or a sense of humour,' Grace murmured.

'I heard that,' Bowles snapped. 'Come on, let's get on with it . . .'

They walked deeper in, past the human clutter.

And right at the heart of the walled compound was a mound of dirt – that was what it looked like, nothing more, a shallow heaping – surrounded by a bank of cameras and other scientific gear, and a ring of human soldiers, each heavily armed in some kind of battle suit – most but not all Chinese and FIS. A drone camera drifted overhead, tiny squirts of propellant exhaust balancing the low lunar gravity.

Tash had seen many images of this. She shivered. *That was it*. The lurker inside its mound – or maybe the mound itself was part of it. An alien technology, just paces away from where *she* was standing. And, assuming it was technology, it was so subtle, so simple, it made the human devices look like children's toys.

Always interested in human reactions, Tash glanced at her companions. Fred Bowles stared in open wonder. Mel seemed more conflicted. She had been here before, Tash remembered; now she seemed more distracted, or dismayed, by the gathering collection of human clutter.

But Grace looked more – calculating. As if weighing up an enemy.

The Astronomer Royal took charge for now. 'Shall we start, Fred? Very well. Cameras set up? . . .'

There was no single camera operator. They all wore microdot cameras on chest and helmet, and now a couple more drones hovered overhead. Tash knew that all these feeds would be combined into a three-dimensional diorama to be sent back to Earth, both for the news channels, and for history.

'So,' Bowles began. 'For the record. Here we are. In Monument Park, Sinus Medii, Luna. We are grateful for the hospitality of China, the other nations, and the FIS, who are cooperating to make this – remarkable – location a safe and secure place. And who have made us welcome today. I will leave it to the Astronomer Royal to explain the significance of this place, and what we are about to see.'

Charlie stepped forward. 'Thank you, Minister.'

She kept her enunciation clear and deliberate, Tash noted with some admiration.

'So. Sinus Medii. Media savvy. The Middle Bay. Once this spot would have been dead centre of the visible face of the Moon, as seen from Earth. The middle, as in the name. But now, as we know, since the Blink, the Moon has been turning slowly on its axis away from its old orientation, so that at times this spot looks away from the Earth entirely.

'Taking what's buried here with it.'

She led the way towards that mound of dirt at the centre of the wall's enclosure. She had to weave a path through a rough inner ring of previously placed monuments, mostly flags, a few statues of leaders or gods. Some more enigmatic offerings: a lump of rock from Iceland, Tash noticed, a basaltic gift to this planet of basalt. All of this was dominated by the huge Chinese structure, though.

Marlowe continued, 'Strange to think that before Blink Day there was pretty much nothing here.' She pointed. 'Nothing but that central mound and what it contains, and only two human artefacts . . .'

The now infamous Surveyor 6, a spindly frame in its own

small walled compound – and the later US spy probe, unnamed, now removed. The Surveyor was individually guarded, Tash saw. Mel murmured in a closed loop that such precautions hadn't been necessary when she was here back in May. But Tash knew that given the revelation of a decades-long cover-up of the evidence it had supplied of an alien artefact on the Moon, the American probe had itself become a secondary target of terrorism – especially by conspiracy theorists who thought there *was* no Galaxias, and all this was got up by an American-Chinese cabal.

'. . . And now, all this,' Marlowe said. 'Monuments. Gifts, if you like. Ambiguous symbols, perhaps. But a human response that has gathered momentum ever since we determined there is indeed an alien artefact buried in that central mound – the so-called lurker – a probe we associate with the phenomenon of Galaxias, by Occam's razor—'

'Keep it basic, Charlie,' murmured Bowles.

Marlowe sighed. 'Very well. Edit. We have evidence of two incursions of alien intelligence in the Solar System: the Blink itself, of course, and now this artefact on the Moon. It's simplest to assume that the two things are connected. We do have *some* direct evidence of that connection, in the lump of water ice that the lurker apparently fired off on Blink Day.

'And we have to believe, do we not, that this – engine – is watching us now, as it may have watched us for thousands of years? Or more – perhaps for hundreds of *millions* of years. The Moon is stable enough for that.' She tipped back; Tash could see she was looking up at the black sky. Marlowe went on, 'And through its eyes, Galaxias watches us. Perhaps. Which is why we, I suppose, at a national and individual level, have come here. An attempt to show Galaxias who we are . . .'

'All this reminds me of the Pioneer plaque,' Mel murmured to

Tash via a closed circuit. 'Fixed to Pioneer 10, remember, which was the first to break out of the Solar System and apparently the trigger for Galaxias to take an interest in us. *That* was an attempt to communicate. Images of people. Science data. Just in case somebody out there ever found it. Here we go again. This is the Pioneer plaque spread out on the surface of the Moon, before the eye of the alien . . .'

'. . . As I look around I see flags. Images. Technological achievements. Statues, mostly of people, not all – there is an exquisite tree carved from coral over there. And apart from the national gestures, there are contributions from other sorts of groups – religions, artists, musicians. Some sent by families, some by individuals. People even want to set up live feeds on screens, just to show the lurker how we live. Well, why not? Certainly this has turned into a display of the diversity and richness of our culture. And now, it is the proud turn of the English Federation to make our own contribution. And *cut*.'

Fred Bowles grunted. 'Well done, Charlie. This is all rather touching, now I see it. But – off the record. All this junk. Wistful. Don't you think? When I stand here and look at it all. Like a child trying to get its parents' attention. And then there's that bloody great oil tank from the Chinese. Off the record still. Does *anybody* have the slightest clue what that is? Charlie?'

Marlowe hesitated. 'Well, it's no oil tank. To me, and this is off the record too – and just on the evidence of what I see here, and some feedback from colleagues I've been asking – I think they might be building something like a tokomak.'

'A what-now?'

'The core of a fusion reactor, or at least one of the old experimental designs. To get nuclear fusion you need to squeeze hydrogen to extremes of pressure and temperature, and the way you do *that*, if you aren't at the heart of the Sun where you have gravity to help, is with magnetic fields. Very intense. And you get *those* by running powerful electrical currents through – well, through an architecture like that.'

Tash said, 'Actually I'm surprised they were allowed to bring something so big inside this cordon. Given the room it takes up and the security implications.'

Bowles said, 'Oh, I imagine there were protests. But the Chinese, on the whole, get what the Chinese want, on the Moon anyhow. I mean, how could we stop them? But *why* would the Chinese want to build something like that, here? Is it safe? Could it be construed as a weapon by Galaxias? Even if that's not the conscious intent.'

Marlowe said, 'I think that's moot. I'm sure this is only a demonstration set-up. The question is why the Chinese want to *show* this to the lurker, and Galaxias. What message are they trying to send? *That's* the question.'

Mel sounded puzzled too. 'Maybe there's more to come. I mean, we know that elsewhere on the Moon, and on analogy sites in Earth, the Chinese are experimenting with automation, industry. Replication, as we know. Maybe this is just another component of that, a part of some eventual . . . complete installation. Which nobody has guessed at yet.'

'And which nobody outside Beijing knows about,' Bowles said with a sigh. 'Well, let's hope that whatever they eventually unveil will do more good than harm. Although for sheer bulk it puts our feeble effort to shame, doesn't it?'

'Oh, come on, Fred, cheer up,' Marlowe said. 'We're English, remember? It's class, not mass, that counts.'

'Quite right, of course, Astronomer Royal. Well said. So let's get this done before this suit starts to itch. I know our allotted site is just over there.' He pointed to a patch of bare ground, delineated by small tokens: symbols of the federal English, Scottish, Irish, Welsh, others.

'I'll lead, sir,' Grace said, stepping forward. 'If I may.'

Bowles appeared to shrug, a gesture largely masked by his suit.

Grace went back to the external gate and briskly organised the handful of pressure-suited locals who had lugged the monument in its container here from the rovers. Now they picked up the package again, hauled it across the much-trampled lunar ground through the gate and into the walled compound, and carefully set it down, standing erect.

These worker bees, marching clumsily by, probably all had PhDs, Tash thought.

Then Grace herself opened the box by punching a key code into a panel. Automated, the box opened and folded itself out of the way.

Tash looked on curiously. With security being as tight as it was, as far as she knew only Grace had the set-up codes for this thing – and Tash herself didn't know what the British gift to the Monument Park was going to be; she hadn't even seen the shortlist.

What was brought out of the casing was a pillar, itself perhaps a metre and a half tall, mounted on a stiff metal rod perhaps twice as long. The pillar, with transparent panels, contained something she couldn't quite see – books, perhaps.

The set-up was obvious. More gofers brought tools from the MoonBus: a standing frame, a drill. Bowles himself was asked to make the final selection of a suitable spot. Then the gofers set up their frame, positioned the heavy duty drill, and let it create a fine hole in the regolith, some metres deep judging by the drill head's smooth descent.

The task looked easy, but took several minutes. Tash did know this rig was adapted from essentially scientific gear, meant for extracting Moon rock samples from deep underground, or for probing the heat flow from the Moon's interior. Expensive, finely tooled stuff, hauled here at huge expense, borrowed for the day, made fit for the purpose of erecting a monument before an alien artefact.

Grace wandered over. 'For the record for you science types, they're telling me this site is typical of the Moon. When it comes to sticking stuff into it, I mean. The surface is dust smashed up by minor impacts, and a few metres down you get huge boulders created by more major impacts. It's all gaps and hard lumps, and you need a bit of skill to drill deep, and securely. But – there we are, they've got it done. Now then . . .'

She went back over and led the next manoeuvre personally. The team lifted the monument from its final casing and removed a soft inner wrap. Then they cradled pillar and stand, and lifted it high until the stand was over the drilled hole, into which it slid smoothly.

'Could have been tricky,' Mel said to Tash. 'An awkward object like that in the lunar gravity. Thick gloves, inflexible suits. But those graduate student types are obviously used to it all. Don't really need Grace fussing around, I wouldn't think.'

'Oh, Grace is pretty essential,' Tash said. 'Because Grace is the only one of us with the whole series of set-up security codes in her head. The monument will be powered – it has to be, to protect its contents from the lunar conditions – and so has to have location codes and identity beacons and such built in. Security protocols, required by the FIS committee that is doing its best to oversee this place. So when the speeches are done Grace will enter a final code to switch it all on, to identify it as harmless to the local security system. And we can leave the contents in safety.'

'What contents?' Mel asked.

'Well, even I don't know,' Tash said. 'One last layer of security.'

She glanced over at Bowles, who was already standing by the monument, ready to make the short dedication speech that he had come all this way to deliver. Another aide called for them both to lift their Sun visors, for the duration of the announcement, so their faces could be seen by the audiences on Earth. Bowles had last-minute second thoughts about that, and ordered all those in shot, including Grace, to lift their visors too, and look at the cameras. There should be no hidden faces in the final image.

When they were ready, Bowles nodded to Grace. She tapped a hidden control in the pillar – whose surface now turned entirely transparent, to reveal what was evidently a very ancient book, open on a wooden stand.

'My name is Fred Bowles, science minister of the Federal States of England, and today representing all the nations and peoples of the British Isles and dependencies. I, with Astronomer Royal Professor Charlotte Marlowe and our team, are here on the surface of the Moon – at the Sinus Medii, the so-called Monument Park – where we are unveiling the British contribution to this remarkable, almost spontaneous effort. A gesture of welcome, of celebration . . .'

Tash knew what would be going through his mind now. It was absolutely crucial for England to get hold of the hosting of the November FIS conference. And this was one of the government's best chances to pitch for that prize. So it was absolutely clear, she thought a little cynically, that Bowles's primary audience was human, not extraterrestrial. And now the gift, the big reveal.

'What we contribute here is a selection from the journals of Captain James Cook. That is, the original manuscripts from the British Library collection.

'You can see that we have arranged for these ancient documents to be protected from the Sun's unfiltered light by this pillar; it will become transparent at a touch, opaque by default. Artificial light will illuminate the whole installation in the lunar night.

'Cook was a British explorer of the eighteenth century. He greatly enhanced the science of exploration itself – navigation, sustenance, the health of his crews – and the knowledge of the world, for the benefit of his own nation, and ultimately for the benefit of humanity in general.

'But there was a dark side to his story. As a representative of an imperial power, Cook "claimed" territories such as Australia for Britain, regardless of the wishes of the peoples already living there. Local people were injured or killed, their artefacts plundered. It was part of Cook's job; he did it effectively and efficiently.

'Why, then, do we choose to celebrate such an ambiguous figure here and now?

'Because we, the modern British governments and successors to the regime that sent Cook out, feel that we humans should show the whole truth about ourselves to Galaxias. We are imperfect creatures – all our past is ambiguous – but we are learning. We can celebrate Cook's explorations while expressing dismay over, and apologising for, their adverse impact. We are scientists. We are technologists. We are explorers. We are immature, even in our dealings with each other. *But we are capable of improvement.* That is what we want Galaxias to understand . . .'

With one gloved hand Bowles touched the pillar in which the Cook papers rested in their casket. A casket that now filled with light, revealing ancient, curled pages.

Tash shivered. Some instinct made her glance over at the lurker mound. *Are you watching, Galaxias? Even now?*

And, she saw, Grace Butterworth grinned widely, as if she had achieved some personal goal.

28

October 2057

Noel Brand opened the door of the flat in Manors to his daughter.

'You're late. Mel and Jane are here already.'

Tash, standing on the doorstep, felt faintly bewildered.

She watched her government-issue smart car drive away, to find its way back across the river to Gateshead, and ultimately Government House. The rain was falling gently. There was a faint smell of ash in the air. It was cold for an October lunch time. But then it was always cold.

To get everything done this morning, to get away from House at all in time to be here for the Lodestone announcement, she had had to follow an intricate timetable, improvising with the usual fudges and pushbacks when things didn't go to plan. All of which had crowded her head until she had got here, at this moment. But now she heard the boom of the wall TV in the background. Somehow that mundane noise was the trigger that dragged her back to reality, as if some invisible piece of elastic had suddenly wrenched her soul here, long after the car that had delivered her body. She was here. And all that planning and tracking and anxiety could just melt away.

'I'm sorry, Dad, I've been kind of busy. Ever since we got back from the Moon—'

'I know, I know.' His tone softened a little. 'I'm sorry. Are you OK?'

'Yeah. Arriving in little bits, maybe.'

'Come here.' Noel stepped out, wrapped her in a reasonable simulacrum of the big bear hugs she had so relished as a little girl. 'You're here, now. With us. Sorry to be a grouse. Come in out of the damn rain. You work too hard, but you can always leave the burden of government at *this* door . . .'

He let her go, and she followed him inside, hanging her coat in the small porch.

But not before, guiltily, fishing her phone out of her coat pocket.

In the living room, Mel and Jane were already here, and the big wall TV screen was bright. It played sombre music, and was dominated by the Jones, Inc., logo, the famous swoosh-and-spaceship. Tash vaguely wondered how many channels were carrying this feed, relayed from the Lodestone, the space station tucked deep in the shadow of the Earth.

Anyhow she hadn't missed any of Serena Jones's latest Pioneer announcement, then – the reason they had all gathered here. Good. To her shame that was the first reaction: to clock her timing. Rather than to react to the people in the room.

Her father and Jane had evidently been sitting together on a sprawl of cushions before the big TV, while Mel was in an armchair, cradling phone and coffee cup in her hands.

Now both Mel and Jane got up and came over to Tash for a hug.

'Last to turn up as always, Auntie Tash,' Jane said.

Mel gave her long red hair a playful ruffle. 'Hey, don't be so rude!'

Jane snorted. 'And it's word for word what you said when

Tash rang the bell, so don't get all hypocritical on me, Mum.'

Noel hung back. 'Good vocabulary, Jane. Hypocritical. If a bit harsh. Would you like a drink of something, Natasha? Coffee, tea – I've got some non-alco brandy to toast – well, whatever it is Jones is going to be announcing today, and I admit I'm a little vague about that.'

'You could get some proper brandy in for my birthday in December,' Jane said.

Mel pursed her lips. 'Yes, we know about your birthday, thank you.'

'Some tea would be fine, Dad,' Tash said.

'Tea it is.' Noel bustled off to the kitchen.

Jane fell back on her cushions. She was tall for her age, now nearly twelve, lithe – a promising high-jumper, Mel had once said – with that shock of red hair to rival Mel's own. 'You can come sit with us and watch the big screen, Auntie Tash. Which is what all my friends will be doing. Or you can sit with Mum in a chair and watch it all by yourself on your phone, the old-fashioned way. I don't mind, really.'

'I heard you, young person,' Noel called from the kitchen. '"The old-fashioned way." Phones, the old-fashioned way now. Ha! My old dad would have liked to hear that. Addicted to his phone, he was.'

Tash said, 'I'll compromise. Maybe I've been around politicians too long.' She made her way to the floor cushions. 'I'll sit with you and the TV, *and* watch my phone, if that's OK. I might get a call.'

In came Noel with a couple of mugs of tea; he stiffly bent over to hand one to Tash, kept the other for himself, sat on an upright chair. 'You mean, you *will* get a call.'

Mel glanced over. 'Do I understand correctly what this is? More details of the Pioneer project, right?'

'Some of them,' Tash said. 'Whatever Serena Jones thinks will sell a few more bits of space kit, probably.'

'So all of your colleagues in Government House will be watching this, will they? Fred Bowles. That bodyguard of his.'

Tash had to smile. 'Grace? She's a political adviser, officially.'

'A political adviser who used to be in the Marines? Have to say I've always felt there's something – more to her than that. She always seems to *know* more. When we were on the Moon . . . Just a feeling.'

That puzzled Tash. 'Fred does cling to her a bit, I suppose.' Maybe Tash herself was too close to see it. 'Anyhow I do know they roped in poor Charlie to advise today.'

'As ever,' Mel said. 'You should hear her complain about the work time she's losing.'

'Yes, but Charlie is still one of the few authentic scientist types Fred and his team will listen to. Or, *can* listen to. She's just too good at what she does.'

Noel leaned over, and ruffled Tash's hair much as Mel had ruffled Jane's. 'You're never off duty, are you? Very proud of you. Serena Jones, though. I read they are calling this new space shot a Sputnik, aren't they? You know, my dad, who I mentioned before—'

Mel nodded. 'Very calculating of Serena Jones, if you ask me. Using names like Pioneer and Sputnik. Plundering space history for dog whistles.'

'Oh, I don't know,' Tash said. 'I think we're all still reeling from the Blink. It doesn't hurt to be reminded of achievements from the past. And I think she means it as a sincere tribute—'

'Speaking of your grandfather,' Noel said, a little more forcefully.

Tash suppressed a smile. 'Yes, Dad?'

'He was actually born on Sputnik Day, you know: 4 October, 1957. So—'

'Oh!' said Jane. 'So he's a hundred. Just.'

'Would have been, Jane. Died – oh, thirty years ago. Tash never really knew him. But, yes, he was born with the Space Age. Of course he didn't remember Sputnik 1 itself. He would say he was told later that the family had gathered around the wireless – the radio – listening to the relay of the beep-beep signal coming down from Sputnik, that one satellite in orbit, passing overhead. With him a babe in arms, newborn. No TV for them, back then, they couldn't afford it! But he remembered the family watching the big space shots together later, gathered around the telly. Black and white, until, I don't know, Apollo 8 maybe? He once showed me a diary he kept during that week when Apollo 13 was in trouble. He was only twelve, I think. Your age, Jane. So you be as "modern" as you like. Just think of him, listening and watching with the family, all those years ago.'

Tash raised her tea mug. 'To Grandad, then. Happy Sputnik birthday.'

They all raised their cups.

And the TV music stopped, mid-bar. They all stared at the big screen.

Where the spaceship-and-swoosh dissolved, to reveal the face of Serena Jones.

She wore a practical blue jumpsuit with that corporate logo on her sleeve. She was *floating*, drifting in the air, her loose grey hair a starburst around her head, against the background of a typical space habitat.

Serena gazed into the camera, not yet speaking.

Jane pulled a face. 'Why isn't she talking?'

Tash smiled. 'Because she doesn't have to. Not for a few seconds. She's got much of the world's collective attention just now. We're watching her, aren't we? And she isn't going to refrain from milking it.'

'Wherever you are on planet Earth, or off it,' Serena said at last, 'good day to you, and thank you for your attention. What I wish to share with you is a significant milestone in the development of Project Pioneer, as we announced it back in May, our response to the Blink and the evident presence in all our lives of the entity known as Galaxias, in all our futures. A response by a coalition of nations, a partnership led by the American unions . . .'

A partnership including the English, Tash knew, and the Russians, and the Japanese, and the Brazilians – almost everybody not directly bound into the parallel and still more mysterious effort being mounted by the Chinese.

'On the technical level too, while we at Jones, Inc. have led the overall development itself, we have enjoyed significant support from partners such as the Jet Propulsion Laboratory in Pasadena, the French Institute of—'

'Boring,' said Jane.

'. . . As many of you will know, we chose to call our conceptual spacecraft – the final product, a vessel that will be capable of traversing distances beyond the scale of the Solar System itself – after Pioneer 10, the first human artefact to escape the Solar System altogether. A fragile little ship that nevertheless seems to have caught the eye of an entity on the scale of a Galaxy.

'And in not many minutes from now we will complete a first step to building that ship. As you can see I'm expecting the imminent conclusion of a proving mission we actually launched fully three weeks ago. A test flight of our new propulsion technology, as it were. It's not fast, as you will see. It's not *big* – not compared to what will follow. But it is the first of its kind.

'So we decided to name our first test shot after a still earlier triumph in space – almost exactly a hundred years back – an achievement which delivered, if anything, an even more shattering conceptual breakthrough for all humanity. Sputnik 1: the very first satellite to reach orbit, launched by engineering geniuses within the old Soviet Union . . .'

Noel grinned. 'Told you so.'

'. . . Well, there were three Sputniks in all. After that the Soviets began new programmes of satellites, under new names.

'And so, a century later, I give you – *Sputnik 4.*'

Jones's image dissolved, to reveal what looked like, to Tash, at first glance, just a sail: a circular disc of some fine fabric, hanging in a starry sky, with narrow lanyards attaching it to a small spherical pod. *Very* fine fabric. Tash could see the stars shining through it. And a *very* small pod, in comparison with the sail's diameter, just a pixel. There was evidently no sunlight; the craft seemed to be illuminated by hovering lanterns.

Jane snorted. 'Is that it?'

'Hush,' Mel whispered. She glanced at Tash. 'Remember the mock-ups we saw at NASA Ames? Well, here's a working prototype, it looks like. Impressive.'

'. . . feel free to explore the data as you like,' Jones was saying. 'You can download a fully interactive model – though there isn't much in the way of detailed engineering to inspect, as you may have guessed.

'The central pod is a standard piece of Jones, Inc. kit. A bus for a lightweight automated satellite or probe. Masses only a few kilogrammes, out of a total of sixty or so for the complete craft. On top of the main bus are spools for the scoop lanyards, and we have mini bots capable of climbing out along the lanyards to achieve simple repairs. The craft has standard instrumentation, such as accelerometers, attitude sensors, position control sensors – everything you'd expect on a test flight such as this. No crew, of course. Obviously. The final version, much larger, will hold three crew.

'And that scoop you see, even though it masses just sixty kilogrammes, is *ten kilometres* across . . .'

Jane goggled. 'Ten kilometres? I've never even walked ten kilometres in one go—'

'Graphene,' Mel said immediately. 'Got to be. Very fine, very light fabric. One carbon atom thick.'

'. . . I know, it looks like a sail. Now, we have already successfully used sails in space, sails that trap the pressure of sunlight. But the principle which drives Sputnik 4 is rather different.

'In fact Sputnik 4 was launched in the long cone of Earth's sunlight shadow, cast behind the night side. A place where there is no sunlight at all. This was a deliberate choice; we wanted to be able to test the scoop without any interference – although in the final Pioneer mission profile we may use sunlight to boost our launch. In the end, though, this ship is designed to work far, far from the Sun, where even that intense blaze of light is diminished to a kind of brighter starlight.

'And the scoop works on a different principle altogether, by gathering—'

'Dark energy!' Jane paused the broadcast. She looked around. 'Anybody think we can skip this bit? She said it all in May, *and* we had to read up about it at school.'

Mel raised an eyebrow. 'So you know all about dark energy? I work for the Astronomer Royal, and *she* doesn't know what dark energy is, not for sure.'

Tash just shrugged. 'Oh, why not? Jane is probably right. Thank the Lord for catch-up. Let's leave it on pause. Dad, I imagine you have some food ready to serve?'

'Of course I do. I baked you a cake.'

'Of course you did.'

'Sit tight . . .'

With a rich fruit cake and more tea distributed, Jane somewhat grumpily resumed the recording. She fast-forwarded until she detected, somehow, that Jones had started talking less about how the Pioneer would be driven, and more about where it was going to be driven to.

'. . . So in summary the essence of the drive is a minor miracle: using its scoop, it gathers up energy from that sparse field, and converts that to a usable form — specifically, kinetic energy. The energy of motion. And *that* is how the dark energy drive works — or at least, that's all our patent lawyers will allow me to say about it at this time.

'And here comes that ship, live in your homes, our pride and joy . . .'

Now the screen split to show a double image: of Jones, and a star field, deep black.

Noel groaned. 'What a ham.'

Tash hushed him reflexively.

'. . . Sputnik 4 was launched in darkness, in the shadow of Earth. For three weeks Sputnik 4 has been sailing, fuelled *only* by dark energy, away from the Sun, away from the Earth. We track its position quite precisely, and it should be exiting the shadow cone soon. From here we should see that clearly . . .' Jones made a show of consulting a heavy wristwatch. 'Any second now . . .'

'That's a Rolex,' Noel said, leaning forward to see. 'Like the first lunar astronauts wore. I remember that. She gets every detail right, doesn't she?'

Against the star field, a broad disc abruptly flared into light.

Tash was amused to hear applause in Serena's own background.

Noel grinned. 'OK, I give in. What a show.'

Mel smiled, but more tightly. 'More like, what a sales pitch.'

Serena was still talking. '. . . But what is more significant is where we intend the dark energy drive to take us. Once our Sputnik mission is done, once Pioneer has finished its trials . . .

'Well, you know the pitch by now. *We intend to emulate Pioneer 10*. Simple as that. We will push our ship beyond solar escape velocity – but this time a ship crewed by humans. Humans on their way to the stars, in defiance of the prohibition Galaxias seems to have handed down in response to Pioneer 10. The very first such mission to carry a crew.'

'Oh, shit,' Mel said.

Jane nudged her. 'Mum!'

'I won't take up much more of your time today. At the November FIS conference on post-Blink strategies, I, sponsored by the American governments, will make a pitch for international support to build, and request assistance with resources for, the full-scale Pioneer 14, to be constructed on these demonstrated principles. I am aware that other proposals will be made – other candidate responses to the Galaxias crisis. Well, we are still a rich world, and need not compete. In fact our response to Galaxias ought to be multiple, diverse – experimental, if you like.

'For that is our nature: argumentative, helpful, supportive, seeking the answers together. In contrast to the dismal isolation of Galaxias.

'We will reveal more of our final design in November. And we trust that others will emulate our openness.'

Mel grunted. 'A dig at the Chinese.'

'So, that's it from me. Thank you for your patience. For now I will close with one more detail, no less significant. As I told you this human ship will be under the control of a human crew. And now we can meet them all . . .'

Into view came three astronauts in blue jumpsuits, with swoop-and-spaceship logos on their breasts, posing awkwardly in some cramped cabin, weightless.

Serena said, 'You'll recognise them. Two survivors of the Al-miriykh mission to Mars: Marina Petko, Ito Katsuo. Victims on Blink Day and now heroes, facing the dark. And, as you know, one of my staff here on the Lodestone — a man who lost his own fiancé to the Blink — Wu Zhi.'

'Oh, shit,' said Mel again.

'Mum!' Jane said gleefully.

Tash eyed Mel bleakly. 'So Zhi *is* going. I had hoped that she'd quietly drop him. I mean, because of the attitude *we've* seen. He's broken, is what he is, and shouldn't be going anywhere for a long time. And I wonder how his mother is feeling right now.'

'I'll break out that non-alco brandy,' Noel said.

'Or something stronger, Dad,' Tash said.

29

November 2057

On the day the FIS conference opened, Fred Bowles's team were to fly in from Gateshead, boarding an RAF helicopter from the pad on the roof of Government House. From there it would be a direct hop across the Middle Sea to New Aberdeen. They were to leave at seven in the morning.

Another conference, Tash thought. Another all-nighter to prepare. Another damn chopper flight, on no sleep. But if you missed the flight, you didn't go.

At the appointed hour, gathering for the flight, they all took shelter in, as Tash said to Mel, what had to be the world's most primitive departure lounge: little more than a shack on this flat grass-covered roof, with no facilities save a lavatory, a water dispenser and not enough hard metal chairs. It was cold too, and the building frame creaked and banged ominously as yet another autumn storm barrelled in from the north Atlantic. At least the cloudy sky didn't trigger her post-Blink phobias.

'Look on the bright side,' Mel said, heavily sarcastic. 'At least you came prepared.'

Mel herself, Tash observed resentfully, was dressed sensibly, in sweater and jeans under a thick, hooded, waterproof winter coat. Whereas the best Tash could do was a heavy coat over a business suit. But then Mel wouldn't be pitched into diplomatic-level meetings the minute they landed at Dogger Island – even if her boss would be, the Astronomer Royal visibly uncomfortable in her own voluminous parka and padded trousers.

'Anyhow, here comes our flight . . .'

The chopper, buffeted back and forth by the rooftop wind, came down with a roar that rattled the windows of the boxy shelter. Tash could see a human pilot at the controls, still standard protocol in military vehicles – and a not uncommon sight now, post-Blink, even on civilian craft. Under a ragged magnetosphere and ionosphere, smart systems weren't to be trusted as they had once been.

Once the chopper was down, clamps pushed out to secure it to the roof, and doors were thrown open. A couple of squaddies briskly lined up the passengers and began passing them through the doors – each of them wand-scanned quickly, for one last security check.

The wind on the roof, when Tash was exposed to it as she crossed the few metres to the chopper steps, was like a punch in the face, and it clutched at her coat, making her stagger. More post-Blink turbulence, she knew, as the atmosphere and oceans continued to slosh eleven months after the great jolt of that sunless day. All boiling down to this viciously cold wind in the small hours of a November Gateshead morning.

A squaddie had to help drag Tash up the couple of steps into the machine.

But once she was inside, and once the last passenger was boarded and the door banged closed – once she sank back into a Skylon-type smart seat which enfolded her like a parent's hug – she felt her eyes slide shut.

She heard murmurings around her – Mel talking to Marlowe, Grace and Fred speaking softly. But soon the conversation died down. Fred had promised that there would be no work on the flight. They had done all they could; they had worked flat out for days, and even over nights; they needed to be as fresh as possible as they faced the task that would swallow them up for more days and nights – a task that would start as soon as they landed.

Tash fumbled on heavy headphones, so that only the deepest bass sounds of the engine reached her. And, as the chopper thrust into the sky, as she was pushed back gently into her seat, she fell into a deep sleep.

She woke once during the flight.

Mel touched her shoulder, pointed. Tash stirred, and looked out of the window. The sky was unusually clear, and she could see that the helicopter was flying over a great dam, a straight line drawn across grey, choppy waters, where fragmented morning sunlight glimmered.

Tash tried to think it through. 'That *is* the North Dyke, right? Five hundred kilometres of dam between Scotland and Norway . . . New Aberdeen is far south of here. We're a hundred kilometres off course.'

'No. Well, yes. Take it easy. We're having to skirt a big storm system. We won't be late; everybody else has the same issues getting there, and they are already rescheduling the conference sessions. I just thought you'd like to see this. I once drove over the English Channel dyke, but that's only a couple of hundred kilometres long, if that . . .'

Tash stared, fascinated. 'This kind of experience reminds me I spend too much of my life in stuffy windowless rooms. Is the water already a little bluer on this side of the dyke? Umm, the south side?'

'Maybe. It's hard to tell through these tinted windows. The

Middle Sea, the enclosed bit of the North Sea, *is* turning into a big freshwater lake, slowly. Like earlier enclosures in the Netherlands. There'll be a whole new ecosystem, ultimately, as well as a defence against rising sea levels.'

Tash smiled. 'They closed off a whole *sea*. Tremendous project.'

'Yeah. Just think, to a North Sea cod we humans must seem to have the power of Galaxias.'

'Hmm. Not entirely a comfortable thought.'

And she sank back into sleep for a blissful few minutes more.

The next time she woke, she was over New Aberdeen.

Dogger Island itself was another extraordinary sight. Huge wind turbine towers thrust out of the water – each, she knew, as tall as the Eiffel Tower – a forest of tall smartwood buildings fenced in by a network of artificial islands and sea walls. The sea had always been shallow here, only tens of metres deep, and now the bed had been sculpted and raised up by human actions.

Mel leaned past her again, looking out. 'What a sight. Heroic stuff from the last generation. And a rare cooperation between Scotland and England—'

'Maybe. But never mind the past. *There*' – Tash pointed down to an array of buildings, smartwood peppered with aluminium and glass and surrounded by air fields and runways – 'there is where, in the next couple of days, we might make a little history of our own.'

'Or not.'

'Or not,' Tash conceded.

The New Aberdeen Conference Centre, the NACC, co-owned by the Dutch, English and Scottish governments and under the nominal management of the Royal Societies of London and Edinburgh, was a series of domes, surrounded by covered walkways leading to landing strips and pads – and with the tremendous turbine towers like a forest above them. The big domes enclosed conference facilities, plus a range of top-class hotels and leisure outlets.

All of which was designed, as Tash knew from government briefings, to entice distinguished guests from overseas to linger a little longer, and spend a little more. Tash herself had never been here before apart from a single one-day helicopter trip, years back. Her father had said it was ridiculous. Like a huge James Bond movie set. Well, there *was* a casino. And it was profitable, or had been before the Blink. It was certainly striking.

Further out, Tash saw, the fringe of this man-made island was indented by docks, and a sprawling company town: New Aberdeen itself, the name a reminder of the folk who had built this place and now largely inhabited and maintained it, a huge transfer from the mainland city of the energies, expertise, even some of the infrastructure of the abandoned offshore oil industry. And these days the old oil fields were, ironically, being used for carbon sequestration: black stuff being pumped *back* into the undersea geology.

But there wasn't going to be a lot of time for sightseeing this time. Not like that day with her father, poking around Neolithic artefacts retrieved from a sea bed that had once been dry land, or peering at tanks of the gen-enged fish that populated this enclosed sea during its transition from salt to fresh . . .

She checked her watch. The conference sessions should already have started, unless the timetable had changed again.

The chopper set down smoothly.

The passengers were disembarked quickly. A military escort and civilian security greeted them at the first of the domes they

312

entered, where they were able to freshen up, dump their flight gear, and open their luggage for inspection – some changed their clothes, hastily, in closet-sized changing rooms before the luggage was taken off to sleeping quarters they would have to find later.

They briskly formed up into teams – Tash joining the one surrounding Charlie Marlowe and Fred Bowles – and dispersed to their assignments.

Fred being a government minister, his very first stop was a roomy meet-and-greet reception area. Under a huge semi-transparent dome, brightly lit, this space was crowded with suits already – and many with glasses in hand, though it wasn't long past noon. Tash recognised politicians from around the world, industrialists, journalists – even an expensive soccer player who had turned out to be an influencer of opinion concerning the impact of Galaxias, 'a great referee in the sky', as she had put it. Floating drones served more drinks. Tash grabbed a glass of water. Somewhere, a piano played.

As soon as they were spotted, people crowded around Bowles and Marlowe. But the pair knew the drill. They pushed forward, like, Tash thought vaguely, oceanic metaphors in her mind, the prow of a trawler, with their attendants – including herself – and would-be petitioners trailing behind like opportunistic seagulls. And Grace Butterworth, with other guards, kept a wary eye out.

Tash found herself staring up at the domed roof itself. Huge Dutch, English and Scottish flags were suspended from a frame below a wooden ceiling, along with the blue FIS flag, the flags of other nations forming a background array. She knew that this ultra-modern building was ultra-smart, constructed almost entirely of enhanced wood, and capable of maintaining its interior climate almost exclusively by feeding off the energy flows from Sun above and Earth below. A smart, modern background behind a chaotic human foreground.

And, post the Blink, it all seemed unreasonably fragile, like a vast bubble.

After a while Marlowe came bustling up to Tash and Mel, bearing a glass of cola. From the look of it her suit was even more uncomfortable than Tash's.

'I need a break already. Quite a show, isn't it? I've already bounced off half a dozen conversations. Like gas molecules in a box. Pretty exhausting, actually. But maybe it's working. I'm finding out that there are sidebar discussions planned on a range of topics – not just the Galaxias response initiatives. It's as if people have been saving stuff up for this big session: let's get it all aired while the influencers are gathered, and with the heads of state themselves on the way.'

Tash replaced her own empty glass of water with a full one from a solicitous drone. 'What kind of stuff, so far? I'll brief Fred if I can.'

'You name it,' Marlowe said. 'More post-Blink mitigation measures, of course, especially the large-scale international stuff. The geologists are saying we must expect a big volcanic episode sometime in the next few years. Dwarfing Rainier, I mean, and even the hypercane undersea event. Preparations are under way for that, in outline, though the likely location hasn't been pinned down yet. Umm – major climate shifts to come, in general, as the new yearly cycle settles down. Deserts and wet zones on the march. They're expecting an upsurge in migration, worldwide.'

'That's not good,' Tash murmured. 'Not to have that back again . . .'

Marlowe shook her head. 'Well, let's hope we can use the experience of the past few decades to do it better this time. Oh, hell, a world in turmoil. *Again*. But then, when is it not? That's even before we get to think about Galaxias itself, and what that means for our future. And here are gathered the brains who are going to manage it all. Or not. All in their suits and thousand-pound dresses. Well, all we can do is our best.' She looked around sourly and stepped a little closer to Tash. 'But, you know, functions like this – it does remind me of what I always disliked about the upper echelons of science in society, at least in England. Where it merges with the money, you know? Old money especially. Summer parties at some august hide-bound institution or other, full of people who are *comfortable* in dinner suits, and noisy small talk over the canapés – and talk probably entirely devoid of intellectual content, if you were to bother to analyse it.

'I'm the Astronomer Royal. At least I got that post on merit, and not because of which school I went to. Well, I think so. And I think I can deal with it, frankly. I can get business done. But I do resent it all.' She added grimly, 'It would be nice to think that this enormous shake-up we face will reform society for good. But if climate change didn't manage it – ah, hell, don't listen to me. Anyhow, come on, you two. Work to do. Follow me.'

She drained her cola, threw the glass over her shoulder, and walked on. Tash cringed, but the glass – actually probably un-breakable, lightweight clearwood – was fielded by a speeding drone, as Marlowe had surely known it would be.

Mel went to follow.

But Tash hung back.

'You're asking for me too? No – wait. Sorry, Charlie. I ought to stay close to Fred. That's my job.'

Marlowe stopped and called back. 'Not for the moment. I got you a pass. Check if you like. Grace knows.'

Tash shook her head, baffled. 'This is a FIS heads of government conference, on humanity's future relationship with a super-powered galactic intelligence. I'm here with a government minister. What can be more important than that?'

Marlowe smiled. 'Personal connections, that's what. Fred Bowles would agree. Communication beyond words.'

Mel asked, 'Connections to who?'

'To Wu Zhi.'

That stopped Tash in her tracks. 'Zhi? He's not even here? He's on the Lodestone—'

'But his mother's here. One of the keynote speakers. If not *the* key. Due to speak this afternoon, I think.'

'I know that,' Tash said. 'Of course I know that. What about her?'

'Right now I have her locked in a room. Not literally, I add for the benefit of the security bugs listening in. But she is in there. And I want you two – Shut-Ins?'

'In-Jokes,' Mel said.

'Whatever. To come help me talk to her. Persuade her. Look, I know you cornered her in Edinburgh that time, and got her to open up a little about the Chinese plans. I know she let Mel poke around that replicator-technology prototype on the Moon, although that was already out in the open. And I know she showed you around that set-up in Oregon, although the Americans had crawled over that already. It's as if she's trying, maybe not even consciously, to reach out to us. So let's help her.'

Tash glanced at Mel, uncomfortable. 'We have tried to get Yan and Zhi to connect. Mother and son—'

Marlowe sighed. 'I'm sorry to seem cynical, or manipulative. But this is too big. We've been pussyfooting around since the Blink. *This* conference is about getting the Chinese onside, any way we can – I agree with Bowles and the rest of them over the significance of that. And Wu Yan has always presented . . . an opportunity, to apply some leverage. Because she shows up, she *speaks* to us, however enigmatically. And so we have to do this, however cynical or manipulative it might seem. So, come on, I'll lead the way.' She pointed a finger at a drifting droid. 'You. Follow. Bring cola.' And she walked off again.

Mel took Tash's hand as they walked. 'Time to bow to the inevitable, kid.'

A couple of lifts and a moving walkway later, they followed Charlie into a small, luxuriously appointed side-office. Or maybe you could call it a hotel suite with business facilities; bedrooms were visible through open doors, and there was even a small kitchen space.

What looked to Tash like a policewoman – Chinese – opened the door to them. A little bubble of Chinese security within the British-Dutch lockdown, she thought.

Wu Yan was sitting, alone, at a table. Glasses and a water decanter before her, like a barricade. Alone aside from that lone cop, who stood by the door, watchful. Yan, tall, elegant as ever, was dressed in a sober brown robe. Serene. Tash always found her hugely impressive, she realised, even if Yan was nothing like her impulsive, emotional son.

For her part Yan seemed surprised to see Mel and Tash walk in after Charlie. Evidently somewhat confused, she made the best of it, stood up, and welcomed them with brief embraces, carefully monitored by the cop. Then, with the drinks-bearing drone outside, the cop closed the door.

'Come. Please. Sit.'

Mel and Tash brought up more chairs, and they, with Charlie, sat opposite Yan.

Yan glanced around. 'Oh – no drinks, save for this water. Would you care for coffees?'

Tash shrugged. Marlowe and Mel both nodded. 'Please.'

Yan looked at the cop by the door. 'Would you mind?'

The cop opened the door, and murmured to the drone that had followed Marlowe, still hovering outside, and it scooted off. When the drone had gone the cop resumed her silent station at the door, staring straight ahead.

'Thank you,' Marlowe said with a grin, 'that's a promising start. In terms of international cooperation. Sorry to be abrupt. And sorry for – well, all this, Yan.'

Wu Yan looked stern. 'This meeting was scheduled with you alone. And in walk these two.'

'I thought they might help . . . Look, this was all my idea. *Mea culpa*. Not approved by Fred Bowles, even. I just thought it was best to try to talk to you before the bun fight. Sorry if it feels like subterfuge.'

Yan folded her arms. 'It feels like emotional blackmail, once again. Over my son . . .'

A soft tap on the door. The cop opened it, and let in the drone, which hovered by the table, bearing a tray, coffee decanter, cream, cups.

They sat silently as the drone settled over the table, deposited its load, and poured out precise cups, responding to requests for cream and sugar.

Once again it left, through the door held by the cop. The cop resumed her station.

'Well, here we are,' Yan said. 'To talk about what?'

Marlowe leaned forward. 'Come now. Professor Wu, as you know, this afternoon is the key to the conference. Your presentation will immediately follow the Pioneer pitch – that's the two big events, everything lined up, before we all get conference fatigue. The *crucial* events we need to get done before the leaders show up.' Marlowe steepled her fingers. 'Now, look, I'm an astronomer, not a diplomat. But I do want this monster chinwag to go as well as possible. We have global problems; we need a global response. And in particular, right now I think we need global *consent* to the high-profile initiatives regarding Galaxias that are being proposed. And one of which, in a sense, you represent.'

Yan smiled. '"Represent" is the right word. I represent only. At best. We have spoken of this before. I cannot speak for the whole team I work with, let alone the relevant government ministries and the national leadership. But if I have been brought here to provide information – I know you are aware of our openness, on specifics. Why, I myself hosted Mel here on an inspection of our solar panel experiment on the Moon. And you had access to the Oregon site—'

'Right,' Marlowe said. 'You allowed limited but appropriate access. It's the way you do things, it seems. Normally. Dribbling out fragments. But, Professor Wu, now is not a normal time. Today is not a normal diplomatic conference. This isn't even a normal extraordinary international conference about a global crisis, if you see what I mean. Because we are moving fast now, aren't we? The Americans' spacecraft programme is ramping up, very visibly. Your industrial experiments on the Moon and elsewhere are gathering momentum. All this in plain view of Galaxias, of the lurker, we have to assume.' Marlowe leaned forward, spread her hands on the table. '*We need to get this right.* We have to assume that every move we make will be taken, by Galaxias, to be made on behalf of all of us, all humanity. Because that's the way *it* would think and act.'

Yan nodded. 'So you wish us both to be open – the Chinese, the Americans. That's what you are saying.'

'Yes. You have told us much, if not in any great detail. But you still aren't telling us your goal. Nothing makes sense without it. *Now's the time*. This conference is your opportunity – because it doesn't get any more senior than this. Don't just talk about the next technical phase. Tell us about the strategy, the ultimate objective. Just as Serena Jones has revealed Pioneer 14, now that she is confident in it. As of yesterday you can look up the damn thing on your phone. If *you* are prepared to speak, then we can open a dialogue with your political leaders. Be as open as you can be—'

'I agree, of course.'

That took Charlie aback, evidently. 'You do?'

Tash shook her head. 'Hold on. You don't know diplomats, Charlie. I think there's a big fat "but" in there.'

Yan smiled. 'And *that* is an expression Zhi has picked up from you, Tash, for better or worse. *I* think we should try to be open as much as possible. Not for the benefit of Galaxias – for the benefit of humanity. I must say, however – you hint at mistrust of the Chinese project, because of secrets at its heart. And I have admitted to such secrets. But we believe what we are doing is too important to reveal, yet, to foreigners. Even if our work should ultimately protect them too.

'But the Pioneer team are mistrusted too, despite their apparent openness. You must know that. Around the world the questions are asked – what do the Americans *really* want? Will they try to make some deal with the ETI, even? Will they seek to steal or monopolise its technology, to gain a commercial, political, even military advantage back home? Now, you and I know this is nonsense. That as an envoy, Jones's little crew will have about as much sway as Pocahontas did at the English court. But nobody said such fears – of a collaboration between America and Galaxias, a betrayal of humanity – have to be based in logic.'

320

Charlie nodded. 'So you agree that openness is desirable.'

She sighed. 'Or course. But despite your eloquence, Professor Marlowe, for reasons we have discussed many times, I cannot go into further details.'

Tash leaned forward. Thanks to a leak from Grace Butterworth, she had one card to play in this discussion. 'But we, the English government, do know one thing about the project. The internal code name for these gadgets you are building. *You call them Acorns.*'

Marlowe's eyebrows rose. 'Really? Once again, I'm glad I dragged you two in.'

Mel frowned. 'I didn't know that.'

'Sorry,' Tash said. 'I wasn't supposed to leak that to anyone. Not even you.'

Mel shook her head. 'Why Acorns? . . . Well, what is an acorn? The seed of an oak tree. One acorn produces one oak tree, which then produces many more acorns . . .'

Yan smiled. 'Perhaps you do not associate oaks with China? We have many native species. The Chinese cork oak, as it is known, is, to my taste, a particularly attractive kind . . .'

Marlowe's eyes narrowed. 'Now you're trying to deflect us, aren't you? Well, here's another leak. *What has Mercury to do with it?*'

Yan merely returned Marlowe's stare.

At length she said, 'May I have a glass of water? Still, please – the table water is sparkling.'

The cop murmured to the drone, then opened the door to allow it to fly off down the corridor once more.

Tash said, 'I wasn't expecting *that*. Mercury? Planet Mercury?'

Mel looked at her, shrugged. 'We detected a space shot, a probe to Mercury, apparently, disguised as a deep-space comms link.'

'A Chinese shot?'

Mel nodded.

Tash glared. 'And you were going to tell us this when?'

'Oh, Fred Bowles knows all about it,' Charlie said. 'Hasn't filtered down to you yet.'

Mel shrugged. 'Sorry, kid. I don't know always what it's safe to talk about. All this damn secrecy. Even between us. It's a wonder we get anything done at all.'

Marlowe shook her head. 'This is all hopelessly vague. Look, Yan—'

There was a subtle tap at the door. The cop opened it, to admit the drone bearing more water on its tray.

And it was accompanied by two armed Chinese soldiers.

'Ah,' Tash said. 'Your asking for water was a signal—'

'This meeting is over,' said the cop, unsmiling.

Wu Yan stood, eyes averted, and left the room.

And Tash knew at that moment that the whole conference, which had barely begun, was going to fail.

'Shit,' said the Astronomer Royal.

30

December 2057

The knock on the door came only minutes before midnight.

Tash had been sitting in front of the smart wall, following the news, alone in the Manors flat, for much of Christmas Day. Now she got up, feeling a little stiff – *you're getting old, kid* – reduced the wall to a murmur with a soft command, and went to the front door.

Outside, Mel and Jane were waiting, bundled up in heavy coats, their breath steaming around their hooded heads.

'Merry Christmas!' they said in unison.

Mel held out a bottle, Jane some kind of parcel. But they both wore head-torches, and after the dim lights of the lounge Tash was immediately dazzled, barely glimpsing their faces.

'Wow! Merry Christmas to you too, whoever you are.'

'Oops.' Mel tapped her own torch to dim it, then reached over to do the same to Jane's. 'Sorry about that. It's just the streets are so dark now.'

'I know. Come in, come in . . .'

As she bundled them into the warmth of the house – relative warmth – Tash looked out over a power-rationed Christmas-night city. As Mel had hinted, the glow of the lamps, bus and tram stops, and other bits of illuminated street furniture, stood out against a greater darkness. Eerie slabs of black on the walls that were long-dead ad posters.

She retreated into the light and closed the door.

Her guests stripped off their outer layers quickly, and hung their coats over a banister. Another oddity they had all discovered through this year of a cooling Earth: houses adapted to climate-crisis warming didn't always have great storage spaces for heavy cold-weather clothing.

In the living room, on the smart wall, muted news channels scrolled. Tash noticed her guests' gaze was drawn to a patch of brilliant white in one corner. The Antarctica landscape, where watchers were waiting for the solar eclipse.

There was a soft chime, and they all reflexively glanced at their phones.

'Midnight,' Jane said. 'Wow, that's the end of Christmas. We almost missed it! Sorry, Tash. Here! Even if it's late.' Jane handed Tash the gift she had carried.

Tash took the gift and ruffled her red hair. 'No problem.' She noticed it wasn't 'Auntie Tash' as it had been even this time last year, say. But then Jane's twelfth birthday had rolled around just a couple of weeks ago. Life went on, Blink or no Blink.

Tash carefully removed a wrapping of fine white paper from the gift, set the wrap aside for the recycler, and held up a plastic bottle – what had been a bottle anyhow, and had now been sculpted, probably with a domestic laser, to create a kind of fantastical, distorted house, with doors and windows.

'We did it at school,' Jane said a little shyly. 'I won a prize. Anyway, even if you don't like it the bottle is an antique.'

Which Tash knew was true. Plastic from the peak stuff years still clogged the arteries of the planet, but actual period artefacts, even mass-produced like this one, were becoming hard to find.

'Oh, I love it. Thanks.' She kissed the top of Jane's head, a habit since Jane had been small, and she wistfully wondered how much longer she would get away with it.

Jane said, 'And sorry if you didn't actually get it on the day. Quite.'

'That doesn't matter.'

'No, it's a bit rude,' Mel protested. 'To just show up so late. And we knew you were on your own. But you know how it is. Hard to get away from family.' Tash knew that Mel's brother had hosted a virtual party for her wider family, from his own home on the outskirts of Oxford.

'Especially when Uncle Paul starts preaching about Galaxias and God and stuff.'

'Never mind that now,' Mel murmured.

'The timing's not a problem,' Tash said. 'You haven't missed the eclipse, which isn't going to happen for another hour or so.'

'Ha!' Jane barked. 'You mean it isn't *not* going to happen for an hour. Does that make sense?'

Tash glanced at Mel. 'Still hoping that Zhi will call? He promised he would. Though I doubt if he'll stay in touch long. You need a drink? You are still staying over, right?'

'If you'll have us – thanks.'

'Well, Dad's away, and I've made up the spare beds.'

'Maybe a synth beer?'

'Me too,' Jane said.

'In your dreams.'

Tash said, 'I'm having cola.'

She shrugged. 'Prefer water.'

'No problem.' Tash hustled for the drinks in the kitchen, just off the living room, while her guests took off more bits of clothing – hats, gloves – and sat down.

'Actually she really does prefer water,' Mel said on Tash's

return. 'This lot are turning out to be an abstemious generation.'

'I don't know what that means,' Jane said.

'It means there's nothing much I can ban you from. They're even worse than us. The Climate Crisis Kids, they used to call *our* generation. Hang-ups about manufactured goods and processed food and drink—'

'Boring,' said Jane, lolling on a bean bag. She took her water, reached up to clink it against Tash's and Mel's glasses, sipped, and looked at the news channels idly.

Royals at Balmoral, Tash saw. Snowdrifts in Surrey. The eclipse-watchers in Antarctica were the only unusual item.

She said, 'How about some food?'

'No, thanks—'

'Hell, no,' Jane said.

'Oh, Jane—'

'We've been eating all day, because of the Uncle Paul thing.' Jane glanced at Tash. 'Unless you've got some chocolate.'

'Maybe.' Tash went back to the kitchen, fetched out a plate of biscuits, returned. 'Only synth stuff, of course. I sometimes wonder how many decades it has been since I've eaten anything that has been anywhere near an actual cocoa bean.'

'This'll do,' Jane said, grabbing at the plate and shovelling in a biscuit, almost whole. Then she took a second and began to lick off the chocolate, cat-like, making smears around her mouth.

Mel leaned over to admonish her again, but sat back with a sigh. 'What the hell. It's Christmas. And it might be a long while before we see even synth chocolate again. What is this, some kind of government issue? A gift for the drones?'

Tash sat and shook her head. 'They wouldn't dare pull such a stunt. Everybody already thinks House is one big hotel, don't they? Where we all lounge around in luxury while everybody else starves and shivers. No, I paid for those biscuits with a hefty chunk of my junior political adviser's salary.'

Mel glanced at Jane, steadily working on the biscuit. 'Well, it's appreciated. It's nice to have some kind of relief from it all, isn't it? Even just for one day. This time last year I would never have thought we would be seeing rationing, power cuts. Not on this scale. Not *again*. We grew up with all this.'

'People are comparing it to a war, rather than the climate crisis,' Tash said. 'That's what the opinion polls say. Dad says as much. His grandfather was a teenager during the Second World War, and he passed on stories of ration cards and queues at the butcher's.'

Jane looked up. 'Was he the Sputnik man?'

'No,' Tash said, 'that was Dad's father. The Second World War one was Dad's grandfather. My great-grandfather.'

'What's a butcher?'

Mel said, 'A person who sold meat for people to eat. Meat from an animal, I mean, not a printer. Oh, never mind. So where is your father tonight?'

'Working on flood relief efforts in Yorkshire. Volunteer. He called a couple of hours ago. He's wet and cold but fine. Sends his best wishes.'

They sat quietly for a while, eating, listening to the murmur of the smart wall, its changing light reflecting from their faces. The time seemed to flow by, Tash thought. The eclipse was due at a quarter past one; maybe they'd all fall asleep before then.

At length Jane asked, 'But *are* we at war? Like your great-grandad. At war with Galaxias?'

Mel and Tash shared a look.

'Good question, actually,' Mel said.

Tash sighed. 'Not legally. I'm the one who works with the

politicians, I suppose. I should know. We aren't in any formal war with Galaxias. We haven't *declared* war. Partly because we don't know how to. There isn't actually a way for the world, for humanity as a whole, to declare war on anybody. No formal, political way, I mean.

'A lot of our governance is still with the nation states – even after all the muddling up of the climate crises. But the states themselves evolve. Why, in Britain alone, we don't have the same nation states as we did a hundred years ago. But the, umm, the rules still apply. The rules of international conduct.'

Jane frowned, around a mouthful of biscuit. 'So, say, England could declare war on Scotland.'

'Exactly. And if we did there would be various international treaties that would come into play – such as about humane treatment of prisoners of war.

'But if we did go to war as a species, as a world, with some extraterrestrial power – well, of course, it's unprecedented. And a mess, diplomatically. Why, we saw that in the November conference at Dogger. I think the high-ups hoped – so I heard from Fred Bowles – that we would come out of that with some kind of unanimity of purpose, or at least a unanimity of response mechanisms, agreed among the nation states and then perhaps mediated by the FIS. The Secretary General as a spokesperson for the Earth, giving some universally agreed statement.' She smiled. 'Dad says it was that way in all the old movies when the aliens invaded.'

'Not all of them,' Mel said. 'Charlie Marlowe likes that old stuff, or rather she likes to pick holes in it. In *The Day the Earth Stood Still*, the 2051 anniversary remake anyhow, the nations of the world couldn't agree—'

'Boring,' said Jane. 'Instead of which—'

'Instead of which,' Tash said, 'the Dogger sessions were

dominated by two nations. Or rather, two powerful blocs: the Americans and their cheerleaders, and the Chinese and theirs. Both of them promoting their own secretive strategy over Galaxias, without giving out enough information for any of it to be fully understood. Neither side could trump the other – or yield to the other. And for better or worse no agency, such as the FIS, had the legal authority to ban their projects, or even endorse them. Well, at least they were talking. It wasn't Yalta, but I think Fred came away feeling it could have been worse.'

'Yalta?' Jane shrugged and looked at the wall images.

Mel said, 'So we accept we are doing both. The space projects. Both Zhi's dark energy warship—'

Jane opened her eyes wide. 'A warship? Cool.'

'Don't exaggerate, Mel,' Tash said, her smile a little forced. 'I deal with the press and the media every day. I have to fend off language like that all the time.'

Mel nodded. 'OK. Sorry. But actually, as Charlie Marlowe points out, and I agree with her I think, with the Pioneer mission anyhow, we are probably responding to Galaxias in the right way, on one level. Responding with *actions*, not words, just as the Blink was an *action*, a communication in concrete form. As opposed to the symbolism of other tokens on the Moon, around the lurker. But on the other hand by allowing the two national rivals to go ahead with their parallel efforts we are sending out muddled signals, to say the least.'

'Then again,' said a voice from the TV, 'we are a muddled species, aren't we?'

They all turned, startled.

Wu Zhi, dressed in a blue coverall, was grinning out of a corner of the screen, while muted news images scrolled around him. All against the background of a huge Jones swoosh-and-spaceship logo.

329

*

Jane jumped and waved. 'Can you see me? Hi, Uncle Zhi!'

'Hi, Jane. Happy birthday, belatedly.'

'You sent me a message on the day.'

'You got that – good. Loving the chocolate moustache look. Is that in at the moment?'

She laughed, blushed, and wiped her mouth with the back of her hand.

'Sorry to bother you. And sorry to hack into your system. You did once give me a key code in case of emergencies, Tash—'

Tash waved back. 'Don't apologise, you idiot. You know you were invited. How's California?'

'Well, it's still the middle of Christmas Day here. Dull. Cold. Not as cold as you are. People in this state are saying they miss the Wildfire Years.

'Anyhow, as I was saying, we're muddled. We aren't even a single, umm, political bloc, which for all we know may have been a stage of Galaxias's own evolution into the, the unified entity it seems to be now. *We* aren't a unity, like it is. So maybe it's appropriate that the gestures we make are somewhat contra-dictory too.'

Tash shook her head. 'Zhi. Zhi!'

'At least it's honest – oh, sorry. What? There's just enough time delay to be awkward, isn't there?'

'It's typical of you, Zhi – we don't hear from you for months, then you just launch into a lecture on galactic diplomacy. How are you? *You*, not the Galaxy.'

A grin, again slightly time-delayed. 'I'm sorry. You're quite right. I do get immersed, don't I? Although you will understand that all this is very personal for me. Which is why my mother encourages me to keep in touch with you guys. You keep me grounded, she says. Sane, in some ways, *I* would say. Even if we may disagree half the time.'

Tash grinned. 'You and us, or you and your mother?'

'I'm not keeping score.'

Mel said. 'How is your mother?'

'Busy, I imagine. We don't have a lot of contact.'

Mel said, 'Well, that's a pity. Sometimes it feels like we've all spent the whole year since the Blink just trying to get the Americans and Chinese to talk about it.'

Zhi grunted. 'Mostly through me and my mother, in fact.'

'You work with what you've got,' Tash said. 'I'm sorry if we were manipulative, though.'

Zhi shrugged. 'OK. Well, there's no rush. The deadline is eleven years away. I guess there's plenty of time to sort it out.'

That left Tash baffled. Deadline? Eleven years?

Mel, a veteran of this kind of confrontation, winked at Jane, and silently mouthed, *Three, two, one—*

Tash snapped. 'All right, damn you! You know me too well. What happens in eleven years?'

'We get Galaxias's response. Possibly.'

He left that hanging in the air.

Tash asked at last, 'Response to what?'

'To our actions since the Blink. Especially our immediate response. You see, we believe that Galaxias and its tech is limited to lightspeed. Remember that? And we also believe from the exoplanet astronomy results that its nearest communications node is at Barnard's Star. Which is—'

'Five point nine six light years away,' Jane said briskly. 'Everybody knows that.' Then her mouth dropped open. 'Oh, I see. I think I know what you're getting at.'

'Right,' Zhi said. 'Right. So a message from the Moon lurker will take a bit less than six years to get out there; any response can come no sooner than a further a bit less than six years beyond that. Starting back at the Blink itself, in January, takes us to the end of 2068. A bit less than twelve years after the Blink. So anyhow we have a period of grace before Galaxias can intervene again, at least in terms of responding to anything we've done. Makes sense?'

'Makes perfect sense,' Tash said. 'While the cat's light years away—'

'Serena Jones has rounded it down to a decade – like Apollo's decade to get to the Moon. But she's planning to get our space shot up and running long before the time is up . . .' He glanced at something out of shot. 'Hey, it's nearly eclipse time. Then I'll have to run, I'm sorry. Back to work.'

Jane snorted. 'At Christmas?'

'We famous astronauts have deadlines to meet. Although they did put a sprig of mistletoe into one of the simulators.'

Jane frowned. 'What's mistletoe?'

'Tell you later,' Tash said. 'Zhi . . . Keep in touch. Don't wait for Easter. Whenever the hell they work out Easter should be. We miss you.'

Mel murmured confirmation.

'I . . . know. I'm sorry. I guess I've been self-absorbed. I did have one hell of a year. Well, we all did. And now I'm hellish busy. But I don't mean to shut you out. I'll stay on the line for the eclipse. A minute to go, right?'

Tash glanced at a clock on the smart wall – it read not quite one fifteen – a screen that was filling up with images of the southern sky now, as the deadline for first contact approached: the moment when the Moon's edge, seen from the Earth, touched the Sun. Or should have.

Tash was distracted by glimpses of Antarctica itself. Camera pans, establishing shots, mostly blue sky over white ground, but in some of the images there were bare, rocky stretches where the ice had receded during the climate-crisis summer, and had yet to advance again in the Galaxias winter. There were even patches of green – lichen, maybe?

Mel murmured, 'This is a rare event – two total eclipses in a year. Or would have been. The last was 1889, the next will be 2252.'

'"Or would have been,"' Jane chanted.

'Right.' Mel smiled. 'Charlie is down there, you know. On Sky-thrust, like in January. Over Antarctica. Watching in comfort.'

Tash grinned. 'Wouldn't you sooner be there, rather than shivering in this government-issue hovel?'

'Well, it would have topped and tailed a year that has been – utterly bizarre.' She reached out for Jane's and Tash's hands. 'No, I'd rather be with you all . . .'

Jane was watching the timings carried by the straplines under the various copies of the Sun image. 'Nearly there. A countdown. Three, two, one . . .'

The Sun's disc, seen through filtered lenses, was of course unblemished.

A moment of silence.

'. . . Two, three, four . . .'

'Now I'm wondering why we're all doing this,' Mel said. 'Half the planet losing sleep, waiting for an eclipse that we *knew* was never going to happen.'

Jane shrugged. 'We knew what the scientists were saying. About Earth's new orbit and all. We just had to see if it was real, that's all.'

Zhi just nodded. 'Exactly, kid. It's real, all right. I love you all. I have to go.'

And his image winked out.

DECADE

2058–2067

31

March AD 2058:
Year 2, Winter (English Regularised Calendar) (retrospective dating)

Tash was enough of a space buff, at second hand anyhow, through her acquaintance with Zhi and Mel, to know what JPL was. The Jet Propulsion Laboratory. Even where it was, vaguely: somewhere in the hills above Pasadena.

But she was surprised when she, Mel and Jane got there on a bright March day, and stepped out of their smart bus into a deep, bitter cold that sank into her bones. In California. Jane huddled close to Mel, wrapping her arms around her mother's torso theatrically.

Zhi himself was waiting for them, on the inside of the security barrier at the entrance gateway. Evidently self-conscious in face mask, gloves, and NASA-blue astronaut's jumpsuit – the blue fabric plastered with Jones, Inc. corporate logos – he herded them through the barrier quickly.

It turned out it wasn't just good manners that Zhi should come out to meet them in person. As they were put through retinal, fingerprint and DNA scans, he told them brusquely that the Jet Propulsion Laboratory, like many government, military and science facilities, had come under random attacks from a variety of post-Blink crazies. It didn't help, Tash often thought, that both of the world's leading players, America and China, actually *were* conducting secretive space projects in response.

'Which is why,' Zhi said, 'I have had to come out to validate you in person, in spite of all my other duties. One last human-eyeball verification, dumb as it sounds . . .'

He led them through a final set of gates, and JPL opened out before them.

Tash found herself distracted by the sheer oddity of the place. Built around a rough avenue ahead, the site was a jumble of buildings of all apparent ages from rough concrete shacks to sleek modern smartwood. A big steel and glass tower, elderly itself, dominated the site. And the place was busy, busy, drones zipping through the air, people coming and going – though from the look of their city clothes, not to mention their age, she guessed that most were guests for the day rather than workers here.

Zhi hurried them on. 'Come on, you're late. But the President is running late too, so the whole schedule is slipping.'

Mel and Tash complied obediently.

But Jane said now as she walked, 'I can't believe you lot. The way you're behaving. Running past all these old – *sheds*. Here's Zhi, who is like your *oldest* friend, and who is going to be shot off into space *again* – why aren't you hugging?'

Mel frowned. 'Now, Jane. What have I told you about psychoanalysing the adults?'

Zhi grinned behind his mask. 'You're quite right, Jane. But – no hugs today! We're in lockdown, we astronauts. We are planning at least one deep-space test flight of the technology before the main mission. A crewed flight, I mean. I'm slated for the big job, which might not be for years yet, but you never know – they are only training up a handful of us crew, and assignments can get moved around. They think it's healthy enough for me to run around in the sunshine like this – the gear I'm wearing is smarter than it looks – but I'm not supposed to come into physical contact with anybody. Even second hand; I couldn't take a gift off you, for instance.'

Jane said bluntly, 'We didn't bring any gifts.'

'Well, that's typical. But they are being cautious.'

Mel smiled. 'I guess Serena Jones regards all this formality as an unwelcome distraction—'

'Actually not at all,' Zhi said. 'I've seen her working close up for some months now, remember. And, along with her many other talents, I'm learning she is a master of PR. And she knows its importance.'

Jane scowled. 'I know what PR is. Telling people stuff so you can sell them other stuff.'

Tash had to laugh. 'Good enough. But what has she got to sell today? I mean, *announce*. Everybody *knows* she's sending off a spaceship at solar escape velocity. And everybody knows you will be on it, Zhi, with the Mars astronauts. She's said all that already.'

'True enough,' Zhi said. 'And *I* don't know what she's got left to say today. She does hold stuff back, so as to grab a little more press attention when she does the reveal. But Serena will have goals she wants to accomplish today – management goals, even political, if not technical. What I do know is that if Serena didn't think it necessary, this circus wouldn't be happening at all. But it is a chance for me to smuggle you lot in . . .'

'Show-off,' murmured Tash. But she was pleased he still felt close enough to have invited them in the first place.

They walked on, deeper into the compound, but slower. Mel in particular was staring around, increasingly distracted.

Jane took her mother's hand. 'Are you OK?'

Mel looked down at her. 'Yes. Yes, I'm fine, honey. It's just this place. I was always a space buff. I feel like I've walked into a movie set.'

Zhi eyed Jane. 'So, do *you* know about this place? There are layers of history here. Do you even know what JPL—'

'Jet Propulsion Laboratory,' Jane said stiffly, pronouncing the words carefully.

'Right. This used to be a military laboratory, which is why it was set up in the hills out of town – or it was out of town then – in the Arroyo Seco, a dry valley. But times changed. The city spread up the hillside, and this remote location became a select suburb. And *then* JPL took on the management of early uncrewed space missions for NASA – including the first Pioneers, built at Ames, run out of here. So you have generations of buildings cluttered in here, all different. And then the climate changed and the dry valley wasn't always so *seco* any more—'

Mel said, 'And here we are just hurrying past it all.'

Zhi grinned, kindly enough. 'I'll take you through the gift shop on the way out. Come on, come on . . .'

They reached one of the larger modern buildings, a big pillbox with huge clearwood panels, subtly tinted to exclude the still bright California sunlight. A lot of the guest types seemed to be filing in here, Tash saw, passing through more security barriers, watched by a sparse cloud of drones overhead.

Security agents soon spotted Zhi. They formed a loose escort around him and his party, and walked them.

And Tash found herself in a kind of welcome lounge, where coffee dispensers crowded for space with displays, evidently of triumphs from JPL's illustrious past. Spindly spacecraft, like dragonflies, were suspended from the ceiling. And beyond,

340

through open doors, she spotted an auditorium, already filling up.

Mel pointed out groups of students, mostly mid to late teens, some in school uniforms, looking around, listening to group leaders, or soaking up the displays. 'For a change, something good Galaxias has done for us,' Mel said. 'An upsurge in science studies. These kids are growing up in a new intellectual environment, where we know there is life beyond the Earth, we even think we know it's intelligent, and think we know its motivation . . . It might be malevolent, but it answers a lot of age-old questions. The Fermi Paradox is resolved, for one. Maybe the next generations are going to be a lot calmer than we are. More rational, like the universe.'

Tash felt more cynical. 'Maybe. If that rational agent doesn't kill us all. Or all the crazies in *their* response to Galaxias don't bring everything crashing down . . .'

Jane, ignoring the models, was drawn to a more prosaic display on one of the tables: heaps of yellowed paper and oddly shaped cards. 'What's all this stuff, Mum? These cards with holes in?'

Mel smiled. 'Well, that's what they used to program computers, back in the day. Maybe a hundred years ago. Even computers that controlled spacecraft. One command at a time coded into these little holes, which they would shine light through . . .'

'On *cards*? . . .'

'Yes, cards!'

Lee Yamanaka, the President's science adviser, came gliding across the room, in a bright Hawaiian-pattern blouse, grinning hugely. 'Good to see you all.' She shook Tash's hand. 'Please send my best regards to Fred Bowles.'

Tash grinned back. 'He'll be watching all this back in Gateshead.'

Yamanaka glanced over at Jane, almost fondly. 'Interested in the punch cards, eh? Actually I do often find that in displays like this the young are oddly drawn to the more primitive arte-facts. Stuff you can imagine making by hand almost, and yet which enabled us to reach the planets.'

Zhi nodded. 'Serena says that. It was how she started herself, making stuff, toy planes and rockets . . .'

Yamanaka held up a hand, touched an earpiece. 'The President is scheduled to hook in soon. I'd better take you in. Your seats are reserved, down front. Stay close.'

She led the way towards the auditorium entrance. Zhi's party followed, Jane tugging her mother's hand.

Near the doors, they merged into a gathering crowd, and had to slow.

Yamanaka walked with Tash. She said softly, 'I must say it feels like it's been a long journey since Blink Day to *this*. The presentation, at last, of a reasonably constructive response to the event. It has been long for the President herself. I happened to be with her that morning, you know. President Cox. On Blink Day.'

Tash glanced at her. 'No, I didn't know that.'

'One for the memoirs, I suppose. It was before dawn for us, remember. I'd been sleeping over, we were in the middle of rou-tine annual budget-allocation meetings. A secret service agent woke me up and said I was called down to the bunker – which is a situation room in the basement. We were in the Winter White House, in Anchorage.

'President Cox was already there, in a dressing gown. Her Chief of Staff was with her in person, and on the line she had the National Security Adviser, Secretary of State, Secretary of Defence, the Chairman of the Joint Chiefs. Further down the line there were links to the directors of the CIA, FBI, Homeland

Security. Oh, and military aides with the Emergency Satchel. The nuclear football. Links to people like some of the big media outlets, the power companies and other utilities. All of that . . .

'The nuclear football, sitting on a table in front of me. Think of that. I remember all those grim faces. It was like a movie set-up.

'And I remember how remote we felt, though, in Anchorage. The mood wasn't – chaotic, I remember, but it wasn't calm either. We just didn't know what we were dealing with, you see. Europe, Africa, Asia just going dark in our screens. We wondered if it was some kind of strike – a massive nuclear event even, scrambling up the sensors . . . We could have panicked, and a terrible situation could have become far worse.

'But we avoided that – with luck and some good judgement, I guess. We just sat and tried to gather data, handle local issues as they came up. And then, as the machinery of government started to work, we found ourselves having to prepare America for a day without a dawn . . .'

They'd made it into the auditorium now, and Tash found herself in a bewildering bubble of noise and bright media-feed lights, crammed with people seeking their seats, drones ducking and darting overhead.

As she led Tash forward, Yamanaka said, 'Even after Blink Day was over and the Sun was back, we were baffled as to how to respond, I suppose. We did fix on a determination to robustify the nation in case of another Blink, even a longer one – the target was a week. Stable door duly bolted. We shared ideas with you English, and globally. And then—'

'And then in walks the famous Serena Jones,' Tash said with a grin.

'Right. Who starts outlining a dream of spaceflight . . . Which turned out to be, not by accident, exactly what we needed to hear. Something with a science justification, political resonance, and positivity. It might even work! And here we are.'

They reached the front few rows, where a handful of security types checked them over once more, and let them sit down.

Behind Tash now, a crowd that only seemed to be getting noisier. Before her, an empty stage with nothing but a single podium, standing against a backdrop of logos – JPL itself, NHSA, the Air Force, the Stars and Stripes, as well as Jones, Inc. and other corporate partners.

Yamanaka had to lean over to be heard by Tash.

'I don't know how well you know her. Serena, I mean. Well, I dare say we'll get something of her personal biography today. Which somebody ought to write up some day, by the way. All part of the image, the sales pitch. Born in the last century, a small town in South Carolina. Kind of place where you fixed your own car, back then anyhow. She made money quickly – actually from running a car service business out of her parents' garage – and she founded Jones, Inc., straight out of college. That's how people like her always make their start. Well, she just chomped her way through the private space industry. Made the earlier bunch of entrepreneurs look like kids selling cookies at a fair.

'So she was already super-rich when the climate crisis bit. 2030s, she threw herself into local relief efforts. 2040s, she worked on larger-scale schemes – the big relocations and re-buildings. Around 2050, having made her name nationally, she worked on the Los Angeles flood barrier, a relief effort so big—'

'You could see it from the Moon, I know. While getting even wealthier.'

'Well, that's the nature of our society. But, you know, I think there's more than money involved here. Jones's generation – *my* generation – have, I sometimes think, something in common with those from a century before. I mean the leaders of the 1930s and 1940s, who managed the New Deal to get the country out of depression, and *then*, after the Second World War, implemented the Marshall Plan and other initiatives to rebuild Europe, Japan. Thereby postponing other wars, probably, by decades.

'What those people bequeathed us, among things, were new management skills, sufficient to deliver projects on an epic scale. So by the 1960s you had people like NASA's Jim Webb, who had cut his teeth on enormous pre-war New Deal projects and post-war reconstruction projects, with an ideal skill set to lead America to the Moon. People look back and call them the greatest generation. And so now—'

'And so now, you think, that climate-crisis generation have the skills to manage another global-scale dislocation in the Blink?'

'Well, look how we've responded so far. Ask me, *they* are the greatest generation. They saved the world. And Jones was one of them. But Jones has a killer instinct too. She did contact Cox just at the moment when—'

Yamanaka's watch chimed, distracting her.

There was a stir in the audience.

Zhi turned and grinned. 'The President just tuned in, from the White House.'

Jane shushed him. 'Look! Here comes Serena . . .'

A slim figure walked out of the wings and headed for the podium.

When the applause had died down, Jones, haloed by silently hovering drones, looked around the audience, one hand shielding her eyes from the overhead lights' glare.

'Wow. Madam President, in Anchorage, thank you for your attention. And a full house here. Thank you all for coming. Although I suspect some of you of the press are owed an apology, you see too much of me . . .'

A welcoming laugh.

'Sometimes it feels like I've come a long way from my childhood in South Carolina . . .'

Yamanaka leaned over to Tash and whispered, 'We should have made a bet.'

'You know, it was my mother who first pointed out to me — she found it on some website — that I had the same birthday as Robert H. Goddard, though I was born over a hundred years later.

'Who was Robert H. Goddard? Well, he's pretty much forgotten now, but he was one of America's great rocketry pioneers. In the bigger scheme of things he was overshadowed by the Russian theorists, and by the Germans' more advanced practical developments during the Second World War.

'But still, even as a young man — even as a tree-climbing kid — he was inspired by stories of Mars and Martians, and he wondered what it would be like to *go* there. To climb some impossible tree all the way into the sky. Well, he didn't grow any trees that I know of, but he did end up with a real home industry of model rocketry — and I'm speaking of liquid-fuel rockets too, not just gunpowder fireworks. All in his back yard — metaphorically, anyhow.

'I'll tell you what attracted me to that story. It was about people *doing* stuff. Real stuff. Robert Goddard *building* things — not just messing with virtual constructs on a phone, as was the dominant fashion back when I was a kid. And I can show you my own first home-made rocket.'

Jones snapped a finger, and a big holo appeared behind her,

a kid aged maybe eleven, her hair drenched, holding a plastic bottle and grinning into the camera.

Tash had to smile.

Yamanaka whispered, 'Told you so. Sales pitch.'

'Just an old plastic bottle and a cycle-tyre pump. The tricky part was fitting a valve to the bottle. You put in some water, then pump as hard as you can, compressing the air, and when that's released, you get a rocket flying up in the air – and a miniature rain shower, as you can see. Kids like to make stuff, is my theory. Permanent stuff, stuff that changes the world. Whether they know it or not. From that, to *this*.'

This time the reveal was more subtle. The air above Jones's head seemed to congeal into a dark mist that then faded down to a starry sky.

Across which sailed a ship.

Sail being the operative word. Tash could see a central knot of technology, what looked like a group of Jones, Inc. standard Shelter modules ganged together. But they were dwarfed by an immense, filmy disc of what looked like spiderweb at first glance, a pale sheet of threads and knots through which stars shone, apparently undimmed. As the image rotated, Tash could see fine threads linking the Shelters to the disc.

Jones was taking small steps around the stage. 'If you paid any attention to your briefing packs – hell, to a dozen presentations before – you'll know that this is a ramjet, designed to exploit dark energy, which is a very thin, all-pervasive medium of – well, stuff. Energy that fills the universe. And, being expansive, it's slowly pushing the universe apart, from within.

'What *is* dark energy? Well, I don't know, or much care. All I care about is the energy field itself – and what I can do with it.' She gestured at the huge sail. 'You've seen this design before – essentially the design we trialled with the Sputnik, massively scaled up. With that big dish we will be scooping up dark energy and turning it into kinetic energy, energy of motion for our ship here. How exactly we do that – well, patent still pending.'

More laughter.

'The design strategy is simple, though. Elementary. That dark energy, sparse as it is, is *everywhere*. We can just keep chomping our way through it, as far out as we choose to go, and we can chomp our way all the way back to the inner Solar System when we're done. That's the point, really. We can never run out of fuel, no matter how far we choose to go.

'Oh, and by the way, about getting my crew home safe.' She glanced down at the astronauts. 'My dark energy drive will continue to function, *even through another Blink*, should that be inflicted on us. One reason we chose to develop the dark energy drive was precisely for that reason. *We don't need sunlight*, not for propulsion, not for power. There will not be another Al-miriykh. Not on my watch.'

More applause. Tash saw that Zhi dropped his head.

'All this has still to be built, tested, but the engineering is already proven. So I have a spaceship. And I have a crew. Folks, you want to stand up?'

Zhi, with what Tash knew was genuine reluctance, got up out of his seat. Glancing around she saw his partners, Ito Katsuo, Marina Petko, stand up from the first couple of rows. Awkwardly, to a growing ripple of applause, they nodded, sat down quickly.

At length Jones held up her hands. 'So we have our astronauts; we will soon have ready their fine ship. But when will we fly? I can tell you now that the President herself has mandated our schedule.'

Yamanaka frowned, restless. 'Not through me . . . I hadn't heard this.'

Jones said, 'And we accepted her logic. You see — *we are working to a deadline.*

'My colleague Wu Zhi was the first to work it out. The Blink came in January 2057, of course — and we think that was a response, apparently limited by lightspeed, to our own first interstellar venture, with Pioneer 10. Well, you see, we know now that Galaxias has an eye in the Solar System. The object we call the lurker, on the Moon. Back in the 1970s that seems to have reported on Pioneer 10 — but it evidently took many years for that report to reach Galaxias's decision nodes, many light years away, and just as long for the response to arrive. By which I mean the Blink.

'And we know the lurker has also reported on how we have reacted to the Blink. We *saw* the shot. Once again we wait for a response, for better or worse.

'But we think the very *earliest* we could expect any response to that is after a lightspeed exchange with Barnard's Star, which we believe is Galaxias's nearest node. And *that* can't happen until late 2068, a little less than twelve years after the Blink. That's ten years from now.

'After which — well, if Galaxias acts again, who knows how our freedom to manoeuvre might be curtailed? So we have a deadline.

'And *here* is the mandate the President has given us to achieve within that deadline.'

She waved a hand, and a screen with three bullet points appeared overhead.

'As we have previously announced. One. The goal. *We will send a crew* — a human crew.

'Two.

'When? *Within a decade.* And finally—'

Yamanaka seemed distinctly uncomfortable now, Tash saw.

Evidently the President's science adviser had been cut out of the decision-making loop here, and hadn't even known about all this.

'And, finally,' Jones went on, 'three. *Where* shall we go?

'Look — we'll be able to fly out of the Solar System in any direction we choose. Any which way would make our point about our defiance. So — where should we send our crew? What course shall we steer?

'I'll tell you. *We intend to challenge Galaxias in its own back yard.*'

Another finger-snap, the gauzy ship disappeared, and an image of a star field coalesced. It looked familiar to Tash.

'Having achieved escape velocity we will go on, still accelerating, far across the Solar System — far out from Earth and Sun — in fact, our nominal target is to travel about three times further out than Neptune, the last of the inner-System worlds.'

Tash saw Mel frown at that. She said, 'Ninety AU, then. Ninety astronomical units . . .'

Jones went on, 'And as for a course, we intend to fly out in the direction of the constellation of Centaurus. *Ninety astronomical units out, towards Centaurus . . .*'

And now, looking at that constellation map, Tash felt a shock of recognition.

'Right,' Jones said, grinning into the camera. 'I bet that made you sit up. Everyone follows the science now. *You* know the significance of that. Centaurus, ninety AU out. *That's where Galaxias put the Sun.* And *that* is where we are going.'

'Oh, shit,' said Yamanaka.

'Oh, shit,' said Mel.

Jane grinned.

Tash, in the front row, was surprised to see, looking around, that most people had got to their feet. Reluctantly, she followed, as did Mel, Jane, Yamanaka. Even the embarrassed-looking astronauts joined in the applause.

'Genius,' Yamanaka said in Tash's ear. 'She's doing just what Jim Webb did with Apollo. Made sure he had the backing of the politicians from the start, with a very clear mandate, three very specific goals: *a man, on the Moon, in a decade*. What, so Congress wants to cut the budget, a couple of years down the line? Then you will miss the goals, as clearly set out today, right here. Just like Webb with Kennedy, Jones has got Cox and her administration locked in – and her successors. Genius. Genius.'

The applause seemed to go on and on.

And Yamanaka said, 'Now all she's got to do is deliver.'

32

June AD 2059:
Year 3 ERC, Spring

The first exit poll announcement, delivered a few seconds after ten o'clock on this June General Election night, was brusque, the result hastily dissected by a group of media talking heads on the Government House lounge's smart wall.

Fred Bowles muted it all with a gesture. 'Shit,' he said. 'They're predicting a seventy-seat majority for Mara Caine and her Reconstructers. Worse than I thought. Worse than I feared. *Shit.*'

Jane Kapur grinned at the word.

Tash saw Mel glare at Jane. Charlie Marlowe seemed oblivious.

'So,' said Grace Butterworth. 'The Talisker or the champagne?'

'You know the rules we set, Grace,' Bowles said. 'The hard stuff if the majority was over forty. The bubbly if it was under that.'

Grace grinned, got up, lifted one of the two trays of glasses off this private lounge's low central table and moved it to a corner of the room. She did this delicately for such a powerful woman, Tash thought idly, with the discarded champagne flutes carried smoothly and without a wobble. Then she cracked open the whisky and began pouring neat, precise measures into a row of shot glasses on the tray still on the table.

'Not that it makes much difference,' she murmured as she did so. 'This isn't any more the real true stuff than that "champagne" over there ever saw a grape. All synthesised from soya stock and—'

'Leave us our illusions, Grace,' Charlie Marlowe said. She was distracted by imagery projected from her own phone to the smart table before her – it looked like the lunar surface to Tash, some kind of machinery under a black sky – but, Tash noted wryly, that didn't stop Marlowe reaching forward and taking a glass.

Tash and the rest followed suit, one by one, as Grace poured.

On this, results night after federal England's general election, they were a close and select gathering in this Fred Bowles's private lounge, deep in the bowels of Government House. Fred himself. Grace and Tash, who he had come to rely on as his closest personal advisers, indeed among his closest allies, in the jungle that was the post-Blink English government. Charlie Marlowe, who Fred still thought of, Tash suspected, as his most reliable, most honest, most comprehensible adviser from the external world of academia – in all things scientific post-Blink, in fact, even far beyond Marlowe's specialist field. Bowles had asked Charlie to be on hand tonight in case a victorious Prime Minister, sitting or new, needed some kind of urgent briefing from the science minister, outgoing or otherwise, a request certainly not unlikely in the turbulent post-Blink world. Here was Mel at Tash's suggestion, as Marlowe's PA – and where Mel went on such a night, if it was informal, so her rapidly growing daughter came too.

Jane held out her hand for a whisky shot.

Grace smoothly switched the glass for a tumbler of cola. 'Nice try, missy. What are you, fourteen?'

'Thirteen. So what am I supposed to do, sit here and watch you lot get drunk?'

Bowles laughed. 'Well, not that drunk. I've given Grace strict instructions. We can have one more shot each at midnight, by which time enough solid results should be in to know for sure . . .'

Solid results. By which he meant, Tash knew, in this post-Blink world, the outcomes of people laboriously counting by hand bits of paper in ballot boxes. Electronic connectivity, among other modern conveniences, was flaky now, if not as hackable as it once was. A shredded upper atmosphere let through more space storms than before, and quakes and storms and other terrestrial hazards did nothing good to atmospheric broadcasts, even landlines. So many of the old ways of doing things had been revived, including running a national election in England using paper marked with pencil crosses.

'One shot at midnight,' Bowles repeated firmly. 'And one at, oh, two a.m. when Caine makes her gracious victory speech. If I'm not called out to be there to hear it. Christ.' He downed his measure in a gulp. 'Going to be a long night.'

Marlowe raised her glass. 'You should have saved a drop for a toast. I mean, you have kept your own seat, if not your job.'

Bowles grinned. 'Thanks for that.'

Jane said, 'So are you going to retire now?'

Mel gave her a look.

'What? I'm just asking. If your Democratic Green party loses you won't have your job any more. That's right, isn't it? You'll be just an MP.'

Mel gave her daughter another look for that.

Bowles sighed, and looked longingly at his empty glass. 'Well, maybe that's the traditional way of it. But I don't think Mara Caine is going to be much of a traditionalist PM — in her throw-back values, yes, and the Britishness she espouses which will infuriate our neighbour nations, as well as the English federal regions – but not traditional in the way she will run her government. Well, we saw some of that during her reign as Home Secretary in the coalition government. Apparently she's going to want a smooth transition, which may mean sitting ministers, or some of them, staying in their jobs – even if we are officially in opposition. It will be like Churchill's wartime government, she says.'

Marlowe smiled tightly. 'I hear Churchill's name invoked by that lot so often they ought to dig him up and appoint him Foreign Secretary. Also, co-opting the talent from the losing side sounds a good way to control any opposition.'

'True enough, as well. We won't get the great offices of state, so-called,' Bowles went on gloomily. 'The Chancellor, the Home Secretary, won't be Greens. But junior ministers—' He shrugged. 'In particular the scuttlebutt is that I'll be asked to stay on. For better or worse.'

Mel frowned. 'I know I'm naive about this stuff. Isn't that a kind of compliment?'

'You could read it like that. Mara is *selling* it like that. But it may mean I will have to implement policies to which I am – ideologically opposed. Put it that way. And as Charlie says, it's a policy that has the advantage of neutering the opposition. We'd have to share the blame.' He glanced over at Marlowe, who was still intent on the images before her. 'So that's why I might need your counsel, Charlie, if there are any immediately bonkers policies that need shooting down. Is that display the Moon, by the way? Must be comforting to have the bigger picture to look at, even on a night like this.'

Marlowe looked up from her smart table, distracted. 'Comforting? I wouldn't be so sure about that. I still don't understand

what I'm seeing here. The damn Chinese on the Moon . . . And
what I don't understand – well, I relish it, if it's a scientific
problem, but if it's something big in the human world, by default I fear it.'

Fred Bowles grunted. 'Between these four walls, the western
intelligence agencies still can't get a handle on it. Not the big
picture.

'They've been up to something for years, on the Moon. Something big and industrial. We know that. The question is, what?
Personally I can't believe that they are planning any kind of
destructive system – a weapons platform on the Moon, either
directed at us, or even at Galaxias, somehow? Nothing I've seen
personally *looks* like that, even if the security services have
been briefing that way for months. The official Chinese line is
still that they are merely advancing a peaceful, civilian-led programme of industrial experimentation. Which – well, I suspect
that is partially true, at least. The question is, what's the real
goal?'

'Maybe we'll know more soon.' Marlowe waved her hands
over her screen, pulling out images that rotated in the air above
the table. 'I think we may be about to see the project revealed,
in a sense. Or at least it may reach a point impossible to hide.
This is why I'm watching it now, antisocial as it may be. I have
a feeling this is all coming to some sort of climax, perhaps even
tonight.

'I'll take you through the sequence we've been observing
– remotely, mostly from the Gateway in lunar orbit – over
the last, umm, thirty-six days,' she added, checking a timer.
When Bowles hesitated, she said, 'Look, sit down and watch,
Fred. What else have you got to do while you wait for the
sack?'

*

So Bowles sat beside her.

And Tash looked over Bowles's shoulder at the table-top display of imagery.

She saw a little three-dimensional diorama. A slab of bare lunar plain, tan brown, with eroded rocky formations – crater walls maybe – smoothed by a covering of dust. A background of sky black as pitch. Judging from the slight shadows, the Sun must be hanging somewhere out of sight to her left.

She felt a pang of recognition. *I went there*, she thought with a kind of longing. *I walked up there. Me . . .*

Everybody was watching, she saw, glancing around. Bowles, for now. Mel, Jane. Everyone save Grace Butterworth, who seemed to have her attention split between the election coverage and a news channel on a wall screen, a so-called Earthwatch feed: a pooled network project, rolling coverage of the post-Blink suffering of the planet, and of humanity. Refugees plodding across a wasteland, somewhere.

'So this is the Moscow Sea,' Marlowe said. 'On the lunar far side. As was. As I said, this sequence begins thirty-six days ago, OK? Some of it natural speed, some of it speeded up . . . Ah, and here it comes.'

A squat craft appeared at the top of the screen, descending smoothly and silently. Invisible rocket exhaust kicked up dust that obscured the lines of the craft, but with no air to suspend it, the dust settled quickly.

For a moment after the landing – as seen by the silent audience in the lounge – the craft just sat there, squat, a fat cylinder with a hull pocked by sensor ports and the lines of closed hatches. It was very toy-like, set in this toy-like diorama, Tash thought. But its sharp shadow shifted, just slightly, slowly, steadily. The Moon's day was still about an Earth month long, post-Blink. So Tash could tell she was watching heavily edited, speeded-up coverage.

Mel nodded. 'This is their so-called Acorn project, I take it.'

'We have to assume so. We have still not been able to learn much about it.'

Bowles said, 'It has no markings. Can we even be sure—'

'It has various radio idents, broadcast continually,' Marlowe said. 'Routine international protocols, mandatory when working on the Moon. Yes, it's the Chinese. And the idents do prove that it is some kind of stage in the Acorn project.'

'What is it doing, though? I can see time passing, the shifting of the shadows . . .'

'Lots of internal rearrangement going on. Presumably,' Marlowe said. 'As it transitions from flight mode to ground mode. *Presumably*. Have patience . . . Ah. Here we go.' Quite abruptly, the craft's hull seemed to peel open, with hatches dropping down or rolling up.

And lesser vehicles poured out, riding on fat wheels like wrapped-up bundles of wire. In the imagery they looked even more like toys than their parent vessels, Tash thought, and Jane was still child-like enough to be entranced, she saw.

Once the vehicles were out, the work seemed to begin immediately, with the spreading of a dark blanket, in sections, around the central craft.

'They work quickly when they get going. Even in real time.' Marlowe tapped her phone to reveal a wider-scale overhead view.

That dark blanket quickly washed out all across the lunar plain, becoming a solid sheet covering the dust. Its perimeter was soon far from the centre, though it was hard to judge scales, Tash thought – and seemed to push further out even as the interior surface gradually solidified.

'It's beautiful,' Jane said. 'Like watching a flower open. A robot flower. A mixture of nature and tech.'

Mel ruffled her hair.

Marlowe grinned. 'You don't often get Chinese tech called beautiful. It is, though, isn't it? When you watch it live you can't see the motion. It's only when you speed it up that the growth of that sheet is evident.'

Fred Bowles pointed at the images. 'That's a solar energy panel,' he said bluntly. 'The black sheet. Yes?'

'Correct, Minister. Mel saw an early lunar demonstration. Mel and Tash later, on Earth. When a unit is fully extended – or fully grown – its radius is around a kilometre, and it's capable of collecting around five gigawatts of solar power. Pretty efficient. In fact it *does* grow from a smaller seed, like a tree from an acorn, by a bootstrapping process. It starts with a small array, and uses the solar energy it captures, and aluminium from the lunar dust, to grow larger arrays. As some of us have seen on the Moon for ourselves. The Chinese have worked with an odd mixture of secrecy and transparency. I suppose it would have been impossible to hide it all.

'Anyhow we estimate that the manufacturing process we are witnessing now is entirely powered by that solar energy capture, with an end-to-end efficiency of around one per cent. That's from the photons of sunlight hitting the panel, to the delivery of the fabricated articles. Which in terms of the performance of that kind of technology is pretty efficient, by the way, though it may not sound it.'

Bowles nodded. 'OK. So what's it doing with all that energy?'

'Here's a speeded-up view.' Marlowe switched to another angle, which showed a flock of smaller craft dashing away from the parent lander to the perimeter of the solar energy blanket. There they started to work the surface: scooping up dust, digging out lumps of rock. These diggers then transferred the material to more specialised craft, like trucks with big hoppers, which in turn transported the material to what appeared to be some kind of processing units. Before long, complex metal parts were being spewed out on the lunar surface – almost comical in the speeded-up imagery, Tash thought. Meanwhile, shadows cast by the Sun shifted slowly but steadily, like the hands of a clock.

Complex parts. But they were parts evidently ready to be assembled into new machines.

'That's what Mel and I saw in Oregon,' Tash said.

'Correct. Developed, trialled there, before they transferred to the more challenging conditions of the Moon. We western-ers have been allowed to see much of this before, in stages,' Marlowe said. 'The self-growing solar blanket, the specialised sub-machines, each with a task that contributes to an overall process. That's thanks mostly to, it seems, Wu Zhi's mother, who for all her denials seems to have an instinct for openness, comparatively.

'The Chinese teams evidently tried it out piece by piece until every component, every process was tested and true. Only then, you see, do you integrate all the elements to ensure they work together?

The image was plunged into darkness, quite abruptly, to be replaced by a kind of ghostly simulacrum, Tash thought, as she watched blurry representations of the trucks and diggers, glowing red, rolling around. 'Lunar night,' she guessed.

'Yes,' said Marlowe. 'Which is roughly the same length it always was, though the Moon's orbit around the Earth has changed . . . I told you this whole sequence spans thirty-six days – Earth days – all apparently pre-programmed. So this went on right through a lunar night, and back into the daylight.' She tapped at her screen, accelerated through more blurry night-time imagery, until the daylight returned.

By now, Tash saw, the original craft, still intact, was surrounded by heaps of components, mostly unidentifiable, lying around in gleaming piles that looked random but surely weren't.

'This was a few days ago,' Marlowe said. I haven't viewed this footage myself by the way, it's that new. I *think* I know what's going to happen, but I prefer to wait and see.'

Bowles, restless, kept one eye on the election coverage. Tash could see that the predicted parliamentary majority for Mara Caine's English Reconstruction Party was growing.

'Shit,' said Bowles. Then he glanced at Mel and Jane. 'Sorry.'

'Heard worse,' Jane said bluntly.

'You know, maybe our little English pantomime tonight is going to distract world attention, even from Chinese super-robots on the Moon. It's the wider political context. You've got to remember the Americans are going to the polls next year. And Cox is already in trouble over there with her constitutional reform package. Well, asking the US Senate to vote itself out of existence was always going to be a challenge . . . Depressing as it is, everybody *will* be paying attention. We're the canary in the populist coalmine.'

Jane was puzzled by that. 'Does that mean Ms Caine is popular?'

Mel smiled. 'Popul*ist*, Jane, not popul*ar*. It means − well, telling people what they want to hear, which isn't necessarily the truth.'

Jane thought that over.

Grace, still locked into her Earthwatch coverage, said sourly, '*I* can tell you what people bloody want. Not distractions. Not politics. They want all *this* to stop. Just stop, that's all. We all got through the Blink, more or less, but it's this ongoing stuff that gets you down. On and on. The weather stuff. Scary robots on the Moon. Waiting for another Blink, which could come at any time. It's worse than those years-long pandemics we used to have. Oh, you can tell me it's not the fault of any government, it's all down to Galaxias. I know that up here,' and she tapped her forehead. 'But not in my heart. My gut. And that's why the government lost. Give the other lot a chance.'

For her, Tash thought, that was quite a speech. Grace seemed visibly angry.

And Fred gave Tash a look.

Tash got up, made her way over to Grace. 'Hey. Let's go make some coffee.'

The main room had a small kitchen offshoot. Tash left the door half-open, as she and Grace crowded inside and started work on a round of coffees. A small screen showed that Earthwatch feed. Grace started rinsing out a percolator.

Tash, setting out cups, felt oddly uncomfortable.

For all she had worked with Grace for a long time, and notably on Blink Day, Tash had never felt all that close to her. And, Tash realised now, she had no real idea what was going on inside Grace's head. Her sometimes startling reactions proved that.

But here they were.

Tash said carefully, 'So, Grace. Are you OK? I've never heard you sound so . . . I don't know. Distracted.' *Distressed* would have felt like the wrong word, for Grace Butterworth.

Grace said bitterly, 'Really? But then, you've never really listened to me at all, have you?'

'I . . .'

Probably not, if she was honest.

She stared at the Earthwatch feed on the wall, trying to gather clues. As far as she could make out there was no immediate new disaster unfolding, for once. But the screens showed a too familiar litany of aftermath. Hapless refugees trudging in columns: families, this time fleeing south from high-latitude homelands in northern Canada, Siberia. The first post-Blink northern hemisphere winter, shaped by Earth's subtly adjusted orbit, had predictably been a long, deep, bad one. So now, in the summer, people were taking the chance to head south. And yet the overstretched governments were trying to assemble help for those new refugees. Temporary camps were blooming across the lower latitudes.

Tash wondered vaguely how many older people there might be in these huge new flows who had been driven to refugee status *twice*, fleeing north from the climate-crisis heat as children, and now heading south again as parents, even grand-parents, abandoning colonies only decades old.

'It's going to get worse,' Grace said. She tapped her phone, and brought up images on the main screen, with scrolling text. 'See for yourself.'

Now Tash found herself looking at geological images. Geysers in Yellowstone. An ash plume over a caldera called Rinjani in Indonesia, whose thirteenth-century eruption might have triggered a Little Ice Age, according to the captions. Steam vents on Tambora, location of an eruption which, apparently, had caused the Year Without a Summer in 1815. Earnest geologists, talking about magma movements and gas pockets. Many of these old volcanic scars were itching now, one way or another—

'The slosh,' Grace said now.

'Hmm?'

'That's what they are calling it. *The slosh*. After the big jolt of the Blink itself, and now the Earth is in the wrong orbit, all the tides and stuff are wrong. The weather, the oceans are all disturbed. And the geological stuff will be the worst. Under the volcanoes and earthquake zones, all that liquid rock sloshing around underground, in the . . .'

'In the mantle?'

'We'll get quakes, some major ones. And volcanoes. The big ones that are due to go pop sometime in the future anyhow.'

A memory surfaced at the back of Tash's mind. *Volcanoes.* 'Naples,' she said now. 'Naples, where your sister lives. There are volcanoes there. Vesuvius?'

'That's on one side of the city,' Grace said dully. 'On the other side is the Campi Flegrei. The field of fire. Another bloody one. There have been magma movements. Whole place might go up tomorrow, or next week, or never. They've banned travel out of the city—'

'And your niece, right?'

She smiled tightly. 'Billie. Born on Blink Day, if you remember. A Blink Baby, they call them now. People are saying they are cursed. Or blessed. Children of Galaxias.'

Charlie Marlowe called out from the main room. 'I heard that.'

Tash and Grace exchanged a glance.

The coffee was ready. Tash poured it out into mugs, and bore the tray back into the main room, followed by Grace.

Marlowe looked over, distracted from the Moon, as she took her coffee with mumbled thanks. 'Cursed children, people are saying, are they? Did I hear that right? In the second half of the twenty-first century? Well, if we are consumed by such ideas and prejudices, perhaps Galaxias is right to confine us.'

Mel touched her arm. 'You shouldn't say that.'

'No,' Fred Bowles said. 'You shouldn't, Charlie. None of us is as rational as we would like to think. People *know* it makes no sense to punish a government just because we were in power when the Blink came, although it's perfectly fair to criticise our response. Nevertheless, that's how people *feel*. You can't condemn them for it; you have to work with it, to educate, to persuade. Let's hope that rationality prevails, in the long run. If not tonight.' And he glanced gloomily at the running coverage of the election on his screens.

The ERP results were mounting steadily, remorselessly – actually beating the predictions Tash had made in her own head for this time of night, not yet one in the morning. And it looked as if the outgoing Prime Minister, at his own constituency, was already preparing to concede the inevitable defeat.

Suddenly Tash felt drained, tired. It had already been a long day – a long few weeks, as the campaign had wound down through its weary stages, a hopeless cause from the beginning. 'Maybe I shouldn't have had that whisky,' she murmured.

Mel looked over and smiled. Tash saw that Jane was nodding off, leaning against her mother's arm. Mel touched a finger to her lips.

Then Charlie Marlowe gave a shout of triumph.

All of them, including Bowles, Grace and a wide-awake Jane, gathered again, and stared at images projected from Charlie Marlowe's screen above the small table. At first glance Tash saw what looked like toy rocket ships, two of them, rising up into a black lunar sky . . .

'OK,' Fred said. 'Tell me what I'm seeing.'

Marlowe looked up at him. She seemed inordinately pleased. 'A bit of remarkable ingenuity by the Chinese, that's what. I think some of us guessed at this outcome, but to actually *see* it . . . Look – you saw the mother ship land on the Moon, in the middle of the Sea of Moscow. Fully automated. Thirty-six days ago.'

She tapped the screen and key images blinked past. That

solar blanket was unrolled, the specialist machines opened up, the fabrication processes began.

'Well, now we know what the end product was to be.' She wafted a hand through the virtual diorama, speeding it up.

And Tash saw how the subsidiary machines clambered around to put together the components they had manufactured, all created on the spot from lunar resources, into what very quickly – and, she judged, it must have been quick even in real time – crystallised into *a copy of the mother ship*. There was even a second solar blanket, she saw, in segments, being rolled up and stowed into the second ship.

As the equipment was loaded the ships' hulls sealed themselves shut, becoming seamless.

For a moment there was stillness.

Then, without warning, the two ships, looking identical now, side by side, rose up from the surface on near-invisible plumes of exhaust gas and churned-up lunar dust.

And then they were gone, leaving only pits and tracks in the face of the Moon.

'Wow,' Jane said. 'That makes me shiver.'

'*Self-replicating technology*,' Marlowe said. 'That's what the Chinese have been building up to. You all saw the whole sequence, across thirty-six days. A single machine landed, on bare lunar ground, and made what appeared to be *an identical copy of itself*, all from sunlight and lunar resources. And the two of them just took off. The Chinese could hardly conceal the stages. We had enough clues, starting with the self-replicating solar blanket itself. But we had no clear idea of *this*, before now, this final experiment – and, evidently, demonstration. Again, something they couldn't hide.'

Mel paged through screens on her phone. 'Yes. There has been plenty of theorising about this, going back a hundred years. Nearly. Von Neumann's theoretical studies. But it's all very well theorising about machine reproduction, quite another to build a process that actually *works*.'

Jane was grinning. 'It's like something living. Giving birth.'

Marlowe nodded. 'Everybody uses words like "living". Yes, the Chinese are mimicking life here. But a new sort of "life", very limited, and dedicated to specific purposes.

'And the main purpose is economic. Well, usually, in most studies. A fabricator can land, and use the local resources and the power of sunlight to make whatever its mission needs – including copies of itself. And the process will repeat, over and over, guided only by high-level commands from its ultimate creators. The only cost, after development, you see, is the delivery of the first machine to be landed on the Moon. Or wherever.'

Mel nodded. 'And then the real potential of the technology cuts in. One factory ship becomes two; two becomes four; then eight; then sixteen—'

Fred Bowles looked bewildered and alarmed in equal measures, Tash thought. He said, 'Charlie? You said the main purpose was usually economic. Not in this case, surely. Then what?'

'Well, replication is also a quick way to make a *lot* of stuff. One becomes two, two four, four eight . . . as long as the resources last. And in the process you consume a lot of stuff.'

Jane said, waving her arms, 'Until the whole Moon is eaten up? And kaboom!'

Bowles looked still more alarmed. 'I certainly hope *that's* not the plan.'

'Oh, I don't believe they are staying around,' Marlowe said. 'I mean, it looks as if all of this, the whole lunar phase, was no more than a final proving test for the technology. And now those two ships are steering off to start another project, or phase – somewhere else.'

Fred Bowles was frowning. 'Somewhere else? Where?'

'We have no firm data yet.' She glanced at Mel. 'At least I don't think so.'

Mel hastily swiped through imagery. 'Well . . . The ships have left the Moon, Charlie. Left lunar orbit, already. Both, apparently, on the same trajectory. See?' She flicked charts from her phone onto the smart wall.

Bowles stared, evidently bewildered, at charts of trajectories and orbits. 'Just tell me, damn it. So they left the Moon. To go where? To Earth?'

'Not there. We can't be sure yet—'

Bowles's phone sounded. He glared into its screen. Then he stood up, neatened his jacket, pushed up the knot in his tie, tapped his ear piece. 'Don't you think you had better bloody well find out, then? Ideally before I go to brief the new Prime Minister, and my new boss, pro tem.' He caught Tash's eye. 'It's starting to happen. I've just been summoned to Caine's constituency. She's there for her own count, and she wants us all there, all the ministers and shadow ministers she can drag in. She's not messing about. Christ, it will be like the coronation of William the Conqueror.'

'I'll get onto the travel,' Grace said, and she went to work on her own phone.

'Tash, with me, and be ready to brainstorm on the way. At least we might have a chance to guess at what she's going to pitch for immediately. Her first-hundred-days policies, the initial positioning—'

Tash held up her phone. 'Already on it. If she goes for everything she's spun in her campaign speeches, we might be looking at rationing, new border controls—'

'Her new English Regularised Calendar,' Bowles said. 'Don't forget that. Oh, joy. OK, I'm ready. Look, the rest of you stay in here as long as you like. Or can stand it—'

'Mercury,' said Charlie Marlowe, standing up herself.

'What's that?'

'The new Chinese probes. We've tracked their burns since they left orbit, and the delta-V indicates they are entering a Hohmann trajectory—'

Bowles snapped, 'In English, for God's sake, Charlie. Mercury? *Planet* Mercury?'

'That's where they are heading, it looks like. A long unpowered coast into the heart of the Solar System. Get there in a hundred days or so – if that's their final destination.'

'Why would the Chinese go to Mercury?'

Mel and Marlowe shared a glance.

'I have no idea,' Marlowe said honestly. 'Maybe we will find out in a hundred days. October?'

'Hmm. I think I'd need answers long before then. I—'

'Transport ready,' Grace barked.

'Good. Enjoy the whisky – oh, hell, bring it with us, Grace. Charlie, please figure out the implications of this somehow. And quicker than a hundred days. *Why Mercury?*' Then, surprisingly, he grinned, once, at them all. 'Listen. Quite a night, in the end. The kind you will remember for the rest of your lives. Welcome to a glorious new England, and the start of the Caine Reconstruction – *and this Chinese* phenomenon, whatever it is – and God help us all. Come on, Tash.'

33

September AD 2060:
Year 4 ERC, Summer

Deep in the shadow of the Earth, Wu Zhi watched as the EarthMoon freighter docked smoothly with the Lodestone.

Launched from Vandenberg in California, the senior North American spaceport since the abandonment of a flooded Canaveral, the freighter itself was a venerable Jones, Inc. workhorse: a design primarily intended to ferry crew and cargo to lunar-orbit locations, now stretched with booster pallets for these bolder journeys into Earth's umbra.

And Zhi didn't have a clue why its passengers had come here.

Had to be something major, and therefore unwelcome, given the urgency of their project. Naturally enough, work on the Pioneer project, as well as its Pathfinder precursor, was mostly suspended for the duration of the visit. That was for security reasons, Zhi knew, even though Pioneer was already by far the most locked-down assignment Jones, Inc., had ever taken on — which was saying something, given Serena Jones's close ties to the US military.

The post-Blink world was a much more wary, suspicious place, and the Pioneer project, intended as at least a symbolic challenge to the diffuse might of Galaxias, attracted a lot of attention from 'the crazies', as Jones, Inc. insiders had come to call them. Some crazies, including some in the military it was said, supported the Pioneer project because they thought it was some kind of weapons system, aimed at Galaxias – and others opposed it for the precise same reason. Some religious types thought Pioneer was possibly blasphemous; you didn't go dissecting God. And still others imagined it was part of some global conspiracy, with an elite lying to the world somehow, or even seeking to ally somehow *with* Galaxias. And so on.

You would think a deep-space station more than a million kilometres from Earth would be about as safe as you could get. But they had had repeated briefings on how that wasn't particularly true, with scenarios such as the alarming ease with which a bomb could be smuggled into a supply-drop drone. So security was always tight.

And so, even after all the effort put into this visit, the disruption to the ongoing work of the Pioneer project, and the sheer expense of it all, Zhi wasn't particularly surprised that only three of the staff aboard the Lodestone were to be allowed to greet the visitors in person. Of the rest of the current crew, none, not even the commander, Ange Costello, were allowed anywhere near the docking port when it finally opened. The ultimate security measure: just don't talk to anybody.

The chosen three were Zhi himself, Serena Jones, naturally enough, and the station chief engineer, Sara West. West was a previously Earthside-based Jones, Inc. employee – short, slim, with crewcut, prematurely grey hair – much valued by Serena Jones, evidently, and brought up here for the duration.

That was all.

Even Marina Petko and Ito Katsuo were excluded, the surviving veterans of the catastrophic Blink Day Mars mission, and now the pencilled-in crew of the Pioneer itself, along with Zhi.

And, after all this fuss, Zhi was faintly surprised when only two visitors from Earth came swimming through the hub lock: Lee Yamanaka, the President's science adviser – and, at her side, Harry Regent, in Air Force blue.

Harry had been aboard the Lodestone on the day of the Blink, and, having handled himself well in the eyes of his superiors, had since been promoted and assigned to new duties Earthside. Now, an experienced astronaut with a military background, he must have seemed an obvious choice for this assignment, accompanying Yamanaka on her mission, whatever it was.

It had to be a big deal. Zhi had known it since learning that Serena Jones had come up here specifically to host it. And now here was the bulk of Lee Yamanaka, dressed in her trademark loose Hawaiian shirt over an NHSA jumpsuit. The science adviser herself, still a member of President Cox's core inner Cabinet, swanning all the way out here to a deep-space station.

But, for Zhi, it was all just getting in the way. He had set his heart on the completion of the Pioneer project. *That* had become his way of working through the loss of Jim on Blink Day, even if it cost the US and AFS taxpayers billions of bucks in the process.

He hoped against hope that this new twist wouldn't somehow derail all that.

Once they were through the lock, Serena Jones herself greeted Yamanaka, with handshakes that were quite formally done given they were all floating in mid-air. Jones hastily introduced Sara West.

The tone was sombre, the greetings subdued.

And Zhi faced Harry. Both grinned, uncertain, drifting in the bright fluorescent light.

Zhi said at last, 'Shit, you look hot in Air Force blue.'

'Asshole.'

Then they broke, collided clumsily, and embraced, hugging and patting each other's back. Just for an instant, Zhi felt an almost overwhelming closeness to this man.

Harry pushed him away, holding his shoulders. 'So. You OK?'

Zhi shrugged. 'About losing Jim? No. Of course not. But being back here helps, actually. And the fact that I'm doing something about it. In an indirect way, anyhow.'

Harry nodded, and, drifting, did his best to straighten up his uniform jacket. 'Well, yeah. We'll always have Blink Day, won't we? But—'

'But you should have stayed in the project,' Zhi said. 'As I did. All that training and experience wasted.'

'Not that I had a lot of choice. It's a different world, now, Zhi. I wasn't so surprised when the USAF drafted me back. In fact, given my profile with NHSA, I was a kind of poster boy for that sort of re-enlistment.'

Zhi frowned. 'Hm. The militarisation of society. We aren't actually at war, Harry.'

'Yeah, but the world is in turmoil. Everybody is waiting for the next post-Blink shoe to fall — maybe a crop failure, maybe some climate collapse, even a terrorist strike. And then all the time you have this abstract threat in the sky. It makes it worse somehow that we can't even *see* it. Galaxias. Just that damn lurker on the Moon. The politicians seem helpless.'

Zhi felt troubled. 'I suppose I have heard similar whispers out of England — you remember my friend Tash Brand, who works for the government there? Mental health issues have become a widespread concern. But still, Cox did say—'

'President Cox is up for re-election this November,' Harry said coolly. He glanced over at Yamanaka and Jones, and leaned closer to Zhi. 'Which is why we're here. You'll find out soon enough.'

Serena Jones called for their attention, effortlessly taking command. They gathered in the air in this cluttered cabin, its walls crowded with equipment.

'Well, now – once more, welcome aboard, the two of you, Lee, Harry. Let's hope we can make sure all the effort and time you have put into getting here were worthwhile. So I think Professor Yamanaka and I ought to have a quick preliminary debrief before we involve the rest of you. Lee, you're welcome to come to what I like to call my ready room. Which is neither ready nor, strictly speaking, a room. Umm, Zhi, why don't you catch up with Harry? Take him to see how we are getting on with the Pioneer. And the Pathfinder, if you like – which is closer to completion.'

Harry raised his eyebrows. 'Pathfinder?'

Zhi explained, 'A precursor project. We flew Sputnik, a technology demonstrator, and now we're trying out the dark energy drive on a crewed craft – Gemini to the Pioneer's Apollo. Fine, Serena. But aren't you afraid we'll leak secrets?'

Yamanaka frowned. 'Let me answer that. First, I trust you. Both. Second, you have nothing here which is not known to the US civilian authorities and the military, so, Zhi, you have no secrets *to* leak. Captain Regent, on the other hand, does have some classified knowledge, but I feel I can trust him not to blab, frankly. Even to his closest friends, such as yourself.'

Jones put in, 'However, that is why, Zhi, I have asked Ange – Lee, that's Angela Costello, our station commander – to make sure she and the rest of the crew stay out of touch with the visitors. That's perfectly manageable for a few hours. This station is a big spoked torus, and even though we mined it for parts for the Pioneer, there are still plenty of alternate routes from one point to another. We can keep out of each other's way.' She checked her old-fashioned astronaut-style wristwatch. 'Shall we say thirty minutes? Zhi, bring Harry back to my ready room after that. Sara, why don't you join us there?'

Sara West stiffened. 'Why? If Ange, the station commander, isn't included? Am I to serve the drinks?'

Zhi knew Sara was close to Serena, and had a high opinion of herself – but he didn't blame her for asking. The clock was forever ticking towards the end of their project's decade-long time allowance. They always all had mountains of work. They were all always aware of time passing.

Yamanaka grinned. 'Good for you, kid. No, not that. Serena tells me you're her top engineer, which is saying something. We need your input. Look, I'll serve *you* the drinks. For now . . . let's just talk. All will, I hope, become clear. Or as clear as anything is in this rather paranoid age.'

Serena seemed to soften. 'Zhi, Sara – I'm sorry to be so oblique. It must be obvious there is something big rolling down the pipe towards us. *I* know very little about it, you know nothing, yet. Whatever it is, it's something which, if I'm honest, I was reluctant to consider at all. For us any side project is a – diversion, at best – from our own main goals. Not to mention a threat to the schedule.

'But we live in extraordinary times. We are involved in extraordinary actions. I think I always anticipated something like this would hit us. It always does. And, as I overheard you say, Captain Regent, this is an election year. We all have our duty to fulfil.' Another glance at the watch. 'Twenty-eight minutes. Don't be late.'

So Zhi led Harry through the maze-like structure of the Lodestone, towards the perimeter of the torus-shaped station, heading for a good viewing point for the half-completed Pioneer.

Harry, back in the days before the Blink, had actually spent longer on this station than Zhi had. But the Lodestone had changed a lot since then, and he was soon disoriented, Zhi noticed with a certain glee, as they made their way around the hub complex, diverting past one closed hatch after another. And as they descended through shafts and moved away from the centre, and the colour-coding of the walls changed to indicate increasing spin gravity − but, with the station no longer spinning on its axis, the effective gravity staying at zero − Harry looked almost queasy.

Zhi grinned. 'If you need to throw up, Commodore Regent, use your hat.'

'Just Captain, asshole. Shit. Goes to show how your body remembers stuff. Once I knew this place like the back of my own eyelids. But now it feels like a fairground ride. They sure made a mess of our station, didn't they?'

'Unfortunately, yes. The times we live in, Harry.'

Harry glanced up at him. 'And people have lost a lot more. I know, my friend.'

They reached the outer rim and made their way along what was effectively a stretch of curved corridor, made up of Shelter units, boxy modules each twelve metres long, four wide, joined end to end by flexible airtight junctions. Once, a stately rotation had delivered a steady gravity of about Earth normal here. But now the rotation was gone, the stars in the pitch-black sky, visible through the many windows, stationary.

'I remember Ange Costello running down here,' Harry said now. 'Around and around, with the rest of us cowering out of her way.'

'Well, the perimeter was nearly four kilometres. Even I ran

a lockdown marathon once . . . You couldn't do it now. It's not a complete circuit any more, since the cannibalisation. Here. Good view of the construction shack.'

They paused and peered out of the windows, drifting from location to location. The installations beyond were brilliantly lit.

Harry screened his eyes, wincing. 'Wow. So bright.'

'I know. Once this was one of the darkest places in the Solar System, remember? The deep shadow of the Earth. The reason we came, the reason we built our big telescopes here. Well, now it's a construction yard. Where we are building *that*.'

And he pointed to a boxy hulk, adrift in the glare of the spots.

Most of it was a 'jig factory', jargon for a kind of frame of trusses, beams and girders set out in the rough shape of the final craft, and into which various components could be manoeuvred with precision, mated, fitted out. Zhi made out the glare of welding torches, wielded by a phalanx of drones that cautiously worked their way along the assembly. The drones ran on rails or cables stretched out along the trusses, smoothly, precisely, with high energy efficiency.

This was the way you built things in space, Zhi knew. Most days no humans went out there at all. It took too long just getting ready for an EVA and decompressing later, and humans were a *lot* more prone to making mistakes.

'So,' he said hesitantly. 'Behold Pioneer 14.'

'Those are more standard Shelter modules, aren't they?'

'You got it. And you can see how that main hull has been put together. It's never going to be pretty. We used forty modules in all.' Drifting in the air, he mimed a square shape with his hands. 'You make a frame of four modules, twelve metres long, four metres thick. And you stack ten such frames, weld them together, to give you a hollow box forty metres long. When inessentials and double walls have been stripped out, the mass will be about that of the old ISS – including the ramscoop, which masses next to nothing. What do you think?'

'I think,' said Harry, the crisp blue of his jacket reflecting in the windows, 'that will be one impressive mother. But ugly as sin. And all of it cannibalised from the Lodestone?'

'Afraid so. Well, the scoop itself is a specialised build, of course. Much of that boxy hull will be living space – we're looking at a mission of a few years. And, you won't like this, we had to cannibalise some of our astronomy instruments to build the sail's central frame, and other vacuum-friendly infrastructure. That broke our hearts, I think.'

Regent winced. 'I bet. But don't blame yourself. It's not an age when science, pure science anyhow, is a priority. Not any more. Which is why I'm back wearing the blue. That dark energy ramscoop, though. I hesitate to ask. I don't suppose you've got around to proving that the technology actually *works*.'

Zhi grinned. 'You always were a shitter. We did fly the Sputnik, you know. That was a decent technology demonstrator. And as for proving we can scale it up – well, that's what the Pathfinder is for.'

'The Pathfinder? Oh, your Gemini . . .'

Zhi pointed to a smaller structure off in one corner of the visual field, overwhelmed by the hull of the greater craft. Just a single square frame.

'Four modules only, stripped down to about forty tonnes. Big enough to take a couple of crew, however. We'll install a scaled-down dark energy scoop, and load up crew – and, well, fly it up and down the umbra, the shadow of the Earth, as with the Sputnik. No sunlight pressure, to prove the dark energy drive.

'And then we plan to make more extensive journeys. You know how it is with a new ship, let alone new technologies. The more you can learn about its handling characteristics the better. Possibly a jaunt out to the orbit of Mars, following a Hohmann orbit, more or less. Yes, Serena does think of it as our Gemini programme, which was a proving step before Apollo. Ito Katsuo and Ange Costello are down as prime crew for the Pathfinder, by the way. Ange is still station commander and deserves some time off the base.'

'Ito's the Mars astronaut. On your prime crew for Pioneer also?'

'Right. So we figure at least one of us should have direct experience of handling the dark energy ram.'

'OK. And then it's off to the Kuiper Belt?' He clapped Zhi on the back, making Zhi grab a handhold for support. 'Well, I'm impressed, old buddy. Not convinced, but impressed.'

Zhi snorted. 'You'd give your right leg to get that gig.'

'If you say so.' He glanced at his phone. 'But I do know that Jones will chew off both our right legs if we are late for her briefing. Come on.'

They moved off, Zhi leading.

Harry called ahead, 'And don't think you can lose me by running ahead, asshole. You made a mess of my beautiful station, but I still know it like the inside of my eyelids – *ow*! Shit, who put that brace there? . . .'

Zhi knew that the space Serena Jones called her 'ready room' was not much more than a standard crew cabin with a few minimal extras, even though it was receiving such an illustrious visitor as the President's science adviser. The cramped compartment with the standard fittings, the fold-down bed and fold-up table, the lockers for spare clothing, personal gear and work documentation crammed into the spaces behind the wall panels. A door to a small private shower room was half open. But Serena had one main privilege, a minuscule private kitchen area with a water spigot, where she kept a coffee printer, with flasks floating in the air, attached by cords to hooks on the wall.

Aside from that it was a work space, a nest of papers and manuals, and screens stuck to every surface, most of them scrolling with text or refreshed imagery even now.

Zhi always thought this was stimulating, somehow. Proof of Serena's own hands-on approach to stuff. And Yamanaka, once she was floating free amid the debris with a coffee flask in her hands, looked interested, even pleased.

Sara West, meanwhile, the growly, faithful engineer, evidently out of her depth, was just as evidently trying to keep out of the way. Embarrassed even, Zhi thought, unsure of her place here. That was what politics did to you.

Harry, meanwhile, on entering the room, looked professionally suspicious. He held up his palm, waved it back and forth, and checked a monitor on his uniform sleeve. 'Excuse me,' he said, not looking up. 'Should really have let me in here before Prof Yamanaka. Protocol.'

'Just doing your job, I know,' Jones said. 'Sorry for being so messy, today of all days. I should have thought you'd need to check it out.'

'As you say. Just my job.'

Yamanaka beamed. 'Well, I can tell you I feel right at home in here. I'm a working scientist, remember – when I get the chance. And, believe me, my offices back home are every bit as messy and chaotic and as gloriously creative as this. *I* never throw everything out either. Why, I noticed this.' She pawed through a cloud of roughly gathered debris in a net in one corner, and retrieved a crude model, a rough wheel shape. 'Drinking straws? Cut down to some standard length and glued end to end . . .'

Serena smiled. 'Well, here you are in the real thing. This was our first conception of the Lodestone, at the Jones, Inc. skunk works in California. I grew up with CGI and virtual modelling, but I was a kid who always liked to make stuff I could touch and hold.'

Zhi grinned at Sara, and they both parroted, 'Water rockets in the back yard!'

'OK, OK. You two have heard too many of my pitches. The principle still stands, though. This is large-scale engineering. But you need to fill your imagination with what the finished product will look like before you can even begin—'

'And in that case,' Yamanaka cut in, waving a hand, 'I hope you have plenty of spare drinking straws around. Because I've come to ask you to change course. Or at least to tack a little in the breeze . . .' None too discreetly she glanced at a time display on one wall. 'We'd better get on with it. I am due to brief the White House in less than an hour.'

Zhi, feeling protective about the project, frowned. 'Brief them about what? What change of course? You know what we're doing here. The whole world does. Because we *told* them, back in the day. This is America's highest-profile direct response to the Galaxias intervention. And Serena made sure the goal was clear. Three people, destination Centaurus, there in a decade. So I don't see what other priority—'

Jones held up her hand, silencing him. 'Let's hear what Professor Yamanaka has to say.'

Yamanaka nodded, somewhat sombrely. 'Thank you. Yes, you're right, Zhi, this is already a very high-profile project. The public supports its goals, and supports the President for backing you – the polls are holding up, anyhow. But things have changed.'

Zhi snorted. 'You mean, President Cox is facing a challenge from that loudmouth Stringer?'

Harry touched his arm, gently. *Shut up.*

'Actually, yes, you're right,' Yamanaka said. 'The President is facing a tough re-election campaign; everybody knows that. Probably any sitting President would in the present circumstances. And, yes, Stringer is questioning the value of Pioneer; yes, the President is having to defend you. But that's not the primary problem.'

'Then what is?' Zhi asked.

She looked at him sadly. '*The Chinese*, Zhi. Your own mother – possibly. That's who.'

Zhi frowned. 'I've heard nothing from my mother save for routine stuff – family stuff – for months now.' He tried not to blush. 'Last time I got a call from her, I was allowed to take it up here, it was because I forgot her birthday.'

A gentle punch on the arm from Harry Regent. 'Asshole. Family 101.'

Yamanaka considered Zhi, not unkindly. 'I don't blame you for being out of touch. Even if not for the security restrictions on communications, you've been very busy up here, obviously. The trouble is, Zhi, we suspect your mother has been busy too. I bet any radio silence from her started around fifteen months ago.'

'Why then? . . . Oh. Mercury.'

'Right. Because that's when the Chinese, very publicly, launched the first of a small fleet of automated craft, from the Moon, to Mercury. That's why. But we still have no real idea what they are doing there.'

Jones nodded. 'I've seen some of the background briefing myself. The trouble is—'

'What?'

'There isn't much of it.'

Yamanaka said, 'True enough. We all saw the final self-rep experiment on the Moon. Well, it could hardly be concealed. But we think that was a crucial proving achievement. The engineers had to demonstrate to themselves, and to their superiors and political controllers, that this thing, their Acorn technology, *worked*, end to end, from the touchdown of one bird, the build, and the launching of two. Even if it revealed a lot of the detail of their project to the rest of the world.'

Harry Regent put in, 'I might say that we've long known the commercial logic of replicator technologies. We in the West, I mean. Sure, replicator tech was going to be expensive to develop – but once you had it, you could get an unlimited number of copies, for no more than the price of the basic resources anyhow. And *then* you could have a strategic advantage. You could use such technologies to take the high ground of Solar System resources, before the rest had a chance. *If* you were first in the game.'

'Well,' Yamanaka said, 'even if they had been working on this stuff before Blink Day, in the end the Chinese didn't play that game at all. Any variant of it. The Moon, it seems, was just a proving ground. As soon as their basic technology passed this final test, off went the two replicator ships, the Acorns, parent and child, off the Moon, back into space. *Then to Mercury.* A move that surprised us all. And then—'

Zhi broke in. 'There must have been some monitoring of their activities. Never made public.'

'Only glimpses,' Yamanaka said. 'But that is why Harry and I are here.'

Sara seemed suspicious. 'Why? This is a project to construct an entirely different kind of spacecraft – and nothing to do with replication technologies.'

Yamanaka glanced at Jones with a rueful grin. 'I am presenting this badly. I apologise for any offence. You must understand this is not my . . . expected career path. I am a scientist rather than a diplomat.

'Here are the facts you need to know.

'Yes, in June of last year the first two Acorn craft left the Moon, and journeyed on a low-energy orbit to Mercury. We know they arrived in orbit around the planet after a hundred and five days – in late September last year. And we know that twenty-four hours later they landed, side by side, in a large feature known as the Caloris basin, a vast impact crater. And, in the year or more since then – well, we've seen very little. At first, anyhow.'

Zhi thought hard. 'What about satellites, probes? I know we had some deep-space inner Solar System probes, studying the Sun, Mercury. Ange Costello would know, that's one of her specialities—'

'Yes, but we had no functioning orbiters around Mercury itself,' Yamanaka said. '*They* might have survived the Blink, when the Sun's gravity suddenly switched off. The free-flyers, which were in solar orbit themselves, were scattered. Not entirely lost, but they have proved useless to observe Mercury's surface in detail.'

'And telescopes? Why, the L-Cubed-T here at the Lodestone—'

'Was actually used for the purpose,' Serena Jones admitted. 'I had to keep it from most of the crew. Ange knew. Remember those Navy guys who came up here, supposedly to advise me on imaging technology to be used on Pioneer? Ange ran the experiments for us.'

Zhi had known nothing of this. And nor, evidently, had Sara, given the way she stared now, open-mouthed.

'Even so we have little more than blurred images of – scars – on Mercury's surface,' Yamanaka said. 'From all such sources. We know what the Acorns *do*. They are replicators. We suspect they are busily replicating away down there – using Mercury resources rather than lunar.

'That must be causing them to modify their technical strategy somewhat, by the way. Mercury is different from the Moon in many respects – a different mineralogy, for one thing. For instance, we think they are, umm, *growing* their solar energy capture panels with glass as a base, fused silicates, rather than aluminium as on the Moon. We can see the sprawl of such fields as they grow. On the other hand the available solar energy is much more intense on Mercury, so progress must be rapid.

'But we can't *see*.' She clenched a fist. 'I can't tell the President what it is the Chinese are up to even day to day, let alone what the long-term goal is. And if it has anything to do with the Galaxias crisis.'

Jones said, 'Replicators on Mercury, though. That could lead to something big. That's the *point* of replicators, in a way. From small beginnings . . .'

'Hm.' Sara tapped a pad. 'So if the replicators reproduced at the same doubling rate as on the Moon – thirty-six days, right? – there might be a thousand installations up there by now. Even allowing for waste, failures. And even if their energy-capture blankets are scaled down from the Moon, given the higher intensity of sunlight at Mercury . . . the whole collection might span twenty, thirty kilometres. Ought to be very visible. And growing all the time.'

Zhi thought back. 'The conferences that have been held.

When we announced *this* project, the Pioneer, an active way of, well, pushing back at Galaxias. There were the Chinese – my own government – preaching caution and patience, the way they believe Galaxias may be thinking too. Covering Mercury with replicators doesn't sound too cautious or patient, does it?'

Sara said carefully, 'I suppose it does depend on the final goal—'

But Harry broke in, speaking softly to Zhi. 'It wasn't just your government who's been lying, pal,' Harry said. 'It was worse than that. *It was your own mother.* Who hasn't seen fit to confide in you, has she? Even though she seems to have been central to the whole replication project. She didn't get in touch even now, even though she must have known we were coming here.' He shook his head. 'Don't answer that. I know she hasn't. Because the security analysts told me so.'

Serena, unexpectedly, drifted over to Zhi and put an arm around his shoulders. 'I am sorry you have had to learn about this in such a way. This evident betrayal.'

Yamanaka studied him. 'And I too am sorry. We have known each other for some time. I had no way of discussing this with you in advance, Zhi, as you must understand.'

Zhi shook his head – covering his reaction, as he pushed this latest hurt deep down inside. 'I'm OK. As you have guessed, all of you, my relationship with my mother is complicated.' He shrugged. 'She has her goals, I have mine. It's been that way all my life.'

He was uncomfortably aware of Harry's reaction as he spoke – a stare, hard, judgemental, calculating.

Zhi said, 'It will never change. But still, Prof Yamanaka, Sara's question stands. What does this have to do with us?'

Yamanaka sighed. 'Well, I've only spelled this out so far to Serena herself, just now—'

'I can guess, though,' Sara said calmly. *'You want us to go to Mercury.'*

There was an intake of breath.

'That's about the size of it,' Serena said.

Even Harry Regent looked startled. Zhi realised he really hadn't been briefed beyond the barest need to know.

Sara actually laughed. 'Of course, Mercury. It's obvious. Or at least, it is obvious that President Cox needs to do something about the Mercury crisis. Because she's got Stringer yapping at her heels, if nothing else.'

'It's not just politics,' Yamanaka said calmly. 'We need to know anyhow, as a matter of national security. Hell, the security of the species. The whole Galaxias affair is an existential crisis for all of humanity. *The President of the United States has to know*. Obviously.'

'OK,' Zhi said, 'so you want to send a probe. But what has this to do with the Pioneer programme?'

Harry smiled. 'Ah, Zhi, you just aren't cut out for military thinking. We can't spy on Mercury remotely. Yes, we need to send up a probe. But any *dedicated* mission is going to show our hand – America's hand. What you want is a spacecraft that is already preparing to fly anyhow, and that could, with a little luck, divert to Mercury without attracting too much suspicion.'

Sara snorted. 'Oh. I just got it. *Do you mean to send the Pioneer?'*

Zhi saw it as she said it. 'But that's absurd. Our goal is the outer Solar System. The engineering of Pioneer is very large scale. Very fragile. We will have a sail the size of a planet! It is an architecture that suits the huge, still spaces out there. It wouldn't survive a close encounter with the Sun—'

Serena leaned forward. 'You're right, of course, Zhi. And I can see you're sceptical too, Sara . . . But they're correct, aren't they, Lee? This is what you've come here to pitch. To use Pioneer for this – scouting mission. Well, I heard about this a few minutes before you two, and I've had time to think, and I believe I have a better idea.'

Zhi felt bewildered by her speed of thought. 'A *better* idea?'

'And a way we can save both projects, Mercury and Centaurus. No, we don't send Pioneer to Mercury.

'*We send Pathfinder.*

'Our precursor. Think about it. Our Gemini, not our Apollo. We send Pathfinder in to Mercury, rather than out towards Martian orbit.' She looked around the room. 'Think about it. We have her more or less assembled already. If we cut some of the science payload, we can extend the mission duration we planned, to, what, a couple of hundred days? We can even provide cover by saying we intend to use solar-sail technology as a preliminary booster option, and we want to try that out. That is actually true. All that will justify a flyby of Mercury, as close as you like.

'*And* we can achieve our technical goals, building towards the Pioneer itself, maybe without any knock-on delays. And certainly without having to commit Pioneer to this precursor mission, before any chance of getting out to Centaurus.'

Yamanaka nodded slowly. 'That could work – if you're satisfied with the technical feasibility. And as for security, yes, we would have natural cover if Pathfinder was already in your published development programme. I can make a call while I'm still up here. See if the President approves the amended proposal, subject to the usual reviews.'

Jones looked Yamanaka in the eye. 'Formally, of course, I have to protest. This is going to put a strain on my crew, my developers here and on Earth – and the timeline. We only have eight years left of our nominal ten-year timescale. I need you to press that point to the President.'

Yamanaka looked back calmly. 'If you're asking for more funds—'

'Damn right I am.'

And Zhi could only admire a master tactician at work. This had come out of the blue at Serena as much as it had for him. But to her this was one vast opportunity, he realised, to be grasped.

Yamanaka wasn't done, however. 'You know you will get what you need, if not necessarily what you ask for. There is time pressure. Ideally, frankly, this mission would be flown before the November election.'

Jones laughed, not unkindly. 'Impossible.'

'Then when?'

'I would say a year from now. For the flyby itself, I mean. Launching in perhaps nine months.' She glanced at Sara and Zhi as if for confirmation. 'You can announce it now if you need to. I'm confident of the project's technical feasibility.'

Yamanaka nodded. 'That ought to help.' She leaned forward. 'I ought to warn you, Zhi. You will have a role to play – whether you fly the mission or not. The President herself emphasised that. You see, we are goading the Chinese tiger here—'

'Ah. That's what you want of me. I've been around this loop before, have I not? I'm bait to attract my mother's attention.'

Harry Regent spoke, unexpectedly. 'I'd say it's your duty to be involved in this, my friend. Even at personal cost.'

Again, that startled Zhi, and he stared back. Not the kind of statement he'd have expected from his old shipmate. Maybe he didn't know this man as well as he thought he had.

People changed. Well, the world changed. He felt as if huge masses were reconfiguring, all around him. But he thought he was going to be more wary of Harry from now on.

Serena, typically, tried to lighten the atmosphere. 'So that's your job, Zhi. Try to sell this to your mother to make sure our Pathfinder doesn't get shot down by killer Chinese replicants from Mercury.' She laughed at herself. 'Great title for a pulp novel from about a hundred years ago. Zhi, don't worry; I promise, you still have a date with Galaxias. But in the meantime we all have our duties to fulfil.' She clapped her hands. 'So. Are we done? Crew, give me an hour with Lee and Harry here to figure out a security strategy and the cover story. Then – well, we have a President to brief and a whole new space mission to plan.

'We truly live in marvellous times. Future generations will envy us.

'Let's get started.'

34

October AD 2061:
Year 5 ERC, Summer

Tash thought she heard Charlie Marlowe's booming voice before she and Grace even came through the door, into the big, gloomy conference chamber that dominated the Cabinet War Rooms.

'That damn comet!' Marlowe growled. 'I get asked about nothing else but Halley, and there's nothing *to* ask about since it's not even there . . . Is this where we throw our coats? . . .'

And she faded out, for now.

Tash looked around, taking in the place. Gloomy, low-ceilinged rooms in a network of basement bunkers and corridors. All of this was deep under Whitehall: a structure of massive girders and concrete that suggested strength and resilience, but over a century old. And already half-full of guests in expensive gear, chatting loudly, glasses in hand.

It was cramped, claustrophobic, even smelled slightly damp. And yet Tash found she welcomed being stuck down this hole in the ground – sooner that than under a big open sky, given her lingering post-Blink phobia.

'Amazing place,' she murmured to Grace Butterworth, as the pair of them pushed towards a table of drinks. 'Amazingly drab, anyhow. Where Churchill held his wartime Cabinet meetings, sheltering from German bombs. Then a museum for decades, a monument. Abandoned to the flooding for more decades. Then drained and fixed up at huge expense to be used as a grubby political symbol for the new BRP government.'

Grace grinned, but tentatively, glancing around to be sure they weren't overheard – and her attention always drawn to the group deeper in the room at the centre of which her principal charge, Fred Bowles, held his own court. 'Bit cynical, that, for you, Brand. I'm the embittered military vet, remember. You're a different kind of cliché. The idealistic junior worker.'

Tash had to laugh. 'Am I that obvious? . . .'

But Grace was looking away again, not focusing.

Tash knew Grace was particularly concerned today about her sister and family, who were still stuck in Naples, on the flank of what was rapidly becoming one of the more restless of the world's massive-eruption-probable volcano candidates. The sister still couldn't get out, and Grace herself couldn't find a way to get her into England, thanks to the draconian travel and migration bans Mara Caine had imposed soon after coming into office two years back. All Grace could do was fret from afar.

'Anyway,' Tash said, trying to be bright, and looking to the centre of the room, '*there's* the reason we're all here. Not Churchill relics – a planet.'

That centre was dominated by a huge image projector system. For now the air above it was populated only by stock images of Mercury, diagrams of the planet's location in the Solar System – and crude graphics of the Jones, Inc. Pathfinder spacecraft, a tiny hull dwarfed by the immense sail-scoop to which it was attached. 'I wonder what Churchill would have made of *that*,' she mused.

'I think the old guy would have been impressed.'

*

They both turned.

A soft American voice, coming from a soldier – no, an airman, Tash recognised from the blue uniform colour. Tall, blond – hat under his arm – handsome in a somewhat sterile way, Tash thought.

'My name's Harry Regent. Forgive me for butting in.'

Harry Regent. She remembered that name. 'Oh. You were with Zhi on the Lodestone. On—'

'On Blink Day, right. And, Tash Brand, right? He often mentioned you, his old college buddies. Knowing you'd be here, I searched for your name badge. Sorry to hold you up if—'

'Not at all,' Tash said. 'We're supposed to be circulating.' She introduced Grace. 'I guess you know I'm a PA of Fred Bowles – the big guy holding court over there – and Grace watches his back.'

The airman eyed Grace. 'Military, right? Or ex? I recognise the bearing.'

Grace smiled warily. 'Royal Marines, formerly.'

Regent nodded. 'I'm impressed.'

'Ha! Really? Maybe I waved at you fly-boys from the trenches in some battle zone, while we got on with the fighting.'

Regent grinned back. 'Unlikely. I never saw action with the USAF before I made it to the astronaut corps. But I got drafted back in, after the Blink. Tougher times.'

Grace nodded grudgingly. 'Tougher times indeed.'

'Even soldiers have family, right?'

A look passed between them, a kind of glance of recognition that puzzled Tash. And vaguely concerned her. If they hadn't met before, how come Regent could make such a spot-on remark to Grace? It was almost as if he had researched her.

Which made no sense. Maybe she was getting paranoid, like the whole world.

But Grace had slipped back into her usual on-duty mode, sipping her drink silently, every so often casting glances over at the knot of people around Fred Bowles.

Tash turned to Regent. 'So. When did you last see Zhi?'

'About a year ago. On the Lodestone, actually. But I was already back in the USAF, even then. Escorting Lee Yamanaka at the time – we were initiating this Mercury flight subproject, in fact.'

'I haven't seen Zhi in – well, more than your year. We keep in touch when we can. And security permits it.' She glanced at the recycling display of stock imagery. 'Strange to think he'll be watching the exact same images as us.'

'But a few seconds later,' Regent said. 'What with the station being on the other side of Earth from the Sun, and so that bit further from Mercury.'

Grace said, 'So we'll hear what becomes of their mates at Mercury before the Lodestone crew do. Space stuff is weird.'

Regent grinned. 'Which is pretty much what my current boss says.' He nodded across the room, to the group of dignitaries clustered around Fred Bowles. 'That short guy over there? Current US ambassador to London. My background is why he likes having me in his personal protection squad, I think. I can pull a gun *and* explain the space stuff, as you call it, Grace. Or at least cover for him when his bluff goes wrong . . .'

'I heard that,' said Charlie Marlowe, loudly, pushing her way through a gathering crush – trailed, Tash saw, by a fraught-looking Mel Kapur. 'So where's the drinks?'

Tash pointed her to the drinks table she and Grace had found. But a waiter approached, and Marlowe scooped up a glass of water off her tray and just gulped it down. She grinned, cynically. 'What, human waiters now? Our glorious new leader really is going for the English-traditional look, isn't she, Tash?

'And – *bluffing* about space stuff – Captain, is it? An *ambassador*? Bluffing? Surely not. It would be nice to think that by now, nearly five years after the intervention of an alien entity in human affairs, our lords and masters would start to learn about scientific matters, rather than how to bluff about them.' She glared around. 'However, look at this lot. Stuffed suits and cocktail dresses, just as it always was. The British upper set always seemed to think an ignorance of science was an actual virtue. And it's got worse under Caine, of course.'

Tash and Grace shared a wary look.

Which Marlowe noticed. 'And shame on any of you who indulges them that way. All these damn questions about the comet, for instance.'

Grace looked puzzled. 'What comet? I haven't heard about that.'

'Halley's comet,' Mel said, taking a drink herself.

Tash was aware that was the first time she'd spoken. Mel seemed distant, distracted – if not distressed. Hard to read, even for Tash who knew her so well.

But Mel went on dutifully, 'Halley. Shows up regular as clockwork every seventy-five years, more or less, usually bright in the sky. First recognised in – the eighteenth century? But there are recorded appearances before that.'

'But not this time,' Harry Regent said. He quickly introduced himself properly, shook hands with Marlowe and Mel – and Mel and Regent swapped a couple of lines about Zhi.

Even that didn't seem to engage Mel's full attention, Tash saw.

'Halley, anyhow,' Marlowe said. 'It was due to make an appearance this year. We've looked, no sign of it, as Top Gun here says.'

Harry grinned at that.

'Obviously an after-effect of the Blink,' Marlowe said. 'The orbits of the planets were shaken up when the Sun went away. Well, so were the comets' paths, including Halley, undoubtedly, on its own long, slow, looping trajectory. The Blink could have detached it from the Solar System altogether – certainly we will have lost some more distant comets.'

'Or,' Harry said, 'of course, some comets might have been deflected to come *closer* to the Sun than before.'

Marlowe frowned. She said more softly, 'Implying, I suppose, that some might have been deflected onto a course leading to an impact with Earth? I can tell from the wings on your uniform that you have served in space yourself.'

'At the Lodestone, yes. But I was more flight crew than scientific—'

'Then you must understand how irresponsible such loose speculation is, at this time, coming from the likes of you. Of us. I mean, just think about it. A given comet may be deflected towards Earth; another may be deflected away. It isn't hard to show that the overall *chance* of a damaging impact is exactly the same as before the Blink. Even to suggest otherwise—'

'People are frightened enough,' Grace said now, sternly.

But Harry Regent seemed unaffected by Marlowe's admonition. He turned to Grace. 'Ma'am, to be frightened of the unknown isn't particularly irrational. Especially as there *is* an agency behind it all. Galaxias, whatever you want to call it, *caused* all this stuff. Isn't it rational to be angry? To be fearful? After all, do you think Galaxias would *care* if the Blink *had* accidentally deflected Halley into a collision course with Earth?'

Marlowe seemed furious. 'Grace is right.' She linked an arm with Regent's and led him away with powerful strides. 'I think you and I need to have a talk about the dangers of scaremongering, Captain . . .'

Grace said, 'And I'd better go haunt Fred.' She moved away.

Leaving Mel and Tash alone. Mel looked away, distracted, sipping her drink.

For a moment Tash couldn't think of a thing to say, to Mel, one of her oldest friends. They stood there in a kind of anxious silence.

Everybody was anxious these days, Tash thought.

It was the apparent instability of the post-Blink planet that frightened people more than anything specific, so her own work with Bowles had taught her. And there was always family to fret about. She was glad she had her own father, late sixties now, so close by. Grace, for instance, wasn't so lucky. And she wondered about Mel.

Another waiter passed, and Tash grabbed a fresh glass of grape juice and handed it to Mel. 'Try this. So. You OK?'

Mel pulled a face as she sipped the drink. 'Christ, this is shit. App food, right? Do I *look* OK?'

'Not to me.'

'Well, thanks for noticing. Charlie doesn't. Hasn't. Never seems to realise that there are times when I have more important things to do than be her bag-handler.'

'Let me guess. Jane?'

'Jane, yeah. She's only gone and got herself arrested.'

Startled, vaguely alarmed, Tash looked over towards Bowles and his entourage, all noisily talking, and pulled Mel into a quiet corner. Away from Grace, for one thing.

'Arrested?'

Mel nodded, edgy, even frightened. 'Truth time. And apology time. I would have come here even if Charlie hadn't ordered me to. To see *you* – you're hard to get hold of these days, Tash – and maybe I could get your help—'

'Arrested for *what*?'

Mel grunted. 'What have you got? This is Mara Caine's Britain now, Tash, in case you hadn't noticed inside your Government House. Half a dozen of Jane's friends – that I know of – have already been in custody, and a couple, I think, are still there. Oh, she's out now, but she's been tagged, and . . . And she won't *listen*. She's fifteen years old, Tash. I—'

She seemed unable to speak.

It occurred to Tash that she had never really seen Mel cry – only, maybe, when the In-jokes had got together in the labour ward after Jane's birth. Jane's mother had been there, and her difficult brother Paul, muttering prayers like a priest threatened with being defrocked. Wow, nearly sixteen years ago, in a pre-Blink world that now seemed like an endless summer in her memory.

Tash took Mel's hand. 'Just tell me.'

'Of all the stupid things, it was Caine's calendar that she objected to. The final straw . . .'

Tash wasn't terribly surprised – even though she had been on the inside in the development of the English Regularised Calendar, as responsibility for drawing it up had been handed to a reluctant Fred Bowles, science minister.

The reconciling of the old human calendar to the new planetary realities was a chore that had been put off by the old government, save for sticking-plaster remedies – the issuing of apps to match up the old calendar dates to the different sunset times and seasonal changes. Well, Mara Caine had 'fixed' that. She was, Fred had dryly observed, the kind of person who liked drawing up rules for other people to follow. But as a scientist Tash half-admired the brutal clarity of Caine's scheme.

In England at least, the new Long Year, twenty days longer than the old, was structured as the astronomers' calendar had been before. In the northern hemisphere the astronomical winter had run from the Winter Solstice to the Spring Equinox – roughly, late December to late March. So now the official 'Year' was to start at the northern Winter Solstice – which, with the new orbit, had already drifted out to March – and the Year was broken up into four Seasons, capitalised, from ninety-two to a hundred and one days each: Winter from the Winter Solstice, Spring from the Spring Equinox, Summer from the Summer Solstice, Autumn from the Autumn Equinox, and around to Winter and another year. The days were simply numbered within the seasons.

And the years, each now three hundred and eighty-five days long, were renumbered too. Year 1 of the English Regularised Calendar started, retrospectively, on the Winter Solstice of 2056 – 21 December, just a couple of weeks before the Blink.

That detail, the new numbering, seemed to enrage people more than any other.

Tash found herself falling into a too familiar defence of the government she served. 'Well, it was a campaign pledge, you know. People voted for it. Nearly five years on from the Blink the old calendar is months out of skew. Something had to be done. I did hear other countries are thinking of adopting it—'

'I know, I know. But there's something so – Orwellian – about calling a day the Fifty-Second of Summer. Not that Jane and her crew would use a word like "Orwellian". You know who actually started the latest protest march? The astrologers!'

'Seriously?'

'Who knew so many people cared so much? Of course they ought to be protesting against Galaxias. But you can't reach Galaxias.' She sighed. 'Oh – none of that matters. So a couple of years ago Jane was rebelling against me. Now she's rebelling against Mara Caine. If not the calendar, there would have been *something*. There was a sit-in – she went too far—'

Tash took a step closer to her friend, and spoke more quietly. 'OK. Look, I'll do what I can if she gets into trouble again. But, Mel—'

'Tash, I didn't come here to—'

'*Mel*. Listen to me.'

Mel looked faintly shocked to hear her speak like that.

Tash hesitated, choosing her own words cautiously.

'You have to see it from the government's point of view,' she said now. 'I mean, it's true that Mara Caine runs a "Cobra government", as you may have heard – it's not just a press label. As if we are in permanent crisis. Not everybody can stand the heat – Fred Bowles can, which is why he's still in a job, even if he is a leftover from the previous regime. And me in his wake, I suppose. We do our best to – mitigate.

'But we actually *are* in a permanent, unfolding crisis. The whole global system is increasingly frayed. Supply chains failing everywhere. Four years on from the Blink, we are seeing migrations again, like the climate-crisis years. And, other portents. In some places the old fossil fuel reserves are being eyed up again. In the Middle East, for instance. Russia has been watching those oil reserves for – hell, I'd have to be a historian to tell you how long.'

Mel frowned. 'And all this is Caine's excuse, is it? What's her line? "England is a small lifeboat, adrift on a treacherous sea. And if you're in a lifeboat, you obey lifeboat rules . . ."'

Tash hesitated, praying she wouldn't say anything any more indiscreet. Even under the old regime she had long been used to being listened to, covertly.

And meanwhile, as far as the danger to Jane was concerned, it was an open secret that a year after Caine's election there were labour camps operating in England. It was, Tash increasingly feared, a system that was *designed* to keep you inside. If only because you were actually more useful, economically, that way.

Mel was thinking, listening, rather than arguing, which was a good sign.

Tash squeezed her arm again. 'I'll do all I can to help. Just be discreet. OK? And *keep Jane from getting arrested again.* Ground her if you have to . . .'

But Mel had turned away, distracted.

Something was happening.

The volume of chatter was rising to a dull roar, and people, glasses in hand, were starting to drift towards the knot of audio-visual equipment at the heart of the room.

Charlie Marlowe clapped her hands over her head, and shouted. 'Heads up! The Pathfinder flyby is due any minute now . . .'

Immediately the drift became a crush.

Grace Butterworth came up with Harry Regent, glancing around at the melee. 'You two follow us.' And she and Harry linked arms and bulldozed their way through the crowd, following Marlowe.

Mel and Tash, hand in hand, trailed in their wake.

The central display, when they were close enough to see it, turned out to be bewildering at first glance. Fed through from JPL in California, the overall Pioneer/Pathfinder project control centre on the ground, images and data had been thrown into the air over that complex projection node – including a few spectacular planetary images, evidently of Mercury. Dull red rock, sharp shadows.

In the end Tash managed to pick out something comprehensible: what looked like a countdown clock, working its way down from five minutes. Five minutes to what, though, closest approach?

Then she spotted one spectacular summary graphic: a ghostly grey-black globe with a fine powder-blue rail sweeping past it, and a small bead of light crawling along that rail. Pathfinder making its pass by Mercury, she assumed.

And in there too, she saw now, among the clutter of data displays, the calm faces of two women, presumably imaged by in-helmet cameras. Ange Costello. Ito Katsuo. Tash had never met them, but knew them at second hand through Zhi. Talking, though their voices were not relayed, their eyes flickering over out-of-shot instrument displays.

'OK,' yelled Marlowe. 'OK!'

When nobody paid attention, she shoved her way out of the crowd, dragged a chair from a stack, pulled it back towards the display, and stood on its seat. Mel hurried to hold the chair's back and steady it, evidently alarmed, a sight which made Tash laugh. At least her own nominal charge, Fred, wasn't as impulsive as that.

'OK,' Marlowe said again, calling over the dying hubbub. 'Show time. Now, as you know, I'm the Astronomer Royal, not the Space Technologist Royal, but I'm the best Fred Bowles could find at short notice . . .'

Tash glanced at her phone, then gave Fred a thumbs-up, and called, as loudly as she dared, 'The Prime Minister is watching from her office, by the way, Charlie.'

Marlowe raised her eyebrows. She did have eyebrows built for raising, Tash had often observed. 'I'm sure that will make all the difference to the crew, a whole astronomical unit away.'

Laughter. But Tash wondered what PM Caine might make of such jokes, if she heard them. Such was the environment these days.

Now, from her chair, Marlowe had to turn her head, twist her body, to see all the displays. 'Four minutes to closest approach to the planet. OK. So let's understand what we're seeing here. That dim globe is planet Mercury, an image sent down from a remote satellite. It's about forty per cent Earth's distance from the Sun – and as a consequence its daytime surface temperature is somewhere over four hundred degrees Celsius, maybe seven hundred Kelvin. Hot enough to melt lead. And that's where the Pathfinder is going.'

She pointed to another display: an awkward square-frame hull dwarfed by a huge sail-scoop ahead of it. 'There she is. But she doesn't look like that now; the big sail is folded away during closest approach. She did use her solar sail to descend from Earth orbit and go swooping down to Mercury – while running her dark energy scoop in parallel. Now she is in free-fall, following a close-approach trajectory. The closest approach will last only minutes.

'In a way, Pathfinder is an extension of Sputnik 4, the early uncrewed trial of the dark energy ramscoop technology. *That* ship had a scoop of graphene, ten kilometres across – massing only sixty kilograms. Well, the Pathfinder has a scoop-sail of an even finer experimental substance, and that sixty-kilogram mass allowance gives you a *hundred* kilometres' diameter sail. At Mercury the sail delivers an acceleration of about twice Earth gravity, since the sunlight is that much more intense.

'But the sail *also* acts as a dark energy scoop, in this configuration, which delivers an additional acceleration of about ten microgees – ten millionths of Earth gravity. That's tiny, and makes no practical difference here, but it's measurable – and it has been measured; the tech works.'

There was a ripple of applause, a faintly drunken whoop.

'From the point of view of the longer-term objectives, that was the purpose of the mission – to test out the performance of the dark energy ramjet, even if it made no practical difference to the mission trajectory. But right now,' Marlowe went on, 'that's all behind the crew, as they go through their Mercury encounter phase. Right – let me see—'

Standing precariously on her chair, she swept her hand through the images in the air until she found one she wanted, expanded it with a spreading gesture of her arms. This showed the square-frame hull, without the sails, and a glittering blanket suspended on a frame above.

'*That* is simulating what Pathfinder looks like right now, tucked behind that reflective blanket, which is there to deflect solar heat. The sail cum scoop is folded up and stowed, and every watt of power she can muster is going into the cooling systems. You won't be able to see it, but there is also a ferocious laser, infra-red, dumping the heat. The blanket is based on technology used for close-approach probes sent to the Sun, sandwiches of multilayer insulation foil capable of withstanding five hundred degrees or more. The images you will soon see of Mercury's surface will be taken by instruments poking through holes in that shield . . .'

Tash murmured, '*That* is their cooling system? A bit of foil?'

Mel smiled, but grimly. 'I know,' she whispered back. 'I spoke to Zhi about it. All this was improvised, to some extent. Pioneer expects to get cold, not hot . . .'

'Ah,' Marlowe called. 'This is direct from Pathfinder.'

A large screen expanded at the heart of the display.

A landscape, dull grey, seen from above. Craters everywhere. Like the Moon, Tash thought at first glance, although lacking the *maria*, 'seas' of old lava dust. Nothing but shades of grey.

'*Mercury*,' Mel said. 'Astounding to think of it. Some of those big old crater walls look melted, don't they? And we sent those two heroes down there into that pit of heat, in a lashed-up improvisation of a spacecraft, just to get a few images like this. All because we couldn't get the Chinese to speak to us.'

Tash whispered to Mel, 'That's politics for you. But she probably shouldn't be saying it . . .'

A murmur of conversation now. People were discussing the imagery, pointing out features to each other. Details of the landscapes of Mercury. Including, here and there, Tash saw, black specks, nestling in the landscape. In another context she might have thought they were imaging flaws, perhaps. In this context – Chinese self-replicators? But there were many, many of them, a stippling on that lethal surface.

Marlowe, still on her chair, held a finger to one ear, evidently listening to a feed. Then she held up a hand, and the hubbub of conversation died away.

'OK,' Marlowe said. 'Remember, this is a live feed as we approach Mercury. The spacecraft is unpowered right now, just following a steep orbital dive down towards the planet itself. The close approach will deliver a gravitational slingshot, which will hurl the craft away from Mercury, and the solar heat, as quickly as possible. I . . .' She touched her ear.

Then she reached for another image in the cascade over her head. Began to expand it with swipes of her hand.

'And I think we are getting some meaningful data on those installations you can see on the surface.'

The pattern of black dots, hard to make out against the grey background, spread out as she went for extreme magnification.

'OK. I'm told that we are now looking down at what appears to be the most significant area of modification on the planet. Modification by the Chinese craft, that is. This is why the Pathfinder was sent to Mercury – and its trajectory was

405

designed to take it over this area at closest approach. To see this. We know the Chinese installations are called *Acorns* . . . Scatters of these black specks have been observed over much of the planet as the Pathfinder approached. But this is the densest concentration . . .

'Roughly speaking,' Marlowe said, 'I'm told we're looking at a mass of over a *million* placements. Those black dots. This is across an area – you can see it's irregular – roughly eight hundred kilometres wide. The spots are placed irregularly too, but not quite at random. None closer than about a kilometre to its neighbour . . .'

Fred Bowles spoke up now. 'Can I ask a question? Two years ago the Chinese sent precisely two Acorns to Mercury. They were self-replicating on the Moon; evidently they have been self-replicating on Mercury. So two has become a million. Does that make sense to you, Charlie?'

Marlowe nodded, grim. 'The lunar machines were able to replicate, from scratch, in thirty-six days. So two become four after thirty-six days, four becomes eight after seventy-two days. After two years, allowing for failures, you could be looking at a million installations, easily, or more.'

'And can you speculate for us about what the Chinese are doing this *for*? What's the end goal?'

Marlowe shrugged. 'Right now your guess is as good as mine. Maybe it's all about industry. Maybe the Chinese mean to get a monopoly on the next great resource lode, all that rich ore sitting right next to a million-kilometre-wide fusion reactor!'

From the crowd: 'Maybe the Chinese are planning some kind of emigration, to get away from Galaxias. Huge generation starships, built of Mercury ore, powered by sunlight. Or maybe just their elite.'

A mocking voice, perhaps Australian. 'If so, good riddance.'
Laughter. Tash looked around to see who was speaking.
But Mel grabbed her arm. 'Something's wrong.'

Tash looked back at the display, which had changed drastically, in seconds. She saw that the main images had dissolved into pixels, the data feeds had stopped scrolling.

The faces of the two astronauts were frozen, as in snapshots.

A murmur of concerned conversation. Tash saw people pulling phones out of their pockets. Never a good sign, in her experience. *Something wrong.*

Tash's instinct was to get as close to Fred Bowles as she could. She grabbed Mel's hand and started moving that way. She was aware of Grace ahead of her, also hurrying towards Bowles, with the slim, upright figure of Harry Regent beside her. The drama was probably something off in space, at Mercury, but you never knew; maybe some saboteur was screwing with the feed to the bunker.

The concerned conversations hushed; faces turned back to the screens.

The interval seemed long. Tash, Mel, Regent, Grace, stood together, watching the screens. Charlie Marlowe just looked on, waiting.

Then, at last, amid the frozen images, Serena Jones appeared, peering into a camera, in a blue jumpsuit, her greying hair a loose zero-gravity cloud around her head.

'My God,' Mel murmured. 'Has she been crying?'

'. . . is Serena Jones, CEO of Jones, Inc., calling all stations from the Lodestone, our station in the umbra of Earth. I hope you can hear me. There is a text download in parallel to this transmission.

'You will have observed we lost the signals from the Path-finder some minutes ago, at just about the time of its closest approach to Mercury. The Pathfinder had released a squad of observer drones before closest approach, and their reports, with some terminal data, are enabling us to make a first assessment of what has happened. We have a remarkable team here . . .

'*Terminal*. I apologise to the families for my thoughtless use of that word.

'We have lost Pathfinder. We have lost the crew.

'It's only minutes since the event. The drones have already sent back enough data to start a tentative reconstruction of what happened. Simply put, our heat protection system failed. There appears to have been a flaw in the attachment of our reflective blanket to the main hull. More failures in other backup system operations . . . Well. The crew had no time to respond before the internal temperatures in the craft rose catastrophically.

'The crew were Ange Costello. Ito Katsuo.

'Costello was the commander of this station, the Lodestone. She volunteered for the Pathfinder mission to widen her skill set. She was able, ambitious.

'Katsuo was a veteran of the near-disastrous Al-miriykh Mars mission. She became the first human being ever to visit two planets beyond Earth and Moon: Mars, and now Mercury. She would have flown the Pioneer to Centaurus.

'I will not speculate about the last moments of the crew. Not now. I will not insult them by lecturing you about their bravery. We will assist the families all we can. The data they gathered will be invaluable.

'As for our task going forward, we have thought through this contingency – we had to – and we have a strategy. *The Pioneer will fly*. And it will fly on time, given the Barnard's Star deadline, now only seven years away. We will hold our own investigation; we will cooperate with external inquiries; we will fix this, and Pioneer will fly. She will fly as a tribute to those we have lost today.

'As for myself, I have served as CEO of the company and as project director for Pioneer. *I will not resign.* Not for now. But I take full responsibility. I will stay on to contribute to the recovery of the project from this setback, and to assist the inquiries that must follow.

'I will revert now to official channels, specifically through our ground control at JPL.

'Lodestone, out.'

Tash had seen government ministers scramble for such responses, in such crises. 'That sounded rehearsed. Already scripted. She must have been ready to deal with the worst.'

Mel muttered, 'Wouldn't you?'

With the transmission over, the War Rooms began to empty quickly.

Some left hastily. Journalists and others with immediate follow-up work to do.

Others nucleated around key figures. Marlowe was one, inevitably, as she spoke, loudly, clearly, and apparently responsibly, on what had just happened. Explaining the observed facts rather than speculating, Tash noted approvingly.

And Fred Bowles, as science minister, was another attractor. He was walking towards Marlowe.

Tash had to be by his side. She said a hasty goodbye to Mel, promised again to do what she could for Jane. Then she looked for Butterworth and Regent.

They were already heading towards Fred Bowles too. Tash followed as best she could. And as they worked through the crowd, they were talking over the noise, loud enough to hear each other — and loud enough for Tash to hear too, as she drew closer.

'. . . can't blame the Chinese for these deaths,' Regent said now. 'I mean, the Pathfinder wouldn't have been sent to Mercury if the Chinese hadn't gone there. But *they* wouldn't have done that if not for Galaxias, ultimately. And the Blink.'

'Damn right.'

'Same for your sister and her family, what you told me about Naples. It's no *human's* fault they are at risk. Not ultimately. Same for any of the other consequences — the geology, the quakes, the mixed-up weather. It's not even the volcano's "fault", because it wouldn't have been destabilised in the first place. Again, it's Galaxias.'

Grace said, 'There are some who say Galaxias has big, noble goals. Keeping the peace in the Galaxy. Over billions of years.'

'You told me about Ella and Billie. Would you take a billion years if your niece's life was the price?'

'Of course not. So what are you saying?'

Tash, ashamed for eavesdropping, but feeling this was somehow important, pushed a little closer. Strained to hear as Regent spoke more softly, under the wider hubbub.

'There are some of us — mostly military or ex, like you and me — who don't approve of the way the governments have responded to all this. Not about managing the emergencies — I mean the response to Galaxias. So they have Serena Jones firing off toy rocket ships out to where the Sun went. The Chinese are fooling around on Mercury. So what? What good does that do? *Galaxias* isn't on Mercury. Galaxias is out there somewhere—'

Grace pressed again, '*What are you saying?*'

He looked at her. 'Would you take the call?'

'What call?'

'Well, I don't know. None of us does. But — something might come up. *Would you take the call? . . .'*

If Grace answered, Tash didn't hear. Because now she had reached Fred Bowles, and within thirty seconds she'd received orders to draft a position paper for Fred to brief Prime Minister Caine on the latest developments, and was running back out of the chaotic room, dragging her phone out of her pocket.

Hoping Mel didn't commit any more indiscretions. Hoping that Jane could be protected.

Wondering if she should say something to Grace. Or about her, to security. She recoiled from the thought.

Confused, conflicted, she pushed through the crowd.

35

June AD 2062:
Year 6 ERC, Winter

The next time Tash heard Charlie Marlowe speak, nine months later, she was addressing another crowd of politicians, diplomats and influencers – and, another echo of the past, back on Dogger Island too. Another scrambled effort by the Federal England and the independent Scottish nation to earn some money and international cachet – and, Tash knew, another attempt by Fred Bowles to do the only thing he could, to keep people talking as the world frayed.

A festival of déjà vu, Tash thought sourly. Sometimes she suspected a lot of people simply longed for the twelve-year Galaxias response deadline, now widely known, to be up, one way or another. Still six years left. *Do whatever the hell you are planning for us. Just get it over . . .*

But Charlie Marlowe was evidently stronger than that. She stood at her podium, blinking in the brilliant lights, and peered around at the audience before her – an audience glimpsed in the audio-visual feeds sent out to the wider world. She had only a stack of notes on paper, a microphone, no visual aids save the default New Aberdeen Conference Centre logo on the big screen behind her. She seemed nerveless, Tash thought. If a little older, a little more worn down, as they all were, probably.

'Thank you,' Charlie said simply, to open. 'Thank you for being here. Thank you in advance for your polite attention today.

'Sadly we live in a fractured, fractious world where such courtesies cannot be taken for granted. It is easy to blame others for our own behaviour. And since the Blink, of course, it has become routine to blame Galaxias for all our woes. Well, perhaps some of that is fair.

'But our response to a challenge from whatever source is our own responsibility. And that response ought to be based on *knowledge*. Not ignorance and fear.

'That is what I wish to speak to you about today. Our latest understanding of Galaxias – and by *our*, I mean humanity's . . .'

In a small office deep in the working heart of the New Aberdeen Conference Centre, with Marlowe's voice speaking steadily and calmly from a small screen embedded in a smart wall, Tash sat with Mel and Zhi. The first time the three In-Jokes had been together since . . . Tash couldn't remember when.

Although they were barely together at all, save in physical presence. Already Zhi had got up, kicking his chair over in the process. After yet more months in microgravity at the Lodestone, after months of pressurised work in the Pioneer project, he was clumsy, possibly over-stressed, and he staggered a little, his under-the-clothing exoskeletal support whirring.

Tash sipped her coffee calmly. 'You can stalk around all you want. The room's booked out for the afternoon. I made sure of that. And the door is locked. I made sure of *that*, too. You aren't going anywhere, except the bathroom. And as soon as Charlie is done you're sitting down with your mother. I mean it. She's here. You're here.'

Zhi was genuinely angry. 'Not for the first time, you set me up. Set *us* up.'

'No,' Mel said dully, staring into her phone – evidently listening to Marlowe's speech in parallel to this conversation. 'No, we didn't. We didn't fix up this conference, just for your sake. We didn't come here for you. It's our jobs to be here. Your mother's job. But here we are anyhow. What were we supposed to do, keep you apart?'

'And it's your job to be here, too, Zhi,' Tash put in. 'You, as one of the most senior figures in the Pioneer project, now they sacked Serena Jones.'

'She resigned,' he said bitterly. 'She owns the company. Not *sacked*. She sacrificed herself for the project. And whatever you say, you conned me into coming down here. Am I just bait again to get my mother here?'

Still Zhi stalked.

'Oh, sit down, Zhi. You think this whole event is about you?'

Zhi shot her a look, a mixture of anger and embarrassment. 'Very well, damn you.' He sat down heavily in his chair, folded his arms, and glared at Charlie Marlowe's image on the smart wall. 'But, talk, talk, talk. That was one good thing about Serena. She built stuff. Not just talked about it—'

'Oh, shut up.' Mel suddenly buried her face in her hands. 'Shut *up*. So it's all mommy's fault, is it, Zhi? Have you ever thought, for one second, how *she* might feel? Can you fix that, as you're fixing your damn spacecraft?' She shuddered, evidently crying – or maybe trying not to.

Zhi and Tash shared a look. They held back, uncertain.

'You have all seen images of the lurker on the Moon,' Charlie told her audience.

'Now, of course, it is surrounded by materials from Earth — cameras and other scientific instruments, monuments, tokens. Our own clunky gadgets — clumsy compared to the elemental simplicity of the lurker. And until the FIS authorities cleared the site quite recently, there was also a wall of people up there: patient observers keeping vigils, in person. People *talking* to the lurker.

'But the lurker itself is, as you know, I'm sure, nothing but rock and water. What does *science* tell us about that?

'We have sampled both cautiously, the water content and the rock base, taking only the tiniest fragments for the benefit of our studies. Well, the water is not simple water, as you might expect. We have to admit we have no idea how the lurker "works". But we do know it is a compact marvel of organic chemistry. And it is biochemistry of a kind similar to our own, fundamentally, though quite different in the detail. Carbon-oxygen chemistry. Proteins in water. Just like us.

'As to the rock base — there we have another clue as to the origin of Galaxias. For, having cautiously drilled out tiny samples, we have been able to *date* it.

'We believe the lurker rock came from an exoplanet — a planet of another star. We can tell that from its elemental make-up; it's like no rock formed in our Solar System. We believe it had a planetary origin, as opposed to it having come from a smaller object like an asteroid, because the lurker rock shows signs of having been *melted*. Unlike most asteroid rock. Perhaps its planet of origin was Galaxias's own origin world. It seems the likeliest hypothesis.

'And the rock has traces of residual radioactivity, in the elements of which it is composed. Melted, and radioactive, just like the rocks of Earth.

'Even today, on Earth, radioactivity contributes a great deal of heat energy – it keeps the core from solidifying. But, with time, of course, in any given mass, radioactivity declines. That's what makes it so useful for dating.

'The lurker rock is much *less* radioactive, gram for gram, than a similar sample of silicate rock taken from the Earth.

'And so we think the lurker rock is *older* than any Earth rock – older in the sense that it solidified long before our Earth was born. Therefore the lurker's planet as a whole must be older than Earth. We can even tell how old.

'Now, the universe itself is nearly fourteen billion years old. Our Sun is less than *five* billion years old. It is believed that the *peak* of star formation in our universe, when stars were being born at a faster rate than before or since, occurred about *ten* billion years ago – five billion years before our own Sun was created.

'And this appears to be the age of the lurker rock – and, we surmise, the age of the home world of Galaxias. Ten billion years old.

'This means that Galaxias probably emerged during what we call the "cosmic high noon", when the universe was as bright as it has ever been, or ever will be. Star formation at its peak, as I said – and the whole expanding universe was much *smaller* than now – only a third the size. Smaller, and crowded, and bright. What a sky it must have been!

'And, as we can tell from the erosion of the lunar ground around it, the lurker Galaxias sent has most likely been in place since the very earliest days of the Moon, of the Solar System itself. So the lurker, an emissary of a much older entity, has watched Earth, not just since the emergence of humanity, but since before the dawn of life.'

*

As Marlowe spoke into the In-Jokes' own awkward silence, Tash could only think of the clumsiest of openings. What the hell, it was all she had.

'This speech is getting a huge audience. And with a young demographic. We've seen this before, haven't we? The upcoming generation finding themselves in a universe where we *know* there is intelligent life, there's a reason for the way we find that universe—'

'Huh,' said Zhi. 'A universe where you can be Blink-bombed at any second.'

'So, Mel – do you think Jane will be watching this, somewhere?'

Mel shrugged, without looking up from her phone. 'Well, I know *where* she'd be watching. On her phone, somewhere in the Fields of Fire outside Naples. Probably lugging a seismometer for some geological crew. Or a food parcel for some refugee family. Whether she will actually be listening in . . .' She shrugged again. 'It would be a kind of comfort to think so, to think we are sharing this much, this experience.

'But – I don't know. She's a very people person, as your dad once said, Tash. She does post occasional messages. Very occasional. And they are always posts, not conversations. Sometimes bits of the science. Seismometer traces. The geologists are detecting big shifting magma pockets under the surface now. "Blink slosh", they call it, apparently.'

Tash knew this wasn't the only suspicious site in the world. But when it came to possible near-term major volcanic events, a major Naples eruption was one fairly high-probability candidate.

'There have been precursor events for years,' Mel went on. 'Almost since the Blink. And for years, the Italian authorities have pretty much fenced in the region, kept the population contained.'

Zhi nodded. 'I read about some of that. No formal evacuations allowed. The Italian authorities fear the pressure on resources elsewhere: food, water. Post-Blink Italy is just as stretched as the rest of the world.'

'Most of what Jane posts back is heartbreaking. Such as pictures of part of a suburb being evacuated because of an ash plume, people who'd already had to move being shuffled from one dismal rescue centre to another. And she's joining the protests against the authorities. Needless to say I don't like her being out there, but I have a feeling that if I tried to bring her back, she'd just disappear. She's sixteen years old now. That's pretty much what sixteen-year-olds do, I think.'

Maybe, Tash thought. But most sixteen-year-olds didn't already have a record from her detainment after the calendar riots nearly a year back.

Tash said carefully, 'I do know that the first time she went out there was with Grace Butterworth. Who does have a personal investment in that part of the world.'

Zhi nodded. 'The sister and niece? Yes, I remember you talked about that.'

'It was through me that they met. Jane and Grace. And so I feel—'

Mel shrugged, and took Tash's hand. 'Don't beat yourself up about that. If it hadn't been you and Grace and Naples, she would have found some other worthy cause to support. Some other victim, somewhere in the world.' She looked away. 'I hope I don't sound dismissive. I know sometimes Jane believes I feel that way. It's just – I'm her mother. I want to keep her safe. That doesn't mean I would actively stop her.' She glanced at Zhi, almost shyly. 'I feel the same about you, Zhi. Going off to the rim of the Solar System in a barely tested ship. I want you to go, and not go, at the same time. Does that make sense?'

Zhi thought it over. 'Probably not. But that's friendship for you, I think.'

They sat in silence for a moment.

Mel was still holding Tash's hand. Now she reached out towards Zhi. And he, in turn, took her hand, and Tash's. They sat in a linked circle.

While Charlie Marlowe spoke of water worlds.

'When we speculate about Galaxias and its origin, we know so little that we must be guided by philosophical principles as much as by the meagre data.

'We have the principle of mediocrity, for instance. Which predicts that if we have a sample of something, a good minimal bet is that the sample is *typical*, not unusual.

'So, in our case, we have just one sample close to hand of a Galaxias artefact — the lurker. But because its, umm, "smart" component seems to be protein-filled water, we surmise that *that is the nature of Galaxias too*. Protein-filled water. And if that is typical of the origin environment, we guess that Galaxias comes from a water world. And as I said it is an *old* world, we think, if that rock sample from the lurker is typical too. Older than the Earth.

'How far away might Galaxias's home planet be?

'Since the Blink our great space telescopes have been examining the planetary systems of other stars, in particular those hosting water worlds. Which is a surprisingly large fraction. And in fact in some nearby systems, such as Barnard's Star, second closest to the Sun, we now see water worlds *where we saw none before*. We suspect some subterfuge, some concealment, now abandoned. Another clue as to the psychology of Galaxias, perhaps.

'Earth itself is a water world, of course. But among such

worlds, planets like ours with comparatively shallow oceans – no more than a few kilometres deep, shallow enough for dry land to protrude – may not be typical. Earth got its water from the relics of its formation, internally from the upwelling of water trapped when the planet congealed, and later externally, from the bombardment of comets and other watery bodies. But it also lost oceans of water in the process – driven off by huge early impacts.

'So Earth is probably unusual. Coming out of such a chaotic process you might expect to find either barren, all but water-less worlds – Venus, for example, lost its water to excessive heating by the Sun – or you might find worlds with much *more* water than Earth. It would only take five times the volume of the Earth's present oceans for the dry land to be covered, to the peaks of the mountains.

'So we suspect – lacking any evidence – that Galaxias's world might be more typical. The likelihood is it will have much deeper oceans than our own.

'There is no reason to put any arbitrary *upper* limit on the relative abundance of water on a given world. Could a world have ten per cent of its entire mass as water, fifty per cent, more? But we do know there is a limit on how *deep* a water ocean can be. On a world like Earth, a depth of a hundred, two hundred kilometres would exert such pressure that regardless of temperature the water would congeal into exotic forms of solid ice – like the substance we call Ice VI.

'So, then. Is that the kind of world Galaxias might have come from?

'Imagine a world of deep oceans – deep enough for those exotic ices to form at the bottom. But under that ice floor, there would be a thin rocky crust over a hot lava mantle, perhaps, like Earth's, and an iron core deep within.

'*How* could life emerge on such a world?

'Our best bet, as we believe of our own world, is that it happened at an interface between hot rock and water – like the vents on our deepest ocean floors, warm, mineral-rich plumes, creating limestone chimneys that can be fifty metres tall. Sources of heat energy, and of useful substances from the deeper rocks: hydrogen, sulphides, metals, all helpfully injected into the water. And here, perhaps, as minerals and organic chemistry churned together in the warm water, life may have emerged.

'And that is why, you see, we expect – or predict – there to be only a thin layer of those exotic deep-water ices on Galaxias's world. Because a thicker layer would have sealed off the useful minerals from the vents in the rock beneath. Or – and I personally favour this idea – life may have emerged in a pocket, a relatively small chamber *under* the Ice VI crust, kept open by geothermal heat. In such a limited environment, cooperation rather than competition – even the early integration of life forms – would probably be optimal, to maximise the use of the sparse resources.

'Thus Galaxias could have been born, as a single, coherent unit almost from the beginning. Perhaps.

'And it escaped. Perhaps.

'How? Perhaps the geology shifted; perhaps there were cracks and vents and channels in the Ice VI crust – channels which enabled Galaxias, or some precursor entity, to escape into the greater ocean. A place that was cold, dark, but teeming with potential. It must have been like our own breakout into space.

'Growth out into that ocean, fed only by the mineral seepages from below, must have been slow. But at some point Galaxias must have grown and spread sufficiently to reach the upper levels of the ocean, below any crust of normal ice. This was the photic zone, a few metres deep, where a much richer source of energy waited to be tapped: the light of that world's bright young sun.

'And Galaxias grew towards the light. Some theorists imagine *trees*, perhaps: tall, slender plant-like forms rooted in the deep mineral sources, reaching up and up towards the light . . . Like a tremendous kelp forest, a hundred kilometres tall.

'The idea of intelligence, especially a technological civilisation, arising on a water world seems strange to us. Don't you need fire to make metal tools? And for fire, don't you need dry land and something to burn?

'Well, maybe. But ocean worlds have other forms of accessible energy – and a great deal of it. We ourselves have experimented with designs of machines – called ocean thermal energy converters – that extract heat from an ocean by pumping up cold water from below, which cools the hotter surface waters, thus liberating useful energy, and then letting the warmed waste water flow back down. A Nile-capacity fountain could deliver megawatts.

'And if all the sunlight energy incident on Earth, say, were used to drive such fountains, their number could be counted in the tens or hundreds of billions – *comparable to the number of neurones in a human brain*.

'Meanwhile, for the development of technology as we understand it – if that were necessary – there would always be the resources of the sub-ice crust and mantle . . .

'All this is hypothetical, of course. Think of this as a proof of existence, as the mathematicians would say. It may not have been exactly like this. But this is *one* way it *could* have happened, one way for a technological intelligence to arise on a water world . . .

'A whole world comprised of a single-individual species. A planet emulating a human brain.

'Thus, the birth of Galaxias.

'Perhaps.'

Even as Marlowe spoke, Zhi, moody and restless, was messing with his phone. Impatiently he threw messages, documents into the air, where they evaporated, evanescent, before Tash could make any sense of them.

She gave up. 'OK, OK. You want to talk? I have tried to follow the project, you know. Pioneer. After the Pathfinder mess.'

'Yes. Since we lost Serena.' He rubbed his face. 'And what a mess it's been. You know that Lee Yamanaka took over the direct running of the project herself? Order from the President. And she's getting us back on track, to be fair.

'But, look —' He hesitated. 'I know Serena studied big, demanding, politically visible projects of the past. You know, I think she *expected* something to come up that would come close to derailing us, because something always does. She called it her "Apollo fire moment". And she deliberately put herself in a position where she would be able to soak that up, to save the project, even at the cost of her own career. Even her reputation.

'I think she knew it was always going to end like this. Hell, I think you could say she even *planned* it that way.'

Mel reached over and squeezed his hand.

Tash nodded. 'It sounds like nothing's going to stop you. Not even the loss of Jones. You really are going off to the edge of the Solar System.'

Zhi looked at her sourly. 'Leaving my mother behind? Ha! That's a clumsy link, even by your standards. Even now you want me to play the dutiful son to Wu Yan.'

Mel pulled back her hand and snapped, 'Oh, for God's sake. Just talk to your mother. Not about the science. Because if you fly off on the Pioneer, you might not get another chance. And, believe me, you will regret that for ever. Or *she* will . . .'

'If we can make guesses as to *what* Galaxias is, can we imagine *where* it came from?

'There is no reason to suppose that Galaxias's ultimate origin is at Barnard's, or any nearby star. As I said, water worlds are common. And, you see, while Barnard's is only about six light years away, the Galaxy disc is some hundred *thousand* light years across. So it is much more likely that Galaxias was born tens of thousands of light years distant from the Earth, not close by.

'We think Galaxias is very *old*, from the evidence of the lurker rock.

'And we think it must have moved out of its water world and crossed the stars slowly, slowly. Diffusing, we call it. We know that because it is lightspeed-limited; it would quickly have run out of local resources if it had moved too fast. Slow and steady.

'Thus it colonised the Galaxy. All of it. And we know *that* because we see no signs of other, younger, noisier cultures. I mean – an antimatter starship would be visible across light years. If life emerged on Earth, and independently on the home planet of Galaxias, it must have arisen *many* times. We see nothing of those other cultures, surely, because of Galaxias's control. As it controls us.

'While all around the universe aged.

'Remember, the sky into which Galaxias was born was the brightest it has ever been, or ever will be. Crowded with huge, bright, short-lived stars. Today, much of the primordial star fuel has been burned off, and the universe itself is expanding, growing dark and cold . . .

'As the universe has aged, visibly, around it, so has Galaxias.

'Think of that!

'How must it have been? To be born in the bright noon of the universe, and to witness its long, inevitable descent into night. All alone!'

Those closing words seemed to hit Mel hard.

'Alone. Oh, God. Well, I envy Galaxias. Because maybe it's better never to have a child than to fear losing one.' She folded over on herself, broke down in tears.

Tash hurried to her, holding her tight.

After a moment, Zhi came too.

They waited until Marlowe finished her speech. Waited longer.

Wu Yan did not come.

That turned out to the final time either of them saw Zhi in person before the launch of Pioneer 14. And the next time they heard his voice was in a message from deep space.

36

September AD 2063:
Year 7 ERC, Spring

'My name is Wu Zhi.

'I am speaking to you from the Pioneer 14 craft, which has just, for the first time, cast off from the Lodestone complex. Still drifting through the deep shadow of the Earth, we await the sunlight.

'And today we begin a mission that will take us out of the Sun's planetary system altogether.

'We are a crew of three, right now sitting side by side in our couches – in a cramped control cabin that doubles as an escape pod, incidentally. For safety reasons we also wear pressure suits, as you can see in the visual feeds. When we are under way, we will open up the rest of our ship.

'I am sure you know who we are by now. But for the record, on this launch day: aboard with me is Marina Petko, citizen of Russia, who is now the last survivor of the Al-miriykh mission to Mars, a mission which fell foul of the Blink.

'Here also is Sara West, citizen of the American Free States, best known as an engineer and business associate of Serena Jones, of Jones, Inc. With her engineering knowledge, as well as her managerial skills, business acumen and general good judgement, Sara has done a great deal to help stabilise and progress the Pioneer project after the Pathfinder incident at Mercury two years ago. Of all of us Sara has the least experience of spaceflight – for her, before this, only the shuttle from Earth to the Lodestone, and tours of duty there. They were extensive tours, however. She is a veteran, and I am proud to have her at my side.

'I am Wu Zhi. I am a citizen of the People's Republic of China. I am the son of the prominent scientist Wu Yan, and I am proud too of her achievements – even if I am as baffled by them, as ignorant of them, as many of you must be, as I live on the wrong side of various security barriers. Well, I have chosen to live that way. For myself, I am best known for my long tours of duty at the Lodestone station, here in Earth's shadow – and where this new Pioneer craft has been constructed.

'I could have no better crewmates.

'I'm checking my mission clock. We have many milestones to achieve in this early phase of the mission – a burst of action for a few days, followed by a calm cruise into the deep outer Solar System, a cruise at least a year long if we are to reach the Blink location ninety astronomical units out, and perhaps travel beyond.

'And it may puzzle those of you who are not yet so familiar with the parameters of our mission – or you have forgotten, over all these years of preparation – that to begin with we will be exploiting, not dark energy, sparse and mysterious, but sunlight, the warm and abundant energy that quickens the Earth itself . . .'

Skythrust Two hovered high over Naples.

From within a viewing lounge, Mel Kapur peered out at the ash column that towered over the city. Pale sunlight played on the column, casting a shadow kilometres long.

Wu Zhi's voice from space, relayed over Mel's phone, was a background sound. Almost soothing, Mel thought. Calm words from a million kilometres away. Calm, and meaningless.

Jane wandered into the lounge. Looked around, sat in a window chair far from everybody else. She wore grubby dungarees, as she had since her pickup. Her hair had been roughly shaved down to the scalp, leaving bright red bristles.

Subtle glances among the adults here in this lounge: Mel, Grace Butterworth, Harry Regent. *Don't say anything.* Don't go pricking her pride, or sparking her temper. Just let her be.

Mel herself carefully didn't react. So far as she knew this was the first time her daughter had left her 'cell', as she called her cabin on Skythrust, since being extracted more or less forcibly from the heart of Naples twenty-four hours before. Mel hadn't actually been allowed to touch her seventeen-year-old daughter, not once, since Jane had been brought aboard. Jane just wouldn't have it. *Not yet*, so Mel thought hopefully. Right here, right now, it was enough consolation for Mel that at least her daughter was with her, in this aerial refuge, rather than down on the ground.

That dangerous ground.

The light shifted. Mel turned back to the window.

After three days, the ash column rising above the Campi Flegrei was growing denser, more turbulent. Was the view still more awesome viewed from the air than the ground? That dark, irregular pillar, so thick in its central sections it looked almost liquid, and yet reaching for the stratosphere like some great arm raising a fist − yes, it awed her, as nothing had since the Blink itself. Like an astronomical phenomenon brought down to Earth. *And you are an astronomer, Mel. Yes, but astronomy is supposed to be about stuff safely far away* . . . She felt like a moth before a flamethrower.

'We need to get down there,' murmured Grace, maybe prompted by Jane showing up. '*I* need to get down there. The last message I got from Ella, she was still *there*, in that soccer stadium . . . And Billie was with her then at least.'

Ella was Grace's sister, and Billie her daughter, Grace's six-year-old niece – a Blink Baby, born on that fateful day itself, and, to some, an object of superstitious dread ever since. They seemed to be the only family Grace had, or that she would admit to. Which was why she had come so far, to try to find them. Grace clenched and unclenched her own fists as she stood by the big picture window of this ornate suite, and gazed down at the cityscape, shadowed by the ash column.

Harry Regent, as ever stiff and upright in his crisp USAF uniform, put a hand on Grace's shoulder. 'Then that's where they most likely still are. In the stadium. Ella knew you were coming. And she knows that if we're able to attempt any kind of retrieval it will be from her last known location. She wouldn't move away without telling you. And she wouldn't let herself be separated from Billie, not at such a time. We have to plan for the best case, I guess. Until we know otherwise.'

Grace just glowered – a frighteningly powerful expression, Mel thought. 'What, *this* is the best case? Billie and Ella lost in a crowd of – what – a hundred thousand?'

'More, maybe,' Jane said. 'It's the Stadio San Paolo – Napoli play there.' She glanced at Harry. 'Soccer.'

Harry forced a grin. 'I did know that—'

Grace snapped, 'When is that damn captain going to make a decision?'

Mel knew she meant the commander of Skythrust.

Harry sighed. 'Well, it's complicated. I spoke to her a while back. Right now she could still send down another chopper – they've been experimenting with gauze covers over the engine vents and so forth. But none of it is tried and tested, the ash is thickening all the time, *and* it blows about in clumps. I'm sure her strategy is to wait for a break, a clear spell, a change in the wind—'

'But overall the ash fall is getting worse, not better. Right?'

'Yes. And that's the dilemma, right there. Because if she waits too long, any pickup's impossible anyhow.'

'Shame it wasn't impossible earlier,' Jane snapped. 'I spent days down there before I was forcibly evacuated, on my mother's orders.'

Mel thought that was about as much of a cue as she was going to get. 'Blame me if you want,' she said.

Jane turned on her. The evidence of the medical work on her face was still obvious, stitches slowly dissolving in the deep cut on her cheek. Jane said savagely, 'I do blame you. I'm old enough to make my own choices, about my own life. I had a job to do. I was doing it well too. I was saving lives, or trying to. Look, I was *useful* down there. *Look* at it . . .'

'OK, I'm looking.' Harry walked over to a window, peered out, and said, diplomatically it seemed to Mel, 'So tell me what I'm looking at. That's one big city.'

Jane, apparently distracted, mildly mollified, got up and joined Harry at the window. Grace followed, and Mel.

Mel leaned over the back of an ornate couch to see.

Naples.

It was built around a bay. She stared down at a half-moon of grey sea, pushing into the land. Mel glimpsed an elaborate water frontage, buildings no doubt impossibly ancient, and a dense carpet of building sprawl behind.

Jane said, 'You're looking at the third largest conurbation in Italy, after Milan, and Rome itself. See the harbour? The city centre is just north of that. A comparatively well-off location.

I was only there because I knew you would have your goons come for me, Mum, and I was trying to hide away. If I'd known you'd stuck a tracking chip in me when I was a *baby* . . .'

The source of long, bleak arguments since the pickup. Mel had no regrets.

'Most of the relief work I was engaged on was further to the north – see the suburbs around the old airport?'

In sunlight diluted by the ash tower, Mel thought she could make out a tracery of runways.

'Shanty town now. Horrific poverty. Diseases running wild through populations of street kids. Even before Blink Day, I was told.'

'I did follow your feeds, you know,' Mel said.

To get here Jane had defied every injunction her mother had laid down. And yet, in the end, the images Jane had sent back had been remarkable. The slim, fragile teenager, in a battered, patched-up hazard suit, carrying inoculation kits towards mobs of half-feral street kids.

But now Jane twisted away. 'You followed me? Why? So what, so you could brag about me with your damn In-Joke cronies? If you had paid any attention to what I was actually doing you'd have let me be.'

Harry said, 'You must have had warnings to evacuate as soon as the ash plume started. I mean, it was a Europe-wide phenomenon after twenty-four hours. Flights grounded from Britain to the Urals. Well, all save airships like this one and a few other specialist craft.'

Jane said tiredly, 'Of course I knew about the warnings. Including from my mother. Yammering away, breaking through every filter I could put on my calls. But what was I supposed to do? Even if I got out myself – you should have seen them, all those grimy little kids. Everyone was just baffled. The world

431

had already let them down. And their government. And *then* the ash plume began. Was I supposed to abandon them too? I couldn't just *leave.*'

Mel suppressed a sigh. 'You'll never know how proud I am. But I'm your mother. *I* couldn't abandon *you.*'

Harry asked, 'How did you find her?'

'Contacts,' Jane broke in. 'She called on her friend Tash. And she arranged for my chip to be tracked—'

'Yes,' Mel said, 'I called in favours. The English were already monitoring Naples. And when I knew where you were, and I found out the Skyship was coming over, and the projections were getting worse . . .'

In the final, terrible few days of anxiety and indecision, Mel, like the whole world, had followed the news from Naples with growing alarm. Indeed, since the Blink, Mel knew, the geologists had watched such locations with dismay as Earth and Moon settled into their new, changed orbits, and the Earth's mantle, that global, underground sea of molten rock, perturbed by the new tidal stresses, became energetic, as if awoken – and had evidently begun probing for weak spots in the overlying crust.

Weak spots such as the Campi Flegrei, near Naples.

The big caldera under the 'Fields of Fire', sitting over a huge magma mass, was already scarred by a massive detonation from the time of the Neanderthals, and had long been a candidate site for a new eruption, sometime in the future.

But that future had been fast-forwarded by the Blink.

A few weeks back it had begun with earthquakes, some major – one runway in the main city airport had been cracked – and some more minor, transient. Jane had lived through these. She had said the quakes sounded like distant thunder, felt like a

432

goods train passing by. American friends said it was like living in California.

Then, days ago, the ash plumes had started.

The ash was a symptom of the magma rising from beneath, pushing up against a lid of rock until it cracked, and an 'ash' of rock dust and flakes was expelled and rose high into the air — even into the stratosphere, from where it had crossed a continent, grounding flights, clogging machinery, and making populations choke. This hadn't been the first volcanic-ash plume since the Blink. But this one, over Naples, had evidently been only a prelude to a more major event, so the geologists reluctantly agreed.

Which was why Mel had been desperately looking for a way to bring her daughter out. It wasn't easy. The gathering ash cloud over the city was not just obstructing overflights, it was also blocking the view from satellites. The rest of the world couldn't even see what was going on at Naples, let alone help constructively.

Then she heard about Skythrust.

The inspection mission had been hastily put together by the English and Australian authorities. The vacuum-lifted Skythrust needed no engines to keep it aloft, of course. Its big, languid directional turbines were thought to be robust enough to be able to withstand the ash-laden air, where conventional aircraft were struggling. Drone robots had quickly been improvised to sweep ash fall off the big solar energy farm on the craft's upper hull. And so on. Skythrust could get closer to the incipient volcano than any other aircraft.

And Mel had pulled every string she could, starting with Tash and Charlie Marlowe, to get a place on the flight.

She hadn't been too surprised to find Harry Regent already aboard, as a military attaché to a group of US-based observers

— and, Mel suspected cynically, because of his high-profile status as hero astronaut. *Hey, we can't send any food or aid or get anybody out, but look at our handsome hero sky-boy!*

It was more of a surprise that Grace Butterworth was here.

The justification was her ongoing role as an aide to the English science minister, and some of Fred Bowles's juniors were on board. Mel understood Grace's true motivation for being here, of course — the same as Mel's own: family.

Well, Grace's *apparent* motivation. As Tash had speculated before they had left England, if vaguely. There seemed to be other agendas at play here. During the slow flight from Newcastle Mel had observed Harry and Grace spending long hours together. Talking, Grace generally angrily, Harry more calmly, yet both with intent.

If Mel didn't know better she might have thought they were plotting something. But she had not the faintest idea what.

Anyhow that had had nothing to do with Mel's own objective for this trip, nothing at all.

Now Grace sighed. 'Look, kid, your mum saw a chance, and she had to take it. I will if I get close enough to Ella and Billie. And I wish *they* were chipped—'

She was cut off by a distant rumble.

They looked at each other.

And Skythrust shuddered hugely, as if gut-punched from below. They stumbled, staggered, grabbed for handholds.

'I hope you can make out what we're showing you, or trying to.

'Obviously we are not yet out in the sunlight. We inch that way, cautiously, behind small tug craft that are pulling us out of the umbra, the long shadow of Earth. But we have already unfurled our sail. Spots from the Lodestone are casting light over that huge, gauzy structure.

'Can you see it? You may need some imagination to assemble these random splashes of light into an integrated structure. It is easier for us, we know the geometry of our craft intimately. Not to mention having simulated this sequence many times over.

'To clarify: for the first part of our mission the structure will act as a solar sail, and only later as a ramscoop inlet.

'The sail, at this moment, is all of forty kilometres in diameter. It is connected to our tiny hull by carbon-fibre threads, a spider's web which sustains and controls the sail in flight. We can adjust its shape, we can send micro drones down the threads if repairs are needed. And so on. The sail far exceeds our tiny habitat in size, but is only maybe a third of its mass. The ship and habitat together weigh around four hundred tonnes. Still — forty kilometres. The size of a major city.

'But the material is smart, and in the course of our flight it will spin itself out into a much larger form, fit for a much more ambitious purpose. Far from the Sun, far out in the dark, to maintain our acceleration it will mine the dark energy field.

'So, as our predecessors have done for a century or more now, we astronauts work through our checklists. Completing tasks that we have studied, brainstormed, planned, with contingencies to work around any failure we could think of. Contingencies rehearsed and simulated over and over, until we could do it all blindfolded — literally.

'But now, at last, the sail is deployed. And now we look forward to our next mission milestone.

'Sunrise.'

Sunrise.

After that first sudden jolt, the ship had seemed to calm. Even now Mel listened with half an ear to Zhi, an In-Joke in deep space.

435

But that word resonated in her head. *Sunrise*. For he had said it just as a kind of sunrise glow seemed to rise up from the land below—

The ship moved.

With a surprisingly sharp lurch given its bulk, Skythrust suddenly lifted into the air. And started to tip.

In this fancy lounge, Mel was still leaning against that ornate couch, which luckily, or by design, seemed to be bolted to the floor. Now she clung to it desperately, and looked around.

She saw Grace, Harry, her daughter, sprawling. They had all got some kind of purchase. Grace seemed to have fallen across Harry, close to the lounge's bar, and they had their arms locked together. And there was Jane, braced against a wall, clinging to a fire extinguisher bracket. Safe and stable, but far away from Mel, or Grace.

Mel grabbed tighter hold of her couch, and pulled herself closer to the window on the side the 'sunrise' had seemed to come from. Lifted herself up to see.

She was looking towards the Campi Flegrei, to the west of the city centre. And it really was as if a glaring, ruddy dawn shone up from the ground. It illuminated the huge, days-old ash column from below, casting strange vertical shadows up through the murk. A staggering sight to Mel, the shadows themselves must have been hundreds of metres tall.

Then the noise came, like a thunderclap but overwhelmingly more powerful—

The floor lurched up under her as the shock hit the Skythrust—

Mel lost her grip, fell on her back.

She landed on the carpet, and slid over the tipping floor. The carpet burned her neck, the palms of her hands. Frantically she reached for the leg of the couch grabbed it and hung on tight, stopping her slide.

She heard Harry calling names, checking if everybody was OK. But the ferocious, continuing roar from outside almost drowned his voice, and their replies in turn.

The floor tipped further. Mel just hung on. She couldn't see Jane, or hear her.

And the floor tilted another way, back again. Skythrust was twisting, turning, tipping, almost tumbling in the air – this massive slab of a ship, she thought, picturing it in her mind's eye, thrown like a leaf in an autumn storm.

The tilt worsened further. Mel shifted her position, trying to hold on tighter.

Mel started to fear that the whole ship might turn turtle altogether. In which case, she imagined, in such an unstable configuration, with the lift pods *under* the bulk of the hull, Skythrust would quickly break up. Even the main decks were meant to hang in the air, not bear weight. She imagined it, the ceiling become a floor beneath her, crumbling and cracking, until she fell out into a tormented sky. A scene just seconds away, maybe. *Jane*, falling—

'No!' Mel tried to push herself away from the couch, to scramble somehow to Jane.

Still the floor under her tipped and lurched.

Until it reached an extreme limit, and slowly, ponderously, started to drop back down. Mel, face down, scratched at the thick carpet, trying to get some purchase to save from sliding.

And she twisted her neck, tried to look around. That roar from outside the hull continued, but the four of them in the cabin, acting from instinct, just held on to the furniture, lying on the tipping floor, watching each other, waiting. Any attempts at speech drowned out by the ongoing explosion beneath them.

At last the nose of Skythrust dropped down, and the craft shuddered to a kind of stability, at a slight lean.

As soon as she could, Mel pulled herself to her feet, and staggered across the room to Jane, who was sprawled on the floor, still clinging to her extinguisher bracket. Jane's eyes were closed. 'Oh, God. Oh, God.'

Mel knelt and held her. Jane stayed stiff for one second – a second which broke Mel's heart just a little more – and then she softened into the hug.

Grace looked bewildered. 'What the hell just happened?'

Harry Regent shook his head. He stood unsteadily, brushed down a crumpled jacket, and looked out of the cabin windows. A strange light played on the planes of his face. 'I think the volcano happened. Come look.'

Dizzy, disoriented – and the right-hand side on which she had fallen feeling bruised as hell, maybe even carpet-burned – Mel worked her way around the wall, handhold to handhold, to Harry's side. Jane followed, and then Grace.

They saw it in the rear windows. The Skythrust was fleeing now.

Fleeing from the mushroom cloud expanding over the Campi Flegrei.

The days-old ash column was already scattered, shredded by greater, hotter air masses rising from below, masses thick with smoke and dust and glowing rock fragments, all lifted high into the air from a brilliant, hellish pinpoint on the broken ground. And at the pillar's broadening base waves of smoke and ash billowed out, flooding across the ground, obscuring it.

Whole inner suburbs of the city were already engulfed, Mel saw. By ash waves taller than buildings.

Jane said dully, 'We talked it all through, down on the ground. Well, we had geologists with us. When an eruption is coming you get this column, masses of material held up in the air by the heat flow from below. As long as that lasts. But when the root energy dies a bit, and the column gives way and falls back—'

The floor gave another lurch.

Mel grabbed instinctively for support. She found Jane's hand, by some primal instinct. Jane let her keep hold.

The ship was accelerating now, fleeing faster away from the central zone.

'Shit!' The anger just burst out of Grace. She ran to a wall and slammed her fist against a window, making Mel flinch – but the window, built for the pressures of extreme altitude, held. 'Shit! Christ! You bastard . . .' Her face was twisted with anger and grief. 'You bastard. We have to get down there. Get Billie and Ella out from under *that*.'

Harry Regent held Grace's shoulders. 'It's not the captain's fault. There is nothing to be done now. She would only imperil Skythrust if somehow she tried to land, even if she stayed around. Not her fault. It's not even the volcano's fault, in any sense. A volcano is a dumb mechanism with no more volition than a gun whose trigger you pull. It's not *its* fault.' He rubbed Grace's back.

His voice was insistent now, Mel thought. Seductive even. She felt uncomfortable to hear it. As if he was leading Grace to some conclusion, in this awful, vulnerable moment. 'Harry, maybe it's better if you let Grace deal with this in her own way—'

He ignored her. '*It's Galaxias,*' he said. 'That is the one responsible, Grace. Galaxias, whose "warning" to get us to stay in line has resulted in this. Death and destruction. The destruction of your sister's home. Your niece's home. Maybe their deaths. *It's Galaxias's fault . . .*'

439

Mel and Jane shared a look that overrode their own differences. *What is he trying to do with her? . . .*

Again the light shifted.

Jane turned to see. 'It's starting. The next stage.'

As they watched, Jane explained it all, in a dull monotone. As the heat of the churning magma at its root finally failed, the ash plume quickly collapsed. The rock fragments, pumice, smoke, gases, ash, all caught up in that huge, failing up-draught of heat, suddenly dropped from the sky. The cloud had been so tall this central fall would take several minutes, Jane said.

And around that huge collapse a dark, lethal blanket spread out across the ground, a grim circle. At its edge was a hot wind, hotter than steam, laden with glowing fragments of solidified lava, gases, even fragments of volcanic glass. This was a pyroclastic flow. Pouring across the landscape at the speed of sound.

Jane told them what was happening, down on the ground. Anybody at ground zero was gone, vaporised. People further out, if they were in shelter, if they survived the first overwhelming flow, would have to endure fifteen, twenty minutes under the collapsing cloud. No matter how they tried to shelter, even if they escaped the scalding solid rain, they would suffocate, in the streets, in their homes, until the air was gone, or the buildings collapsed.

Mel shifted her position, trying to see the wider panorama. Much of central Naples was already erased by the black mass of the flow, she saw, a huge spillage. And even beyond, wider ash falls began, hot, heavy. Kilometres away, people would be pounded by falls of hot stones, a relentless, rustling rain, caving in roofs, burying people. The four of them stood by the window, watching helplessly as Skythrust rose and fled.

In the background still Zhi spoke on, a meaningless whisper from above the ash-choked sky of Earth . . .

*

'We will sail on sunlight – for now. Our acceleration is small – less than a third of one per cent of gravity. But we will keep that acceleration constant, as the Sun recedes, by allowing our smart sail to expand, thus catching more and more of the Sun's increasingly scattered spawn of photons.

'Our first target is a location in the Kuiper Belt, ninety astronomical units out – ninety times as far as Earth is from the Sun, indeed three times further than the orbit of Neptune, outermost planet. There we will seek evidence, at least, of the entity Galaxias. For that is where the Sun was taken, on Blink Day.

'The mission to that point will take more than a year and a month. The plan, for now, is that we will not decelerate – not unless we see an obvious target to slow down for.

'And if we do find nothing, we intend to go on – as far as we need to. As far as we can.

'Some months further out, however, we will make a transition, when we reach a point where it will be more efficient for us to use our dark energy drive. With this drive we no longer rely on sunlight, or on any inboard fuel supply.

'Meanwhile aboard the habitat itself our recycling loops are efficiently closed. We have the means to go as far as we like – always knowing that we have the ability to return, however long it may take.

'Of that long journey we have completed, so far, a single day. A day in which our minuscule acceleration has already sent us a hundred thousand kilometres from Earth.

'But already we approach a significant milestone. In just five days we will pass solar escape velocity. Like the Pioneers before us.

'Are you watching, Galaxias?'

*

When the hot wind reached the Gulf of Naples and the sea, water was flashed to steam. Across the coasts of the Mediterranean, tsunamis rolled.

In the days that followed, a fine but persistent ash fell across the city suburbs and beyond, eventually accumulating enough weight to crush surviving buildings, smother any fleeing people, and bury their homes and crops. Across tens of kilometres.

The first estimates were that three million humans died in the first days. A history more than three thousand years deep erased. It was a new Pompeii, people said.

In the nights, aboard the silent Skythrust, Mel held her daughter for hours, as Jane wept, then finally slept.

37

October AD 2064:
Year 8 ERC, Spring

It was a full year before Tash herself visited Naples — the first of the In-Jokes to come here since Mel at the time of the eruption, even though, Tash knew, Grace Butterworth had frequently returned.

And once again Skythrust Two drifted through the murky sky above the city. Or, a year on, the scar that had been Naples. A scar visible from space, Tash knew. From the Moon.

While Mara Caine made a speech.

'A year since the eruption,' the Prime Minister said from her podium. 'And over seven long years since the Blink. And we're still here. Still coping. Still helping each other as best we can. Right? . . .'

That got the predictable ripple of applause — even, Tash saw, from Governor Lang and his entourage. Lang was the main challenger to Cox's vice-president in the year's presidential election. And as she spoke on, Tash knew Caine could look confidently out over a crowd of faces in this big open-air arena, under a pallid blue-brown sky where Skythrust hovered, implausibly huge. This was the media circus that had been set up at the centre of the English-American relief zone at Salerno: an extensive place, a mixture of misery and bureaucracy —

and, Tash thought, with a depressing air of permanence.

Viewing from the air, as they had sailed over in Skythrust, Tash had seen converging roads, road blocks, fences, barriers, the characteristic outer features of a refugee compound. And a swarm of dots moving into this infrastructure: people, still streaming down from the Naples area, filtering through the logic of refugee processing. Every 'dot' as vividly alive as she was.

But the crowd facing Caine now were not those wretched refugees. These were reporters, influencers, politicians, business leaders. Like Tash and her party, they all wore face masks, protection from ash and plague vectors, and they sat in chairs prearranged in wide-spaced rows. To Tash it was uncomfortably like a pandemic drill at school.

And the image on the big screen suspended from Skythrust had nothing to do with Naples. There was the butterfly-like Pioneer 14, lit by a distant Sun – an image transmitted from a free-flying camera drone launched from the ship itself – an image of ethereal beauty, over the squalor of the ground. An imagery that felt wrong, Tash realised, suddenly, belatedly. Tactless.

She uneasily glanced at Grace, sitting beside her – Harry Regent, inevitably, on her other side. Since the Blink, and with a growing sense of her own importance back in Government House in faraway Gateshead, Grace had been known to heckle staff, even politicians, when she thought they were losing touch with reality.

But Tash saw that Grace and Harry were paying no attention to Caine right now. Both had their phones out, Harry's apparently milspec, an impressive-looking bit of kit. And they were paging through images, documents: names, faces.

Refugees. Grace was still looking for traces of her family.

Tash had actually been able to assist Grace in her search.

After the main eruption a year back, Tash, with other staff loaned by the English government, had done some work in an advisory capacity on refugee processing. After a few days of hasty improvisation – when there wasn't much recording of anything beyond hand-written message boards – the refugees stumbling out of Naples had been passed through what were called 'processing shells', essentially a sequence of triage filters. The first level was said to be the most brutal, at which corpses were removed: mothers and fathers separated from the bodies of their ash-choked children, carried all the way out of the city. Hastily set-up medical triage followed – and after that, more controversially, a nationality filter. And after *that* there would be nothing to do but wait in some tent city – if you were lucky – and accept whatever hand-outs were on offer, and hope.

But, Tash knew, after the first chaotic hours and days, at each of these processing points as much information as possible was taken on every individual that was passed through, or even turned away. Personal details, images, names, addresses, DNA swabs. Even of the dead. The early, improvised contact boards were imaged too, and fed into the system.

What Grace was clinging to now was a slim hope: that her sister and niece lived, but were lost in the clumsy bureaucracy of refugee processing – lost, hidden away in this scarred landscape, somewhere. No matter how much more unrealistic that hope became, day by day.

So now, Grace and Harry paged through record after record, search after search, seeking any link, any mention of Grace's sister and niece in a crudely organised, frequently crashing database.

While Mara Caine lectured her prestigious audience on the state of the world. Tash knew her words off by heart.

445

She peered up into the sky: an orange-brown dome, in which the Sun hung, a clearly defined disc, pale, wan. Tash knew that most people thought the persistent, globe-wrapping haze layer was high-altitude volcanic ash. That wasn't surprising given that ash falls had blanketed much of southern Europe, even into Asia: from south Italy to Russia, Turkey, even the Ukraine. As the crops had failed, millions had been displaced. More misery, on an astounding scale.

But all that ash had mostly washed out within a few days of the eruption. It was secondary products belched out of the caldera that were doing the longer-term damage, especially volcanic sulphur that had reacted with water vapour in the air to create a haze of sulphuric acid – which stubbornly refused to clear, even a year on.

So, in the long summer after Naples, harvests globally had been down by about three-quarters. And in the northern winter a savage early cold had set in, only slowly, grudgingly lifting in the spring.

Other effects had not been so obvious, she had learned. With the temperature down, there was less evaporation from the land and sea, so, globally, less rain. Thus, over the land, there were droughts, dust storms, forest fires such as hadn't been witnessed since the worst of the climate-crisis years. The monsoons had been disrupted too, with India, China hit hard: anywhere downstream of the Himalayas, where many of the great Asian rivers rose, was suffering from drought. A global emergency, if the other after-effects of the Blink hadn't created one already.

And, across the planet, even far from Naples, there had been refugee flows on a scale not seen since the 2030s, bringing hunger and epidemics, nightmares from a previous generation . . .

But Tash was distracted by the feed from the Pioneer. Now

the spacecraft image gave way to a group shot of three astronauts side by side, smiling faces, comms hats on, name badges evident. A classic pose, Tash thought, that might have been mounted a century before in some Apollo capsule en route to the Moon.

Mara Caine accepted the interruption, smiled, and welcomed the astronauts.

'Hello, Earth. Hello, Prime Minister Caine, Governor Lang, other honoured guests at Salerno.

'Greetings from beyond Neptune!

'I am speaking to you now – or I was twelve hours ago, by your timing, courtesy of lightspeed lag – from the NHSA spacecraft Pioneer 14. My name is Wu Zhi. With me, the rest of the crew, Sara West and Marina Petko.

'We are all well. The spacecraft is functioning as specified. We have no concerns.

'It is three hundred and seventy-three days since we left home. Nearly a whole new post-Blink year, for Earth. And, fittingly, we have reached the Blink Point. Ninety astronomical units from the Earth.

'Where we have a decision to make . . .

'End packet.'

The spacecraft image returned. There was a ripple of faint applause, as Mara got back to her feet and spoke on. Tash knew that the data from Pioneer, lightspeed-delayed by twelve hours, was being sent down in compressed packets, partly for efficiency, and partly to give ground-based speakers a chance to work around the news from the sky . . .

But, sitting here now, Tash still felt all this was a mistake. The show was clumsy – and, worse, lacking in empathy. Just like

447

the impression given by the presence of the cruise-liner-chic Skythrust itself, in the sky above the ravaged city.

And as Mara Caine spoke on, Tash found she was unsure of the wisdom of her remarks as well, as she tried to remind her audience of the worldwide context, the background to a global effort to help the Neapolitans. An effort that in reality was increasingly resented unwilling donors. Mara wasn't about to say it out loud now, Tash knew, but even worse was expected next year, if the volcano winter didn't end soon – well, even if it did. *This* year refugees could be accommodated, to some extent, because of existing food stores. By next year those stores would be depleted.

Tash suspected people had grown angry about this, even resentful. As if it were all the *fault* of the Neapolitans. Which was why, presumably, the English still backed a coarse populist like Mara Caine and her English Reconstruction movement, a party that hadn't even existed a decade ago, and had shown little sign of competence in government. And why the Americans looked like they were going to back Jeff Lang in this year's election, the chosen candidate of yet another start-up patriotic-nationalist party, whose pledge was to 'reunite the country' by taking the American Free States back into the union. He hadn't actually used the word 'forcibly', commentators noted – not yet anyhow.

And so on. In her worst moments Tash wondered if humanity was always bound to turn to its darker side when times got a little hard. If so, maybe Galaxias was right to try to quarantine the Earth – if that was what it had been aiming at.

Or maybe she was too critical. These were unprecedented times. They all just had to do the best they could, she thought.

Zhi returned.

*

'The Blink Point. Twelve light hours out towards the constellation of Centaurus, to where the Sun was apparently transported on Blink Day. We came here to find out if there was any trace of Galaxias here, any equipment, residual radiations, anything. And, damn it, just to prove we could do this, travel to the scene of the crime, despite anything Galaxias could throw at us.

'But . . .

'We have found nothing. Nothing here, in this unexceptional corner of space.

'However, I can reveal now, we do believe there are – targets – further out, beyond this empty location.

'From our unique vantage point we have been able to see – something. A hint of enormous masses, or some more mysterious objects, out in the dark. Dark masses which we see only by deflections of the motion of objects in the Kuiper Belt. Very subtle deflections, observed by triangulating measurements with those made from Earth.

'Can this be some hint of the giant machinery which Galaxias used to move our Sun? In *our* Kuiper Belt?

'We have debated our options with our primary mission controllers at JPL and Moscow. The decision has yet to be made formally. But we three are united in our determination. We continue to accelerate. We will go on, for some way yet at least, beyond the Blink Point, into the dark. Seeking traces of Galaxias. For if Galaxias is not here – then where?'

A voice from the audience spoke up. 'You go, kid!' A rebel yell.

That contribution got a smattering of applause.

And Grace Butterworth, staring into her phone, swore softly.

*

Tash turned and whispered, 'Grace? What is it?'

But Grace, her lips compressed, her eyes unblinking, did not reply. Clinging to her phone.

Harry Regent checked his own phone, leaned over and said softly to Tash, 'We found her.'

Tash's heart beat faster. 'Who? Ella?'

'Not Ella,' he murmured. '*Billie.* Just the kid. Just Billie. And what we found – well, see for yourself.' He handed her his own phone.

Where Tash made out an image of an image, a scan of a photograph of a child's face. Eyes closed. As if sleeping peacefully.

There were a couple of other bits of paper in the image. Text scrawled in a clumsy hand that was difficult to decipher. Tash swiped to enlarge the image, squinted. BAMBINA DI BATTER, she read. And beneath, a more official-looking document, with a bar code, a printed list of details. Including what was clearly a death date. The photograph itself had been ripped, as if torn from some previous mounting.

'It's her?'

'It's her,' Harry said. 'We were able to follow up the details on the bar code, identify the DNA record . . . The details just came back. It's her. No sign of the mother.'

'Oh, hell, Grace—'

'There's more,' Harry said in a stern whisper. 'You can see the posting has been removed, physically. Posted up elsewhere, and then recorded on an illegal site. Where we found it.' He pointed at the screen. 'This, written by hand. Can you read that?'

Tash looked again. '"Bambina di Batter." I have no Italian—'

'Blink Baby,' said Grace, speaking at last. A harsh whisper. 'That's what it means. Blink Baby. Somebody is going through the refugee records, looking for Blink Day birthers like Billie.

Gathering the records in one place, physically, and posting them together, like this.'

'It's a kind of cult,' Harry said earnestly. 'I think. If you be-lieve the Blink Babies are somehow connected to the actions of Galaxias.' He grasped Grace's hand. 'We don't need to think the child was murdered. Not by any cultists. The records indicate asphyxiation, crushing, some burning, as if she were trapped under the ash fall—'

'Those idiots didn't kill my niece,' Grace said. '*It* did.' She glanced up at the Pioneer image on the screen. 'The thing *they* have gone looking for. Galaxias killed my niece, as sure as if it was driving a truck that mowed her down.'

'And it has to be made to pay,' Harry Regent said.

'It has to be made to pay.'

Tash stared at them both, wondering what consequences would flow from this discovery.

Up on the big screen the astronauts appeared again, clean and smiling in deep space, waved back at Earth, and said farewell in a variety of languages, to a ripple of applause. They seemed utterly unreal to Tash, even though she had known Zhi for so long, and so well.

A breeze blew, stirring ash into the air. All around Tash, people tightened their face masks.

The astronauts disappeared.

38

January, AD 2065:
Year 8 ERC, Summer

For Wu Zhi, Day 513 of the Pioneer 14 mission started out as a good day. Because for Zhi, 513 was a scheduled Garden day.

He felt good about it from the moment he woke, in the Jones, Inc. Shelter module that had been designated as his personal space. Simply because, in the endless cycle of triple rotations which they had all been enduring for seventeen months already, today was *not* one of the one-in-three working days he was assigned to general maintenance, which mostly consisted of scrubbing mould off the walls.

And *not* one of the one-in-three days he was supposed to spend on the Pioneer's bridge, monitoring the ship's status, checking engineering and science feeds. Smiling cheerfully for some PR broadcast, maybe — more likely than not from newly elected President Jeff Lang, who seemed to use the Pioneer as a kind of mirror of his own fame.

Zhi's main problem with the bridge, though, was the view out of the windows. The feeling of isolation in there could be crushing. There was no sense of motion, of movement or acceleration. Their dark energy drive's thrust was just about enough to settle dust, but not enough to *feel*. Nothing to see of the inner Solar System, looking back, save the Sun, itself no more than an unnaturally brilliant star, that and the distant stars, and, looking forward, the backside of their huge ramscoop.

Nothing to do but work your way through the latest material sent up from Earth, always painfully upbeat – while constantly being reminded of that huge gulf of distance that separated the Pioneer from home, most of all by the lengthening lightspeed delay in comms with the ground. *Twenty-four hours*, each way, now. Even Marina Petko, who had gone as far as Mars, had been only ever light-minutes from Earth. Bad mission design, he sometimes thought, psychologically flawed. But he had had a hand in that design, and could hardly complain.

You would think it would be that much worse for Sara West, their tame Jones, Inc. engineer, a tremendous intellect, tremendously courageous – and yet who had not even gone so far from Earth as the Moon before this jaunt. But of the three of them he sometimes thought Sara was the *least* affected by the isolation.

Although it was hard to tell. She was notoriously taciturn. She had seemed to open up a little more as soon as the plants she tended in the Garden started growing. She was a city girl, it seemed, without so much as a window box to bring a little life into her home. In her Texan drawl, she would say, 'Shame I had to scoot all the way out of the Solar System before I discovered I have green fingers . . .'

Anyhow, Zhi didn't have to face any of that today. For today was a day *he* could spend in the Garden that comprised most of the habitable volume of the craft, the trays of green growing stuff in their enclosed environment that kept the humans alive and, probably, sane.

He was well aware that part of the attraction of the Garden for him was that it was so similar to the set-up on the Lodestone, where he had been stationed for so long, even before the Blink. The basic engineering was the same, with a megawatt of power supplied by a compact fission plant to sustain the water pumps, the air dehumidifiers and cleansers, the lamps that provided the heat and light needed by the growing things. And the Pioneer's Garden *felt* much the same, with its mixture of growing crops, including hydroponics – staples like rice and potatoes, the more exotic rainforest species that added flavour, vibrant colour, even medical support.

So now Zhi pulled on his heavy-duty coverall, and looked out his tiny personal toolkit. He knew there was a baulky filter in one of the hydroponics beds. Get the heavier, dirtier stuff out of the way first . . .

He was just about to leave his cabin when he got the call from Marina, on the bridge.

'Zhi? You'd better come up. We have a problem.'

Shit.

He just hung there, weightless, for five seconds. Then he dumped the toolkit.

He left his coverall on.

When he got to the small, cluttered bridge, Marina, dark, intense, was working numbers. She didn't look up when Zhi entered.

He stayed by the entry port. He had developed a habit, when some problem came up, of waiting, just looking, giving himself time to take it all in, before firing off questions or interrogating systems. So now he saw that the windows had as usual been cleared to transparency to reveal the real-time view ahead. Which was, essentially, a scattering of distant stars around a central disc of darkness, itself spattered with a more regular array of lights: marker beacons on their immense scoop-sail.

He did glance now at the readouts describing the state of the scoop, their single most advanced piece of technology – and the most crucial, the only means they had of getting home.

Once the sail had been much smaller in their field of view. At first it had been used as a mirror, a brilliant array that had spanned forty kilometres, deriving a motive force from the intense sunlight that it captured. But as the light intensity had diminished with distance from the Sun, the sail had spread further, a smart material growing, thinning, designed to capture the same amount of total energy hour by hour, day by day – becoming at last a wall across the sky, a wall now with the radius of a small planet.

And *then*, after fifteen months or so, they had transitioned to dark energy running. The smart material had reworked itself again, thinning more, spreading itself further still, turning itself at last into a kind of webbing, not quite translucent. But across that webbing were embedded exotic neutrino sources. These were actually tiny, quantum-level, zero-net-energy particle accelerators, and were the key to exploiting dark energy.

Dark energy, the field that was slowly driving the whole universe apart, was a phenomenon of a higher-dimensional space called the bulk – that, at least, was the mathematical description of it, as Zhi understood it. The universe was expanding like the surface of a higher-dimensional balloon, whose volume was up there in that bulk, a balloon which was inflating more and more. And *that* was where the dark energy came from: up in the bulk.

So each of the sail sources produced a stream of an exotic kind of neutrino, decoupled from normal matter-energy, that could reach *up* into that bulk, and – somehow – extract and store the tiniest scrap of that dark energy. All those scraps, brought down from the higher dimensions and turned into kinetic energy, like fruit plucked from out-of-reach branches, were what drove the ship forward.

Something like that. Zhi had always hated trying to render all that down into a summary the public could absorb. School kids and politicians. Actually, the school kids generally got it quicker.

So the Pioneer was a dark energy ramscoop. In principle it could fly on, without any external input save the dark energy, until it sailed beyond the local galactic cluster, or even further – pushing ever closer to lightspeed. Clearly it worked; here they were. A miracle ship. A miracle ship with a lousy view, ahead anyhow.

And a miracle ship that, maybe, today, wasn't working.

'So,' he asked at length, 'a problem?'

Marina was still paging through numbers on a screen in front of her.

Zhi looked over her shoulder, saw nothing obviously amiss.

She murmured, 'May not be a problem at all. News from Earth, however. An anomalous deceleration, they say.'

'Copy.' He heaved a sigh. He settled into a seat as his illusory gardening day finally shattered in his imagination, and a grain of worry formed. *Anomalous* was never a good word to hear in space. 'This deceleration, then . . .'

She gestured at the console before her. Pulled graphs, columns of numbers into the air with waves of her hand. 'It's real enough. But slight. See here . . .'

Their acceleration, even with their monster ramscoop sail, was tiny, and the marginal deceleration TsUP had noticed was tinier yet. A fraction of a fraction. But it was there.

Zhi said, 'A quarter of one per cent of our nominal dark energy acceleration.'

'Yes. But measurable and steady. *Rising*, if anything, the ground are saying.' She peered ahead, troubled. 'Some fault

456

with the scoop, perhaps? With the neutrino sources? Some kind of evaporation effect from the scoop fabric? That could create a counter-force like this. Perhaps there was some systematic design flaw, not revealed during the manufacturing processes? Or covered up.' She pressed her lips together, troubled.

Zhi shook his head. He had learned that Marina, a product of a Russian industrial base that was still riddled with graft — or, at least, more so than America, China and other advanced economies — was too ready to assume technical failure, through human incompetence or even malevolence. 'I don't think the data indicate that. Look here . . .' He paged through more numbers. 'The tension in the scoop itself, and in the cables, doesn't indicate that kind of flaw. There's no anomalous stress between the ship's components. It's not as if the sail is pulling harder, or less hard.'

She shrugged. 'So then, what?'

He tried to open up his imagination. He had the sense that he was facing a novel problem, requiring a novel solution.

'So, if our scoop isn't failing,' he said slowly, thinking aloud, 'and the structure is retaining tension, it's more as if some external force is acting on the *whole ship*, scoop, lines, habitat and all.'

Marina frowned. 'A force like gravity?'

'I think that's exactly right,' came Sara West's voice over the comms. Her face appeared in a monitor. 'Sorry to butt in. I've been listening in. I figured this was more important than de-sludging air filters just now.'

'Can't argue with that,' Zhi said.

'An external force like gravity would exactly have this kind of manifestation. Pulling on all parts of the ship with equal acceleration — or deceleration. Whereas a failure of the sail, say, ought to cause a relative shift of the components.'

'Gravity,' Marina said, sounding puzzled again. 'How could that be? Gravity fields come from heavy masses. This is a deceleration, remember. There is no heavy mass behind us until you get to Neptune, and even that's not in the right place.' She thought. 'A while back we did notice the odd deflection of those TNOs.' TNOs: trans-Neptunian objects, lumps of ice, potential comet cores, floating around out here in the dark. 'That could indicate the presence of some anomalous mass, pulling stuff aside through gravity.'

'A mass we couldn't model,' Zhi reminded her. Meaning they couldn't find a plausible solution, within understood physics.

'Yeah. OK. If we had passed some planet-size mass in the dark, we would have noticed!'

'Right,' Zhi said, trying to think it through. 'Even detected it from Earth, decades ago, probably.'

'Yes. Earth agrees.' Marina tapped a finger on one screen. 'So – see here? Most of the guff they've been sending up has been reports of failed attempts to model it with some conventional deflector. But *here* . . .' She pulled out a short report. 'Some smart guy at TsUP smuggled in a suggestion that the source could be *ahead* of us, rather than behind. Pushing, rather than pulling, you see.'

Zhi said, 'A source made of what? Never mind. So what does TsUP recommend we do now?'

'Well, they bounced it off the brain-domes of the boffins at JPL. Do you want the full academic study complete with references, the abstract, or just my own headline?'

'Headline.'

'"Wait and see."'

'Ha! OK, then.' He looked down at his grubby coverall. 'I guess that's what we do. While I get on with my gardening.'

Marina still sounded troubled. 'Wait and see? How long for? We need some kind of target here. A trigger for action.'

Zhi nodded, hesitating. 'Fair enough. Sara, you say the deceleration is a quarter of one per cent of the sail's pull right now. Let's keep modelling, measuring. See if this mysterious push changes. Increases – or even decreases. If so, how. Does it obey any kind of power law? And if we get to, say, one quarter of the sail's pull . . . Well, maybe we will know what action to take.'

Marina pursed her lips. 'I think TsUP would say that would be recklessly late.'

'Well, TsUP aren't here, are they? And besides it's not clear to me what we can actually do about this. We monitor, we model, we wait. Agreed?'

An American grin over the comms, a Russian shrug.

'Good. To the Garden for me.'

In the days that followed, on the ship as on the ground, the pushback, as it was coming to be called, was measured, modelled, studied, with various mathematically inclined brains, human and artificial, trying to find some model that fit both the data and the laws of physics. The effect was so small that the data were patchy, though trends emerged in time. The deceleration looked simple enough on a graph – a steadily rising curve, approaching a straight line on a logarithmic scale.

Zhi had the feeling that the ground staff were enjoying figuring out the puzzle, as long as it was doing no immediate harm.

But the crew were physically immersed in the mystery. It seemed to Zhi that it was as if the Pioneer were inching into a head-on breeze. Even though he couldn't possibly be able to *sense* any deceleration, physically. But the deceleration, though slight, was real, consistent, measurable – and slowly rising.

It was as if the unfolding phenomenon became embedded

in Zhi's own consciousness, as he went over the various hypotheses, the numbers, in his head, over and over. He had the ground run wider literature searches, trying to find other theoretic models, other scraps of speculation that might fit the observations.

But then, scraps of speculation were all they had about the nature of Galaxias anyhow, which they had come to investigate. Maybe, he thought, in the recesses of his head, they were starting to find out something, at last.

And meanwhile, day by long day, the mission went on.

Zhi continued to take comfort, or at least distraction, from the one day out of three he spent in the Garden. That and exercising in the zero-gravity facilities, or cooking up whatever fancy meal for the others he could invent from their limited stock of ingredients, another skill that was a remnant of his months aboard the Lodestone.

Or he would just roam around the ship, the hull, this peculiar half-improvised assembly of forty Shelter modules in their stack of square frames.

After a couple of days of data-gathering, the first firm-ish conclusions emerged from Earth. The pushback roughly followed an inverse square power law. It strengthened with diminishing distance the same way gravity would if you were approaching a body like the Sun or Earth – the closer you got, the stronger it got – but in this case the force was a push, not a pull. A push from something ahead of them, at an apparently empty point in space.

And the models indicated that the pushback would rise to Zhi's arbitrary target of a quarter of the scoop's dark energy acceleration at twelve or thirteen days after the initial observation. So it would be reached around Day 525, when the ship would be nearly a hundred and eighty astronomical units from the Sun – almost exactly six times as far out as Neptune, twice as far out as the Sun's Blink Day location.

The theoretical studying continued. But Day 525 became embedded in everybody's heads as a kind of threshold, beyond which nothing could be predicted.

And in the interval before that date, reluctantly, driven by an obscure kind of guilt, Zhi frequently turned his attention to Earth.

Day by day his in-box was generally full of news, if twenty-four hours out of date.

Tash, Mel and other sources had been fulfilling an honesty pledge they had made before launch. They sent Zhi and the rest as much data as they had on the state of the Earth, and answered any questions as fully as they could – nothing censored. Little of the news was good, but as Tash had argued, this was the world they aspired to return to some day, so the astronauts ought to be told the truth.

The truth, two years after Naples.

By now, it was thought, globally some of the high-level acid haze was at last dispersing, more sunlight getting through. But the first year after the volcano, a year of drought, had been followed with a lurch to the other extreme in the second year, with months of excess rainfall. As rivers burst their banks, and the rains washed away what spindly crops were growing, all around the world national borders began to close against new, hard-pressing washes of refugees.

Starving children.

Pandemics stirred up, by peoples on the march.

War threatening.

And in his home country, he learned, there was increasing concern about Russia, with its restless populations already retreating south from climate-crisis-era, one-generation-old northern-latitude colonies – and once again eyeing the expansive lands further south still, beyond the Chinese border. Zhi carefully chose not to discuss politics with Marina Petko.

All this because of the Blink. Zhi's hatred of Galaxias grew visceral.

Thinking of China, though, made him think of his mother. Wu Yan was still involved in her supremely strange project on Mercury. TsUP kept him informed on the progress of the replicator swarm there. By now the machines had all but devoured the crust and were burrowing down into the mantle of liquid rock, *beneath* the crust – evidently adapting quickly to the changing conditions, the densities and temperatures – and copies kept rising in a cloud around the planet. Still nobody was clear what the ultimate purpose was.

His mother sent Zhi no information about that.

Indeed, he heard nothing directly from her at all.

Thus time passed. Hours, days, counted off on the ship's clocks.

As predicted, as they neared a distance of one hundred and eighty astronomical units from the Sun, the 'headwind force' rose steadily and smoothly, until now it was indeed approaching Zhi's nominal trip-wire of a quarter of their dark energy acceleration – and in fact was already starting to take a significant bite out of their accumulated velocity, which had peaked, after the best part of a year and a half of steady acceleration, at nearly a half per cent of the speed of light.

TsUP and JPL had started to call the phenomenon the Barrier.

And Sara West said she had figured it out.

'I think so, anyhow,' she said, almost nervously. 'A bit of speculation in one of the ground's reports set me on the right path . . .'

All three of them were in here today. The Garden, the mould on the walls, could take care of themselves for a few hours.

Sara's hands sculpted light in the air over the bridge's control surfaces, mathematical light, spinning and twisting columns of numbers, tentative graphs. Zhi and Marina stared in bafflement.

Sara said, 'The pushback has been rising with time, OK? The more time goes on the faster it rises. I linearised it to get the power law – look, you can see it. Inverse square, simple as that, just as TsUP figured independently. A lot of scatter from the uncertainty of the measurement; these have been small incremental effects, and we don't know the dynamics of the dark energy scoop well enough to be absolutely confident of how it responds to the pushback . . .'

Zhi picked out one term from all that. '*Inverse square*. Let's go back to basics. Like gravity, yes? Start at some distance – one unit. You get a given gravity pull, a given intensity. Go out two units and the gravity falls not by half but by a quarter. Go out three times as far and it's a ninth—'

'This is elementary,' Marina said, a little coldly.

'I know. I *know*,' Sara said. 'What stopped me seeing it clearly was that it's backward to the way we are accustomed to thinking.' She looked out of the window, to the black, blank wall of the sail. 'I think I know what's out there. The Barrier. *It's negative matter.* A mass of about the size of the Sun, I figure, with a negative gravity field. Has to be. That's what is pushing us back – the ground were right, it wasn't a *pull* at all. Negative matter is—'

'I know.' Zhi nodded, growing excited. 'Of course. Shit, I should have remembered, Mel told me about this . . . For sure, somebody should have thought just to ask Charlie Marlowe. Never mind. A negative gravity field, just as Charlie retrospectively deduced to have been acting on Mercury, just before the

Blink. It's some kind of signature of Galaxias tech, maybe. It makes sense. We should have got there quicker than this.'

Marina was still frowning. 'So what is negative matter?'

Sara said, 'Well, it's been pretty much hypothetical until now. Never observed in nature – until, I'm reading now, the tentative Blink Day evidence at Mercury, as Zhi says. There's a theory that it might be manufactured at the event horizon of a black hole, where a pair of particles might be created, positive and negative mass cancelling each other out, with the positive partner being swallowed by the hole . . .'

Marina said, 'If you could get to the *point*—'

'It's not antigravity – not quite. Gravity is a positive force. Every mass exerts gravity on every other mass, and gravity always attracts. Yes? But a negative-gravity mass *repels* all other matter. That is, it repels not just our kind of matter – positive matter – but other clumps of negative matter also.' She smiled. 'Imagine it. A negative-gravity star out there, dark, brooding. And the closer we get to it, the more it tries to push us away. Half the distance, four times the push – inverse square.'

'You say this stuff *repels itself*. So how can it clump?' Marina waved a hand. 'How the hell can there be a solar mass of it out there? Why doesn't it just – disperse? Blow itself to pieces?'

'Good question,' Zhi said smoothly. And he remembered non-scientist Tash Brand asking the exact same question, long ago and far away 'The theorists have this covered. The answer must come from the fact that negative matter obeys other physical laws. So it's not like dark energy in that regard, which is subject only to gravity. The best theory is that negative matter can be electrically charged. Maybe there are great clouds of it out there, held together by electrostatic charges, which overcome the gravitational repulsion—'

'Very well.' Marina nodded. 'What, then, is it doing here?'

Zhi and Sara exchanged a glance.

Zhi said, 'I think the answer is obvious. Especially as it was detected in the vicinity of the Sun around the Blink. To collect such a mass of this stuff, to control it so precisely – why, to use it as a technology – would have to be a galactic-scale project. Conducted by a galactic-scale agent. *I think we have found Galaxias*. Or its works.'

'Indeed,' Sara said. 'Oh, I should have said. According to this modelling the source is pretty close by.' She gestured towards the sail. 'About one astronomical unit. We are already as close to this source as Earth is to the Sun.'

Zhi had imagined he was beyond being shocked.

'A solar mass of it? That close?' He paged through imaging updates. 'We can't see through the sail, but we have plenty of cameras on the leading side . . .'

Sara shook her head. 'I should have checked.' She tapped a screen.

Up came a magnified image of a star field. A black circle at the heart.

'Ta-da,' she said quietly.

Zhi said, 'It's there. *Shit*. Sitting there all this time. There is a lesson we should have learned from the Al-miriykh. Every so often, look out the window.'

Sara shrugged. 'It's much denser than the Sun. Physically smaller – about a sixteenth the diameter. I'm trying to check the mass estimate – I mean the size of the *negative* mass – with gravitational lensing, which ought to be more obvious than with the Sun itself, given it's so small. Lensing – the deflection of the light of distant stars by its gravity field.'

Zhi nodded. 'Like Einstein's famous solar eclipse experiment, where they proved relativity was correct – mass bending space . . .'

'Of course this – negative Sun – would push starlight away, rather than attract it. Detectable even so.'

Marina put in, 'And the TNOs? The anomalous scattering? Could your negative Sun do that?'

'I think so,' Sara said. 'Simply by pushing TNOs out of their orbits. As opposed to dragging them in, like a normal-matter rogue planet, say. Everybody would have been looking for a pull source, not a push source – and so they were looking in the wrong place. I do need to check the modelling more carefully. I—'

'And what about the lurker on the Moon?' Zhi's mind was racing now. 'The projectile it fired out after Blink Day. Could that be a similar effect? Some kind of – negative matter drive?'

Sara smiled. 'Possibly. I'd have to model it. It would be elegant to hypothesise a single technology to justify all these effects.'

Zhi said, 'I think we need a break. Time to take all this in. One hour.'

Sara shook her head. 'I should keep observing, refining the modelling—'

'OK. Do it. One hour. Try to get some rest too. We'll convene then. And we'll put together some kind of report for Earth.'

Reluctantly, they agreed.

So they broke.

Zhi tried to relax, but couldn't, despite his own advice.

He ate, drafted a report for Earth. Brainstormed queries, hypotheses, concerns, listing them on his phone. He had always enjoyed working in remote stations, even the Lodestone, where he was not under the constant command of mission controllers on Earth. But now, just for once, he longed to be able to talk to JPL or TsUP, to somebody in charge, without whole days of time delay.

Also Mel Kapur, Tash.

Even his mother. Though he found it hard to admit it.

They reconvened on the bridge after the hour.

Sara was first there, and when he arrived Zhi wondered if she had rested at all.

'So,' Marina said briskly, bustling in after Zhi. 'Given this magic repulsive-gravity force.'

'The Anti-Sun,' Sara said.

Zhi smiled, hearing the capitalisation in her voice. *Anti-Sun. We've named it. First step to dealing with it.*

Marina said, 'If this is the work of Galaxias, what does it have to do with the Blink?'

Zhi rubbed his face. 'Actually I have some ideas about that. I looked up negative matter myself . . .

'It's thought you could build a *drive* with the stuff, with theoretically infinite capability. A negative matter rocket.' He grinned, and held up two fists. 'It sounds crazy the first time you hear it, but it's logical. Suppose my left hand is the Sun, the right the Anti-Sun. The Anti-Sun pushes at the Sun, which moves further left.' He moved his left fist that way. 'But the Sun *attracts* the Anti-Sun. So the Anti-Sun follows, going left too.' His right fist followed his left. 'And they just keep chasing each other.'

He shut up, and let them pick holes in that.

'Rubbish! You're getting kinetic energy from nowhere . . .'

'Not to mention momentum . . . What about the conservation laws, Zhi?'

'You ought to have got *that* yourself, Sara. The negative matter has a *negative* energy content. Negative momentum too.

So you start with no kinetic energy, and stay with no kinetic energy, even while the two stars chase each other around the cosmos. Start with zero. Plus and minus add to zero. End with zero.'

Marina continued to frown. 'Very well, but what has this to do with the Blink? In which, it seemed, our Sun was *instantaneously* transported out here – well, at lightspeed.'

Zhi shrugged. 'I don't know. But it can't be a coincidence that the Anti-Sun, here, has the same mass as our Sun. And that it lies, pretty much, on a straight line out from our Sun through the Blink Point. *This Barrier must have something to do with it.* Even if it's just the equivalent of – hell, I don't know – a primitive but necessary technology, to support the rest. The concrete pad at the base of a rocket launch gantry . . .' He glanced out of the window. 'Maybe we are only at the edge of it, here. Perhaps out there are huge engines we have yet even to glimpse. Whole hierarchies of them, surrounding the Solar System. An – infrastructure. And we can't even see it. Or only this one element.'

'Next question,' Marina said. '*Are we going to crash into that thing?*'

That shut them up.

Zhi had the impression that she had been bottling up the question.

'The negative Sun. I mean, we are heading towards it with what is presumably still a good fraction of our incoming velocity—'

'No,' Sara said. 'We won't get that close. The negative gravity field will become intense as we close in . . . My preliminary estimates show we will probably be pushed away long before any impact with – well, whatever is there. Four or five radii out. We shouldn't get any closer than that. And we won't come to any other harm. Remember, this thing has the mass of a star, but it is *not* a star. There seems to be no radiant energy – no light, no heat. I estimate that we will come no further than about half the Moon's distance from Earth.'

Marina snapped, 'How do you know?'

'Because we are moving too *slowly* to get any closer.

'It's counter-intuitive. At least for us creatures of normal matter. We know about escape velocity – you would have to be travelling six hundred kilometres a second to escape our Sun, from its surface, for instance, to get away from its gravity field. Any slower and you would fall back. Here it's different. Here you would have to *fall* in, *faster* than six hundred kilometres a second, to force your way through the push of the antigravity field and reach the surface. Does that make sense?'

'I guess,' Zhi said uncertainly.

'Now, the Anti-Sun is smaller in size than our Sun – the radius is about a sixteenth – though it has the same size mass, but negative. It's actually smaller than Jupiter, and I will leave the reason for *that* to the physicists. Because it is smaller, the surface capture velocity is that much *larger* than the Sun's escape velocity.

'Anyhow it's too powerful for us to reach. We simply aren't coming in fast enough. Basically we will be pushed away, by the antigravity field, as we approach. In the process, at worst we might hit a few hundred gravities. But, remember, *we should come to no harm*. The antigravity is an inertial force. As the ship is pushed, so are we within equally pushed, and we will continue to float around safely. We won't feel a thing.'

Marina frowned. 'Easy to say that. What about tidal forces? At closest approach, even a small distance may make a differ-ence to the size of the forces working on us—'

'Negligible,' Sara said. 'I checked. Well, probably negligible.

469

I'll go over it all again. We may need to lock down the scoop before closest approach, though; that's a pretty fragile, extended structure. I *believe* we will emerge unharmed. There is the question of what to do later.'

'Later?'

'After the closest approach. It's possible we could just turn around and begin the long journey home – boosted by the Anti-Sun's field, before we let the dark energy ramjet take over again.'

Zhi frowned. 'Or?'

'Or we could stay here. In this odd – system.'

'How?' Marina snapped. 'This is not a gravitating body. We cannot enter a stable orbit around it . . . Can we? Hell, no, of course we can't.'

'True,' said Sara. 'But – look, we have our scoop, the dark energy thrust. I told you, I figure that acceleration will balance the negative-gravity repulsive force at – well, about *here*, half an astronomical unit out. And so – you get the idea?'

'I think so,' Zhi said. 'The Anti-Sun pushing back would be exactly balanced by the scoop pulling us forward.'

'Yes,' Sara said. 'In fact the Anti-Sun seems to be pushing at the dark energy field itself – as if there's a breeze coming from it, for our ramjet to tap.'

'It would be like the Lodestone,' Zhi said. 'That's held in place in the umbra of Earth by a balance of forces . . . it would be an unstable equilibrium, right?' He held out his forefingers, pressed them against each other – mimed a slip, a slide. 'But we could manage that actively. The ship is smart enough for that. It may be useful for humanity to have long-term observers, here, at the nearest thing we have to an outpost of Galaxias. Who knows what we may discover?' He eyed Sara. 'From what you say it sounds like we need to make a decision to commit to this course now – I mean, before we wait for a forty-eight-hour round-trip conversation with Earth.'

'Indeed,' Sara said. 'We must use our own judgement.'

'We can always set off for home later,' Marina said. 'But . . .'

'Go on,' Zhi said.

'Well, this antigravity field is a pretty gentle barrier, isn't it? Even for a ship like ours, made of spider-web and thistledown. It's not an *aggressive* technology. It's as if—' She held up a hand, mimed a scoop. 'It's as if Galaxias is guiding the moth from the candle flame.' She spoke softly, her Russian accent coming out more strongly.

'That's one interpretation,' Zhi said, more coldly. He found it hard to think of the entity that had killed his fiancé and so many more people as *non-aggressive*.

Sara asked, 'An alternative interpretation being?'

'Think about it. OK, we set off from the Sun, headed roughly out to the Blink Point, and on through. What were the chances that this solar-mass object would be right here, *right in our way*?'

'Ah,' Sara said. 'Good point. You couldn't shield the whole Solar System this way, with solar-mass blockers everywhere. So Galaxias – came to meet us.' She held up her own hand in a stop gesture. 'Galaxias is shielding us from the flame. But we are not allowed to go any further.'

'Correct.' Zhi let that sink in. Then he said, 'OK. The purpose of the trip was to explore Galaxias's capabilities, its intentions. Well, now we know. It is bottling us up. With *kindness*.

'Well, we have a way forward. And we have work to do. Let's go over the arguments again, then draft some kind of update for Earth. And then . . .' He glanced out towards the huge, occluding shadow of the sail. 'Until we're ordered home, this ship is going nowhere.'

39

July AD 2066:
Year 10 ERC, Winter

After a flight across the North Sea from the mainland to New Aberdeen, without any problems as far as Tash could tell, the RAF helicopter smoothly began its descent.

The bird itself had been heavily modified since Tash had last taken a ride, with very obvious ash-screening filters over the engine inlets and what appeared to be robust supplementary armour layered over the outer hull. In the cabin, a peculiar webbing was embedded in the interior walls: Grace called it a Faraday cage, a new shell of protection against beamed cyber-attacks.

And as they flew they had been accompanied by a swarm of spotter and missile-carrying drones. Tash had the sense of a watchful infrastructure, from satellites overhead to warships in the ocean, and, she could see as they descended, human sentries on the Middle Sea dams.

Three years on from Naples, with the volcano's aftermath still unravelling – it had been the single worst post-Blink disaster by far – the world was an introverted, paranoid place, criss-crossed by refugee flows, marred by low-level conflict. Hungry, cold and sick. It was, in longer memories – such as her father's – like a throwback to the crisis years of the 2030s, when the great powers eyed a failing world, and each other.

Which, Tash knew, was a key subtext to this latest conference on Galaxias and all its works. Or so she supposed. She had been kept in the dark, excluded subtly even by Fred Bowles, more than she was used to. She knew the surface objectives were scientific and diplomatic – or at least she inferred that Fred hoped so, in his usual consensus-building, bridge-crossing fashion. After all, he had already achieved the major coup of persuading the Chinese government to send a delegation, led by Wu Yan, in the hope, presumably, of getting them to talk at last about whatever they were doing on Mercury, seven years after the first landings on the planet.

And speaking of introversion, paranoia, and being kept in the dark, Tash had got barely a word out of Grace during the flight. Even though they sat together for the whole crossing, just ahead of Charlie Marlowe, and a couple of rows behind Bowles, their boss.

Grace had self-evidently never recovered from the loss of her sister and niece in the aftermath of Naples. It didn't help, Tash supposed, that almost every minute of every day she did her job, Grace was reminded of those losses. Grace kept keeping on, Tash saw. For now anyhow. But even so . . .

Even so, Tash found herself becoming, reluctantly, ever more wary of Grace and her moods, Grace and her increasingly furtive, taciturn ways. She and Grace had worked together for ten years already, and all the way through the Blink. And yet it felt as if they were growing further apart, not closer.

Tash was, in fact, suspicious of Grace. Though she couldn't have said specifically why.

A distant boss with an agenda he wouldn't or couldn't share. An unreliable, scary colleague at her side. Everything seemed to be fraying. She wished she had someone to talk to about it.

Ideally Mel or Zhi, she supposed. But right now Zhi was still nearly two hundred astronomical units out in space, in a Pioneer 14 spacecraft slowly developing into a permanent station, its new purpose to observe the enigmatic artefacts of Galaxias – if that was what those remote negative-gravity structures were. And Marlowe herself had apologised to Tash, as they had boarded the chopper, for the absence of Mel, who was working back at Bouldershaw Fell. 'I couldn't spare her, too much stuff back at the ranch, especially since we had that anti-science crazies' petrol-bomb attack . . .'

Well, where Grace was concerned, Tash resolved to stay wary, but to try not to brood. And she would do her best to support Fred Bowles any way she could – trusting him, even if he didn't feel he was able to trust her.

The pilot called the landing.

Tash sat back, pulled on her ash-filter face mask, and peered out of the window at the approaching conference centre. *Again . . .*

As soon as the chopper had landed on the conference centre roof, Grace and another couple of military guards – marines, anonymous behind masks – clambered out to lead the party across the landing pad to elevators down to the interior floors. A new feature since Tash's last visit was a gaudy spire that thrust up from the centre of the roof.

Tash clambered out behind Marlowe and Bowles. They were greeted by a harsh, cold, damp wind, peppered with what felt like sleet to Tash, as it battered her face. This was July, but such was the drift of the calendar by now that it was a seasonal winter – as correctly mapped by Caine's new regularised calendar.

But there was some spectacle out here. Tash saw now that the ugly spire – probably a mask for an antenna complex – actually rotated, revealing a huge banner draped from one flank:

ENGLAND
WORLD CUP 1966
CENTENARY CELEBRATION

The words were set against a shifting, dissolving montage of images of young men in red sports shirts, cheering and laughing, set in brilliant sunshine.

Marlowe essayed, 'Soccer players?'

Bowles nodded. 'I take it you don't know the game, Charlie.'

Tash shrugged. 'Nor me. Not really. My dad has mentioned it.'

'Minority sport now, but all the rage a hundred years back. One of the great mass spectacles we don't do any more. And it gave an English team possibly its finest sporting moment. So some history books say. We were planning to host a large-scale event this summer to mark the centenary. Maybe recreate the final with holograms, even robots.'

Marlowe grinned. 'Another of Mara Caine's quasi-patriotic stunts? Which of course will only repel the Scots and Welsh and Irish she wants to draw back into the old British union.'

'Well, Naples put a stop to that.' Fred gestured at the immense banner. 'I went along with the display, though. I thought we should throw up everything we have to make this latest symposium as memorable as we could. As symbolic, as significant. Colourful. There's always an anniversary if you look hard enough.'

'Every little helps, I guess,' Tash said.

He grinned, rueful. 'Well, you know me by now. But of

course it's also a reminder that we don't get sunny July days like *that* any more.' He sounded tired.

Marlowe said gently, 'They even abolished July.'

Tash felt tired. She would be forty the following year. We're all getting old, she thought. She looked again at the football players, holding aloft their golden trophy, on what looked like an unfeasibly sunny summer afternoon. Some part of her longed to be there. Back then, in 1966.

They were approaching the elevator doors now. Tash tried to focus.

She saw that among the military types waiting was Harry Regent, a surprising sight. He stood out in his blue USAF uniform among the English marines, and detachments of English and Scottish police. As she walked up, following Marlowe and Bowles, Tash clearly saw Regent and Butterworth nod to each other, then prepare to walk side by side in the vanguard of Fred's escort . . .

And they *shook hands*.

Just briefly, it was over in a second, but they had done it.

That startled Tash. In the post-Blink, post-Naples world, you avoided physical contact, instinctively; plagues and pandemics were afoot, even some weaponised. And, from a security point of view, it wasn't impossible to pass data genetically encoded in droplets of sweat, blood.

You didn't touch people. However innocently. Certainly not in circumstances like these. Not without massive precautions.

Could she have been mistaken? . . . *No. Come on, Tash.* Here were two military officers – or in Grace's case ex-military – and they'd shaken hands, bare skin, palm to palm. And in the open, as soon as they met, as if they feared they might not get another chance.

What the hell might *that* mean?

Not for the first time Tash wished Mel were here, or Zhi. Somebody she could talk to, implicitly trusting. Because she felt a cold, hard knot of suspicion coagulate, deep inside.

In fact she wondered if she *should* talk to someone. A marine? One of the civilian police who stood back from the group as they passed? Even Fred himself? But she was aware of one senior copper, a burly middle-aged man – a superintendent, she thought – suspiciously watching *her* hesitate. She hurried on.

They reached the opening elevator doors. More officials came swarming out to cluster around Fred and his entourage – they had to line up to be scanned, each giving that day's verbal security code, *three one four one* – and the moment was lost.

As soon as she was inside the building, Tash's phone vibrated in her pocket. A curt message from Fred, evidently preset for the moment of landing.

Thirty minutes comfort break. Then, office 3A.

She swung by her own room, dumped her small pack, used the bathroom, spent five minutes on yoga moves to work the flight out of her stiff body, changed.

Tash knew 3A well by now. It was one of Fred's favourite spots, deep within the bowels of the centre. Once he had explained his rationale to her. 'Remote enough from the main public areas to be private, physically. Super-secure, screened from signals save through a single fibre – that speaks to just one phone that you'll be carrying, Tash. A single door, easy to secure. On quieter days it's officially a rehearsal room for presenters, so it has all the A-V-virtual facilities you could need. Great place for people to talk. Even if you have to force them to do so. Oh, and thanks to Grace, one of the best coffee machines in the building.'

Yes, Tash thought moodily now, thanks to a Grace who might now have other things on her mind than her boss's caffeine intake. Again confused, distracted – and vaguely suspicious – she put the thought aside.

She collected her stuff, including that security-issue phone, and was at 3A within twenty minutes of Fred's thirty.

Grace was already there, sitting outside the door. A basic security set-up. Tash knew the current protocols, systems of layers upon layers, shells of alert attention surrounding people like Bowles – including, simply, somebody sitting outside the room he was in. Grace didn't acknowledge Tash, but then she wasn't supposed to when the protocols applied. At least there was no sign of the increasingly sinister Harry Regent, Tash thought.

But, when she walked into the conference room itself, she was surprised by the attendees.

Aside from Grace, the token security seated outside the door, and Tash herself as more or less a note-taker and formal witness – the government's rule was still that all official or semi-official encounters of government ministers with foreign nationals had to be witnessed – the only players were Fred Bowles himself, Astronomer Royal Charlie Marlowe – and Wu Yan.

'You're late.' Fred waved Tash to a seat.

She wasn't.

'Sorry, sir.' She glanced at her phone. 'Your room authentication code, sir. Five nine two six.' An extra minister-level layer of security, with additional protection at each scheduled locale the minister visited.

But before she could sit, Yan stood, turned, and approached Tash.

Yan was ageing too, Tash thought. She looked tired, careworn. But still she stood tall and proud, folded in a long, characteristically sombre brown robe — she was like a Chinese treasure ship, thought Tash. Magnificent and dignified.

Her face worked as she came to Tash, and held her two hands. 'It's so good to see you. Even in this circumstance.'

That last clause puzzled Tash. Yan smelled, Tash thought, of some rare, exotic flower.

'And you. I—'

Yan let her go, and put her finger to Tash's lips. 'I know. I miss him too. I think of him every day. Every minute. But there isn't the bandwidth for much messaging, especially imagery, from the Pioneer. Little to spare for anything non-essential, so far away. So I relish the messages you share with me. Your friend Melissa too.'

Tash smiled. 'He'll come home some day.'

'Oh, I know. He has travelled far before, and has always come back. The trick, I believe, is not to let him know how much he is missed.'

'I think he knows—'

'Please.' Fred snapped out the word. Then, clearly uncomfortable, he forced a smile. 'Please, sit. I'm sorry. We don't have much time.'

Yan stepped back from Tash, and sat. And she said, sounding sad to Tash's ears, 'Not much time before you hand me over — well, who to? Your police? MI6? I am a foreign national. The FIS police, perhaps?'

Tash just stared, bewildered.

Yan looked back at her, and evidently took pity. 'You don't know, do you, Tash? My presence here is not voluntary. I was urged to come here to — well, to contribute to yet another of Mr Bowles's very worthy conferences. That was false pretences. Instead I was arrested as soon as I landed—'

Charlie Marlowe spoke for the first time since Tash had walked in. '*Arrested*? What outrage is this?'

Tash, baffled herself, thought Bowles looked embarrassed, even distressed, but determined.

'I'm sorry for the subterfuge,' Bowles said. 'The formal arrest wasn't my idea, believe me. We can spin it as diplomatic immunity. We can say we are protecting you from the FIS cops and your own people . . . But *we must talk*.'

Yan asked him seriously, 'You are afraid, aren't you? Afraid enough to do such a thing? What is it you fear?'

Bowles looked at her frankly. 'The number one scenario, worst case, right now? A Russia-China war.' He held Yan's gaze.

She said, 'I know little officially. Nor, probably, should I comment. But it is not a hard extrapolation to make, given the state of international politics. The refugee flows we have already intercepted heading south from the Russian north—'

Marlowe grunted. 'Given the state of the world, I doubt *any* such war would end until we are reduced to throwing chunks of shattered masonry at each other's heads. But why go to these extremes now, Fred?'

Bowles eyed her bleakly. 'Charlie – *it's Mercury*. There are suspicions, which I know are running round in government circles in Russia, probably elsewhere.' He grunted. 'Security is so tight I sometimes think I know more about what the Russians are thinking than I do about the Americans – or the English, my own bosses. The Chinese have evidently turned Mercury into some kind of vast, swarming industrial complex. Right? Well, to what end? There's one very plausible, very paranoiac theory that it's got nothing to do with Galaxias at all.

'I'm no scientist. I'm a politician. And to a politician the simplest hypothesis is – *weapons*. Maybe Mercury is being turned into one giant weapons factory. All that sunlight energy, all those rich minerals – hell, you all know this stuff far better than me.' He glared around the room. 'Can't you see, Charlie? That's the way the Russians are thinking. What if it's all a cover-up? Layers and layers of lies – well, it wouldn't be the first time. Even if Galaxias exists as we understand it – what if Mercury is all about developing some kind of weapon aimed at a terrestrial foe? *At Russia?*' He pointed at Yan. 'I won't put up with blanket denials any more. We *know* some of those replicator machines of yours have already lifted off the surface of the planet.'

Yan smiled, almost tiredly. 'That is true. They are leaving the planet. But not heading for Earth—'

'The trouble is you're evidently at a stage where you can't hide what you're doing any more – well, that's been true since you started dismantling the damn planet – and nobody can stop you anyhow, right?'

Yan was frowning. 'What is it specifically that you want of me, here and now? What must I do to earn my release?'

'That's easy.' Bowles leaned forward. '*I want you to tell us what you are doing*. Finally. Charlie's here to help me understand. Tell me. Tell us now, because I want to help you sell it.' He sat back. 'I want to *believe* your motives are – reasonable. Whatever the hell you're doing. So I'm forcing you, Yan, as best I can, to share it with us. Here and now. And then maybe, just maybe, we can stop this from pushing us all into some stupid, unintended war.'

Marlowe grunted. 'While Galaxias laughs, probably.'

Yan eyed Bowles. 'Do you have your Prime Minister's backing for this action?'

Bowles laughed hollowly. 'What do you think? Oh, Mara wants to do something about China's "weapons programme" all right. *Her* idea of a precedent to avoid is the failure to stop

Hitler's military build-up before the Second World War. We could end up going to war over suspicions, Yan.

'But she also wants plausible deniability if all this goes belly up. So I'm out on a limb here, and if this goes wrong – well, given the bigger picture that won't really matter, I guess. I – ah, the hell with it.' He folded his arms. 'Tell me, or not. That's my pitch. Oh, if you refuse, I'll let you out of here, and you can do as you like. The arrest is all a bluff. It's just that it's our last chance. Possibly. Probably.'

Wu Yan sat quietly for a while. Then she looked from Bowles to Marlowe, and over her shoulder at Tash.

Tash thought everybody was holding their breath. Was this a pivot of history? Would people in the future look back on what was happening in this room, just as Fred had implied, like the failed diplomacies before the great wars of the twentieth century? . . .

And Yan smiled.

'Not a bad strategy, Fred. And actually the idea of breaking a few rules appeals to me. I may not look it, and my son would never believe it, but I was somewhat reckless in my youth—'

That was when Tash's phone vibrated in her pocket.

Fred looked at her sharply.

The phone was the mandatory security issue, the only phone in the room open to incoming calls or data, via that one fibre channel. With a whispered apology, she dug out the phone, on mute.

Glanced at the message.

Put down the phone.

Fred was watching her; the others waited.

She tried to think, to take in what she'd just learned. This was way above her pay grade.

Fred prompted, 'Natasha—'

'There's a report of an explosion, on the Moon.'

The others exchanged glances.

Then the door opened, Grace Butterworth walked in, and sat on a chair opposite Wu Yan.

Tash was utterly bewildered.

A bomb on the Moon?

And now Grace, breaking basic security protocols? At least, Tash saw, she carried no firearm; her holster was empty. The room itself wouldn't have let her in otherwise.

But she shouldn't *be* in here. Tash glared at her. 'Grace? What the hell?'

Grace just looked back. 'Special measures.'

'What special measures? I—'

Fred snapped, '*Where* on the Moon? Speak up, Brand. We can deal with Grace later.'

She blurted, 'In the Sinus Medii. That's all I have. In the Monument Park.'

The others exchanged glances.

'The Monument Park,' said Marlowe. 'The area around the lurker. So if it's deliberate—'

'An unfounded assumption,' Wu Yan said.

'So far, maybe,' said Marlowe dryly. 'I imagine accidental explosions on the Moon are pretty rare. And if not accidental, if this *was* deliberate, who was the perpetrator?' A glance at Tash. 'Casualties? What damage is there? What was the target?' She took a breath. '*Was it the lurker?*'

Tash glanced at her phone again. 'I've got no more than I've told you,' she said. 'Do you want me to monitor this?'

Bowles sighed, and said wryly, 'It hardly sets the tone of the meeting I hoped to have here. But that's life. Keep an eye, Tash, and let us know what we need to know. OK. You were about to break some rules, Yan – I think? Just as the bomb went off.'

Marlowe looked at him. 'You're serious? You want us to keep talking, in the middle of all this?'

Fred nodded. 'I've been under worse pressure. On Blink Day for a start. You keep working. Charlie, Yan, please . . .'

Wu Yan made a visible effort to focus, closing her eyes briefly, concentrated. If she was perturbed by the presence of Grace Butterworth opposite her, Tash recognised with some admiration, she wasn't showing it. Fred was aware, though; he kept watching Grace warily, exchanging glances with Tash – evidently as confused as she was.

At length Yan said, 'Very well.

'Consider Galaxias.'

'If we are to deal with its presence in our lives, we must understand it. Even now, much of what we know of it is guesswork. But we do know some things.

'Remember, above all, *Galaxias is alone* – or so we infer from what we know, or believe we know, of its physical origin, on a water world. Alone, the only one of its kind. Yes, Charlie, you led the framing of this hypothesis, and we agree with you. And that shows in its actions in many ways. For instance, communications. Galaxias is *one*; it has never had the need to communicate with others as we do – with codes and symbols, in sound, writing, electromagnetic waves. Galaxias *acts*. Like pushing at a rock to see if it will tip over.'

'OK,' Fred Bowles said. 'So Galaxias shoves our star around to see if we stop – doing whatever alarms it.'

He was apparently relieved to be dealing with celestial abstractions once more, Tash saw. She admired his concentration.

'Yes,' Yan said. 'And be aware, by the way, that Galaxias's own origin might limit *its* imagination more than we understand. Possibly transporting the sun of a water world would do less harm to any inhabitants of that world than it does to a world like ours.'

Marlowe nodded. 'That's a good point, and it's been made before. A Blink applied to a water world might generate one almighty global slosh, essentially harmless – rather than the crumbling of a world like ours, with a thin crust over a mantle of active liquid rock, and shallow seas liable to flood the land. Doesn't help us, though . . .'

Bowles said sternly, 'A pretty drastic oversight.'

Marlowe nodded, conceding the point.

'Galaxias was born alone, then,' Yan went on. 'And, remember, born at cosmic high noon – we believe from the lurker dating – a time when the sky was dense and bright. But since then it has seen the universe expand and cool and dim, all around. Huge empty spaces, in which it remains alone.

'Think of that. Galaxias has no defenders, nobody to watch its back, metaphorically. Only itself, alone, adrift in a dying universe – dying from its point of view, a long-drawn-out dying that Galaxias has witnessed itself. Ask yourself. How would that *feel*? How would it shape your psychology? So Galaxias is cautious. Even paranoid, in our terms. A Crusoe stuck on his island for all eternity.'

Bowles thought that over. 'And the first thing Crusoe did was build stockades, as I recall. OK. But is that all there is to Galaxias, Yan? Does it have any ethic beyond some brute need to survive?'

'Possibly,' Yan said. 'There has been some speculation on the nature of universal ethics – values that might be shared by differently embodied intelligences. Galaxias is solitary; its own survival must be the key priority. But, given that basic goal, it may have varying strategies, varying ethical principles. Such as the notion of thermodynamic ethics, where you seek to maximise the value of all the free energy in the universe – or all that is left. Or, a related idea, you might seek to maximise the generation of information, of memory – of thought. Let the universe become as *conscious* as it can be. In the case of Galaxias, perhaps it dreams of taking all of the cosmos into its single consciousness. And if that's so, the first priority is not to waste resources, mass, energy. For these fuel galactic dreams.'

Bowles grunted. 'Galaxias doesn't seem to be aiming to maximise human consciousness at the moment.'

'No, because it may see us, in the short term, as an obstacle to a longer-term cosmic goal in that regard. As it may have observed with other cultures previously.'

Marlowe nodded. 'We spoke of this before. We briefed you, Fred. Your people. The danger of an immature culture expanding its resource usage exponentially, as we have, until it blossoms out into space, still expanding until it reaches a lightspeed limit – and expansion must stop, and it all collapses, probably, in war, starvation. Ripping a hole in the cosmic resource store in the process.'

'That's it,' Yan said. 'Galaxias may have observed this – *harm*, as it may see it, before. And it may have a fear of its recurrence. We Chinese have a long memory. My grandparents spoke of how they were forever wary of the return of *luan*, the chaos, of the twentieth-century wars. And earlier centuries had their own chaos.'

Luan. Tash remembered how Mel had told her that Zhi himself had used that word, when briefing Lee Yamanaka at the start of all this. Mother and son.

Marlowe nodded. 'Which, you think, is pretty much how Galaxias feels all the time.'

Wu Yan shrugged, a graceful gesture, Tash thought.

'At least we can empathise. Galaxias is a galactic power. Clearly. We cannot wish it out of existence. The Americans' Pioneer is a fist waved in the face of Genghis Khan. Brave, but futile, if not deadly. No – we cannot defy – *we must accommodate*. And to do that we must understand its fears.'

'*Its* fears,' Bowles murmured. 'What of *our* fears?'

Marlowe said, 'All of which, Yan, is a preamble to telling us what you are actually trying to do at Mercury.'

'Well – essentially, I suppose, we intend to do what Galaxias did.'

Tash was baffled. 'Which means—'

'Which means *we intend to move the Sun.*'

There was a startled silence.

Tash looked around the room. She had to laugh. 'Cue jaws literally dropping. Well, you got us, Yan.'

That was when Tash's phone shivered again.

They were all aware of it.

She glanced at the phone, and looked to Fred.

Fred nodded to her to report.

'The bomb,' she said now, staring into the phone. 'And it *was* a bomb, it's been confirmed. Some kind of battlefield nuke. No word yet on its origin, its manufacture, or the perpetrator. But it seems to have been a drone strike. Very precise. And it did hit the lurker site.' She was aware of their stares as she hastily paged through more data. 'No word on casualties yet. No clue as to the perpetrator—'

Bowles frowned. 'Impossible. *Nothing* should be able to get through in that way. I was briefed on all that when we set up the British marker. The signal we send out from that monument

487

is meant to be a pivot of a surveillance and robustness network, feeding into the international shielding . . . Unless that itself was hacked—'

'Grace,' Tash said, suddenly understanding. She stared at Butterworth, still sitting silently where she shouldn't have been. 'You were there, on the Moon, that day, when we dedicated the monument. Weren't you, Grace? With Harry Regent. *You set this up*. There and then. You sabotaged the British marker. Didn't you? Even though you were entrusted with the security codes themselves. And you just waited for the right moment to come around, to use whatever hook you had left in it – the right moment to drop the shield.'

Grace didn't react.

Fred Bowles looked devastated. 'Of course – of course. My God, Grace, how could you? I trusted you with my life. Not just then, over and over—'

Suddenly it seemed to Tash he had never looked older, more worn down. Nine years since the Blink in the stresses of government, and most recently years in the endless cage-fight that was Mara Caine's Cabinet, were taking their toll, she thought.

Grace just stared ahead.

Bowles seemed to pull himself together. 'All right. There's nothing we can do about that, sitting here. I think we should continue our discussion. This sharing. We have to focus,' he said, sounding as if he was capable of anything but. 'Yan, please – Galaxias? What did you say? You intend to *move the Sun*? You'd better start at the beginning.'

'Very well.' She steepled her fingers, closed her eyes. As if gathering her thoughts.

'We are not building a weapon. Of course not.

'We are building a Fogg engine.'

*

Tash couldn't resist going to her phone, the only working device in the room, to look that up.

'Two *g*s in Fogg,' Yan said with a smile. 'I can tell you how it works, roughly, though of course this will take many generations to perfect, and deploy. Many, *many* generations actually to move the Sun. We do not have Galaxias's magic solar-transporter technology.

'But it can be done, even by us. Given time.

'It is a spaceborne design. Essentially we will manipulate the Sun's own magnetosphere, to turn the whole Sun into a kind of rocket. A very feeble rocket, given the Sun's mass. The Sun will not be lightspeed-beamed, not by us. It will move slowly, slowly. *But it will move.*'

They sat and took that in.

Tash tried to understand. 'What's a magnetosphere? Sorry. I mean—'

Marlowe said, 'The Sun's magnetic field, Tash. An immense structure in its own right, rooted in the Sun's physical body, created by giant flows of charged particles in its interior . . . And I mean immense. The planets have them too. Why, if Jupiter's magnetosphere was visible from the Earth it would be a structure five times larger than the full Moon.' She laughed, bleakly. 'I should say, than the full Moon used to be.'

'That's it,' Yan said, and she smiled. 'Whether you approve of what we are doing or not, you can't deny the magnificence of the endeavour. For, with our little machines, we are seeking to manipulate a structure larger than the Sun itself.'

Marlowe snorted. 'But that's just a means to an end, correct? . . .'

Throughout these exchanges Tash kept an eye on Grace, who didn't move a muscle, her face blank, empty. Tash was sure she wasn't hearing a single word of this fantastic scheme. Tash's awareness of Grace's multiple betrayals today was like a spike in her head.

'So tell us how you will do this,' Marlowe went on. '*How* will you manipulate the magnetic field of the Sun?'

'With an electric current. Which we will create with a ring of ion accelerators circling the Sun's equator. Particle beams. The accelerators will be positioned in a close orbit around the Sun, at about one-seventh of the orbital radius of Mercury—'

'But that alone is a huge undertaking. How will you build so many? . . . Ah.' Marlowe slapped the table top. 'Replication. And *that* was what you have been manufacturing on Mercury. You were building what we thought were tokomaks, fusion chambers, from Mercury ore.'

'Or bombs,' Bowles murmured. 'No – these will be your accelerators. Self-replicating accelerators.'

Yan said, 'We may dismantle Mercury entirely, to construct the stations we need. Ultimately.'

Bowles barked a laugh. 'Dismantle a planet! That's not a thought I expected to hear today. Still in the dark over here, though, chaps.'

'So,' Yan said. 'Let me make this clear for you.'

She held up one fist, above the table, and sketched rough vertical semicircles in the air with the forefinger of the other hand, around the fist, from top to bottom.

'Here is the Sun. Here is the magnetosphere, the flux lines around the Sun, anchored at the poles. And here is a Fogg engine.' Now she sketched circles around the equator of her fist. 'So you run a strong current through an equatorial ring of accelerators, around the waist of the Sun. Which will create a toroidal magnetic field around the whole star. Like a doughnut. And *that* will squeeze the magnetosphere.'

'Ah!' Marlowe said. 'I see. And the ring of accelerators – these are your Acorns, self-manufacturing on Mercury. The numbers must be . . .'

'Heroic,' Yan said softly. 'We will raise a swarm of a hundred *trillion* machines, each massing a few thousand tonnes. Self-replication is rapid once it starts; but we estimate this will take no less than millennia to complete.'

Bowles laughed, tiredly. 'Oh, just millennia!'

Some one-thousandth of the mass of Mercury will be consumed, in this first phase.

'Then the swarms, flocking like swallows, will fly down from Mercury to an inner close orbit. And the machines will begin their work. With powerful particle beams they will generate immense star-girdling electric currents, which in turn will distort the Sun's magnetosphere – and with *that* we will manipulate the solar wind.'

'Ah.' Marlowe glanced at Bowles. 'For the benefit of the tape, that's a flow of charged particles that streams off the Sun, continually.'

'Thanks for the clarification,' Bowles said dryly.

'I see,' said Marlowe to Yan. 'And you direct that flow, presumably by firing it out of one or other of the solar magnetic poles, and *that* is your rocket exhaust. OK. I think I have enough to do some order-of-magnitude figuring.'

She got her own phone out, started tapping, threw it on the table. 'Useless! Damn your security.

'OK. In my head. Suppose the mass flow emerges, from one pole, at solar escape velocity, which is – a little over six hundred kilometres a second. Now, I know that the mass lost to the solar wind is about two million tonnes per second. Sounds a lot, but it would, what, take a hundred million *years* to lose a mass the equivalent of Earth. And the Sun is a third of a million times more than *that* – or so. You won't run out of propellant any time soon. But you aren't going to get much of a push out of it, after all that work.'

'True,' said Yan. 'So we increase the flow. Of the solar wind, our rocket exhaust.'

'How? By dropping bombs on the Sun?'

'Not quite. By heating one polar region with lasers – or possibly matter beams. We have already tested this aspect with flyby spacecraft. Flying close to the Sun, that is.'

Bowles frowned. 'You kept that quiet. That you are *already* meddling with the Sun.'

'All relevant results will be released after the formal meeting . . .' Yan smiled. 'The programme delivered good science data too. *That* will make you happy, Astronomer Royal. As to the engineering, with a continuous heating process – and there will be plenty of energy to be harvested by our equatorial ring of solar energy stations – we believe we can increase the mass flow by a factor of a hundred thousand, perhaps.'

Marlowe looked faintly desperate. 'A hundred thousand! OK. OK. Let's assume you achieve that. The Sun's going to be a rocket, flying across the Galaxy like some stately galleon—'

Bowles asked, 'And the planets? When Galaxias took the Sun, the planets were left to drift, weren't they? Will the planets be left behind?'

Yan shook her head. 'No, no. The planets are bound to the Sun gravitationally, and will stay that way. We will take the suite of planets and moons with us – and the comets, the asteroids, all save a few distant stragglers, perhaps.'

Marlowe nodded. 'That makes sense, Fred. The Sun is *already* moving, following a long orbit around the centre of the Galaxy. The planets stay with it as it orbits – just as the Moon stays with the Earth as it orbits the Sun.'

Yan smiled. 'Precisely. Why, most people won't even notice the new motion. Not until the velocity builds up, the displacement, not even visible for millennia, longer . . . Of course our own estimates of performance are only guesses. We can expect the, umm, *engine* itself to evolve. We have given our replicators the capacity to learn, to experiment. Perhaps we can achieve much greater efficiencies. Much more powerful magnetic fields. For instance, particle flows energetic enough to emulate conditions after the Big Bang, when the fundamental forces were still unified: gravity, and quantum forces . . .'

Marlowe frowned. 'Only *just* after the Big Bang. A trillionth of a trillionth of a trillionth of a second . . .'

'Our best current guess as to how to achieve that is to build a photon-photon collider, with a length comparable to the width of Jupiter's orbit, and absorbing, say, ten per cent of the Sun's luminosity. No doubt there are more efficient designs. But if you could achieve *that*, the magnetic fields available to manipulate the Sun—'

'Let's leave that for the future,' Bowles said dryly. 'Can we stick to what you can actually foresee? So you're pushing the Sun – and for millennia, you're hinting. Pushing it *where*? . . .'

Marlowe said, 'No, let me try to figure it out. A check on the logic. So let's use the rocket equation. We know the rate of mass loss, we know the exhaust velocity. What would make a significant difference to our position? Suppose we want to emulate the Sun's speed in its orbit around the galactic centre. Around two hundred and thirty kilometres per second. That will require a mass ratio of about one and a half . . . Why, nearly a third of the Sun's mass will be consumed.'

Tash was starting to feel utterly bewildered by this talk, in this context. This monumental abstraction of the manipulation of huge masses and timescales.

Against the reality of the news of a bomb, news still trickling through her phone.

Against the blunt protocol-breaking presence of Grace in this room, only metres from Fred Bowles.

But that had always been the conceptual challenge of dealing with Galaxias. The cosmic-scale threat folding down into the petty human world.

She struggled to concentrate. To ask an intelligent question.

She said, 'A third of the mass of the Sun, Charlie? Is that bad? To deplete the Sun like that?'

'Actually, no,' Marlowe said gently. 'Not necessarily, if you manage it right. Its luminosity might drop, and we may have to move the Earth closer a little bit.'

Bowles had to laugh. 'Move the Earth! A little bit! Well, that's fine then.'

Marlowe shrugged calmly. 'Small beer compared to the rest of it, Minister. And a smaller-mass star actually lasts longer. Burns its hydrogen fuel more efficiently.'

Bowles shook his head. 'Clinging on to my sanity here. And how long would all this take? Using up the Sun, moving the damn Solar System?'

Yan just smiled, and raised an eyebrow at Marlowe.

Marlowe said, 'That much mass at that rate . . . say a hundred million years. And we might have travelled — wow. Maybe tens of thousands of light years.' She looked at Yan in some admiration. 'Are these the orders of magnitude of the journey you are considering? To a first approximation?'

'To a first approximation. You do understand, Professor.'

'I understand it's a hell of a stunt. That would be enough to take the Sun, and Earth with it, halfway across the Galaxy.'

'Or,' Yan said evenly, 'out of it.'

Silence.

'And I suppose,' Charlie said dryly, 'that's the point?'

'I feel another conceptual breakthrough coming on,' said Fred Bowles. 'Tash, could you fetch me a glass of water?'

Tash glared at Grace. Some instinct made Tash reluctant to move too far away from her. Even to move too quickly.

But Grace just stared ahead, blank.

Holding her secure phone, Tash went for the water.

When Tash returned from the suite's small kitchen area, with a jug and glasses for them all, Marlowe glared, her arms folded. 'Yan – you'd better explain your overall strategy.'

'Very well,' said Yan placidly. 'Essentially, it is as I indicated. We are trying to reassure Galaxias that we are harmless.

'But humans, you see, are fickle creatures. All of us. Even if we made some commitment now, to live constrained lives under Galaxias's not very benevolent gaze, how could we be *sure* that some future generation, or individual despot, will not decide to defy Galaxias's dictates after all, and go burning up a chunk of the galactic disc in a frenzy of consumption?

'But – our Galaxy is more than the main disc. There are clusters of stars, great dense aggregations of them, suspended above and below the disc, particularly in the region of the core.'

Marlowe sat back, apparently marvelling. 'So that's it. You're taking the Sun, Earth and planets and all, *out of the galactic disc altogether!* Off to a globular cluster. And out of the reach of Galaxias, I guess you are hoping?'

Bowles frowned. 'I am barely following this. *How do you know that?* If this Galaxias has spread across the Galaxy, what's to have stopped *it* hopping up into these – star clusters?'

Yan sighed. 'We can't know for sure. Not yet. Maybe someday we will learn to detect its presence directly, and its absence . . . But this is our intuition. Those of us who have studied Galaxias most closely. We *think* Galaxias will stay in the main disc. This single ocean of stars, an extrapolation of the single planetary ocean in which, we think, it first evolved.'

'Yes,' Marlowe said, 'that makes sense. Galaxias is a unity, physically. It won't be motivated to colonise offshore islands. Yes, it's a fair bet it will be confined to the main disc. Something we can confirm in the distant future if not before . . .'

Tash said, 'Can I ask you – what *is* a globular cluster, though? What would it be *like* to live there?'

Marlowe nodded. 'In such a cluster the stars swarm close, Natasha. There would be thousands more stars visible to the naked eye than in the night sky of Earth. Many of them brilliant, too.' She shook her head. 'So, a pretty view. A cluster may or may not be a great place for life to emerge. The clusters evolved early, their stars are old, and the clusters lack heavy elements . . . No supernovas to trouble you, however. It may be that fewer planets per star would form than in the main disc – that lack of heavy elements. There might be more close approaches of one star to another, so more chances for planets to become detached from their stars. But close-in worlds like Earth should be safe enough. And with all those nearby stars, it would be a great place to build a civilisation – *if* you can avoid the light cage.'

Tash smiled. 'Sounds like you'd like to see it, Charlie. *How* many millions of years do we have to wait?'

'You can always dream, Tash. You can always dream.'

Yan said carefully, 'Clusters are not ideal places for life, perhaps. But any such obstacles are preferable to extinction. And *that* is where we will lodge the Earth. Because *Galaxias* will not be there.'

Bowles nodded slowly. 'I'm picking my way through this. Let's get back to the basics. All of it, the shifting of our planet

– shifting the *Solar System* – or at least, this project which is a precursor to all that – is essentially an attempt to communicate with Galaxias. Correct?'

'Exactly. As we have said, Galaxias communicates with us, not in words or symbols, but with actions.'

'The Blink. I got that.'

'Its meaning could not have been clearer, could it? So we must respond in the same way. *We will tell it we will leave the Galaxy.* We can only tell it this by *doing so* – not quickly, for we can go no faster – and besides, moving quickly, even if we could, might alarm Galaxias in any case – but we must start the process now. And visibly.

'So we test the components of the scheme, step by step. We perfect our Acorn technology on the Moon. We bring it to Mercury, and begin the process of replication and launch, refining and improving as we go. Why, the machines themselves are smart, and learn; each successive iteration of them will become more efficient, more effective.

'*We*, our generation, will see little of the result. It will be many centuries before the great stellar rocket is even ignited, perhaps by descendants of our crude designs, massively upgraded. Thousands more years after that before the displacement becomes noticeable. But—'

'But the intention will be clear,' Marlowe said. 'You believe. Clear to Galaxias, that is.'

'That's the idea. We will do all of this in full view of the lurker, by the way. So that it sees, and Galaxias sees.' She frowned. 'At least that was the intention. But the lurker is gone, it seems.'

Bowles put in, 'But what about future generations? How will they know what to do, how to carry on? Even if they *want* to. That's another issue. I can't get my own nephew to eat his supper, let alone save his yet-to-be-born grandchildren.'

Yan shrugged. 'That is a cultural challenge, I agree. We must educate. Create — markers. Monuments. Reminders. All *we*, this generation, can do is set humanity on the right path to the future.' She glanced at Fred. 'The children will have to learn to live without our guidance. Every parent understands this.'

'As you have brought up Zhi,' Tash put in gently.

Yan smiled. 'I didn't say it was easy. I—'

That was when Tash's phone pinged again.

Tash heard a scuffle at the door. Then a loud hammering.

Grace didn't move. Just sat, staring forward.

Fred Bowles stared at the door, and at Grace, apparently confused.

But Tash, relying on memories of her own minimal security training, understood. And realised that what she had most feared when Grace had come in the door was unravelling.

She said, 'Everybody keep still. The security people have figured out we are in trouble. And I think this is being read as a hostage situation.'

Bowles glared. 'What the hell are you talking about?'

'Please, Minister. Just stay seated. Stay where you are. You too, Charlie, Yan.'

Marlowe and Yan complied, looking grim, more concerned than scared. At least they were relatively safe, on the other side of the table from Grace's position, Tash realised.

But everything about the layout of the room, its occupants, seemed different now. And fraught with danger.

I should have acted earlier. I didn't want to believe this was happening. Damn, damn.

But nobody was dead yet.

She stood, cautiously, picking up her phone as she did so

498

— letting Grace see her hands at all stages. If Grace was to make a move against her, it would be now.

'Grace. I need to go to the door. Is that OK?'

Grace stayed still, glaring ahead at Yan, expressionless.

Tash braced herself, and went to the door, taking slow paces, showing her hands. By the door, she spoke into the phone, putting it on speaker. 'Who's out there?'

A gruff male voice. 'My name is Superintendent Finney. Police commander on the island. Your daily code is five nine two six.'

She looked at Fred.

He nodded at her curtly. 'Open the door.'

Tash looked over at Grace, who sat still, unmoved.

'OK, Grace, I'll take that as consent. Superintendent, I'll open the door. On my count. Five. Four.'

Grace made her move on *three*.

After long minutes of stillness, she stood up, knocking back her chair, and vaulted neatly over the table. And she got hold of Wu Yan, got one arm locked around her neck — and put a blade of some kind at Yan's throat.

Bowles, already standing, backed away a step. Marlowe stood up, her mouth open.

'Stay still!' Tash yelled. 'Fred, Charlie — stay back! Stay where you are!'

'Two—'

'Hold, Superintendent,' Fred called, hands in the air, taking charge. 'Things have changed in here. OK, Grace. Look, we have to let them in. Otherwise they will just come in blasting. Is there any point to that?'

Grace met his gaze, then looked away.

For one second Fred kept looking at her, his disgust and dismay evident to Tash.

Still Grace didn't react.

Tash wondered if she had any thought-out strategy at all. Or if this desperate bit of hostage-taking was any more than a reflex – if Grace had done this thing, however hopeless, because she had no other options left. Or maybe, Tash thought, she had something against Wu Yan herself.

The officer called again. 'Mr Bowles?'

Bowles shouted back, 'We have a situation in here.' He kept his eyes on Grace. 'Superintendent. Come in. But carefully. All right, Grace?'

She didn't reply.

The door opened.

Two officers, armed and in armour, bustled in and stood to either side of the doorway, quickly surveying the room.

The commander, Finney, followed them in. He was the man Tash had spotted on landing, who had been suspicious of her own hesitation. Bulky, fifty-ish, evidently competent. Tired-looking, Tash thought.

Grace still stood behind Yan, with arm lock and blade at her throat.

Guns were trained on Grace.

Yan had closed her eyes, and was breathing deeply, Tash saw.

Fred nodded. 'All right, thank you for that, Grace. Superintendent—'

Finney sighed. 'Sorry to tell you this, sir. We're here to assure your safety, and we have to apprehend Grace Butterworth. It's all to do with what's going on up on the Moon.'

'The Moon,' Marlowe said sadly. 'At Sinus Medii. The lurker, the Galaxias artefact? Correct?'

Finney said gravely, 'Destroyed, I'm afraid. By a drone missile

500

– we are still trying to locate the source. But we know about the destination. Minister, it was guided to its target by the security signal coming out of the British monument up there.'

'Ah.' Bowles looked as if he had been punched. 'So they hacked into our signal. Which was supposed to *protect* the site, the lurker. They used it actually to *guide* the strike?'

Finney shrugged. 'No fence is more secure than the people patrolling it, sir. In this case today's government pass code used – we aren't sure how – by Captain Harry Regent, US Air Force. And we think *he* got it—'

'From Grace,' Tash said. Memories flooded back. '*Shit*.' She glanced around. 'Sorry, Fred. Sir. Superintendent. *I saw her do it*. Pass something on. When we landed here, and Regent met us – I saw them shake hands. Regent and Grace.'

Now Grace spoke for the first time. 'But I still needed to get your day code, Mr Bowles.'

Tash thought that over. 'Right. And that's why you had to come into the room, to – hack the secure phone somehow. And somehow you passed it back out? The code. Out from this supposedly secure room.'

'*That's* a hole that will have to be fixed,' Bowles said.

Tash said, 'And I didn't report any of what I knew, or suspected. I'm sorry, Fred. If you want me to resign—'

'Oh, don't be ridiculous, Tash,' Bowles said. 'Half the party must have seen the same damn handshake. The coppers should have clocked it, with all due respect, Superintendent. One has to be pragmatic. And I'm going to need you more than ever in the hours and days to come, I think.' He shook his head. '*Grace*, though? After all we've been through, how long we've worked together?'

Grace didn't respond.

Marlowe said, 'Well, I'm just bewildered. Maybe I'm naive.

Why would anyone do such a thing? And go to such elaborate lengths?'

'And why the knife now, Grace?' Fred asked softly. 'Why all this? Why threaten Wu Yan? If you think you can bargain your way out . . .'

Grace, stony-faced, would not answer. Tash wondered, now, how she had managed to smuggle a knife into this room in the first place, a smart space supposedly proof against any such threats. Went to show how good Grace was at her job, she supposed.

Finney said, 'We think we know some of it, sir. There's been quite the conspiracy.'

'Just tell us, Superintendent,' Bowles said, patiently enough.

'Not all the details are clear yet . . . There are plenty of groups, including military but not exclusively, we think, who believe we are being too soft in our response to Galaxias. That we should strike back. You have survivalists, religious fanatics, conspiracy theorists. A real cabal of doubters. But they all agreed the only thing they could strike *at*—'

'Was the damn lurker,' Marlowe said. 'Which is like responding to Hitler invading Poland by kicking a dachshund in Regent's Park. How bloody stupid.'

'But very human,' Tash said. 'I think Grace believed she lost her sister and niece because of Galaxias. Indirectly anyhow. The Naples volcano.'

Grace just stood there, face blank, still holding Wu Yan, the blade.

'But it wasn't just the volcano,' Tash said. 'Was it, Grace? The niece was a Blink Baby, which ended up with her memory being – dishonoured. Did you want revenge, Grace? No matter how illogical. That's what Harry Regent played on, isn't it? How he played *you*.'

Bowles growled, 'Oh, Butterworth, you idiot.'

Grace smiled back, tiredly, coldly, and finally spoke. 'I had motives of my own, sir. Maybe Harry will say I played *him*.'

Tash wondered how much sleep she had had recently, planning all this.

But still Grace had that knife at Wu Yan's throat.

Yan, in a broken whisper, said, 'Please. Grace. I have a child too. I . . . I will not resist. May I speak, at least?'

Grace didn't move.

'This is a tragedy,' Yan whispered, even as she stood there, held by Grace. 'More than that. A disaster.'

Grace shifted her position slightly. One of the police officers stepped forward, but Finney held up a hand to stop her.

And Marlowe, sitting close to Yan, cautiously reached out to the Chinese scientist and held her hand. Watching Grace all the way. Grace didn't try to stop her.

Marlowe asked, 'Why so, Yan? Why a disaster?'

'Our Fogg engine project. It is meaningless unless Galaxias *sees* what we are doing, or are trying to do – in fact the *demonstration* of our intention is more significant in terms of the outcome than anything we have achieved so far. We have to show Galaxias we *mean* it. Fred, you understood that. The whole thing is really a message, in concrete terms, to send to Galaxias.'

'Oh,' Fred Bowles said. 'And the only eye Galaxias had open in the Solar System, that we know of, was the lurker.'

'Which we have now – blinded. The whole point of this is communication. What will Galaxias think of us now? This is epochal. An existential disaster.'

She said these words, Tash saw, even as a little blood seeped out from the skin of her neck through Grace's gloved fingers.

'No,' Charlie Marlowe said firmly, and Tash could see an idea being worked through even as she spoke. 'No. It isn't true. I mean, the Moon *isn't* the only location in the Solar System where humans face a Galaxias artefact. Not any more. *Your own son*, Yan. He's there—'

Tash said eagerly, 'Of course. Pioneer 14. At the Anti-Sun. We have a crewed ship sitting there, faced by that weird object. Your son!'

Yan sounded faintly bewildered. 'I . . . yes, that is true. But we have no evidence of observing stations out there. Equivalents of the lurkers.'

'Galaxias is going to know we are there,' Marlowe said confidently. 'I bet its installations out there are covered in lurkers, or the equivalent, sending reports up to that interstellar messaging network. And if that's so—'

'If that's so,' Tash said eagerly, 'you can tell Galaxias your whole story through packets sent up from Earth, relayed by the Pioneer crew. By Zhi himself, by your son. We can't bring back the lurker. And let's hope we don't get punished for *that*. But we can keep talking, keep showing Galaxias your good stuff, Yan. Keep getting your message through. *We are no threat to you . . . Look! We're leaving the damn Galaxy!*'

Tash stole a glance at the three coppers in the room, who looked utterly baffled by this talk.

Grace and Yan were still frozen in their lethal tableau.

But Marlowe was enthused. 'This is your vindication, Fred. For all the times you tried to bring China and the West together, to talk. Mother and son, even. Because now we *have* to work together. Yan here and her son up on the Pioneer – they have to talk.' She shook her head, apparently marvelling. 'You were right.'

Fred Bowles shook his head. 'Well, I'll put the knighthood on hold for now. Grace – come on. End this—'

Grace said, or hissed: 'Galaxias killed my niece. You want to appease it. *Collaborators.'*

And, with a spasm-like plunge, she drove her blade into Yan's neck.

The police had Grace on the ground in a second.

The Superintendent caught Yan, and lowered her stiff body into a chair.

Tash was astonished by the amount of blood, vivid red, that spilled on the floor.

40

July AD 2067:
Year 11 ERC, Winter

Tash was late for Mel's funeral.

And that was despite the smart government-issue car having made an efficient job of driving her from Government House in Gateshead, all the way to the opposite corner of England, and this small, ancient church outside Salisbury, close to Mel's childhood home. Of course traffic was never heavy nowadays, although the car had projected a blue police icon to clear the way a couple of times.

Even so, by the time the car rolled to a halt outside the walled cemetery, it was getting dark, this brief winter day ending – a July day by the old calendar – another day deep in the heart of another winter that still felt anomalously long, a decade after the Blink's huge wrecking of the seasons of Earth.

As soon as the car released its locks, Tash was out, pulling her heavy black coat around her.

And here was her father, leaning on a stick, waiting for her, outside an ancient wrought-iron gate.

She held still for the usual perfunctory kiss on the cheek. Then he led her through the gate and up a short path of cracked paving stones to the dark pile of the church.

'Got a cab,' he said, wheezing heavily. '*You* nearly bloody missed it altogether.'

The wheeze was a relic of one of the respiratory conditions that had run around the country a couple of years ago – a disease actually related to Mel's own final illness. Noel was only seventy-three, she reminded herself; he might have been a decade older. And Tash, only forty herself, felt the weight of her years too.

She linked her arm with his, and they hurried up the path as best they could.

'Well, I'm here now. That's what being an adviser to the Prime Minister gets you. On the one hand over-running meetings, on the other hand priority ministerial-grade transport. On the *third* hand, not that high a priority. No more chopper rides, for instance . . .'

Sometimes she actually missed Grace Butterworth. Grace had known the system far better than Tash ever would. *She* would have found a quicker way to get here. But Grace was in a high-security military prison, location unknown, and was never likely to emerge.

They paused in a stone porch with notices about baptisms, funerals, service times and pub quizzes. A heavy wooden door opened into the church. Noel breathed hard, and Tash pushed back her hood, shaking out her hair.

'Well,' Noel said, folding back his collar, 'I would say poor Mel was honoured to have you come all this way. But you're not the only VIP here. You'll see. There're people packing up to leave already. Too bloody cold. But I suppose you lot know all about *that*.'

Tash kept her counsel, knowing what he was fishing for. News of the ice packs forming around Iceland and Greenland, for instance. Fears that the Gulf Stream might be closing down.

In one of her final conversations with Tash, Mel had tried to explain all this to her. There was a gathering fear among the climatologists that, under all the weather chaos post-Naples, in the longer term the cooler post-Blink northern summers were precursors to a slide into a new Ice Age. This, apparently, was how it had begun in previous glaciations, with patches of ice lingering through the northern spring and summer, reflecting back a little more of the Sun's heat year by year . . . But the subtle changes in Earth's rotation and orbit – the precession and tilt of the spin axis, and the eccentricity of the orbit – were all messed up now, making predictions harder. 'That's the fear,' Mel had admitted. 'Nobody knows. But we're not there yet . . .'

That was Mel, always trying to end on a positive note. Tash felt a sharp, deep stab of grief, of loss.

Noel studied her. 'You OK?'

She found she had to blink back tears. 'No. But whatever the state of the world, we're here today. Together,' she said quietly, squeezing his arm tighter. 'And that's all that matters.'

He patted her hand on his arm. 'That's my Tash. Late or not. Come on.'

They opened the door, walked up the aisle.

The church was a squat, cold, stone pile, with a gloomy light admitted through grimy stained-glass windows. It was not unlike St Joseph's in Gateshead, Tash thought, where she still called in every now and then, mostly remembering Blink Day when she did so. And like St Joseph's the church looked nineteenth century, Tash thought, an expansive age that had bequeathed an awful lot of the country's surviving monumental heritage – as she had seen for herself, especially in the last few months she had spent accompanying the new Prime Minister Fred Bowles on tours of the nation, and too many funerals.

But still it was cold, gloomy, unwelcoming. The handful of people here were mostly congregated in the pews towards the front, but a few were scattered at the back, locals perhaps, or old friends from Mel's childhood, shy of the family and adult acquaintances. One man Tash didn't recognise, older, sat entirely alone at the back. There were no clergy here, no organ playing. And no coffin.

Tash was getting used to such sights as part of Prime Minister Bowles's entourage. Since the Blink ten years ago, even in comparatively secure and stable Britain the death rate had steadily climbed. And funerals had changed. Now most hospitals had crematoria: no more shipping possibly infectious corpses around the country, no more graves, no more gravestones. Church services centred on urns of ashes, or no physical token at all. Tash did know there was to be a small ceramic plaque fixed to a new memorial wall outside, a wall slowly building its way across the old churchyard. A post-Blink custom. A plaque for Mel.

They kept walking forward, slowly.

And Jane was here, Tash saw now. Unmistakable, she was standing in the centre aisle, tall, her vivid red hair cut neatly short, but not shaved as it had once been. Mel's daughter stood with friends before the altar, cradling her own baby − another Melissa, Tash knew, just a few months old.

Now she turned, evidently recognised Tash, and nodded, but her smile was cautious. Tash had always had the sense that as Jane had grown up − she was twenty-one now − she had come to disapprove of her mother's old friends. Maybe every child somehow resented a parental past they could never share. At that thought she squeezed her own father's arm.

And now, as she pressed deeper into the gloom of the church, Tash saw who her father had meant by other VIPs.

Sitting in a pew, Charlie Marlowe twisted around to see Tash and Noel approach. Charlie, still the Astronomer Royal, was pretty unmistakable, even from behind: a broad back swathed in a brilliantly coloured jacket – no mourning black for her – and that startlingly bright scalp of crewcut, silver-dyed hair.

'About bloody time,' she murmured. 'And don't give us that stuff about working for the Prime Minister—'

'She already has,' Noel said.

'—because so do I, and I was here on time. Mind you, Jane's father has been and gone – ever meet him? I don't think they were ever close. Even your friend Zhi, stuck out in the Kuiper Belt, managed to send a message to get here at the right time.'

Tash gave in with a nod, but she said, 'Actually he's already on his way home . . .'

Since the Moon lurker had been destroyed, and Pioneer 14, out in the Kuiper Belt, had been recognised as the only conduit through which humanity had any chance to feed information to Galaxias, as well as the best place to study its engineering, the Pioneer had been turned into the core of a permanent installation, with fresh crew and facilities on the way out from Earth – and Zhi was to be the first to be brought home.

And thinking of him suddenly made the loss of Mel real, vivid, for Tash. After all, she hadn't even been able to speak to Zhi since the news of Mel's death, in a critical care ward in a Chilean hospital. Mel had been working with Marlowe at the high-altitude Andean observatories, and had been caught by a local epidemic.

Thinking of Mel, Zhi, she found tears welling in her eyes. 'I . . . oh, dear.'

'Oh, love—' Her father limped over, and, cautiously, folded his daughter in an embrace.

Marlowe looked away.

Now Jane emerged from her small knot of mourners and approached. Her baby was in her arms, wrapped in a soft white blanket. 'Tash. Thanks for coming.'

'Oh, I'm sorry, I didn't mean to be such a mess—'

'It's OK,' said Jane, kindly enough, showing her baby. Her face was expressionless. 'Take all the time you need. But oh, – excuse me. There's somebody I need to speak to at the back.' She passed, and walked on down the central aisle, carrying the baby.

She knew that after her post-Blink adventures at trouble spots like Naples, Jane had become a medical student, looking to become a teacher specialising in public health. She'd already planned a doctorate, partly under Charlie Marlowe, on the effects of the new lunar cycles on human psychology: a very post-Blink career choice, and quite different from her mother's physical-sciences path. She'd grown up in a different time – a different epoch, Tash thought. Just as smart and wise as her mother. But more focused on people on the short term – especially now she had the baby.

Tash had a sudden, vivid memory of how Jane had been, only a few years back. The bright, cheeky teenager at In-Joke Christmases.

'Suddenly I'm nearly blubbing like a kid. I'm forty years old, for God's sake.'

'Well, I rather think that's the point, love,' her father said gently, sitting down stiffly on a pew. 'It is a funeral, you know. You lot, you In-Jokes – I was always so glad you had such close friends, Tash. Supportive friends. It's what you need in life. But I always knew as well that eventually – well, you would have to leave some of that behind you.'

Tash, getting back some composure, looked to the back of the church, where Jane was talking to that solitary man.

'One of us would die, you mean. I guess you're right, Dad. About growing up. I know it's really stupid, but I remember when Jane came along – well, it all changed, even then.'

'Don't beat yourself up. I saw you with her often enough. Mel hardly saw her brother, remember, so Jane had no wider family to speak of. I think at its best you and Zhi were honorary aunt and uncle to little Jane, when she came along.'

'But it's complicated,' Tash said.

'It's always complicated,' Noel said sternly. 'That's one thing this old fart can promise you about life.'

'That's right,' Marlowe said, standing heavily, one hand on the back of a pew for support. 'You get used to it. Noel, let me come sit with you, us old folk together.'

Jane returned, baby asleep in her arms.

Marlowe, taking her seat beside Noel, glanced to the back of the church. 'Jane, who was that, by the way? At the back there. Not that it's any of my business. But I did get to know many of Mel's friends—'

'He's my uncle.' Jane shrugged. 'Uncle Paul – my mother's brother. I barely know him.'

'Good of him to come, I guess,' Tash said cautiously.

Jane shrugged. 'He did me no harm. He was pleased to see the baby today. Don't imagine I will see him again. My mother hardly ever spoke of him. Or my father.'

Tash found she didn't even remember the father's name. For Mel, it had been an awkward relationship with a man neither Tash nor Zhi had ever met – a short affair in her postdoc years, an accidental pregnancy, an impulsive decision by Mel to keep the baby.

Jane said, 'I ought to write all this down for the future. Little Melissa will want to know about it some day. I would.'

Marlowe said now, 'Actually that's my own new project, in a

sense. Sorry to overhear. Writing stuff down for the future. Or one of my projects, as mandated by the great Fred Bowles. Such a relief to have a PM at least *acquainted* with science, don't you think, Tash? And in the Blink aftermath, as they used to say, he is having a good war. Deserved the top job, when Caine was finally toppled.'

Tash prompted, 'Charlie? Your new project?'

'Yes. Sorry. Rambling. Anyhow the project – they're calling it *Legacy* – is all about memory, humanity's memory. Our memory of the Blink and its aftermath, and what we're doing about it.'

Tash had heard of this. But she hid a smile at Marlowe's bright intervention. She did have a way of coming up with conversational nuggets like this, somehow appropriate to the occasion, inclusive, and yet – uplifting. As well as interesting.

'After all,' Marlowe said, 'as even government ministers have worked out by now, the Chinese Acorn project is a long-term development. We need to show our commitment to it, long term – because that's the whole point, to prove to Galaxias that we are not and never will be a threat. But it's *very* long term. Most people haven't remotely grasped that yet. So, at the very minimum, we have to find ways to *remember* what the hell we're doing.'

Jane frowned, jiggling her baby. 'I thought it was a massive project already. All those Chinese machines digging up Mercury—'

Marlowe said, 'But this is just the start of a longer-term process. It will take a thousand years at least just to establish the complete belt of particle accelerators around the Sun, before we even start to move the bloody thing. Of course that might change. My bet is we will come up with something smarter than this first strategy– or the smart replicator cloud will figure it out for itself.

'Still, for now, that thousand years of basic manufacture is our first conceptual horizon. And that's a *long* time in human terms. A thousand years ago, the Normans were conquering Saxon England. Our institutions – nations, religions – can last that long. But they don't always manage it.

'But beyond that – our first meaningful stellar encounter will be with Barnard's Star, where we will make a closest approach of about two light years, in about *ten* thousand years. Which is longer than any human civilisation has lasted, to date. Maybe, after a fresh Renaissance or two, our descendants will have to rediscover what we did, and why . . . And if it takes *a hundred million* years to get out of the Galaxy, as some estimates suggest, you are looking at time periods longer than *mammals* have been around. So what we are wrestling with now is ways of making sure we *remember*, on such timescales. Or trying to.'

Jane frowned. 'I'd never thought of that. It seems . . . impossible. Intuitively. And yet we have to do it, clearly.'

Tash recognised her constructive curiosity, so like Mel's sharp intelligence.

'I mean, even little Mel here won't remember the pre-Blink world. So – write it all down?'

'On what, though?' Marlowe asked. 'Our digital records are notoriously evanescent. We could create tremendous stores of records on more or less indestructible parchments, say, kept in more or less indestructible vaults. But even if that survives – could your remote descendants *read* it? Languages evolve on a timescale of a few centuries. Even the meanings of images change. In five hundred years, what do you think a map of the London Underground would seem to signify?

'And after a few thousand years, all this, all we have lived through, might be sinking into myth and legend. Falling out of history and into the domain of archaeology, even at best.'

She glanced around at the fittings of the church. 'Or religion. Do you remember how the Blink was compared to biblical phenomena, like Joshua's miracle day when the Sun stood still? Which actually was – maybe – some remote, distorted memory of a solar eclipse. And as for the Acorn project, maybe some new spacegoing civilisation, not understanding the purpose of this big cloud of clunky old factories around the Sun, might go out and start mining it for materials.'

'Like Hadrian's Wall,' Tash murmured. 'North of England. Where I work. That was robbed for building stone from as soon as the legionaries withdrew.'

Jane frowned. 'So we have to create – memorials. Markers of some enduring material like the Roman concrete I saw in Naples, that has lasted millennia. With engravings of, of—'

'Of what?' Marlowe said gently. 'We need to describe the Sun's journey, and its meaning – and establish at least a basic timescale. Images might be the best way. So, for example, you could show how the constellations should have shifted after ten or twenty or a hundred *thousand* years. Continental drift on Earth is quite predictable, so you could use maps of the changing Earth as markers spanning *millions* of years. You could even use the Andromeda Galaxy as a clock – *that* rotates in a timescale of *multiple* millions of years. The passing of time in science diagrams.'

Noel pursed his lips. 'If I were a god-emperor of the year 5,000 AD, I might want a monument like that to be brought to my palace. Or even smashed up to *build* my palace.'

'Good point,' Marlowe said.

'So maybe you make it cheap and nasty,' Tash said. 'You use plastic. I know a little about *this* idea. I remember Mel was working on this before she died.'

'So she was,' Marlowe said respectfully. '*That* never goes away, until it's subducted beneath the drifting continents. Create millions, billions of little – tokens – each one inscribed with some kind of message. Layered, so if you were smart enough you could dig out meaning after meaning.'

Jane smiled. 'Turning the world's junk into race memory? I like that.'

Tash nodded. 'I remember you gave me a Christmas gift once. A sculpted plastic bottle?'

Jane laughed. 'I remember that. How embarrassing.' She rocked her baby again. 'Well, we like Grandma's idea, don't we?' And little Mel gurgled and laughed. 'Calm down, you. I think she's getting tired.'

'Me too,' Noel said, shifting stiffly. 'It feels like my rear was cold-welded to this pew.'

'Oh, Dad,' Tash murmured. But she went over and helped him up.

Jane hesitated. 'Thank you for coming. I mean it. You were good friends to Mum, and I do remember the good times we had. Family stuff, the Christmases, as you say. She would have appreciated this. Look – I splashed out and hired a suite in a hotel in town. I'll ping your phones. Join us later, for a few hours anyhow. Drink some decent tea, whatever you like. In the warm.'

'That sounds a good idea to me.' The Astronomer Royal stood grandly. 'Come, Noel, let's go and get warm.' She linked Noel's arm in hers, and she swept down the church, like, Tash thought, a ship setting sail.

But they were met in the aisle by the man from the back of the church. The brother, the uncle. He stood now, blocking their way. Tall, a pinched face, and wearing a heavy overcoat. Tash thought she could just make out a remnant tinge of red in his rather long white hair. And he had the dog collar of a priest or vicar at his neck.

For a moment they stood, slightly wary of this silent man. Tash became aware that he was staring at Charlie Marlowe.

'This is my uncle Paul,' Jane said stiffly, evidently uneasy herself. 'Paul, this is —'

He bowed his head. 'Astronomer Royal. I have followed your words.' He lifted the collar of his coat to reveal a gaudy button-badge.

PUNY YAHWEH

Tash tensed. Not for the first time she wished she had Grace Butterworth at her side — the old, pre-fanatic, pre-tragedy Grace.

But Charlie stayed calm, and smiled. 'Paul? Well, I see we have differing points of view. How — healthy. Why don't we sit and talk? Come — I think the pews are a little warmer towards the front of the church.'

She linked his arm — he towered over her — and they walked back through the church.

So they were left alone, Tash, Jane, baby Mel.

Jane exchanged a glance with Tash. 'Phew,' she said.

And Tash smiled. 'You sounded just like your mother just then.'

'Before you go. Come see her marker stone, outside. Just us.'

Tash nodded. 'That would be an honour.'

As they spoke the baby looked at them wide-eyed, from one face to another. And when Tash stroked her cheek with a fingertip, she laughed with curious joy.

41

January AD 2069:
Year 12 ERC, Spring

In the years that followed, as Zhi slowly sailed home, Tash only shared a few brief message exchanges with him. She had the sense he was simply enduring the solitary journey until he made it back to Earth – where, of course, his mother no longer waited for him.

And the longest message came in the regularised Spring of Year 12.

'. . . I suppose you're wondering why I asked you here today.

'Simple answer. *Galaxias*.

'Remember Blink Day, and how we – well, *I* – figured out the response times from Galaxias, to any observations made by that lurker on the Moon? Observations of how we first reacted to the Blink? Reports sent by that chunk of smart ice in the Sinus Medii . . .

'We thought that Barnard's Star was the nearest reply node, six light years away. So any immediate response could come no sooner than twelve years after the Blink – six years at light-speed out, six back. And *that* gave us a deadline, an interval of freedom maybe, to do what we could before that response arrived. Twelve years' grace. We used that in the Pioneer project pitch, remember? We had to get out to Centaurus before that deadline was reached.

'Well, check your calendar. People haven't shouted about it, but the deadline is up. Twelve years on.

'And, guess what: *we saw Galaxias's response*, right on the lightspeed schedule. Last Tuesday, actually. My buddies on the ground patched me through the observations.

'We got new lurkers.

'One came slamming down into the Sinus Medii, near the wreck of the old. But there are five more now, scattered around the lunar equator. So it can keep an eye on us even as the Moon turns on its axis.

'You can imagine the security perimeters around *those* babies.

'And nothing else, as far as anyone can see. Galaxias is just watching us, as it always did. It may or may not have accepted our galactic escape plan. It must *know* about it, however.

'In any event, maybe we'll learn more when we get to Barnard's Star − or rather, when Barnard's gets to *us*, since it's drifting towards the Sun anyhow. Boring science note.

'I guess that's it. Give my love to your father, all our friends.

'We'll talk again . . .'

They never did.

GALACTIC YEAR

Year c. 190 million ERC
(c. AD 200,000,000)

42

A silvered star reached escape velocity from the globular star cluster once known to humanity as M-12.

Essentially a compact spacecraft, a star entirely encased in technology, it thus became the first artefact destined to return to the galactic main disc since the arrival of humanity at the cluster.

The creatures who had built this craft, composites of biology and sentient automation, were not human.

Their biological component did not even have any evolutionary descent from the human.

But their remotest ancestry had originated on Earth. And they had rediscovered what humans had once done. And why.

Now, a breakout had begun.

On Barnard's b, an eye opened.

And on Altair e.

And on an oceanic moon the fourth planet of the star 55 Cancri.

And on planets scattered across the plane of the Galaxy, all of them ancient super Earths, all oceanic, all infested with life.

On the origin world, at last.

Eyes opened. To see motile stars, descending.

And A hard rain fell across the face of Galaxias.

Afterword

A convincing recent account of the climate emergency is Gaia Vince's *Adventures in the Anthropocene*, (Vintage, 2015). A recent study on the possible impact of a large (VEI 7) volcanic eruption on the modern world was given by C. Newhall et al. (*Geosphere* vol. 14, pp. 572–603, 2018). The building of dykes to enclose the North Sea as a climate-crisis protective measure has been proposed by Sjoerd Groeskamp in the *Bulletin of the American Meteorological Society* (February 2020).

Mark Wolverton's *The Depths of Space* (Joseph Henry Press, 2004) is a useful reference on NASA's Pioneer missions. A study on the feasibility of airships using vacuum-lift balloons was recently published by Benjamin E. Jenett et al. ('Discrete Lattice Material Vacuum Airship', AIAA 2019-0815, published online on 6 January 2019). My depiction of a Skylon spaceplane was informed by a visit to Reaction Engines Ltd at Culham, Oxfordshire, UK, in February 2020, where a team led by Alan Bond made a party of science fiction authors very welcome.

The Lodestone was inspired by an Earth-umbra station design by Stephen D. Gunn, FBIS (to be published). The concept of a 'statite' was patented in 1993 by Robert L. Forward (US Patent 5,183,225). The magsail details are derived from papers by one of the concept's originators, Robert Zubrin ('The

Magnetic Sail: Final Report to the NASA Institute of Advanced Concepts (NIAC)', 7 January 2000). The concept of a magnetic radiation shield has been explored in another academic study ('Modular Space Vehicle Architecture for Human Exploration of Mars using Artificial Gravity and Mini-Magnetosphere Crew Radiation Shield', Mark G. Benton, Sr et al., AIAA 2012-0633, 2012).

The use of self-replicating technology on the Moon has been studied at least as far back as 1981 (R. Freitas et al., 'A Self-replicating, Growing Lunar Factory', in *Proceedings of the Fifth Princeton/AIAA Conference May 18–21, 1981*, edited by J. Grey and L. Hamdan, American Institute of Aeronautics and Astronautics). There are many more recent references. Dark energy was considered as a candidate basis for exotic propulsion in NASA's Breakthrough Propulsion Physics Project from 1996 onwards (see M. Millis et al., *Frontiers of Propulsion Physics*, AIAA, 2009, p. 20). The Jones drive depicted here is my own irresponsible speculation, written up as 'The Wormship: A Dark Energy Ramjet', *Journal of the British Interplanetary Society*, vol. 74, pp. 56–63, 2021. A useful introduction to negative matter, with further references, was given in *Indistinguishable from Magic* (Baen Books, 1995) by Robert L. Forward, who originated the idea of negative matter propulsion.

The idea of using the Sun's own solar wind as a rocket was proposed by Martyn J. Fogg ('Solar exchange as a means of ensuring the long-term habitability of the Earth', *Speculations in Science and Technology*, vol. 12, pp. 153–7, 1989). This in turn was based on an earlier proposal to modify stars by removing some mass to extend their longevity (by D. R. Criswell in *Interstellar Migration and the Human Experience*, Ben Finney and Eric Jones, eds, University of California Press, 1985). Of more recent designs of 'stellar engine', M. E. Caplan (*Acta Astronautica*, vol.

165, pp. 96–104, 2019) would use an enhanced solar wind to fuel a fusion rocket that would in turn push the Sun.

Of the exoplanets, 55 Cancri f is an authentic observation, though the presence of an oceanic moon is speculative. My depictions of the (fully revealed) planetary systems of Altair and Barnard's Star are largely fictitious. No exoplanets have been found at Altair at time of writing. Barnard's Star has one known exoplanet (Barnard's b). For speculation that Barnard's b could be a habitable water world, see 'Barnard's Star Planet May Not Be Too Cold for Life after All', posted on Space.com by N. Redd on 10 January 2019. The Jovians depicted here reflect earlier apparent discoveries, later discredited (Piet van de Kamp, *Astronomical Journal*, vol. 74, pp. 757–9, 1969, and see *The Lost Planets* by John Wenz, MIT Press, 2019).

Regarding theories of extraterrestrial life, useful summaries of the nature of water worlds, among other planetary types, are given by James Trefil and Michael Summers in *Imagined Life* (Smithsonian Books, 2019). The (hypothetical) planetary oceanic brain of Galaxias is my own speculation.

A useful recent survey of SETI, the Search for Extraterrestrial Intelligence, is M. Cirkovic's *The Great Silence* (Oxford University Press, 2018). The idea of universal (i.e. beyond human) systems of ethics has been explored by Clement Vidal (*The Beginning and the End,* Springer, 2016).

The idea of using 'lurkers' – patient, long-lived space probes – to search for life and intelligence in space was first suggested by Ronald Bracewell in 1960 ('Communications from Superior Galactic Communities', *Nature*, vol. 186, pp. 670–1). A more recent paper on searching for such probes was by J. Gertz, 'ET Probes: Looking Here as Well as There', *Journal of the British Interplanetary Society*, vol. 69, pp. 88–91, 2016. On the search for probes on the Moon, see A. V. Arkhipov and F. G. Graham,

'Lunar SETI: A Justification', SPIE, vol. 2704, pp. 150–4, 1996. The idea of an ET nodal system of communications was described by J. Gertz, 'Nodes: A Proposed Solution to Fermi's Paradox', *Journal of the British Interplanetary Society*, vol. 70, pp. 454–7, 2017.

The Kardashev scale, a classification of hypothetical alien civilisations based on their energy usage, was first published in 1964 (N. S. Kardashev, 'Transmission of Information by Extraterrestrial Civilisations', *Soviet Astronomy-AJ*, vol. 8, p. 17, 1964). Soviet astronomer Nikolai Kardashev died in 2019, aged 87. Concerning the lack of visible K-III cultures in other galaxies, see M. Garrett, 'The Application of the mid-IR radio correlation to the G-Hat sample and the search for advanced extraterrestrial civilisations', *Astronomy and Astrophysics*, vol. 581, id L5, 2015. The idea of galactic colonisation by a slow 'diffusion' was suggested by W. Newman and C. Sagan in 1985 ('Nonlinear Diffusion and Population Dynamics', in Ben Finney and Eric Jones, eds, *Interstellar Migration and the Human Experience*, University of California Press), and more recently revisited by J. Haqq-Misra and S. D. Baum in 2009 ('The Sustainability Solution to the Fermi Paradox', *Journal of the British Interplanetary Society*, vol. 62, pp. 47–51, 2009). The problem of the 'lightspeed cage' limit to fast interstellar expansion was first set out by S. von Hoerner in 1975 ('Population Explosion and Interstellar Expansion', *Journal of the British Interplanetary Society*, vol. 28, pp. 691–712).

A study of star cluster M-12 is 'How to Steal a Million Stars', ESO press release, http://www.eso.org/outreach/press-rel/pr-2006/pr-04-06.html. A recent study of the habitability of globular clusters was reported in *Nature* news, 6 January 2016 ('Alien life could thrive in ancient star clusters' by Alexandra Witze, doi:10.1038/nature.2016.19124).

An annular solar eclipse has been put forward as a tentative explanation for the Sun 'standing still' in the sky over Canaan, as reported in the Old Testament Book of Joshua (10: 12–13), by Colin Humphreys and W. Graeme Waddington (*Astronomy and Geophysics*, vol. 58, pp. 5.39–5.42, 2017).

All errors and misapprehensions are of course my sole responsibility.

Stephen Baxter
Northumberland
July 2021

Credits

Stephen Baxter and Gollancz would like to thank everyone at Orion and beyond who worked on the publication of *Galaxias* in the UK.

Editorial
Marcus Gipps
Brendan Durkin

Copy editor
Elizabeth Dobson

Proof reader
Jane Howard

Audio
Paul Stark

Contracts
Anne Goddard
Paul Bulos
Jake Alderson

Design
Joanna Ridley
Nick May

Editorial Management
Charlie Panayiotou
Jane Hughes

Finance
Jennifer Muchan
Jasdip Nandra
Afeera Ahmed
Elizabeth Beaumont
Sue Baker

Marketing
Tanjiah Islam